THE
WONDROUS
AND THE
WICKED

BOOKS BY PAGE MORGAN

THE DISPOSSESSED TRILOGY

The Beautiful and the Cursed

The Lovely and the Lost

The Wondrous and the Wicked

THE
WONDROUS
AND THE
WICKED

Page
Morgan

Delacorte Press

Text copyright © 2015 by Angie Frazier
Front jacket photograph © 2015 by Anna Mutwil/Arcangel Images
Back jacket photograph © 2015 by Jose Ignacio Soto/Shutterstock

Visit us on the Web! randomhouseteens.com

Educators and librarians, for a variety of teaching tools,
visit us at RHTeachersLibrarians.com

Library of Congress Cataloging-in-Publication Data
Morgan, Page.
The Wondrous and the wicked / Page Morgan. — First edition.
  pages cm
Summary: "Turn-of-the-century Paris is in turmoil, with demons
prowling the streets, unless the Waverly sisters and their gargoyle protectors
can stop them. Except there is an otherworldly power rising up that
could mean the end"— Provided by publisher.
ISBN 978-0-385-74315-0 (hc) — ISBN 978-0-307-98083-0 (ebook)
[1. Supernatural—Fiction. 2. Gargoyles—Fiction. 3. Sisters—Fiction.
4. Demonology—Fiction. 5. Paris (France)—History—1870–1940—Fiction.]
I. Title.
PZ7.M82623Won 2015
[Fic]—dc23
2014012858

The text of this book is set in 11-point Hoefler.

Printed in the United States of America
10 9 8 7 6 5 4 3 2 1
First Edition

To my sisters, Lisa
and Sarah,
forever

The lamps along the Quai des Orfèvres were dark. That was the first signal for Marianne that something wasn't quite right. She moved with caution through the inky black. It was a familiar street, one she'd walked countless times, and yet the impenetrable dark made it feel like uncharted territory. Glass crunched under the soles of Marianne's boots, and she stopped walking.

Had the lamps been *smashed*?

She drew her cloak tighter as wind rolled over the quay wall and shook the brittle leaves of some poplars lining the Seine. Vandals had likely pitched rocks at the lamps, nothing more. Had Marianne known, she would have asked Monsieur Constantine's driver to let her off closer to her home at Place Dauphine. Instead, the slim brougham had stopped, as usual, a block away, on the Pont Saint-Michel. For a month she had been walking the extra few minutes home along the quay road to make sure her mother and father would not see Constantine's fine carriage. They believed she spent two evenings a week giving piano lessons to a young girl in the Latin Quarter. Marianne could never tell them the truth: that she was, in fact, at a gentleman's chateau on the outskirts of Paris, learning to curb her appetite for blood.

Marianne picked up her pace, wincing as her boots ground over more shattered glass beneath the next lamppost. If she could shift, like some of the other Dusters with hellhound blood, she wouldn't be so nervous walking alone in the dark. But she hadn't shifted yet, beyond a few instances of fur sprouting on her arms and a half inch of nail growth once. Marianne was impatient for it to be over and done with, but she prayed the first time wouldn't happen until she was alone and far away from home.

Ahead, she saw the faint glow of lights from the residential square directly across from the law courts of the Palais de Justice. In their apartment, Papa would likely be smoking a cigarette and reading to Mama from *Le Petit Journal* as she arranged the table for supper. If Marianne hurried, she might be able to get home in time to listen to an article or two. For a moment, she forgot the dashed lamps along the quay road and thought only of her papa's steady, clear voice.

A flicker of movement in the sky drew her gaze up to the roof of the law courts. Two imperial stone eagles, perched on either corner of the columned façade, had cast their shadows over Place Dauphine for as long as Marianne could remember. Seeing them now, stamped darkly against the cloudless, moonlit sky, didn't surprise her. What did was the third, unfamiliar winged statue set between them. It stopped her cold. Where had *that* come from?

The wings on the new statue snapped open and a long tail undulated into sight. Marianne barely had a moment to comprehend that it wasn't a statue at all before the creature launched itself from the roof—and dove directly toward her.

Marianne screamed and whirled around. She wouldn't be able to reach the square now, not without colliding head-on with the beast. She broke into a run down the center of the quay road, back toward the well-lit Pont Saint-Michel. There she could see passing carriages, pedestrians. Safety. The utter blackness . . . the smashed lamps . . . No one looking out their window right then would witness Marianne running from a winged beast. No one would see anything at all. *We are likely being watched,* Monsieur Constantine had cautioned her just that evening. *Be vigilant.*

A hawklike shriek rang out overhead, shearing through the whistle of wind in her ears and her own panting breath. She couldn't run fast enough, couldn't scream. There was no point. The creature was already upon her. A bright shock of pain carved into her back, punching through skin and muscle, and then two sharp talons cracked through her breast.

Marianne gasped for air as her body, impaled on the beast's talons, was lifted from the street. But the air had turned to water. Warm, thick water that raced up her throat and pooled in her mouth. She coughed and struggled to breathe as the lights upon the Pont Saint-Michel grew fainter, her body colder. How strange. Blood had been all she'd wanted for months. And now she was drowning in it.

CHAPTER ONE

PARIS

LATE MARCH 1900

Ingrid should have brought a sword.

She crouched in a most unladylike manner on the narrow quay beneath the Pont de l'Alma, considering ways to pry a manhole cover free. The tarnished brass disk had to weigh at least five stone. She needed to lever the blasted thing up if she wished to descend into the sewers before daylight broke over the city.

Entering miles of dank, serpentine sewage tunnels alone was a risk at any time of the day, but Ingrid needed to slink her way in, and she preferred to do so without being seen. She had to find her brother. Grayson had been gone for nearly a month, and she'd started to have that old bubbling awareness again. The caged restlessness that always beset her when she simply *knew* her twin was in trouble.

The sewers were as good a hiding place as any, and Grayson had most definitely been hiding. For a month he'd been on his own in Paris, avoiding Ingrid and their mother. Had Gabby still been in the city, instead of in London, Ingrid was certain he would have steered clear of their younger sister as well. Anything to avoid facing the reality of their grim situation: that he and Ingrid were Dusters—humans who had been given demon blood at birth. A rogue guardian angel had gifted them this blood, and with it, inhuman abilities. Ingrid could create electricity at her fingertips. As for Grayson . . . his ability was a bit more complicated, and much more dangerous.

Well, she was finished waiting for him to come home. She needed her brother—even if he *was* a hellhound some of the time. Ingrid would find him and drag him back to the abbey by the ear if she had to.

She untied the silk drawstring pouch cinched around her wrist and withdrew the petite hand dagger she kept for emergency use. When Vander Burke had given her the four-inch blade of blessed silver with its polished ebony handle a few weeks prior, he'd intended for her to use the weapon to fend off hungry Underneath demons trespassing in the human realm. Ingrid, however, was perfectly content using it to try to lift this sewer manhole cover.

She scraped the point of the blade along the rim of the cover, searching for a gap. It was nearly impossible to see in the predawn darkness. The point slipped into a crevice and Ingrid pushed against the weight of the brass disk with all her strength.

"You are not going down there."

She paused at the low, surly voice. She'd wondered if Marco might follow her. Butlers didn't usually keep such close tabs on the members of the family they worked for, but Marco was more than just the butler at l'Abbaye Saint-Dismas. And Ingrid was more to him than just his employer's daughter.

The dagger had barely raised the cover an inch, but she continued to hold it propped open.

"Not by myself," she replied, glancing quickly over her shoulder to where he stood. "My gargoyle wouldn't be so negligent as to allow that."

Marco came around to stand before her. The dark gray merino of his butler's livery was a few shades darker than anything else around them. Sunrise was closer than she had thought.

"If you'd help me with this, please?" she asked, pushing on the handle again. With his strength, Marco could easily rip the cover up and toss it aside.

Instead, he set his foot on the cover, forcing it to slam shut and her dagger tip to pop free.

"And as your gargoyle, I am forced, once again, to keep you from getting yourself killed." He crouched down until his eyes met hers.

Marco's dark features were even darker than usual in the coming blue of dawn. Ingrid had once feared the scowling face before her. Even more, she'd feared him when he would take on his true form—a thick, cinnamon-red jacket of reptilian scales, featherless sienna wings, and long, wickedly sharp talons. At one point, not very long ago, Marco had considered killing her. That was before he'd been assigned to the abbey and become her gargoyle protector. Before everything that he was forbade him to harm her.

"I'm not afraid of what I might find in the sewers," Ingrid said, though the tunnels were rife with demons. Her last visit beneath the city had been with two demon hunters, Vander Burke and Nolan Quinn, and she hadn't known the first thing about protecting herself.

Things were different now. Ingrid knew how to use her demon half, powered by the blood of a lectrux demon. She knew how to summon electricity and store it in her fingertips, and more importantly, how to release a current of lightning without completely draining her reserves. If she came across a demon threat in the sewers, she was certain she could subdue it.

Marco leaned forward. "Then why, Lady Ingrid, could I taste your fear in the back of my throat?"

She clenched her teeth and beat back a wave of nausea. Marco himself didn't make her uneasy. It was his vivid connection to her that did. He could sense her so intimately that if he held still and drew up her scent, catalogued within his memory, he could feel the beat of her heart echoing his own. He could feel her every breath, the shift in her pulse, even her emotions. He could find her and be at her side within moments.

These things were all meant to help him keep his human charge from harm. Still, Ingrid didn't want him to have such access. She didn't want him to be her gargoyle.

She wanted Luc.

Ingrid turned her head toward the Seine to avoid Marco's stare.

"I'm worried for Grayson, you know that," she said. "I have to find him."

"Human, your impatience is infuriating," he growled, standing tall. "The only thing you're going to find down there is a quick fissure straight to Axia's hive."

Ingrid let out a sigh and stood up. The crown of her head reached just below the starched points of his white collar. Marco wasn't entirely wrong. She was certain there were plenty of fissures in the sewers that led to the Underneath. She was also certain that Axia, the fallen angel who had created all of the Dusters, had not forgotten about Ingrid and the angel blood still circulating through her veins. Axia wanted that blood back. It was hers, after all.

Axia had also given Ingrid and Grayson her angel blood at birth, unlike her other seedlings, thinking to safeguard it from the toxic Underneath should the Angelic Order ever banish her to that realm. After sixteen years, the angel blood had finally grown strong enough within the twins' bodies for Axia to reclaim. With it, she could return to the human realm for something she called the Harvest. What that was, exactly, was still a mystery to Ingrid. It wouldn't be good, that much she suspected.

Axia had already reclaimed Grayson's angel blood. If she reclaimed Ingrid's portion, she would be able to begin her Harvest.

"I'm not going to hide on sacred ground forever," she said to Marco as she slipped her dagger back into her purse.

"And your brother isn't going to come back to you until he is ready."

Ingrid cinched her purse and curled her hands into fists at her sides. "He's in trouble."

Her brother's hellhound blood had made him do horrible things. He'd killed a girl in London. Ingrid couldn't imagine the guilt Grayson had to be suffering. What if he couldn't live with it? What if he decided *not* to live with it?

"Think me cold and callous if you choose, but *you* are my human charge. *He* hasn't been since he quit the rectory and started residing elsewhere," Marco said. "I warn you: if you attempt to climb down that sewer hole again, I will strip off my clothes, coalesce, and fly you back to the abbey kicking and screaming. Trust me—you don't want that." His deadly serious gaze softened as he flashed his teeth. "Or perhaps you do. I am rather stunning when unclothed."

Even poor light couldn't hide her blush from his night vision. Marco picked up on the pinches of color and laughed.

"My mother should toss you out on your ear," Ingrid said. "You are by far the worst butler I have ever met."

Marco gestured toward the wide stone steps that led to the street. She groaned and reluctantly started walking toward them.

"Lady Brickton adores me," Marco replied, following her. "And I am a marvelous butler."

She supposed he was rather efficient. He had no excuse not to be, not with over four hundred years of various servant duties under his belt at his former territory. That didn't mean Ingrid felt the need to praise him.

"Mama is terrified of you," she said. Her mother knew what Marco was. She also knew that as the Dispossessed assigned to the abbey and rectory, he would not be going anywhere even should she dismiss him.

9

"Terrified is exactly how I prefer my humans," he countered. "I need to work on finding a way to frighten you into obedience."

"Threatening to remove your clothes was quite enough. I—" Ingrid's retort fell silent on her lips as a man appeared at the top of the quay steps.

Since arriving under the bridge, she had only needed to pause for one vagrant who had shuffled by, wheeling along a wooden cart filled to the brim with his meager belongings. Ingrid had hidden in the shadows until he'd passed, the dark having been a much better veil a half an hour ago.

There was no avoiding this new stranger. The rising light cast him in shades of blues and purples, and Ingrid could tell by the cut of his trousers and heavy greatcoat that he was not some ragtag vagrant. She paused at the bottom of the steps, thinking to stand aside and allow him to descend first. *This isn't London,* she reminded herself. This man wasn't going to recognize her. Though she'd been in Paris for over four months, she wasn't a true part of society here. No one but her mother would care that she was on a quay this early in the morning.

Marco stepped close behind Ingrid, his brawny chest brushing against her shoulders. Though he said nothing, she felt him rigid with menace as the stranger took the first few steps down.

"Relax," she whispered, but at the tail end of her plea came a familiar sharp *twang*.

She knew the sound: the spring release of a crossbow.

Marco caged Ingrid with his arms and with unnatural speed pivoted her away from the stone steps. He moved with such swiftness that he drove the breath from her lungs and her vision blurred. Marco stumbled as something hit him, and with a grunt and a growl, he shoved Ingrid.

"Run," he rasped. "Go!"

His thrust propelled Ingrid forward, but she stumbled to a halt, disobeying her gargoyle yet again. Had that man actually *shot* at them? She turned back toward the steps in time to see

Marco's human body erupt into true form. His butler's uniform ripped apart at the seams as his spine cracked and lengthened, his legs grew and bulked with muscle, and a pair of massive wings unfurled out of his back. He flexed those wings, raising them into great sails, and shredded the last clinging remnants of his jacket. Ingrid stared at the dart embedded in Marco's ribs.

Marco's battle screech echoed off the quay wall as the stranger tossed his spent crossbow aside, drew a sword, and slashed it toward Marco's enormous form. With one swipe of his talons, Marco sent the sword clattering to the ground. He raked his claws toward the man again with unrelenting ferocity. Ingrid swiveled around and squeezed her eyes shut, but she still heard it: the rip of flesh, a short squeal of agony. And then silence. An awful silence, slowly being pushed back by the pounding of her pulse and the burble of the swollen Seine.

Ingrid turned toward the quay steps, certain of what she would see. Marco's wings drooped slightly as he twisted at the waist and wrenched out the embedded dart. The stranger lay on his side next to Marco's long, spiked tail.

"Is he . . . is he dead?" Ingrid whispered. Marco couldn't answer her while in gargoyle form, and he wouldn't be shifting back into human form here, not with his clothes in tatters.

Instead, he threw the bloody dart and the man's discarded sword and crossbow into the river. The current swallowed them. Marco scooped up the limp body with one arm. He then stalked toward Ingrid, fury powering every step. She pulled in a breath and held it as the eight-foot gargoyle, his wolfish face crumpled into a scowl, surged toward her. She knew he wouldn't hurt her, but she'd never been more terrified of him.

Marco broke into a run. His wings snapped open and caught a gust of wind a mere second before he hooked her around the waist with his free arm. Ingrid slammed against his chest, and she clung to him as he lifted off the quay and into the low blue light of dawn.

CHAPTER TWO

The man wasn't dead.

He'd groaned during the flight to Hôtel Bastian, the rising sun nipping at Marco's tail the whole way to rue de Sèvres. Marco had landed on the roof of the town house with such force that the Alliance member standing sentry had actually cried out. He'd recovered quickly and run inside to alert the others, leaving the door open, the invitation explicit: gargoyles were not often permitted inside Hôtel Bastian, but this was obviously an exception.

The injured man hacked a wet cough as Marco shrugged him off his plated and scaled shoulder, dropping him carelessly on a steel table inside Hôtel Bastian's medical room. More blood leaked through his teeth and over his lips.

The gashes across his chest were fatal; of that Ingrid was certain. Marco's talons had ripped a path from the man's right collarbone to his left ribs, and with every heartbeat, blood rushed from the carved trenches, drenching his overcoat and shirt and—

Ingrid stared at the sash, wide as a cummerbund, wound around the man's torso. Even soaked nearly black with blood, she could see what color it had originally been: bright crimson. The color of the Alliance.

Marco had brought them here, to Paris Alliance faction headquarters, for a reason.

Ingrid heard the thud of feet approaching the room and expected Marco to shift back to his human form. But he remained true and turned to face the door. The first person to rush in would meet with the sight of a gargoyle's intimidating height, brawn, and fury.

This wasn't the first time the Alliance had tried to kill her.

Nolan Quinn charged through the door of the medical room. He was occupied with tucking in the rumpled tails of his linen shirt and strode right by Marco without more than a swift glance of acknowledgment. The gargoyle emitted a snort of disappointment through his long, wolfish snout.

The man on the table gurgled on more blood, and Nolan swore under his breath. "What happened?"

"We were on the quay beneath the Pont de l'Alma—" Ingrid began.

"What demon did this?" Nolan barked as he threw open a cabinet door and pulled down a familiar black glass bottle.

"Mercurite won't help. He doesn't have demon poison in him," Ingrid said. Nolan slammed the cabinet door and spun toward her.

Gabby had once told Ingrid how much she adored Nolan's eyes, as bright as a morning glory and as sharp as one of the Alliance's blessed silver blades. Ingrid, however, squirmed beneath them now. He shifted his glare toward the gargoyle standing behind her.

"Marco had no choice. This man tried to kill us."

Nolan lifted his chin and the anger drained from his face. He set down the bottle of mercurite and approached the table.

Nolan inspected the wounds but didn't attempt to staunch the bleeding. Ingrid figured he knew a dead man when he saw one.

"What is your name?" Nolan asked him. "Who sent you?"

Another Alliance member rushed into the medical room, giving Marco his desired reaction. Hans, the new faction leader in Paris, pulled up short and stumbled past the pair of half-open wings. Finally satisfied, Marco crumbled from his true form. His wings pleated and sank into his back, his barrel chest and hulking thighs slimmed, and his slate scales disappeared beneath dark olive skin.

Ingrid turned aside. It was startling how accustomed she'd become to naked men waltzing about. She'd long lost any desire to peek.

"Why does his name matter? He'll be dead in less than a minute," Marco said, joining the conversation now that his vocal cords allowed him to speak instead of screech. "He attempted to kill Lady Ingrid and he is Alliance. What your father told us was true, and this proves it."

The man jerked and arched his back. He hissed a long, reedy death rattle, and then his spine hit the table.

Marco grunted. "He shouldn't have lasted this long. It's not good for my ego."

Hans moved to Nolan's side and frowned, causing two deep creases to bracket the space between his eyebrows.

"Are you certain he tried to kill you, Miss Waverly?" Hans asked.

After Carrick Quinn, Nolan's father, had died in the jaws of a hellhound, Hans had come up from Rome and taken command of the faction. So far, he'd been quiet and unsmiling the few times he and Ingrid had met.

"Does the wound in my back look like a paper cut from when he shot an invitation to tea from his crossbow?" Marco growled.

Ingrid squeezed her eyes shut. Marco's quick temper would not help things. A lot had changed within the last month. Nolan and the others had put up with Luc's presence from time to time, but ever since Ingrid's sister had accidentally killed the Dispossessed elder there had been a complete breakdown between the gargoyles and the Alliance. The tenuous accord Lennier had nurtured between the two groups for centuries had all but shattered.

"Enough," Hans said in his soft yet authoritative voice. He had his eyes on the crimson sash. "Were there any witnesses?"

Ingrid hadn't yet decided whether she liked Hans. She hadn't liked Carrick, and for good reason—the man had released a mimic demon and given it orders to attach itself to her, torment her, and ultimately, kill her. He and the rest of the Directorate had agreed that the sacrifice of one human was acceptable if it meant that Axia could never reclaim her angel blood and set her Harvest in motion. They had no more of a clue about what Axia's exact plans were than Ingrid or anyone else, but they had decided that the safest route would be to spill Ingrid's blood and never find out.

Nolan's father had tried to redeem himself in the end by going against Directorate orders and attempting to save Ingrid's life. Clearly it had worked. Here she stood, still alive. However, Carrick had told her flat out not to trust anyone from the Directorate. Hans wasn't a part of the Directorate, though he did have their ear.

"No," Ingrid answered. She hadn't seen anyone else on the quay, and she hoped no passersby had witnessed Marco's transformation or the brutal killing. If they had, the poor wretches would likely have nightmares for the rest of their lives.

The door to the medical room winged open once more, and the only female Alliance hunter in Paris strode in, her cropped black hair wildly mussed and flattened on one side, presumably from a bed pillow. Chelle stood at least a head shorter than Ingrid, her petite frame drowning in a baggy shirtwaist and wide-legged canvas trousers. As if her eccentric clothing required one last detail to top it off, she was also barefoot.

Chelle approached the body without hesitation. No one needed to tell her what had happened. It was all there for her to piece together: The red sash. The deep slashes delivered by a set of talons.

"Well, has anyone looked yet?" she asked.

Ingrid frowned. "Looked for what?"

When no one answered, Chelle sighed and boldly lifted the man's limp arm. Her frankness and tenacity more than made up for her unintimidating stature.

She pushed the man's coat and shirtsleeve down, revealing a tract of coarse black hair on the top of his forearm. On the pale flesh underneath, something had been inked into his skin. Ingrid craned her neck. It was an arrow, the head aiming toward the man's blue-veined wrist and the fletching curved in half crescents toward the crease of his elbow.

Nolan moved away from the table, muttering a long string of curses. Chelle dropped the man's arm.

"What does it mean?" Ingrid asked.

"Only one sort of Alliance member receives the Straight Arrow," Chelle answered. "An assassin."

Ingrid looked upon the dead man with new horror. Carrick Quinn had spoken of Alliance assassins. He'd said the Directorate would send one to end his life for betraying their orders. Ingrid had feared that they might send one for her as well once they discovered the mimic demon had failed. But after a month had passed with Marco practically adhered to her side and no trace of danger, she'd let herself breathe again. Too soon, apparently.

"Let's not speculate," Hans said, pinning Ingrid with his cool glare. She had relayed Carrick's confession to Hans, but it had gone unaddressed.

Like many Alliance fighters, Nolan's father had been exposed to mercurite, a tincture of mercury and silver used to destroy whatever poison a fighter became infected with after a bite or gash from a demon. But mercurite was a poison of its own. After years of use, it started to eat away at the hunter's internal organs, including his brain.

By the time Carrick had set the mimic demon on Ingrid, he'd been suffering badly. Even Nolan had noticed how different his father had been acting. They all believed he'd been half mad with mercurite poisoning, and of course, the Directorate had denied ever having voted to have Ingrid murdered.

Even she had started to question Carrick's confession. The body on the table, and the tattoo on his arm, removed any lingering doubt.

Marco moved closer to Ingrid, mindful to keep his bared body out of her side vision.

"It's hardly speculation," he said. "The Alliance wants my human dead, and this proves what we've already tried to tell you."

The knotted tangle in the pit of Ingrid's stomach tightened a little more every time Marco called her that. *My human.* As if she belonged to him.

"Or this man could be connected with the Dusters that have been disappearing," Hans murmured. "Miss Waverly is a Duster, after all."

At Ingrid's last session at Clos du Vie, where she practiced gathering and storing electric pulses in her fingertips, Monsieur Constantine had mentioned that a few of his students had not arrived for their scheduled lessons. They had not been seen at their homes, either.

"He isn't connected," Marco said. The finality in his voice brooked no argument.

Chelle tapped the sole of one bare foot against the tile floor and glared at Marco. "Of course he isn't. We already know who is. Or I should say, *what* is."

Ingrid risked a glance over her shoulder. Chelle's hostility toward the Dispossessed wasn't new, but she was accusing them of harming Dusters. Oddly enough, Marco didn't make a sarcastic retort. He cut his eyes away from her, toward the body on the table.

Nolan had taken up the unpleasant task of searching through the dead assassin's coat and trouser pockets, most likely for any identifying information. "Marco is right. Assassins aren't trained to hide the bodies of their targets, and none of the missing Dusters have been found," he said. "Though a seasoned assassin would have known better than to approach his target *and* her gargoyle."

Finding nothing, Nolan reached for a length of linen toweling. His hands were smeared with blood from his search.

"The ink on his arm does look fresh," Chelle noted. "He could have been newly initiated."

"I said we should not speculate," Hans barked. "Now go wake the others. I want to know who this man is. Perhaps someone will recognize him."

Chelle swallowed her retort and left the room.

Hans kept his gaze on the dead assassin. "I'll contact the Directorate. Until I receive word, perhaps, Miss Waverly, you should remain in your home."

He didn't wait for Ingrid's response. He stole out of the room and left her gawping. Stay in her home?

"He doesn't know the Waverly women very well, does he?" Nolan said, raking a hand through his tousled black curls. Then his amused grin faded. "Have you heard from your sister?"

Ingrid shook her head, startled he'd mentioned Gabby. He hadn't, not once, in the last month.

He rubbed his mouth, his palm scraping over the shadow of a beard. "I need to send a telegram to the London faction," he said, his eyes glazed. Concern pulled his dark brows into a slant.

"You don't think . . . *Gabby* isn't in danger, is she?" Panic flooded Ingrid's body and suffused her with heat. "Do you think an assassin might go after her?"

Why did Gabby have to be so far away? Bloody London! Her

sister had been banished from Paris for her own safety against any retaliating gargoyles, but what could keep her safe from an assassin? And what about Grayson? The restless urge to find him, the notion that he was in trouble, made sense now. What if—

A hand clamped her shoulder. Marco. He'd felt her cold rush of fear. "Stop. She isn't the one with angel blood, and I would bet my wings that is what this is about."

Nolan paused at the door. "I didn't mean to alarm you, Ingrid. I just have to make sure she's all right." Without another word of comfort to spare her, he disappeared into the corridor.

Ingrid stood beside the table, alone in the medical room except for the naked gargoyle at her back. Hans had advised them not to speculate, but it was indisputable to her what had happened that morning: an Alliance assassin had attempted to kill her on orders from the Directorate. They still wanted her dead. And here she was, standing in the lion's den.

But she was safe. With Marco, she had a shield, someone who could read her primal instincts perhaps even faster and more effectively than she could. She had known the sound of a crossbow releasing its arrow, but she hadn't been able to move or think quickly enough. Marco had, and without hesitation he'd taken the shot meant for her.

"You saved my life," Ingrid whispered, still staring at the assassin's body, at the deep gashes to his chest that had stolen *his* life. She didn't feel as if she could say thank you to Marco. She wasn't thankful that someone lay dead in front of her.

"It's nothing," Marco replied in that bored tone of his. She was most certain it *was* something to the gargoyle, though. When had he last killed a human?

Ingrid moved off to the side, toward a window, unable to stare at the body any longer.

Yes, she was safe with Marco, and perhaps she and Marco bantered more easily than she and Luc ever had, but there was still something missing between them. A warmth, a tenderness.

The ever-present want—*need*—that had been between her and Luc. They had tried not to notice it for a while, and then, when that hadn't worked, they'd tried to overcome it. To actually touch and kiss and love one another. Because Ingrid did love him. And he loved her. He'd confessed it to her the morning the angels had taken him away to some other territory.

"Where is Luc?" Ingrid asked as she parted the black velvet drapes and looked out.

An older gentleman stood smoking a cigarette on a terrace directly across the street. The balcony doors opened, and his wife handed him a scarf and a hat. Just regular people doing regular things. Normal. Something Ingrid would never be again.

"I know you know where he is," she went on.

She reached into her skirt pocket and rubbed her thumb along the curved fragment of stone she kept with her at all times. It was the irregular-shaped piece of Luc's shattered stone shell that she'd picked up in the belfry, the place where his stone-crusted body had hibernated for over thirty years. The fragment was the only piece of him she had left, and she often found herself rubbing its smooth underside as if it were a talisman.

"Marco, can't you understand? I need to know."

He spoke through gritted teeth. "Why? He couldn't have saved you this morning. He isn't your protector any longer. I am."

Ingrid closed her eyes, knowing she'd hurt him. He pretended not to have feelings, but she didn't believe it for a second.

"You'd best get used to me, Lady Ingrid, unless you feel like joining your sister in London. Trust me, I wouldn't attempt to stop you."

"I didn't mean it that way." She sighed, letting go of the stone fragment. "I know how much you do for me—"

"What I am *forced* to do, may I remind you, Lady Ingrid."

By the angels, yes, she knew. Marco was compelled to protect her. And perhaps that was her answer. Perhaps the moment Luc had been removed from the abbey and rectory he'd stopped caring. Had he confused protection with love? It wasn't a new thought for Ingrid. Every day that passed without a word from Luc drove that fear a little deeper into her heart.

"I know it's dangerous . . . what I feel," she said after a stretch of silence. She spoke to the pane of glass, her fingers balled into the velvet drape.

"I know he can't . . . perhaps doesn't . . . feel it, too, but I'm not asking to see him. I just want to know where. I promise, I'll stay away, but—" Ingrid stopped herself. *But I love him.*

Marco was her gargoyle, but he was still a Dispossessed, and the Dispossessed had strict rules among their own kind. General relationships with humans were frowned upon. Romantic relationships were forbidden, and punishable by death. Gargoyles were not immortal. This was simply their second life, one that stretched on and on for an eternity, or until they were killed— something that was usually difficult to accomplish, with their steely scales and stony muscles. However, a horde of gargoyles could easily rip another gargoyle apart.

Marco said nothing, and after another stretch of silence, Ingrid turned around. The medical room was empty. Marco had left noiselessly, though she didn't know if it had been before her bumbling half confession or after. Or during. All she knew was that she was alone in a room with a dead body.

Strangely, she didn't feel any lonelier than usual.

CHAPTER THREE

LONDON

The moment the door to number 75 Eaton Square shut behind Gabby, she let out a breath and stormed toward her father's waiting carriage. All she wanted was to climb inside, pull the shade, and forget the last thirty minutes of her life.

The driver, busy conversing with a passing maid, did not see her. Gabby was moments away from clearing her throat to gain his attention when the carriage door opened from within. The steps were already down, so Gabby ascended quickly, ignoring the driver's spluttering apologies as he finally saw her and belatedly offered his hand.

"I just want to leave. Quickly," she stressed, and ducked inside the carriage.

She sat down, leaned against the cushions, and released a pent-up groan.

Rory Quinn, seated on the opposite bench, took out his pocket watch and checked the hands.

"A full half-hour. Yer patience must be improvin'," he said with a grin.

Gabby closed her eyes. It wasn't Mirabelle's fault. She'd been one of Gabby's closest friends before the move to Paris. Perhaps that was why Gabby had finally felt compelled to accept her invitation, after ignoring scores of others that had arrived at Waverly House in the days following her return to London. Surely Mirabelle would be sweet enough to overlook the grotesque scarring on the left side of her face. She wouldn't mention the puffy white tracks that ran in a hooked arc from Gabby's eye to the corner of her mouth. The ones she tried to keep hidden beneath dark veils, all of which she'd slashed on a diagonal. No, Mirabelle hadn't mentioned them.

But her two other, unexpected guests had felt no such reservations.

"No more teas. No more parties," Gabby said, her gloved fingers smoothing the dark emerald tulle of the day's veil.

Rory had seen her scars plenty of times, but she still didn't wish to showcase them. He'd been with her all month, living in Waverly House, acting the part of bodyguard quite well. His presence went along nicely with the story of how Gabby had received such dreadful wounds—that some deranged murderer had attacked her with a three-pronged hook before making off with and killing her lady's maid, Nora. Rory was simply an extra measure of protection Lord Brickton had put in place for his daughter, considering the murderer had never been found.

Of course, the murderer had never existed. A hellhound had killed Nora and torn up Gabby's face, and even though Lord Brickton knew as much, he still refused to speak about anything remotely supernatural. That was, whenever he bothered to be at Waverly House. Which wasn't often.

"Teas and parties don't suit ye anyhow," Rory replied as the driver rocked onto the bench and whistled to the grays.

"They did. Once," Gabby said softly. She sat up and attempted to hold a proper posture.

After a full month of being back in London and one horrible outing to a ball, during which she had suffered relentless inspection and false sympathy, Gabby had retreated to Waverly House and taken to living as a hermit. All of London society knew she was there. They all knew she was avoiding them. And to her surprise, Gabby didn't give a fig.

Rory sat with his knees wide and his coat undone, revealing the vest of blessed silver daggers he wore instead of a waistcoat. He was no gentleman. He was a demon hunter, and a fine one, at that. Nolan had assigned him as Gabby's protective escort, and he took the job most seriously. Wherever Gabby went, Rory attended her. He had even claimed the bedroom two doors down from hers at Waverly House, much to her father's displeasure. Lord Brickton had been far too intimidated by the demon hunter to refuse him the room, though.

"Listen," Rory said. He rubbed his fingers against the knees of his tan trousers. "The London faction tracked me down while ye were takin' tea."

"You mean while I was resisting the urge to chuck my tea at Mirabelle's friends," she muttered.

Gabby had barely swallowed her first scalding sip before the two girls had brought up the scars. Mirabelle had flushed fiercely at their silly questions. Did the scars still pain her? Was it very difficult to look into the mirror? Was there nothing a surgeon could do to reduce their size?

The carriage turned a corner and lurched, shaking Gabby from the humiliating memory of standing up and excusing herself after a second round of questions, one of which touched on her handsome Scottish bodyguard.

"They got a telegram," Rory went on. "From Nolan."

A cascade of stones poured into the pit of her stomach. There was a flutter of hope in her chest, though piteously small.

"May I see it?" she asked. Nolan hadn't written a word to her all month. Gabby had sent one letter. A simple thing, saying she'd arrived in London, that she was safe. Her pen had hovered over the fine stationery while she thought of how much she missed him. How much she loved him.

She had signed off with a safe *Yours, Gabby* and sent it before she could humiliate herself. When no reply had come, she was glad she had held back.

"It's encrypted. Ye won't have a clue what it says. The London boys decoded it, though, and it seems yer sister had herself a spot of mischief this morn."

Gabby sat up straight. "Is she hurt? Was it Axia?"

Rory held up a hand, his palm bare. Demon hunters didn't wear gloves. Too slippery on the handles of their weapons. "She's just fine. Her gargoyle was wi' her, and it wasnae Axia."

Gabby relaxed her spine, relieved. Though not wholly. Axia was still a threat to Ingrid, still able to send her demon pets to the human realm to try to fetch her to the Underneath. Gabby should have been there, in Paris, at her sister's side. Not hidden away in a big old house on Grosvenor Square.

"It was an Alliance assassin," Rory said.

The carriage ground to a stop, and so did Gabby's breathing. Before her mind could even form a thought, Rory again held up his palm.

"She's safe. The assassin's dead."

"The Directorate sent him," she said, remembering what her sister and Marco had told them about Carrick Quinn's confession. Gabby had believed them, of course, though it hadn't gone over well with the rest of the Paris faction.

"They canna know that," Rory said as the carriage broke through a knot of traffic and started rolling again.

"Of course they know. Who gives assassins their orders?" Gabby challenged.

Rory sighed. "The Directorate."

She cocked her head and crossed her arms. "There you have it."

Rory removed his bowler and his mess of wavy ginger hair sprang forward, nearly covering his eyes. He didn't like hats, she guessed. He was always taking his off and running his fingers through his hair, holding the bowler in his lap until he stepped into public view. Gabby figured the brim impaired his side vision, and for a demon hunter, being aware of one's surroundings was of paramount importance.

"I need to go back," Gabby said. Her body might have returned to London, but her heart was still in Paris.

"No."

Rory was probably used to telling her that by now, she thought.

"Ingrid writes that the Dispossessed don't know their tails from their wings. They don't have a new elder; they don't have any order at all. It's been a month. The flame of vengeance must have turned cold for them by now, don't you think?"

Rory leaned forward. The blades strapped to his vest shifted as well. "Vengeance is a flame that stays lit, Gabby, even if it's only the bluest of embers. One breath of air is all it takes. Yer stayin' here."

Nolan's cousin could be intimidating when he wanted to be, and right then, his frosty gaze and the tight muscles of his jaw urged her into silence. Fine. She wouldn't argue. But she truly did not think—*could not* think—that she would be forever barred from setting foot in the city of Paris. What if Mama, Ingrid, and Grayson never left? Mama had her art gallery to see to, Grayson would never wish to be near Papa again, and Ingrid . . . well, Ingrid had Luc. A gargoyle. Yes, her cautious, intelligent, levelheaded sister was in love with a gargoyle. Luc had been taken away from the abbey and rectory, but Gabby knew Ingrid would not be so easily deterred.

Gabby missed them all more than she'd imagined possible.

To be cut off from them . . . from Nolan. Perhaps that was what he wanted. The thought turned her throat into a hard knot. She turned so that Rory could see only the veiled half of her face. She peered out the window. They had not traveled north toward the stately homes of Grosvenor Square. Gabby noted the salty tang of the river Thames, smelled the bite of an oil and grease factory and the familiar malty scent of a brewery. Rory must have directed their driver to take them to Battersea.

"I don't know if I'm up for sparring today," she said, forcing her voice steady as their carriage clattered along the industrial road lined with brick and clapboard buildings.

"Yes, ye are," Rory replied. She shook her head, but knew he was right. There was nothing she liked more than sparring. Rory had been taking her to an abandoned Battersea dry dock for the last three weeks, and there, Gabby had resumed her weapons training for when—*if*—she was allowed into the Alliance.

Whenever she held a sword or dagger in her hand, she felt essential, as if she was doing something important rather than whiling away her time in exile. The exertions of swordplay, from wielding the heavy blade and parrying with quick steps to lunging, thrusting, and absorbing the impact from Rory's opposing blade, left her muscles sore and her chest heaving. She was by no means competent, but she wasn't as green as she'd been in Paris, either.

The carriage drew to a stop, and after letting them out, the driver continued. Most likely to a tavern for a pint of ale and a meat pie, Gabby guessed. He'd been accommodating their secret outings in return for an hour of freedom.

The long, narrow building jutted out over the swirling brown Thames and had an open access point to the river. Its clapboards were whitened with age, wind, and weather. Inside, the slipway, shaped like a wooden cradle, had once held ships in dry dock.

Rory had stored Gabby's short sword in his coat. He withdrew it and, without warning, tossed it toward her. She lunged and caught the handle of silver inlaid with mother-of-pearl. The pommel, a hollow sphere of silver filigreed scrollwork, was tucked tight against her wrist. She pointed the tip of the sword at Rory's head.

"I might have sliced off my fingers had I caught that poorly," she said, her heart already beating faster.

He raised his arms and withdrew the two short swords resting in a cross-sheath at his back, under his coat. He swung them in an ostentatious display, the blades circling through the salty air.

"I've taught ye better than that, *laoch*."

The Scottish word meant "warrior," and Rory had taken to calling her that the way Nolan had called her *lass*. She closed her eyes briefly and pushed Nolan from the front of her mind. He couldn't live there forever.

"Come at me," Rory commanded, his swords at his sides. She would never get a strike in, that much she knew. He was too stealthy, too fast.

She unpinned her hat and tossed it to the floor. The cold air coming off the choppy Thames through the access gap ruffled her dark hair and gusted over her cheeks. Rory paid her scars no attention. He never had, and Gabby knew, without his having to say it, that they weren't a distraction for him the way they were for so many others. Sometimes, if she didn't smile or squint, she couldn't feel the tightness of the scars. She could even pretend they weren't there.

Gabby walked a circle around him, trying to find a way in. Some method of surprise. She locked eyes with him, forgetting his two swords and her one. So much of Rory's training so far had been about mind play. Hunting required the skill to predict your opponent's next move and the ability to mask your own.

Gabby lowered her sword until it was at rest, as both of his were. Still holding his stare, she took a step toward him. The aged wood floor groaned beneath her. Rory's brows pulled together almost imperceptibly. She'd still seen it, though. He was trying to read her. Trying to predict her tactic. She took another step and Rory's glacier-blue eyes sharpened.

Just one more step and she'd be close enough to swing her sword up so the tip was at his navel. He'd block it, of course. Rory's strict attention wavered, diverted to Gabby's left cheek and the track of scars. Trying to distract *her,* now, was he? Playing on her deepest insecurity. It wouldn't work. She knew he didn't see her the way Mirabelle's friends did, as pitiful and pathetic. Nolan had once said that every scar told a story. Every scar was a victory. She wanted to believe him.

Gabby cut her sword up. The silver tip whispered against Rory's coat before he blocked her strike with his right blade. The trance was broken. Gabby hopped back with a wild smile.

"I did it!" She belted out a laugh. "I had you!"

A wry smile pulled on the side of his mouth. "What makes ye think I didna plan to give ye that taste of confidence?" He pressed forward.

Gabby bounced back and to the side, deflecting a teasing jab of his sword. "I saw it in your eyes, Rory Quinn. You were distracted."

Her shoulder hit a rusty iron hook the size of her head hanging from the beamed ceiling. She shoved it toward Rory with another laugh. He ducked and moved out of its return path. Gabby kept her eye on the hemp rope swinging back into place a moment too long. Rory slapped the flat side of one sword against her waist before she could curl away, out of reach.

"Now who's distracted, *laoch?*"

The lick of his sword hadn't hurt, but it shamed her into making a forward thrust of her own. His blade clashed against hers, and they glided, their silver blades singing together as they circled each other. They were both grinning like fools. With every step Gabby took around the dry dock with Rory, the awful visit to Mirabelle's faded, and her keen longing for Paris, her sister, and Nolan diminished—at least for the time being.

Rory's smile, something he seemed to save for these practice sessions, wavered and then fell. He withdrew his blade from hers, and the loss of his equalizing pressure made Gabby stumble. He pivoted on his heel and faced the sliding warehouse door that he and Gabby had closed less than ten minutes before. It was open now.

"Show yerself," Rory ordered.

Someone else was here? Gabby stepped to the side for a better view of the door. Rory's sword slashed up and barred her.

"I thought you said this place was abandoned," she whispered, worrying that they'd been caught trespassing.

"It is."

A tickle of premonition ran along her spine and Gabby spun around. A man stood near the dry dock's access point, his back to the mud-colored Thames. Rory pivoted again, holding his swords down and behind him, out of view. Gabby did the same.

"State yer business here," Rory said. No questions. Just a command.

The man stood with arms crossed over his broad chest. He looked indignant, as if he had every right to be there. Perhaps this was private property after all.

The man moved out of the opening and onto the raised floor beside the slipway. Without the bright gray sky behind him, Gabby could better see his features. He had a light ginger beard and mustache, and he wore a clean suit. Nothing fine; rather, the plain cut of a house servant.

"I wanted to see the one who killed the Paris elder," the man said. His eyes locked with Gabby's.

Rory's blades purred through the air as he brought them into view again. Gabby's grip on her sword's handle weakened, her breath suddenly short.

"Gargoyle," she rasped, though only loud enough for Rory's ears. He gave a slight nod.

This man was a Dispossessed. She'd known there would be

gargoyles in London. The Alliance here had said they were on decent terms with the local Dispossessed. She just hadn't met any of them yet.

"Now ye've seen her," Rory replied coolly.

The gargoyle continued to look past Rory, his attention solely on Gabby.

"I've got more to say." He looked and sounded as human and British as Gabby. But he wasn't human. Not anymore. She knew that in less than five seconds, this man in front of her could shed his skin and become a massive and deadly beast.

"Then say it," she said, regaining her grip on the smooth mother-of-pearl handle.

"It's about Lady Ingrid Waverly and the attack on her this morning. I've had a communication from Marco, of the Paris Wolves." Before either Gabby or Rory could ask how, he explained. "I had a territory in Paris once. Got reassigned back here, but we're still in contact."

Rory's arms remained steady, his twin blades poised.

"He sent a warning for you not to return under any circumstances," the gargoyle continued. "Your presence would only put your sister in more danger."

Gabby had been Marco's human for a mere forty-eight hours, and yet somehow he still knew she would wrestle with the notion of coming home. His foresight vexed and impressed her in equal measure.

"So yer saying the Paris Dispossessed still seek vengeance for what happened to Lennier?" Rory asked with a gloating, sidelong glance toward Gabby. She huffed and looked away, not liking that he'd been right earlier. Perhaps it would never be safe to return to Paris.

"Of course they do. If an Alliance member rubbed out our elder, we wouldn't quit seeking vengeance."

Gabby clenched her jaw. "I'm not Alliance."

She wouldn't bother trying to explain to this gargoyle that

killing Lennier had been an accident. Her worst mistake ever. Lennier had helped her find Ingrid. He'd saved her from getting mangled in a carriage wreck, too. Lennier hadn't deserved a dagger to the heart, and Gabby still felt sick with guilt every time she remembered the way he'd crashed like a stone to the earth, shedding his albino scales to adopt the flaccid and pale skin of an old man.

But what did this gargoyle care? He'd come to deliver a message. If he was anything like so many more of the Dispossessed, he'd rather wash his hands clean of humans entirely.

The gargoyle came around another beam, to the edge of the slipway. He pressed his light ginger brows together and looked down at her. "The blessed silver blade in your hand says differently. You hold that, and in our eyes, you're Alliance."

Rory finally lowered his swords. Gabby trusted his senses. If he believed this gargoyle wasn't going to attack, then she would believe it as well.

"Is there word of a new elder?" Rory asked.

The gargoyle cut his eyes away from Gabby and spared the demon hunter an indifferent look. "Marco says two Dispossessed are vying for elder, and one of them would gladly use a vengeance kill to claim the role. That's why you should, in his words, 'stay the hell out of Paris.'"

Finished with his message, the gargoyle started back for the slipway opening. Only one of the two contenders would kill her? Gabby moved past Rory, jumped over a few stacked boards, and followed the gargoyle.

"Why would the other gargoyle not kill me?" she asked, hope blooming and leaving her a little light-headed. If he didn't wish for her death and he became the new elder, perhaps he would allow her to return and live in Paris safely.

"Because you were his human once," the gargoyle replied.

Startled into distraction, Gabby tripped over a bowed floorboard and narrowly missed plunging her foot through a rotted section of the floor along the slipway, the spooling waters of the Thames showing below.

"*Marco* is vying for elder?" she asked.

"No," the gargoyle answered, stopping at the entrance to glance back at her. "The Dog called Luc."

CHAPTER FOUR

Luc wasn't in the mood for visitors. He never had been, not when he'd resided at l'Abbaye Saint-Dismas, and definitely not now. Visitors were forced upon him anyway, a constant stream of them coming and going at all hours of the day and night, sauntering through the arcaded entrance off the Luxembourg Gardens and dropping down from the sky into the courtyard.

How had Lennier withstood it?

After the elder's death, Hôtel du Maurier had been in urgent need of a guardian. And in the eyes of the Order, Luc had been in urgent need of reassignment. Still, when Irindi, the angel of heavenly law, had directed him here, to this ramshackle residence that had been abandoned by its human owners decades ago, Luc had laughed. The Order couldn't be serious. They wanted *him* to take over gargoyle common grounds?

It had been a month now, and Luc still hoped Irindi would appear and send him to his true reassigned territory. This just had to be an extra dose of punishment for breaking all the rules the Dispossessed were supposed to live by.

Luc stood at a window inside Lennier's second-floor apartments and braced his arms against the cold glass. There were at least fifteen men in the small, enclosed courtyard below. Had it been night and not afternoon, they would have been in their gargoyle forms, crowded wing to wing around the cracked and dry Hydra monstress fountain.

Their eyes were all turned toward Luc, watching and waiting for their leader, Vincent, Luc's current and most unwelcome visitor. He turned and faced the Notre Dame gargoyle that had intruded on him a half an hour before.

"You're wasting your time," Luc said. "I've been given Lennier's territory, not his role as elder."

Across the room, Vincent sat on a sofa in front of the marble fireplace. He kept his eyes on the cold ashes in the hearth.

"That is obvious. At least, to me it is," he replied. "The new elder must earn the title. The Order cannot hand it out like a prize."

It was a title Vincent had been coveting. When word had traveled through the Dispossessed that Luc had been given guardianship of Hôtel du Maurier, the rumor that he was also to be the new elder had somehow been fanned into existence. Gargoyles and their damned gossip.

Once ignited, the rumor had spread like wildfire. It had all seemed to happen around Luc rather than to him. The first few weeks in his new territory had passed as if he were being held underwater. He'd seen the gargoyles swarming the grounds of Hôtel du Maurier at night. He'd known they'd come to see him, the gargoyle that had taken Lennier's place. He just hadn't cared enough to speak to them or tell them that they were wrong.

"Irindi didn't say anything about being elder. She gave me a territory, nothing more."

They were the same words he'd finally been able to grind out two weeks after being removed from the abbey. He'd said them again and again since then, to anyone who would listen. Had he been more coherent in the days after leaving the abbey, perhaps he would have been able to stamp out the whispered assumptions. Instead, he'd sat brooding in silence at the head of the dining room table Lennier had never used, ignoring the visitors flooding into the front sitting room.

The only one he'd spoken to had been Marco. Luc had asked if Ingrid was safe. And then he'd told Marco to keep her away.

"Nevertheless," Vincent said, pushing his tall, reedy human form up from the sofa. "The Dogs and Snakes, along with some of the other lowly castes that have organized their little crusade to see you into the role, need to know where you stand. They need to be shown. Definitively."

Whenever Vincent spoke like this, enunciating each word as if Luc were an imbecile, his lower lip drew down and exposed his small, yellowed bottom teeth. Right now, Luc resisted the urge to put his fist through them.

Vincent came to common grounds every few days. His tireless quest to convince Luc to openly announce his support for him as elder had long since rubbed Luc's patience to shreds. The Dogs and Snakes and some other lower castes had thrown their weight behind Luc for reasons he couldn't understand. Gaston, the representative for the Dogs, had tried to explain that they believed Luc could forge a stronger bridge between the Dispossessed and the Alliance. Stronger than even Lennier had been able to manage. The Alliance here in Paris liked Luc. They trusted him. The same couldn't be said for Vincent.

"They do know where I stand," Luc replied. "It isn't behind you."

Vincent's thin nostrils flared, the way they did every time Luc refused him.

"The Chimeras and the Wolves are with me, Luc, and you know their numbers are stronger than all of yours combined."

Luc strode past Vincent, toward the door to the dim corridor. Outside of these apartments, the grand town house was in near ruins. The handful of rooms Luc used was well kept, though lacking in modern touches like electricity and plumbing. Gargoyles required neither of those things, and anyhow, Luc had existed in far worse conditions.

"Marco is not with you," Luc said. The Wolf was by no means Luc's friend, but Ingrid was a Duster, and it was obvious to all the Dispossessed—and many of the Alliance—that Vincent had begun picking off Dusters one by one.

Vincent formed a smug grin. Luc wouldn't have minded smashing his fist into that, either.

"Marco is no longer the voice of the Wolves. He's become too obsessed with his new human toy, that Duster abomination, to maintain his standing within his own caste." Vincent stepped away from the hearth. Luc had already opened the door for him, though he would much rather have tossed him through one of the windows.

"Tell me, Luc," Vincent said as he approached. "Do you think he has touched her yet?"

Luc gripped the doorknob hard enough to fissure the sculpted glass, his body shivering with the desire to erupt into true form.

"I have eyes on them," Vincent went on, no doubt enjoying Luc's fury. "Just as I had eyes on you."

"Get out."

Vincent's lips hardened back into a thin line. "Pledge your support to me."

"Go to hell. You're killing Dusters, and I won't support that," Luc answered.

Vincent swept up to the door, his long black cape reminding Luc of a pair of wings. "You took a human consort, and *I* don't support *that*."

Luc released the fractured glass knob, aching with the urge

to coalesce. He imagined sinking his talons into Vincent's throat. Silencing him forever.

"Do you think any of the others will side with you once they know the real reason you were removed from the abbey?" Vincent asked. "Even your own Dogs will turn against you."

Marco had fed the Dispossessed a convincing story: that with only three humans remaining on abbey grounds, Irindi had decided the territory required just one protector, and since Marco had so recently been reassigned, she'd chosen to send Luc elsewhere. The lie had rolled out of Marco without hesitation, though Luc knew it hadn't been meant to protect him. If caught in an illicit relationship with a human, a gargoyle would meet his final death. The human would not be forgotten, either. Luc had seen human consorts torn to ribbons in the past. It had been long ago, during darker times, but neither he nor Marco had wanted to take the chance that sentiments had not evolved.

Marco's explanation had been widely accepted, but clearly not by everyone.

Luc was certain he'd been careful with Ingrid. A gargoyle could feel another gargoyle's presence by the pounding chime at the base of his skull. Whenever Luc had touched Ingrid, or kissed her . . . when he'd told her he loved her . . . they had always been alone.

"You know nothing," Luc said.

"I am offering you your life. Refuse me again and the truth will be made known. Do you honestly want to test Marco's ability to protect his human against a horde of gargoyles?"

His human. The words gouged Luc more deeply than Vincent's hollow threat. The abbey and rectory had been Luc's territory for more than three hundred years. His human charges had come and gone, flowing in and out, and he'd had stretches of hibernation in between. No human had ever awakened Luc the way Ingrid had. Not just from a stony sleep, but from a monotonous existence. She'd given him a purpose. Ingrid was *his,* not Marco's.

"Bring me your proof," Luc said to Vincent.

"Perhaps I'll bring the girl herself," he returned.

Luc bristled and surged up against Vincent's chest. He had never felt so murderous. "Touch her and I will rip out your heart."

Vincent laughed as he stepped into the hallway. "Ripping out hearts seems to be Marco's job, not yours." Seeing the confusion on Luc's face, Vincent chuckled again. "Or haven't you heard? Your lovely demon-blooded human was set upon by an Alliance assassin this morning. Oh, but you can't feel her anymore, can you?"

Luc slammed the door in Vincent's face.

The moment he'd been severed from Ingrid, Luc lost the ability to surface her soft scent of sweet spring grass and earthy black soil. The absence of it had torn a gaping hole in his gut. Not being able to protect her, to even be near her, kept that hole yawning wider and wider with every passing day.

At least Ingrid was safe. No thanks to him, but he supposed it shouldn't matter. If the Alliance still had their crosshairs on Ingrid, she needed Marco.

Luc couldn't protect her any longer, but perhaps there was a way he could stop gargoyles like Vincent. But to actually become elder? To attempt to take Lennier's place and command the respect and loyalty of hundreds of Dispossessed?

Luc turned to face the cold hearth. He wanted his abbey back. He wanted Ingrid back.

Not this.

The demon hunter walked a tight circle around Grayson Waverly, so close that Grayson felt the hunter's shirtsleeve graze his own. Grayson stood completely still with his hands at his sides. He raised his eyes toward the ceiling.

"This will never *not* be awkward," he muttered. "Will it?"

Vander Burke made another slow rotation, his attention fastened on something Grayson couldn't see: demon dust. According to Vander, the dust hovered in the air around Grayson's body at all times. It curled behind him when he walked, leaving a glittering trail in his wake. Like that of all other hellhound Dusters, Grayson's dust was deep scarlet. The color of a hellhound's eyes. The color of the thing Grayson most desired.

"I suspect I come out of these meetings slightly more uncomfortable than you," Vander said as he moved past Grayson's shoulder and out of sight.

Grayson closed his eyes and cursed himself. "I'm sorry. You're right. Thank you, Vander."

The demon hunter said nothing as he came back around into Grayson's line of vision, then stepped away.

"There." Vander held out his arms. "That should take care of you for a day or so."

Grayson ran his hands down the front of his shirt. Already he was breathing easier. He had arrived in Vander's small room on rue de Berri, adjacent to the American Church's sanctuary, where Vander had been studying a quarter of an hour before. Grayson's muscles had been aching, his skin itching, and the scent of Vander's blood had made his throat hot with hunger. He'd barely been able to stifle the urge to shift.

Vander had taken one look at him and, without a word, gotten to work. It wasn't difficult. All Vander had to do was walk through Grayson's dust field. If he stood close enough, for long enough, his own demon dust absorbed Grayson's. That was what mersian demons did, after all. They consumed the dust of other demons, and with it, their abilities.

"Like I said before," Grayson said, picking up his jacket from where he'd slung it over the back of a caned chair. "Thank you."

Vander sat on the edge of his narrow bed. The room was cramped, every available corner stuffed with things he'd brought with him from his flat above the old bookshop: stacks of books, boxes, and a long table crammed with a microscope and test tubes. Grayson eyed the clothing that hung on wall pegs and the sweaty glass terrariums atop the bow-front dresser, the drawers so overflowing with books and newspapers they couldn't shut all the way. Books in dresser drawers and clothing hanging haphazardly on the walls. Grayson shook his head and grinned. Yes. This was a room he could understand.

"You don't have to thank me," Vander said as he rolled down his sleeves. He'd been hunched over the microscope, changing a glass slide, when Grayson had arrived.

"You've been absorbing my hellhound dust for the last few weeks and making my life less of a living hell. Yes, I do have to thank you," Grayson replied.

Every time Vander absorbed hellhound dust, he would take on some hellhound symptoms of his own. He'd been stoic about it at first but had eventually admitted to being able to smell the unmistakable tang of blood. And to feeling a thirst, too, Vander had said. Or perhaps it was hunger. He hadn't been able to decide which. Grayson didn't wish his symptoms on anyone, but he hadn't been able to refuse Vander's generosity.

He'd been sitting on the steps of rue Foyatier in Montmartre when Vander had found him. A bracing February wind had been rushing up the stone steps, cooling Grayson's temper after his first visit to Monsieur Constantine's chateau. Léon, another Duster, had convinced him to try at least one session. It hadn't been so awful, Grayson admitted, until Constantine had started asking for details about what had happened the month before, in that Daicrypta courtyard in Montmartre. Why in the world had Grayson imagined he could command two hellhounds? The hounds had wound up killing Nolan Quinn's father, and Grayson was to blame.

Rather than answer Constantine, he'd left Clos du Vie, and in the dark, Grayson had shifted into hellhound form. He'd run along the perimeter of Paris before sneaking down into the eighteenth arrondissement. Vander tracked Grayson's dust from the Cimetière de Montmartre, where he had been dispatching a possessed cadaver. After promising not to tell Ingrid that he'd found him, Vander had offered to take some of Grayson's dust. After one full day of smelling only air and not blood, of not feeling the slightest urge to change into his demon form, Grayson had gone to the rue Foyatier steps again. He'd hoped Vander would come. He had.

Vander buttoned his cuffs now and glanced up at him. "I wish you'd let me tell her."

Grayson stood by the closed door. He slid his arms into his jacket even though he was still sweltering. A ten-degree hike in body temperature was considered normal when one was half hellhound.

"I'm not ready," he said, his voice soft. "Not yet."

"She misses you."

"And I miss her." The muscles along his shoulders tensed. He didn't care for this part of his meetings with Vander. Today, the guilt cut more sharply than usual.

"She was under that bridge this morning looking for you," Vander said, standing up. He'd told Grayson about the attack while he'd been absorbing his hellhound dust. "She was going to go into the sewers. You know what could have happened to her in there."

Grayson rubbed his palm over his cheek and tamped down the urge to give in—to go back home to Ingrid and Mama at the rectory. He didn't *want* to stay away. He was doing it to keep them safe. For the past few weeks, Vander had been taking the edge off Grayson's urges, but the effects were temporary. They always came back. Sometimes it happened slowly, over the course of one or two days. Other times they rushed back like an ocean tide after less than twelve hours. He was a mess of sporadic hunger and guilt, of hope and injured pride. He couldn't control his demon half without Vander's help, and in all honesty, Grayson didn't trust himself yet.

"Are you sure she wasn't hurt?" Grayson asked.

"I haven't seen her yet, but Nolan said there's not a scratch on her." Vander had been acting cool toward him today, and this was the reason. He didn't know where Grayson and Léon had been living, but he wanted permission to at least tell Ingrid that her twin was safe. Grayson knew his sister, though. She'd push for more information. He also knew Vander was too far gone in love with Ingrid to put up a decent fight—he'd give in and tell her everything.

When Grayson remained quiet, Vander let out an irritated breath and took his coat from one of the wall pegs.

"I'm meeting Ingrid in twenty minutes," he said, shrugging into his long, faded winter coat. Even if Vander had money, Grayson didn't think he'd spend it on a new coat or suit. For a brief moment, he thought of his father, Lord Brickton, and what the stuffy old goat's expression would be if he learned his daughter was planning to marry a poor reverend.

Not that Vander had proposed yet.

"I'll understand if you don't want to meet anymore," Grayson said as Vander crouched to slide a long, narrow trunk out from under his bed. "I know it isn't easy for you to keep secrets from Ingrid or to feel what I normally feel because of this damn blood."

Vander twirled the small dial of a lock set into the trunk. Left, right, then left again. The hinges sighed their release.

"I want to help you, Grayson." The trunk opened to reveal an impressive collection of blessed silver weaponry nestled in form-fitting velvet cushions of midnight blue. Vander removed the hand crossbow he usually wore underneath his coat, two silver darts, and a light rapier.

"Besides, I don't exactly mind recovering from our meetings," he added with a wry grin.

His "recovery" involved seeing Ingrid and entering into her dust field just enough to drown out the hellhound symptoms. Lectrux abilities were apparently much easier to live with.

"Where are you meeting?" Grayson asked.

Vander sheathed the blessed weapons and held up his hands, palms out. "Don't worry, big brother. We'll be in full public view. I won't be able to do more than hold her hand." He shrugged one shoulder. "Probably."

Grayson feigned a scowl but quickly let it dissolve. He liked Vander Burke. He was going to be a bloody *reverend*. What older brother—even one who was only six minutes older—wouldn't want his sister to fall in love with a reverend?

"Before you leave," Vander said, adjusting his spectacles, "I have some potentially good news."

He nodded toward the table at the foot of the bed, and the needle and syringe kit Grayson had become acquainted with during his last de-dusting. Vander had been wondering, even before hunting Grayson down in Montmartre: If his dust could absorb another person's dust, what then could his blood do? Could it absorb the potency of a Duster's blood? At their last meeting, he had tied a rubber tourniquet around Grayson's bicep, and, using the needle and syringe from his kit, drawn a vial of his blood. He'd planned to draw a vial of his own blood, mix the two samples, and then watch and wait.

"You warned me not to expect much," Grayson said, though he'd let his hope run wild anyway.

Vander hunched over the microscope and used the thick steel knobs to focus the lens. "My warning still applies. However"—he stepped aside and gestured for Grayson to have a look through the eyepiece—"the samples aren't clotting."

Grayson held his breath. That was promising, at least. Vander had explained how blood from one person did not always mix well with blood from another. Transfusions were risky, according to the phlebotomy text he had been reading, because there was a high likelihood that the joining bloods might clot, spread through the recipient's body, and stop the heart altogether.

"We're a match," Grayson said, bending over the microscope and adjusting the focus until the multiplication lenses showed the blood cells pressed between each slide. They were perfect little pillowy cells.

"We can try a small injection." Vander failed to mask the thrill his new experiment gave him. "Come to Hôtel Bastian tonight, after most of the patrols have gone out."

Grayson clapped Vander on the shoulder and refrained from thanking him yet again. The demon hunter raised his finger.

"But like I said—"

"Don't get my hopes up," Grayson finished for him. He grabbed his hat from the cane-back chair and tipped it toward Vander before slipping into the corridor.

The smell of musty carpet and rotting wooden crossbeams set in the plaster walls didn't bother him as much on the way out as they had on the way in. His dust had been reduced, and for the time being, he felt comfortably distant from his curse.

The stairwell took him to the street-side door and deposited him on the sidewalk.

"Better?"

His friend Léon leaned against the limestone exterior, ankles and arms crossed. Léon had walked with him to rue de Berri but, as usual, declined to go up to Vander's room. He wanted nothing to do with dust reduction. Not too long ago, Léon had nearly allowed the Daicrypta to drain his blood in order to be rid of it. Like Grayson, Léon had lost control of his demon half once. Grayson had taken the life a prostitute in London, and Léon had killed his own parents and younger brother.

But now, after having spent more time with Constantine and a handful of other Dusters, Léon felt at ease with his demon side.

His arachnae blood gave him fangs, deadly venom, and the surprisingly useful ability to create silken web at his fingertips. All controllable, apparently.

"I can't smell your blood," Grayson answered. "And considering your blood smells like a pair of dirty socks, yes—much better." He ducked as Léon made a swipe for his hat.

"I do not understand," Léon said, his French accent heavy. They spoke to one another in English mostly, since Grayson's French wasn't much better than Ingrid's. "Without your dust, how are you to protect yourself?"

They started toward the wide boulevard of the Champs-Élysées. Grayson knew Dusters had been going missing the last week or two. He'd eventually gone back to Clos du Vie for another lesson with Constantine, and it had gone more smoothly than the first. Grayson had returned many times now, and at his last session, the old man had warned him to be vigilant.

"Still no word from Marianne?" Grayson asked to avoid Léon's question. The girl had hellhound blood, like Grayson, though she hadn't fully shifted yet.

Constantine had started combining his students into small groups, allowing them to form acquaintances. The old man had thought the approach might be better than having his students learn how to control their base instincts and desires individually, feeling isolated and freakish.

Léon shook his head. That made four Dusters in just the past week.

"The rumor is that gargoyles are doing this," Léon said as they came upon the busy Champs-Élysées.

Grayson hadn't met many gargoyles, but he couldn't imagine Luc would have anything to do with killing Dusters. If Marco had not become bound to Ingrid, the Wolf might have developed an appetite for Duster blood. Not now, though. Yann, a griffin chimera that had attempted to kill Grayson once, couldn't be trusted. He'd been Lennier's comrade and likely still craved retaliation against Gabby.

"If that's the case, we're bird bait," Grayson muttered. Léon huffed a laugh.

"But if you had your dust like you *should . . . ,*" he said, not needing to finish his thought.

Grayson stuck his hands in his pockets and stepped around an ankle-deep puddle of slushy gutter water.

"I want to be human, Léon."

Léon was the only one who knew about Grayson's meetings with Vander. The other Dusters he'd gotten to know through Constantine's lessons were like Léon—practically proud of their demon dust. They acted as if they felt special instead of just strange. They didn't understand how the blood ate away at Grayson.

"You cannot be, *mon ami,*" Léon replied softly.

Grayson hadn't told his friend about Vander's latest theory or the blood test. If it worked . . . if Vander's blood could cancel out Grayson's demon blood, even if for a little while . . . it could be the answer to everything.

They crossed the boulevard and Grayson turned left, heading toward Place de la Concorde. Léon drew to a stop.

"Are you not coming back to the room?" he asked. "Pierce and the others are meeting us there soon."

He and Léon had moved into a crummy little place on the left bank a few blocks away from the Eiffel Tower and the mass of exposition buildings erected around the Champs de Mars. It was one room, with no running water and a single brazier for heat, but without funds, it was the best the two of them were able to afford. Their Duster friends preferred the place to their own homes, considering most of them still lived with their families.

"In a while," Grayson answered. A ball of nervous energy tightened in his stomach. "I need to try to find someone."

He felt slightly guilty that it wasn't Ingrid. However, Vander was about to meet with her anyway. Fresh out of dust, Grayson didn't want to waste any time. Ingrid and Mama had not been the only people he'd been avoiding. Or missing.

"The Alliance girl," Léon guessed.

Grayson's smile came involuntarily. "Her name is Chelle."

Léon rolled his eyes. "I know her name, you fool. You talk about her even when you sleep."

"I do not," Grayson said, but Léon was too busy laughing.

"You are like one of Shakespeare's plays. All tragic and star-crossed and depressing. She does not even like you, *mon ami*."

Léon was right about that. Chelle didn't like him. There had been one moment, though, when she'd seemed as if she might be softening toward him. A moment when, if Grayson had possessed the nerve, he might have kissed her. But that was before he'd confessed to ripping out a girl's throat back in London.

Chelle was going to skewer him. He still had to see her, though: her clenched jaw and dark, flashing eyes. He yearned to hear her impertinent voice commanding him to go away.

"You are going to humiliate yourself," Léon said.

Grayson shoved him hard enough to send him into one of the icy gutter pools. Léon swore in French, still laughing.

"I know I am, but I'm tired of looking at your sorry face all the time," he called, racing away before Léon could counter-attack.

Léon waved in surrender, kicking his legs and shaking out his soaked trousers and shoes. As they parted ways, Grayson swallowed the urge to turn around and walk back to the shabby room with his friend. It would be easier than seeing Chelle. But if he could control himself this time with Chelle, perhaps he'd try stopping by the rectory soon.

Ingrid didn't need him. She was safe with Marco and Vander. But *he* needed *her*. And he needed to prove that he could be the Grayson she remembered and trusted.

CHAPTER FIVE

The Champs de Mars didn't usually look this way. At least, that was what Vander was telling Ingrid as they strolled down the crushed-gravel esplanade toward the iron behemoth that was the Eiffel Tower. Vander, who stood more than an arm's length from Ingrid, gestured to the palatial three-story buildings surrounding them.

"They're constructed out of plaster," he said. "Quick to go up, and even faster coming down, I suppose."

The buildings, all connected by arcaded façades and domed entrances, had been built specifically for the Exposition Universelle, opening in just over two weeks. Ingrid's mother's art gallery would be opening that week as well. She and Mama had spent the last month working furiously to ready the abbey. The stained-glass windows had all been repaired, each alcove chapel cleaned out and dusted, and the organ tuned, and men had come in to construct walls to run between the nave and the side aisles, where most of the art would be hung.

Ingrid had exhausted herself with the work, taking up much of the manual labor on her own. A scandalous thing for a lady of the British peerage, but it had been a way to drive out thoughts of Grayson and Gabby—and Luc.

"It seems a shame," Ingrid said of the exposition buildings. "They're beautifully done. Especially the Château d'Eau."

She glanced over her shoulder toward the head of the Champs de Mars. The soaring Eiffel Tower sat at one end of the esplanade and the ornate Château d'Eau at the other. A grand, tiered fountain surrounded an extravagantly carved dais set in the center of the chateau. She'd heard that the fountain would be illuminated at night once the exposition began, as would the Eiffel Tower.

The glass roof of the Palace of Electricity rose behind the chateau. All the electricity required for the fair was going to be generated right there, inside that one, enormous building. It topped the straight line of the Champs de Mars like the top bar of the letter *T*. The engineers were likely testing the generators, because she could hear the low hum of machinery. There was a subtle electrical charge in the air.

"How are the gloves working?" Vander asked after a beat of silence.

Ingrid held her hands clasped before her as they walked, the soft, buff kid gloves looking as fashionable as those of any of the other ladies strolling the esplanade. Of course, those other ladies would have been hard-pressed to find a pair such as these in any Paris shop. Ingrid doubted they would find the paper-thin metal disks sewn into each fingertip very practical. However, when one wished to contain sparks of electricity erupting from one's fingertips, those disks came in rather useful.

Ingrid clasped her hands tighter and felt the stiff, unyielding tips of each finger. "Quite well. I haven't accidentally electrocuted anyone in days," she replied, winning a laugh from Vander.

They had designed the gloves together after Ingrid had joked about needing to carry around a lightning rod in order to contain her volatile ability. An idea had lit Vander's eyes. "A lightning rod at each fingertip," he had returned.

The little disks absorbed the runoff energy that happened to leak out, but Ingrid was getting much better at controlling her electric impulses.

"Were you wearing them this morning?" he asked.

Ingrid paused as they crossed under the shady base of the tower. He hadn't mentioned the attack until now. Earlier, when they had met for their stroll at the gigantic Ferris wheel, the Grand Roue de Paris, Vander had said nothing. He'd charged up to her, directly into her dust field, and had cupped her cheeks with his ungloved hands. They'd stood like that for a half a minute or more, just staring at each other, Vander's warm hands so inappropriately pressed against her skin. Ingrid had been terrified that he might actually kiss her. But he'd let her go and stepped away, Ingrid's relieved breath shuddering between them.

"Does it matter if I was wearing my gloves?" she answered now. "Vander, it was an Alliance assassin, and yet Hans *still* refuses to admit the Directorate sent him."

"You shouldn't have been under that bridge."

Ingrid bit the inside of her cheek to keep from groaning. She was worn out from listening to everyone tell her how idiotic she'd been. It especially bothered her that they were all correct.

Vander invaded her field of dust once again to take her elbow. He brought her to a halt at one of the tower's wide pillars. Reluctantly, she met his warm, golden-brown gaze. She despised admitting she was wrong. Thankfully, Vander didn't allow her the chance.

"I should have listened to you," he whispered.

Vander stood a full head taller than Ingrid. He tilted his face toward hers. Men and women walked arm in arm all up and down the esplanade, but Ingrid still felt as if she and Vander were standing more intimately than was proper.

"I wanted to believe Carrick had lost his mind when he told

you those things about the Directorate." Vander sighed, and the quick puff of air caressed her ear.

The Alliance was the only family he had. Ingrid knew he hadn't wanted to believe they would stoop so low.

"I don't know whom to trust," he said, his head still tilted toward hers.

A smile pulled at her lips. "That's easy. You can trust Nolan and Chelle and Constantine. And don't forget Marco." Vander scowled and Ingrid gently nudged him. "You don't have to *like* him."

Vander caught her hand against his chest before she could pull it away. Now that she knew what his dust did, she could feel the subtle shift in her own body whenever he stood too close to her: the rise of gooseflesh along her arms and legs and the comforting warmth low in her stomach. He hadn't risked absorbing this much of her dust in a long while.

Ingrid's eyes flitted to his mouth. He was going to kiss her. It had happened twice before. Both times, the touch of his lips had weakened her, and then she'd felt guilty when her thoughts had inevitably meandered to Luc. Yet kissing Vander had felt good. So wrongly good.

She forced her hand out from under his and stepped away.

"Ingrid—"

"And me," she whispered before he could say anything more. "You can trust me as well."

"I already knew that," Vander said, accepting her rebuff like a gentleman. He stayed out of her dust, or what was left of it, but the intensity of his stare made Ingrid feel as if she were being drawn back to him. "And I hope you know that if it ever comes down to keeping loyal to the Alliance or protecting you, I'll choose you."

It will always be you. Vander had made this vow to her before. They had been devising a way to rescue her father from the corrupt Daicrypta doyen, Robert Dupuis, and Vander had brusquely admitted that he didn't give a damn about Ingrid's father. He only cared about her. He would choose her. Always.

"I do know," she said.

Vander Burke loved her. She knew this, even though he hadn't said the words straight out, the way Luc had. Luc. There he was again, always stepping into every thought, every conversation and meeting she had with Vander.

He was *gone*. Vander was *here*. And he wanted Ingrid.

"The best thing for us to do," he said, finally resuming their stroll, "is to keep working on the draining machine."

Carrick Quinn's secret partnership with the Daicrypta had allowed him access to the designs for a dreadful blood-draining machine Dupuis had planned to hook Ingrid up to. The machine, Dupuis had explained, would draw out Ingrid's blood, separate whatever inhuman cells it recognized, and then return Ingrid's pure human blood to her body. The only problem had been that angel and demon blood made up most of Ingrid's blood cells, and the human blood returned to her would have most likely not been enough to keep her alive. Dupuis hadn't cared about that, though. All he'd wanted was the angel blood.

"I can come to Hôtel Bastian today if you want to draw some more of my blood," Ingrid offered.

She had been steadily letting Vander draw and store her blood over the last month while Nolan constructed the machinery. So far, they had three pints stored. Robert Dupuis's invention wasn't completely evil. If it was used safely and tested appropriately, they could remove the angel blood from Ingrid's body and then destroy it. And if they could do that, Axia would have no reason to come after her. Neither would the Alliance.

Nolan and Vander planned to test the machine on the stored pints of blood before actually hooking the needles and tubing up to Ingrid herself.

Vander picked up his pace. "Not today," he said, his eyes on the Château d'Eau straight ahead.

Ingrid waited for him to explain why today wasn't a good day for a visit, but he stayed quiet.

"Is everything all right?" she asked. Perhaps she had offended him when she'd evaded his kiss after all.

"It's just . . . I have to be at the church tonight," he answered. "I'm being ordained Sunday, remember."

As if she could have forgotten. Vander Burke: bookseller, demon hunter, budding scientist, and reverend. He truly was amazing.

"Of course I remember. Can I attend?"

He visibly brightened. "Would you?"

"I'd love to. Vander, I think it's so wonder—"

Ingrid had gone two more strides before she realized he had stopped walking. She turned to look at him, but his eyes weren't on her. They were trained on the esplanade before them.

"What is it?"

He pushed his round, wire-framed spectacles higher on the straight, strong bridge of his nose.

"Dusters" was all he said.

Ingrid followed the direction of his gaze. The exposition architects and construction teams had left trees and grass between the esplanade and the quickly built plaster buildings, and right now Vander watched a small group of people congregating beneath one such tree. Three young men and a woman, all roughly the same age as Vander and Ingrid.

"All of them?" she whispered.

Vander nodded. If they knew one another, they must have been Constantine's students. Ingrid had kept her sessions private, though she was never alone. Marco was usually there, or Vander.

"I wonder if they know Léon," Ingrid murmured as one of the group's members said something the others found amusing. The arachnae Duster had been the last person with whom Ingrid had seen her brother. Constantine, claiming a duty to protect student privacy, refused to tell her whether Grayson and Léon were still in contact. A simple no wouldn't have violated any sort of privacy, which led her to believe the two young men *were*.

"There are scores of Dusters in Paris, Ingrid," Vander said, crossing in front of her.

"And yet it's a small community," she countered, stepping aside so she could view the Dusters once again. They were walking as a group toward an arcade that would take them out of the Champs de Mars.

Ingrid slipped around Vander's shoulder and started after them.

"The likelihood that they know Léon is slim," Vander said, falling in after her. "Even slimmer that they know Grayson."

Her brother had shunned lessons with Constantine before, but would he have completely segregated himself from others like him? She didn't think so. If she could find Léon, she believed she would find her twin as well.

"Wouldn't you agree that following them is safer than scouring the sewers?" Ingrid asked as she came upon the arcaded exit walkway between two exposition buildings. The group had crossed the street just beyond, and she picked up her speed. Vander easily kept up with her, but she could sense his discontent. She didn't understand why he was so against approaching some fellow Dusters. All he needed to do was explain that he, like Monsieur Constantine, was able to view demon dust, and then Ingrid would simply ask if they knew another Duster named Léon, or perhaps Grayson.

She and Vander trailed the group across avenue de la Bourdonnais and up rue de Grenelle. They gained on them but couldn't catch up completely. Unless, of course, Ingrid wanted to break into a sprint—something her cornflower-blue cotton walking dress, coutil corset, and heeled boots simply would not allow.

They had nearly come within shouting distance of the group when one of the young men opened a door set next to a *fromagerie* on rue Amélie. It would lead up to the apartments above the shop, Ingrid knew. The group filed inside, one by one.

Vander snagged Ingrid's elbow, drawing her to a halt. He instantly let go, however, having consumed too much of her dust already.

"And if they do know Léon? If they *can* lead you to Grayson?" Vander pressed. He let out a pent-up breath as a bicyclist and his attached rickshaw cut by along the narrow street, the tires sliding uneasily along the slushy stones. "He's part hellhound, Ingrid. He thirsts for blood. That can't be easy for him to accept. Maybe he just needs more time."

Did Vander not think she knew this? That she hadn't considered all this and more, and that it was why she had allowed five weeks to pass without a single inquiry on her part?

"And has anyone—even Grayson—considered that perhaps I need my brother?"

She turned on her heel and approached the door, breathing in the ripe odor of the cheese shop. She needed to make her family whole again. For herself, for Mama, and for Gabby, who waited impatiently in London for news.

Vander didn't stop her from opening the door, or from taking the first few steps up the stairwell that immediately presented itself. A scream split the air and Ingrid froze. Vander's hand circled her wrist. A second scream and then a panicked shout sounded from the upper floors. Something heavy crashed, and more thuds and screams followed. The sounds spiraled down the stairwell, straight into Ingrid and Vander.

They rushed up the steps, their feet pounding the worn tile. Vander moved with rapidity and ease, while Ingrid dragged her short train and wheezed for air. Chelle's trousers made complete sense right then.

The screaming ceased, but Vander and Ingrid continued to wind their way up three flights of stairs, past closed doors, the apartments likely empty of their residents during this weekday afternoon.

As Ingrid caught up to Vander, he held out his arm. The door at the top of the steps was wide open.

"Dust," Vander rasped. "Not theirs."

"A demon?" she asked.

Vander shook his head once before reaching into his coat. He removed his sword, a thin rapier, and ascended the steps slowly, purposefully. He hadn't instructed Ingrid to stay put, so she climbed after him. Vander reached the landing, whirled past the open door at his right, and pressed his back against the wall. He then peered around the doorframe.

His clenched jaw loosened and horror brightened his eyes. She scooted past the open door the same way he had, planning to place herself right behind him. The blood stopped her. It colored the inside of the apartment, splattered over a threadbare carpet and the plaster-and-beam walls. She clapped her hand over her mouth when she saw the bodies on the floor. All four of them. They lay prostrate, their limbs tangled as if they'd all fallen together in a heap. Their clothes were soaked with blood, a glistening crimson pool forming around them.

"Van—" Ingrid's voice broke off when she saw another body across the small room. He was seated on the floor, his back to the wall and slumped to the side. The gore from his torn-apart stomach and chest had splashed his face, but Ingrid still recognized him.

"Oh my God," she whimpered.

It was Léon.

A thump from up the next set of steps drew Vander's attention. The steps led to a door half the size of a normal apartment door.

"He's on the roof," Vander whispered.

Ingrid averted her eyes from the bloodbath. "Who is?"

"The gargoyle that did this," he answered.

Ingrid finally understood. He'd seen *gargoyle* dust.

"Go," he said, already taking the steps up to the roof door. "Hail a hansom and get back to Hôtel Bastian. Tell Nolan what's happened."

"Vander, stop! You can't—"

"Go!" he shouted again, and then was gone, through the door and onto the roof in pursuit of the gargoyle.

Ingrid wavered on the landing. She couldn't help Vander with this. He was the hunter, not her. He was right. She had to go, had to alert the others. Taking one last glance around the shabby apartment from the open doorway, making sure there was no other body she had overlooked—one with blond hair and a face she knew better than her own—she ran back down the curving stairwell.

A door opened as she passed by the last landing, but she didn't stop. She barreled down the final flight of steps and straight out onto the sidewalk beside the *fromagerie,* her chest heaving, her legs weak. She had thrown herself into the path of two older women, who peered at her wild display with narrowed, disapproving gazes.

"Pardon," Ingrid said, barely above a whisper. She pushed back the blond tresses that had fallen out from under her pinned hat and searched for a cab. She saw wheeled carts and rickshaws and a private carriage, but nothing she could flag down.

Ingrid peered up at the apartment building. The alley between this building and the next was so slim Vander could have easily jumped from roof to roof. She needed to move. Needed to find a cab. She hurried toward the cross street up ahead.

"Ingrid!"

She reeled to a stop, causing the man behind her to stumble to the side in order to avoid colliding with her. She ignored his mumbled curse and stared across rue Amélie. *That voice.*

"Ingrid, over here. Quick," it came again, and this time she saw a shadow dipping into the slim break between two buildings across the street.

Grayson?

She crossed the street, jumping over the thin stream of waste-water and sludge running down the center gulch in the road.

She'd known her brother would be with Léon! But, oh . . . what had happened? Had he been meeting the rest of the Dusters here? She entered the gap between the two buildings, and it immediately forced her to take a diagonal route to the right.

"Grayson?" she called, one of her gloves running along the limestone of the building she followed.

Ahead, the alley cut to the left. Just before Ingrid turned the corner, she pulled to a stop. She closed her eyes and cursed herself. *Stupid, stupid, stupid!* It wasn't Grayson. He wouldn't be running from her, leading her away from the safety of the street.

It was a delusion demon, just like the one that had once used Grayson's voice to attempt to lure her into the catacombs beneath the abbey.

Ingrid took a step back, but as she did, something hooked her ankle and tugged hard. She yelped as her foot flew forward, out from underneath her. She hit the ground on her side, her elbow jamming into the packed dirt. The thing that had wrapped around her ankle pulled again, hauling her around the corner and ruching up her skirt as she slid along the wet ground.

She dug her gloved fingers into the dirt for purchase, and kicked and thrashed her leg, but she wouldn't come free. Lifting her head, she saw a pale brown tentacle curled around her ankle. The tentacle was attached to a gelatinous glob the same dirty-dishwater color. It moved with an undulating ripple, pulling itself along by more writhing tentacles.

Ingrid ripped off her gloves but then remembered Vander and how he'd absorbed so much of her dust during their stroll. She released what she had, aiming for the delusion demon, and the lines of electricity that spit out of her fingertips were enough to stun it. She wrested her ankle free and scrabbled to get up. She spun around, lunged forward—and came face to face with the red lantern eyes of a hellhound.

The beast was as tall as Ingrid, its giant maw open to showcase the wicked curve of its protruding fangs. The stench of its breath and its black, greasy fur hit her and she stumbled back, her foot treading upon one of the delusion demon's squishy tentacles.

The hellhound raked its head to the side, and one of its bottom fangs opened her shoulder. Ingrid screamed and clutched at the wound, demon poison already burning its insatiable path through her neck and chest. It fired down into her arm, consuming the pathetic reserves of electricity.

The hellhound took hold of the fabric of her skirts and petticoats in its mouth, and then once again, Ingrid was jerked off her feet and dragged down the alley. A fissure. The beast was taking her to a fissure and all she could do was rasp a scream of pain. The rough alley ground suddenly gave way, as if the beast had dragged her off the edge of a cliff. And then she was falling, weightless, the demon poison coursing through her, filling her completely. Allowing her entrance into the Underneath. Straight into Axia's waiting arms.

CHAPTER SIX

All this time, Luc had believed that the stone statues that topped the abbey's twin bell towers and lined its pitched roofs were dog-headed gargoyles. He knew each one of them by heart. Every snarling mouth and extended tongue, every pair of wings, tucked, outstretched, cracked, or not present at all. There were missing talons and ears here and there. One gargoyle, jutting out above the courtyard's transept door as if it were bursting through the stone façade, had lost its head altogether.

Perhaps that had been the wolf-headed gargoyle, Luc considered as he approached the abbey and rectory. For Marco, a member of the Wolf caste, to have been assigned to this territory, there had to be a wolf-headed statue somewhere on the grounds. Every Dispossessed transformed into a certain caste of gargoyle, and every gargoyle's territory had to have at least one matching granite statue.

The angels, all-knowing as they were, determined which gargoyle caste each newly damned soul would belong to. In their first lives, Wolves, like Marco, were the fiercest and most persuasive; Dogs, like Luc and Gaston, loyal and dauntless; Snakes, cunning and flexible. The lesser castes, such as Monkeys and Goats, were of not much significance in their first *or* second lives.

It was the Chimeras, the anomalous blend of two animals, that Luc was thinking about as he approached the tall iron gates surrounding the abbey. Vincent's caste concerned him. Their numbers were equal to the Wolves, and among the Dispossessed, large numbers meant more power. If the Wolves and Chimeras had truly joined forces, Vincent should have already been elder. The fact that he'd again come begging for Luc's support that morning made little sense. Luc needed to ask Marco for the truth.

Luc peered through the bars of the iron gates. The abbey hadn't looked so fine or sturdy for at least a century. The stained-glass windows gleamed, and the arched front doors were new and painted glossy red. Even the gargoyle statues appeared to have been dusted and cleaned for Lady Brickton's new gallery.

He walked on, to where the iron fence ended and a row of tall hedges began. The hedges enclosed the courtyard, rectory, and carriage house, protecting them from street view, but there was a gap in the hedges for the Waverlys' landau. Luc walked through, officially entering another gargoyle's territory.

Marco was here. Luc felt his presence, just as Marco was feeling his. Luc took a deep breath. Ingrid's sweet grass and dark earth, and even that biting tang of demon dust, remained nothing more than a memory. If she was here, so be it. Luc knew he couldn't hide from her forever. He'd thought time away would lessen the ache, but it had only served to sharpen it.

Luc stepped lively, eyes cast down, forcing himself not to think of her. Which only made him think of her more. He stormed into the carriage house and slammed the door behind him.

"Take out your aggression elsewhere, brother," came Marco's unruffled tenor from the loft above.

Luc climbed the bare board steps and found Marco reclining on the cot that had once been his. He held a book over his face, his nose stuck within the pages.

"Are you the voice of the Wolves or aren't you?" Luc asked. He didn't have the patience for preamble today.

Marco licked his index finger and flipped to the next page in his book. "Do you like what I've done with the place? I thought it needed a Wolf's touch."

Luc let out his breath and took a quick look around. Nothing had been rearranged. The loft was exactly how he'd left it.

"Answer me. Do the Wolves stand with Vincent or not?"

Marco clapped the book shut and sprang up from the cot in one fluid bound. "The Wolves do as I tell them. Our alliance with the Chimeras ended the moment Yann attempted to kill Lady Gabriella. We do not stand with Vincent now."

Marco, dressed in the black merino trousers and white linen shirt of a butler's livery, tossed the book to the floor. With a lift of his brow, he added, "We don't necessarily stand with you, either."

Good, Luc thought. At least someone was being reasonable.

Marco strode to the loft door and rolled it open. It was late afternoon, and the sun looked like liquid fire slipping through the naked tree branches.

"Vincent has made threats," Luc began. He didn't know how to proceed. Marco might have known the truth about Luc and Ingrid, but that didn't mean he liked or accepted it.

Marco stared out over the rectory, his back to Luc. "Of what sort?"

"Ingrid."

Marco turned his head, the muscle in his jaw jumping. "Threats against her?"

There was a reason Marco led the Wolves. He was the strongest, fiercest, and fastest gargoyle Luc had ever met. Vincent should have been begging *him* for his favor instead of Luc.

"If a certain rumor he decides to spread takes hold, I'll be destroyed," Luc said. "I need to know you'll get her out of Paris."

Marco turned fully from the loft door now. "What does he know?"

"He suspects," Luc replied. The fewer words exchanged, the better.

Loving a human was a shameful thing. It was one of the first rules Luc had learned after emerging from death into this new existence. As elder, Lennier had welcomed Luc with a short list of hard-and-fast rules. "You protect. You don't have to like it, but you have to do it," he had said, his long white hair flowing like twin silvery rivers over his shoulders. "You are no longer human like they are," he had gone on. "You are of a higher order now, and attachments will not be tolerated."

Lennier had been ancient even then, and he had witnessed firsthand what resulted from such attachments. They weakened the gargoyle until he trusted his human enough to share his secret, in turn jeopardizing the rest of the Dispossessed.

"We will act swiftly and without mercy, against both the gargoyle and his human," Lennier had explained. All to stop the knowledge of their existence from spreading.

At least, that had been the official reason spoken from the lips of authority. As the years, then decades, and finally centuries passed, that official reason had been practically buried beneath the brutal truth: there were many gargoyles who clung to excuses to satiate their base mob mentality. Luc had never participated in these mobs, and they had been happening less often as time wore on. However, Luc knew the Wolf's talons were not so clean.

"I will take her as far as my chains allow," Marco said after a moment of silent deliberation. He then quirked his lips. "But don't let that worry you, brother. I'm sure the Seer would be overjoyed to take her the rest of the way. He's with her right now, as a matter of fact."

The thought of Vander Burke whisking Ingrid away to some

safe haven stabbed shards of glass into Luc's chest. He must have been scowling, because Marco's goading smirk fell off.

"This is your own doing. You have my silence and my vow to keep Lady Ingrid safe. And that means safely away from *you*," Marco said, good humor gone. "But if you continue to—"

It took a second for Luc, his eyes fastened as they were on the rafters while Marco ranted, to realize something was wrong. That Marco wasn't just searching for his next words. By the time Luc dragged his gaze down from the ceiling, Marco's eyes had gone a deep umber, and his pupils had slimmed to vertical slits. He stared into a dark corner of the loft, and Luc knew he wasn't seeing anything. He was *scenting* something.

"Lady—" Marco's human words cracked off into a grating shriek.

Ingrid.

Marco peeled off his clothing, too slow to save his trousers from ripping apart at the seams. Luc didn't need Ingrid's scent surging through him to know exactly what was happening. Daylight be damned.

Luc pulled the trigger in his core and unloosed his true form. He shed his clothing in practiced harmony with the pull and coil of new muscle and lengthened bone, of sliding tendons and ridging vertebrae. His jet scales shimmered from crown to ankle like a form-fitting cloak, and then, with his clothing bundled under one arm, he was racing after Marco's tail as it whipped through the open loft door and up into the sun-streaked clouds. The two of them were dark shadows racing through the sky, so fast, Luc knew, that in a blink of a human's eye they would be there, then gone.

But they would still be seen. Too large and fast to be birds. Too real to be figments of the imagination.

Luc focused on Marco a short distance ahead. They were over Saint-Germain and closing in on the crowded, narrow streets just past the Esplanade des Invalides. Marco had to be berating himself for letting his guard down. For thinking, after a thwarted attack that morning, that the odds of a second were slim.

Marco lost altitude and folded in his wings as he careened through a narrow gap between two buildings. Luc pulled in his wings, and a moment later his talons touched down in the dim, dank alley. He and Marco weren't alone.

Luc shed his scales in a matter of seconds and faced Vander Burke, whose blessed sword hung in his hand. "Where is she, Seer?"

Vander turned in a circle, his eyes everywhere but on Luc. He didn't answer. Luc forced his way into Vander's line of sight.

"Where is she?" Luc repeated.

Vander finally met his glare. "I don't know. We found Dusters, dead in the apartment building across the street, and dust. Gargoyle dust." He glanced over Luc's shoulder, where Marco was still standing in his scales.

"I went after it and sent Ingrid to catch a hansom back to Hôtel Bastian."

"Alone," Luc inserted, his fury on a fast boil.

Vander ignored him. "Her dust trail led here. And it's not the only dust I see."

Dust lingered. Vander could see traces of the colorful particles hours after a demon or Duster had left a certain spot.

"Another gargoyle?" Luc asked, but Vander was already shaking his head and swallowing hard.

Marco's human voice entered the conversation, his body having shifted. "She's gone."

The break in his voice, the sound of utter defeat, left Luc cold. Vander sank into a crouch, propping himself up with his sword. He pressed his head against the handle. "Her dust trail ends here."

A fissure.

Luc went utterly still. He wanted to kick the blade out from under Vander's balancing weight and plunge it through his neck. He wanted to scream and rage and destroy. But right then, he couldn't even breathe.

"I can't scent her," Marco said.

"Don't," Luc said. If either of them spoke another word, he might actually attack them both: the useless, pathetic excuse for a demon hunter and the neglectful gargoyle who'd gotten cocky and careless.

"Stand up," Luc growled. Vander pulled his forehead back and raised his eyes to Luc's. Slowly, rising inch by inch, he stood, locked in Luc's fiery stare.

"Axia needs her seedlings. I don't think she'll kill Ingrid." Luc hated that the Seer hadn't said this with begging desperation. Vander remained calm, his tone placating. "She'll reclaim her angel blood and then most likely return her. As soon as she's back, Marco will scent her and find her."

"Not before I suffer an angel's burn," Marco grunted.

"Forget your burn!" Luc shouted, releasing the bundle of clothing still tucked under his arm. Unlike Marco, he didn't enjoy walking around in his birthday suit and had long since learned to carry his discarded clothes whenever he went in true form. He tugged on his trousers. "And forget your excuses, Seer. I know you keep demon poison at Hôtel Bastian. Bring it to me."

He would ingest it just as he had the last time Ingrid had been taken into the Underneath. With the poison in his system he would go to the familiar Métro stop, now nearly constructed, find the fissure that he knew to be closest to Axia's hive, and descend into it.

Marco's heavy hand moored Luc's shoulder. "Take that poison to go after her and every gargoyle in Paris will know that what Vincent says is true."

Luc shrugged off his hand. Desecrating his body with demon poison the first time had been acceptable, but only because

Ingrid had been his human charge. Now he had no excuse. No excuse that wouldn't get him mauled to death by gargoyles.

"Know *what* is true?" Vander asked, rounding on Luc this time.

"You're not really so thick, are you, good reverend?" Marco replied.

Vander stepped back and sheathed his sword. "Those Dusters back there," he began. "They were murdered by a gargoyle."

"And you think this concerns me when my human is most likely being drained by an evil angel hag?" Marco returned.

The peal of bells and police whistles drowned out Vander's argument. The predictable roar of shouts and screams signaled that the bodies had been discovered.

"We need to leave," Vander said. Luc was more than ready. He couldn't stand to look at the Seer another second. With his shirt and boots back on, Luc turned toward the alley entrance. It wasn't visible, the zigzagging line of the alleyway making this place a perfect doorway to the Underneath. He'd walk back to the abbey and wait. Marco, his clothing still a pile on the floor of the carriage house loft, would have to fly. Luc would go nowhere until Ingrid's scent surfaced in Marco's nose, signaling her return—and he didn't care what the other Dispossessed thought.

Blue light flickered behind Ingrid's closed lids. There was no place left for the demon poison to fill, no corner inside her spared. The pain had plowed so deep it had struck bone.

The flickering blue wasn't cold like a winter tide or a shaded forest brook. It was hot and dry, and when Ingrid tried to move, she let out a moan. Lord, everything hurt.

She parted her lashes and the blue light grew brighter. She knew where she was. She had been here before, on this same hard-packed dirt floor. The small, cavelike room inside Axia's hive hadn't changed.

Ingrid should have been in a panic. Her pulse should have been hammering and her body sweating, and her mind should have been racing to assess the possibilities for escape. Instead, she lay on her side, her cheek against the floor, dirt caking her parched lips. All she felt was the crushing weight of failure. Axia had managed to trick her back into the Underneath after all. Hopelessness cramped around her chest and squeezed her stomach until she felt ill, on top of feeling defeated and incapacitated by pain.

Ingrid's leg ached the most. As the fog of the demon poison began to clear, she recalled that the hellhound had raked its fang across her shoulder, not her leg. Another sharp twinge of pain assaulted her as she strained to lift her head. She peered down the length of her body and saw a dark mass huddled by her legs. *Robes.* They shuddered and writhed.

Ingrid's stockings had been torn away and her skirts and petticoats bunched up to expose her pale knee. The agony of her calf seared brighter, the anguish radiating from one spot: her demon mark.

The robe's wide hood obscured Axia's face, but Ingrid could feel the fallen angel's fangs lodged deep in the flesh of her calf. Pulling. Suckling. Reclaiming.

A swell of nausea and exhaustion, chased by more pain, brought Ingrid's head back to the dirt floor. She couldn't move. And if she couldn't move, she certainly couldn't fight. It was too late anyway. It was over. Axia had won.

CHAPTER SEVEN

Gabby sat at her writing desk with a candle in one hand and a stick of red sealing wax in the other. The candle's flame turned the hard, squared-off tip of wax into a thick rain. It dripped onto the creamy linen envelope below. She let another few drops pool up before pressing the heavy pewter W monogram stamp into the quickly cooling wax. It was the second letter she'd written to Ingrid in as many days.

Gabby had returned from the Battersea dry dock the afternoon before in a tear to get up to her room and shout at her sister through the muted confines of a letter. Had Ingrid known that Luc was vying for the position of elder? If so, why had she not mentioned it? Gabby couldn't imagine that her sister would overlook all the possibilities. If he was named elder, Luc could command the gargoyles in Paris to cease thinking about revenge for Lennier's death. He could devise a way to bring Gabby back to Paris and keep her safe.

It was only after Gabby had sealed and addressed the letter

and sent it off to the post that she realized she hadn't written a proper greeting or inquired after Mama or Grayson. She hadn't even asked if Ingrid was well after her run-in with the Alliance assassin.

As she addressed this second letter, the paper heavy with apologies, Gabby thought again about Luc as elder. The notion was difficult to imagine. Luc just seemed so . . . solitary. Quiet. Not like a leader at all.

There was a movement at Gabby's bedroom window. She slapped her pen against the desk when she saw the bird perched on her windowsill. If the window hadn't been closed to the drizzly snow, Gabby would have reached for the dagger sheathed under her skirts at her calf and hurled it at the bird's oil-slick breast.

It wasn't a raven, as it pretended to be, but a corvite. A demon messenger bird. And it had been spying on her for the last week.

"What do you want?" she asked it.

The corvite's head turned toward the sound of her voice. Its long, hooked beak smacked into the glass. Anyone who stared into a corvite's eyes would notice the blood-red ring around each black pupil. But really, who stared at birds all day? Gabby certainly hadn't. Not until she'd known that not all birds were of this world.

Why was Axia sending her little messengers here? Gabby pushed back her chair and stood.

"Get out of here!" She waved her arms. "I'm not a Duster, and I don't have angel blood, so leave me alone!" She rushed at the window and threw up the sash.

The demon bird squawked and beat its wings at her before leaping from the sill. It swooped toward the back lawns, its throaty caw trailing off into a low growl. A draft of wet wind raised the hairs along Gabby's arms as the corvite's wings flapped deeper into the night. It would be back eventually. Gabby left the window open. She'd be ready for it.

Two solid knocks landed on her bedroom door. Gabby

glanced at the mantel clock, the hands lit by the fire in the grate. What did Rory want at half past ten? She moved across the white-carpeted room, knowing her new lady's maid, Kendall, had a gentler touch on the wood, and had already taken her leave for the night besides. Her father, whenever he was home, never sought her out at all.

Her guess had been correct. Rory stood on the other side of the threshold, dressed in a dark charcoal hunting kit: checked trousers and a four-button jacket, a lighter gray linen shirt, and a gray bowler. He'd even exchanged his usual tan vest for one of black leather.

"Where are you going?" she asked, her brow rising at the bulging canvas bag in his hand.

He'd been taking her in as well: she wore an emerald silk wrap cinched tight over a matching nightdress, with little white slippers poking out underneath the hem. In any other London residence, a young man simply could *not* knock on a lady's bedroom door at this hour of the night and then proceed to stare so openly at her lack of proper clothing. But all the usual rules didn't apply between Gabby and Rory. When he looked at her there were no flickers of admiration or desire. No curiosity. He had no intentions beyond protecting her, and for that reason she felt as comfortable with him as she did with Grayson.

Rory shook his head.

"Ye canna hunt wearin' that." He stepped into her room without an invitation.

Gabby closed the door. "Hunt?"

She followed Rory to her bed, where he promptly upended the canvas bag. The contents slid out and landed in a clinking heap on her pillowy duvet. Gabby gawked, instantly recognizing the strange-looking crossbow and a silver mesh net.

"Where did you get those?"

The last time she'd seen a net and crossbow like that, she'd been in the expansive courtyard within the Daicrypta mansion in Paris, surrounded by disciples who wanted to drain Ingrid's blood. They had all been armed with this same weapon. Gabby remembered how the nets had sailed out of the crossbows, unfolding as they spun toward their targets.

"Chelle managed to nab it from the Daicrypta courtyard," Rory answered. He lifted the crossbow and ran his hand down the stock's straight silver plane. "The Alliance in Paris've been tryin' to figure what it's made of."

Gabby approached her bed and noticed that the net had four long, slim metal bars in its center, like the ribs of an umbrella. One of those bars had been made slightly longer than the other three. The mesh between the bars was a simply done crosshatch, woven to leave rather large gaps, wide enough to put one's hand through. The net wasn't made of metal wire but of a strange, thin tubular material. And trimming the net was yet another tube, this one wider. She saw recurring slits along that tube and remembered how Ingrid and Vander had been sealed to the earth when they'd been captured beneath the nets. Gabby figured the tube had spikes hidden inside that came out to plunge into the ground.

She lifted a portion of the crosshatched net, expecting it to be heavy, but the material didn't weigh more than one of her bed's bolster pillows.

"Does the net gather up somehow? Before it's shot out of the crossbow?" she asked.

Looking rather smug, Rory took the cumbersome netting from her by gripping the bottom of the longest metal bar. He pressed a steel-capped button located where all the bars joined in the center. Rory's long bar stayed immobile, but whatever mechanism he'd engaged sent the other three bars swiveling around it, like ribbons on a Maypole. They wound tightly around the stationary bar, twisting and expertly tucking the mesh net as they closed. When it had all finished, Rory held what looked like an exceptionally long, thick crossbow bolt. Again, similar to a bound umbrella.

"Why did Chelle send it to you?" Gabby asked.

"She knows I like new toys," Rory answered with a lopsided grin. He shrugged. "Suppose she thought we might have fun wi' it, too."

She looked again at his dark gray hunting attire. "What, *tonight*? Rory, I'm not certain I'm ready."

Practice sparring at the dry dock during daylight hours was one thing. Demon hunting at night was something altogether different. She'd gone out on her own in Paris one evening in February, wanting to prove to Carrick Quinn that she could hunt and be useful to the Alliance. Instead, she'd clashed with an appendius demon and gotten herself stuck with the poisonous horned tip of its arm. Nolan had needed to use mercurite to destroy the poison before it burned through her body and killed her. Gabby still wasn't sure what had caused her the most anguish: the poison, the cure, or the humiliation of failure.

Rory packed the Daicrypta crossbow and bound net into his canvas bag.

"'Tis time to go out, Gabby."

With startling finesse, Rory ripped a dagger from his vest. He pivoted on one heel while sinking into a crouch and chucked the dagger across the room, toward the open window. Gabby heard the short, surprised shriek of a corvite but didn't see the demon bird itself before it exploded into a cloud of emerald death sparks. Rory straightened his legs and strode to the window.

"That thing was beginnin' to annoy me," he said, retrieving the dagger that had clattered onto the brick window ledge when the demon had vanished.

He took a cloth from one of his coat's inner pockets and ran it along the blade, black with demon blood. He acted with such quiet certitude, such stealth. Gabby wished for the same skill. She knew he was right. It was time she moved to the next level.

Gabby nodded. "I'll get dressed."

* * *

The London docks were no place for a lady. Gabby walked along the Wapping Basin quay wishing she didn't feel so much like an earl's daughter. She hadn't in Paris those few times she'd been out with Chelle tracking demons. But Paris had been more than just a new and different city. There, Gabby had entered an entirely different world. It had given her permission, in a way, to be an entirely different person. Here in London, in the city she had always known, the old Gabby kept trying to creep back in.

Her heeled boots clacked along the stone quay, and the river water slurped in and out of the dock's entrance basin with a constant push and pull. The small, three-acre basin was silent otherwise, having mostly fallen out of use with the larger ships coming in to port farther upstream at the Shadwell entrance. Rory had chosen this spot for its privacy. He walked next to her, the two of them draped in near blackness. There was only a handful of lamps lighting the rows of four-story warehouses, and another string of them up ahead along the jetty and the Western Dock, where light ships and barges heaved gently in the water.

There were a few people milling about, but nothing like the pandemonium the docks must have been like during the day. Gabby saw shadows moving between warehouse lanes and around corners. Not demons, she thought. One had a sack thrown over his shoulder—a rag-and-bone man. Another had the messy upswept hair of a loitering prostitute. Muted laughter came from one of the ships moored to the Western Dock. Sailors.

"My cousin would spear my guts and roast 'em over an open flame if he knew I'd brought ye here," Rory said, voice hushed. "He wouldna like that I've been trainin' ye, either."

His eyes roamed the docks and saw, Gabby knew, more than she did. Rory was competent, and she trusted him, but she still wished Nolan could be the one teaching her how to hunt. He had been going to. When his father had told Gabby she couldn't be part of the Alliance, Nolan had vowed to train her in private.

"I don't think he'd mind so much anymore," Gabby said softly as they made a right and moved parallel to a row of brick warehouses. She breathed in the sweet scent of tobacco stores in the cool, still air.

"Nolan's being a bloody dunderhead right now, but I know my cousin. He's gone half daft he's so in love wi' ye, *laoch*. Just give him a little more—" Rory paused on the narrow walkway between the warehouses and the Western Dock's high quay wall. His arm came up, level with Gabby's shoulders, and stopped her from taking another step.

"Ye don't want to step on it," he whispered, his attention fixed on the ground before them.

Gabby followed his gaze. In the low light it appeared to be a slug. The largest slug she'd ever seen. It was about the length of her hand and the width of three fingers, and it moved with surprising speed, cinching and stretching, its two feelers pointed in the direction of the tobacco warehouse. It wasn't alone. A line of them crawled up from where the quay wall dropped off into the watery Western Dock.

Without speaking, she and Rory stepped to the edge of the wall and leaned over. The slugs were climbing up the slick, mossy stone, coming from a pale mass floating in the water.

"That's what I thought," Rory said, with an unmistakable edge of excitement. Gabby felt only revulsion.

There was a body in the water, slapping gently against the quay wall. It was so completely covered by slugs that its clothes and skin looked like they were writhing.

Gabby's hand settled on the pommel of her sword, sheathed inside her long coat. "What are they?"

"They're part of a bigger demon. A mollug," he answered, sinking into a crouch. He watched the slugs wriggle away from the quay wall in a perfectly ordered line. The line curved behind a pyramid of crates and slatted wooden boxes set in front of one warehouse door, then disappeared.

"What do you mean, part of another demon?" Gabby asked.

"The mollug itself canna move quickly. It sheds its exterior—scores of these smaller slugs—and sends 'em to attack and paralyze its prey," Rory explained, hitching a thumb over his shoulder to indicate the body below in the water. "They're returnin' to the mollug now. Once they reattach, the mollug'll come out for its dinner."

Her stomach kinked as Rory took the Daicrypta's crossbow from inside his long coat and held it out for Gabby. She stared at it dumbly.

"Go on," he said. It was larger than Vander's hand crossbow, and when she took it and felt her muscles struggle to adapt, she imagined it was probably much heavier as well. She wore no gloves, and the polished steel stock slipped in her sweaty hands.

"We couldna've asked for a better demon to test this contraption on," Rory murmured.

Gabby let out a breath. He was right, especially if the mollug was too lethargic to capture its own prey.

"All right," she said, holding out her hand. "Just show me how to load the net . . . bolt . . . thing."

Rory smiled and reached inside his coat for the bolt. Gabby stepped forward to take it—and felt something squish beneath her boot. Rory swore as Gabby lifted her foot and saw the flattened remains of one slug.

A high, keening wail slipped out from behind the stacked crates.

"Take it." Rory shoved the bolt into Gabby's hand. "Load it, quick."

The wail died down, but Gabby's ears still rang.

"Load it how? I need you to show me," she said, her panic

rising as another sound came from behind the crates. A grating, dragging sound, like the bottom of one slatted wooden box being shoved along the quay stones.

"Pull the bowstring back," Rory said. Gabby dropped the bolt to the ground in order to lever the hemp back. She hadn't yet hooked it into the latch when she saw movement at the crates. A pale, undulating blob emerged. It was taller than Rory, and without any normal features like arms or legs, or even a head. It was just a huge, jellylike tumor—and it was coming for them.

"Load the bolt into the groove," Rory said, his curt instructions striking like errant pins at a dress fitting. He stood immobile, his eyes on the mollug as it heaved forward, its flat bottom slurping along the stone. One by one, the slugs climbed up onto the mollug, tucking themselves close together to form a kind of shell.

Gabby picked up the long bolt and tried sliding it into the groove atop the stock.

"It's not working—Rory!"

He didn't move to help. "Pay attention to the bow, Gabby. And turn the bolt around."

She flipped the bolt and slid it into the groove easily just as the mollug increased its speed. It was less than five yards away from them now. She lifted the stock against her shoulder and aimed for the creature.

"Pull the trigger," Rory said.

Gabby placed her index finger against the curved trigger and squeezed. The trigger stayed put. Her stomach bottomed out.

"Rory!"

"Again. Harder," he barked.

Gabby crushed the trigger as hard as she could and yelped as the crossbow bucked against her shoulder. The bowstring released, propelling the bolt down the flight groove and toward the demon. The net whirled open and came down hard over the mollug. The net's rim slammed against the ground, and Gabby heard the spikes crack through the stone, sealing the demon in place.

Rory clapped his hand against her shoulder, jostling her forward.

"Nicely done, *laoch*."

Gabby regained her balance and jammed the stock of the crossbow into Rory's stomach. "We could have practiced first!"

He coughed and pulled the weapon from her hands. "That *was* practice."

He toed one of the slugs out of his way as he walked to the captured demon. The ones that hadn't made it back to the mollug retreated from the net now, into the shadows and back toward the quay wall.

"Besides," he said, clearly amused. "I knew ye could do it."

A man's voice sounded from close behind them: "Why shouldn't she have been able to do as much?"

Gabby whirled and saw three men watching her and Rory. Two tall, burly men flanked a shorter person. For a heartbeat Gabby thought the center person was a child. But then the figure stepped forward.

"Diffuser bows are extraordinarily easy to manage," he said, his voice that of a grown man.

Rory had abandoned the netted mollug and was now back at Gabby's side. The stranger knew the Daicrypta crossbow; he had a name for it. Which could mean only one thing: he was a member of the Daicrypta.

The man wore a dark suit and a cape the color of midnight. It was a handsome, expensive design, if a little dramatic. Red silk piping ran along the edge, and wide red ribbons tied at his throat. Truly, he looked like a magician. A very short magician.

"The net," he said to his companions. The two bruisers approached the mollug.

"What are you doing?" Gabby asked as one of them crouched by the base of the net.

"Simply retrieving what is mine," the man answered. Standing closer now, Gabby could see he had a youthful face. Not a day over twenty-five, if Gabby was to guess.

"I captured that demon," Gabby said, though she instantly regretted her petulant tone.

"And you are welcome to it," the man replied. "I would have the net and crossbow, if I may."

He extended his hand toward Rory, who still held the weapon. The Scot huffed and stared at him, incredulous.

"Why should I give it to ye?" he demanded.

"Because you stole it," he answered without hesitating. "And considering it was my father's invention, I think it only fair you return it to me."

Though his accent was slight, Gabby could hear a French inflection here and there.

The net's spikes retreated from the quay into the tubular rim, and suddenly the mollug was writhing again. The net fell away, helped along by the two bruisers, and the creature undulated toward Gabby and Rory with renewed vigor.

"Are you mad?" Gabby shouted, skittering backward. The caped man only laughed.

"Not at the moment. I'm rather amused, actually. You have a demon hunter standing beside you, do you not?"

Rory growled, his free hand going for one of his trusted blades. The dagger whistled through the air, and a thundercloud of green sparks signaled the demon's demise.

"The diffuser crossbow," the man said, extending his white-gloved hand once again toward Rory.

He held the weapon up. "First I'll have yer name."

The man kept his hand raised and waiting. "Hugh Dupuis."

Something inside Gabby snapped to attention. *Dupuis.*

"Your father—" she began.

"Was Robert Dupuis, Daicrypta doyen and head research facilitator in Paris," he rattled off. "I believe you met him once."

CHAPTER EIGHT

Ingrid felt the sting of hard, frozen ground against her cheek first. The pain came next, ballooning inside her as she woke. Her leg was in agony, her calf a ball of flame. The flickering blue light of Axia's cave had gone. It was dark here, wherever *here* was. The smell of winter air and dirt and grass browned by snow filled her nose.

She was out of the Underneath. Returned home.

Ingrid pressed her hands against the crusty ground and tried to push herself up. She was too weak, however, and her arms collapsed. She lay still, heart racing. Even opening her eyes seemed to drain her of what little energy she possessed. There was a lamppost nearby, the glass orb streaming yellow, vaporous light over a long park bench and a handful of pigeons roosting on its curved back.

Ingrid closed her eyes again and tried to think of what to do. She was too cold and tired to flinch when the roosting pigeons squawked and scattered in a flutter of excitement. A rush of air fanned down over her, tousling the hair that had fallen loose around her face. The familiar rustle and snap of wings from close overhead caused tears to well up behind her closed lids. Marco had found her.

Her body moved, nudged gently by what she knew were talons, not hands. Ingrid mewled as even that slight touch renewed the pain in her leg and calf. She forced her eyes to open as Marco's arms wedged underneath her and lifted her from the cold ground. His scales were desert hot in comparison, and as he drew her to his plated chest, she felt the tug of a memory. Marco had never held her like this before, and yet she knew these arms. Knew the warmth of this steel chest, and what it felt like to be cradled against it.

Ingrid looked up, already knowing what she'd see. A pair of peridot eyes, pale and bright as jewels; shimmering jet scales tightly woven along his face; and short, clipped ears set high upon his head.

"Luc," she managed to whisper before her head fell against his chest once more. Luc had come for her. She didn't know how he'd known, but he was here and she was safe and there wasn't anything for her to worry about any longer. So Ingrid let her eyes close and Luc took her into the night sky.

The soft down of a pillow had replaced Luc's hard, reptilian scales when Ingrid found consciousness again. She was warm, buried underneath the weight of a thick duvet. *Her* duvet, she saw after opening one eye.

She stirred under the covers, and by the clear honey light coming in through the window, she determined it was early morning. She heard the even, rhythmic breaths of someone sleeping and pushed herself up onto one elbow. Luc had flown her here. *Luc.* After a full month of not seeing or hearing from him, he'd come for her when she'd needed him most.

It wasn't Luc in her room now, though. With a start, she saw Vander in a chair at the foot of her bed, his arms crossed, his legs wide, and his chin tucked into his chest as he slept. The sun lit his golden-brown hair, mussed from where he'd likely raked his hands through it again and again. She wondered what Vander had said to her mother to gain permission to sit watch here without a chaperone. The fact that he was to be ordained soon must have certainly come into play. A smile touched her lips, until she twisted to sit up and felt the soreness of her shoulder where the hellhound's fang had sliced into her.

The memory hit her like a fist. Ingrid batted the heavy duvet off and yanked up the hem of the nightdress that someone had changed her into. Her calf didn't burn with the same fury that it had in the Underneath or when she'd woken in that darkened park, but the spot was tender. Luc had likely healed her wounds with his blood, because the skin along her calf was unmarred by the fangs Axia had plunged into her flesh.

Ingrid closed her eyes, a hand pressed to her temple. How could she have been so stupid? Racing into that alley, chasing Grayson's voice. And now Axia had reclaimed her blood. All of it? Ingrid didn't know. She didn't feel any different than before, other than the sweep of panic making her hot and then cold again. What would happen now?

"Ingrid?"

Vander shot up from the chair, sleep rasping his voice.

"She has it," Ingrid said, her thumb rubbing the two strawberry ovals on her calf. "She took her blood back. She had me in her cave again and I couldn't move, I couldn't make any electricity, and the demon poison, it burned—"

Vander came to her side and lowered himself onto the bed. The mattress shifted and dipped.

"I'm so sorry," she said, gasping for air around the tight, aching ball of a sob lodged in her throat.

Vander's hands cradled her neck and jaw, his fingers

combing through her hair. He forced her head up, her eyes to look into his.

"Ingrid, you have nothing to be sorry for."

She shook her head, though his hands held her tightly.

"She has her blood and now she'll be coming here, for her Harvest. I gave her exactly what she wanted, Vander."

He pressed his fingers into her skin more firmly. "She *took* what she wanted. Do you believe any of us care about that right now? You were taken into the Underneath. You were gone a full day. I'd started to worry that you weren't—" Vander stopped, his thumbs sweeping over the curves of her jaw. "I should be the one apologizing. I shouldn't have left you alone."

A whole day? She'd been in the Underneath for that long? Vander let go of her but remained on the edge of her bed.

"You're here," he said. "You're safe. That's all I care about."

They were simple, straightforward statements. They helped to calm her. Ingrid kept her hand on her calf, rubbing at the small ache underneath her demon marks. Vander followed the motion with his eyes. She gave a start, realizing her leg was exposed from knobby knee to bare foot.

Ingrid let go of her calf and grabbed the hem of her nightdress, ready to tug it back into place. Vander's hand came up and rested atop of hers, stopping her.

"Is it healed?" he asked. He then took the liberty of skimming the soft curve of her calf with his palm.

Ingrid sat frozen in place. Though her eyes watched him inspect her demon marks, it wasn't Vander she was seeing in her mind. It was Luc, that first night in the abbey when he'd revealed to her what he was. A hellhound had nipped at her calf, and Luc had demanded to see the wound, roughly tossing up her skirt hem and grabbing her leg. She saw Luc, lifting her off the cold brick and gravel walkway so her bare feet wouldn't have to endure a painful walk back to the rectory. Luc, storming into Axia's hive, coming to take Ingrid home to safety. Luc, his damaged wings hanging limply in the Daicrypta courtyard, his bond to her severed, and yet there to help her anyway. And there in the park also, her body belched up from a fissure, too weak to move. He was always there.

He would always come for her.

Ingrid shoved the hem of her nightdress down, dislodging Vander's hand.

"It's fine," she said.

Vander adjusted his spectacles before standing up and moving away from the bed.

"We have Marco to thank for that," he said.

Ingrid paused in bringing her duvet up around her waist. "Marco? But I thought . . ."

Vander went to the window and pushed back the gauzy drapes. "Luc was with Marco when he found you," he said, his words clipped to sharpened points. "He couldn't stay."

Ingrid propped herself against the pillows, relieved. She hadn't imagined him, then.

"He had to return to his territory," she said.

Vander stayed silent at the window, looking at the churchyard lawn as if there were actually something interesting to see there.

"You know where he is. Don't you?" Ingrid asked.

She hadn't had the nerve to bring up Luc's name or ponder his new territory with Vander these last weeks. She'd also been careful to keep Luc's stone talisman in her pocket and out of Vander's sight. She knew his feelings for her, and he knew of hers for Luc. It would have been awkward to discuss her heartbreak with someone who was likely rejoicing inside, so she'd stayed quiet instead.

"Lennier's old territory," Vander finally answered. He turned away from the window and added, "Luc didn't want you to know."

She leaned into the pillows, stunned. He'd been close this whole time. Guardian of gargoyle common grounds, a mere ten-minute walk away. She pictured him in Lennier's sitting room, in front of the hearth. In the guest bedroom where they had kissed and held one another in the four-poster bed—the very action that had decided Luc's fate as guardian of l'Abbaye Saint-Dismas.

Of course he hadn't wanted Ingrid to know. He would understand how tempted she'd be to go to him, and he wouldn't want her at gargoyle common grounds, not when any number of Dispossessed could be there.

Vander left the window. "I have to get back to Hôtel Bastian. Things are . . . busy."

The way he'd hesitated took Ingrid from her thoughts of Luc. "What is it? Do you know which gargoyle killed Léon and the others?"

He picked up his jacket from the back of the chair and avoided her eyes.

"Vander, you can tell me. I can handle it." Another thought stilled her. "Or is it Axia? Has something happened while I've been sleeping?"

How long would it take for the fallen angel to set her Harvest in motion?

Vander shrugged on his jacket, the blessed silver crossbow inside weighing down the faded tweed. "No and no. It's Alliance matters, that's all. You need to rest."

She pressed her lips tight and cocked her head, as if to say *I don't think so.* Vander started to laugh a moment before the door to her bedroom creaked open. Ingrid's mother stepped inside all smiles and bright eyes. Ingrid was about to ask why when someone else came in on Mama's heels.

"Grayson!" Ingrid pushed back the duvet once again and leaped up. Her brother reached the bed in time to catch her before she fell. Her leg didn't hurt, but she wasn't steady on her feet just yet, either.

Her mind whirled, her vision spun, but it didn't matter. Grayson was here and he was holding her. She breathed in deeply, and with the air came a rush of anger. She pulled back and cuffed his arm.

"Where have you been? You could have at least sent a note saying you were still in Paris. That you were still *alive*."

Grayson sighed and hung his head, nodding once. "I know. I'm sorry, Ingrid."

Mama stood in the doorway, watching them. She was still smiling, without a trace of anger anywhere on her lightly lined face.

"I have already spoken with him," Lady Brickton said, her corseted figure cut into an hourglass. Plump and firm and trim all at once, like a pincushion, Ingrid often thought. "And I am holding him to the promise he has made me. Mr. Burke?"

Mama held the door open, graciously indicating that it was time for Vander to take his leave. Grayson turned his head to watch Vander in his side vision. They didn't make eye contact, and Vander, Ingrid noted, fled the room rather quickly, without so much as a hello for her brother. If he was upset about Luc, she would just have to worry about it later.

Mama closed the door behind herself and Vander.

"I was supposed to be there," Grayson said the moment they were alone.

He pulled away, his jaw tight. His eyes were red-rimmed, as if he'd been crying.

"It was my flat. The one I share with Léon."

"Oh, Grayson." She reached for his hand. He let her take it, wind her fingers through his, and squeeze.

"I took an omnibus to Hôtel Bastian instead. To see Chelle."

She tried not to show her hurt. "You've been seeing Chelle?"

He brought their joined hands into his lap and started twisting the ring on her center finger. The single pearl set in silver had been their grandmother's.

"No, and she wasn't there, so I still haven't seen her. By the time I made it back to the flat . . ."

Even if he had been seeing Chelle, she couldn't be upset with him. Not right then. He'd come too close to being among those slain Dusters.

"You made Mama a promise," Ingrid said. "What was it?"

Grayson quit fiddling with her ring and stood up. His light blond hair flopped forward and nearly covered his brows. It had grown past his ears and had an easy wave to it at this length.

"I can't come back here to live, Ingrid. Accepting the rectory as my home again will bind Marco to me." He said the gargoyle's name with a heavy dose of acid. "I don't want him, and he doesn't need another human to guard right now anyway. But do you really think Mother would let me go off without having a place lined up?"

"I can't imagine she would," Ingrid replied, refraining from saying anything more. Like how worried their mother had been over his absence.

Grayson seemed to hear the words anyway.

"I don't know if you're safe with me," he said.

"I wish you trusted yourself as much I trust you."

He couldn't make a reply to that, it seemed, so instead, he leaned over and kissed her forehead.

"Mother's already found a flat across the street for me to let. I promise I won't disappear again."

She jabbed him lightly in the stomach before he could straighten back up. He pretended to double over in pain.

"See that you don't," she said. "Now that Axia has all of her blood back, I have a feeling we'll need one another."

CHAPTER NINE

Grayson leaned against one of the steel tables inside Hôtel Bastian's medical room, his right sleeve rolled up and cuffed past his elbow. It was the same shirt he'd been wearing for the past month: white linen with small ivory buttons and a short club collar. Grayson had never had to wash his own clothes before, and he was certain the numerous times he'd plunged the thing into brown tap water at the flat hadn't done the expensive bespoke shirt, made just for him on London's Savile Row, much good. But he was also sure it wouldn't have caused it to shrink.

Grayson's muscles had bulked over the last few weeks, causing the seams to bite into his shoulders and the buttons at his chest to pull when fastened. It couldn't be blamed on an abundance of food—he and Léon had scraped by, living on bread and cheese, eating well only on visits to Constantine's chateau. The change in his musculature had to be attributed to the numerous times he'd changed from human to hellhound. Sometimes the shift had been on purpose. Other times, he hadn't been able to fight his body's urge to let go. Grayson wondered if his muscles had hung on to a little bit of the hellhound bulk to make shifting less of an ordeal.

"I'm glad you went to her," Vander said from where he stood at one of the glassed in cabinets. He had his kit out and was drawing blood from a vial into the glass barrel of a syringe.

Grayson hadn't gone to Hôtel Bastian for his first mersian blood injection, as he and Vander had planned. The massacre at the flat and Ingrid's abduction into the Underneath had made them both forget. Seeing Vander in Ingrid's room at the rectory that morning had reminded Grayson, so he'd made his way to Alliance headquarters after tucking Ingrid into bed to rest some more.

Grayson flexed his bicep. The length of red tubing tied tightly around his arm stretched and whitened to pale rose.

"You were right. I should have gone back to the abbey a long time ago. If I had, she wouldn't have followed my friends to the flat. She wouldn't have been anywhere near that alley," Grayson said.

Vander came toward the table with the barrel full of what Grayson knew was mersian blood. "'That which hath been is named already.'" Vander glanced up with a wry grin. "Ecclesiastes."

"I could use a translation." Grayson held out his arm and attempted not to look at the long, thin steel needle.

Vander positioned Grayson's arm and rubbed the bulging blue vein he intended to stick.

"What's done is done," he said, piercing Grayson's skin without hesitation. A press of the plunger and the barrel's contents slowly emptied.

"Please, Reverend, no more biblical code," Grayson teased.

The last drop of mersian blood disappeared from the glass barrel and Vander removed the needle tip. A bead of blood welled up on the injection site and gravity pulled it down Grayson's forearm.

"It's always about blood," he said as Vander removed the rubber tourniquet and held out a wad of linen. Grayson staunched the blood and began to wrap the linen around his elbow. "Angel blood, demon blood, Duster blood. For once I'd like it to be about something else. Like, I don't know . . . food. Or whiskey. Why couldn't Axia just crave a shot of good whiskey?"

Vander smiled but didn't laugh. He was taking apart the needle and syringe, preparing to dip the pieces in a jar of carbolic acid.

"What now?" Grayson asked, and somehow Vander knew he wasn't thinking about the mersian blood spreading through his system. He was asking about Axia. About the Harvest.

"Word has come from Rome." Vander let the needle's components settle into the jar of syrupy, red-tinged antiseptic. "The Directorate is sending us an emergency troop of Alliance hunters. They want Paris secured if Axia is to make a strike."

Grayson finished with his bandage and rolled down his cuff. He would have thought the more hunters, the better, but Vander didn't sound relieved.

"You don't want them here?" Grayson asked.

Vander wiped his hands on some linen toweling and, without a reply, moved to a squat, freestanding zinc cabinet tucked into the corner of the room. He then took a key from his waistcoat and crouched to insert it into the padlock latching the doors.

"Two mornings ago, an Alliance assassin tried to kill Ingrid. Assassins don't work on their own; the Directorate gives them their targets." The padlock fell open and Vander swung the zinc doors wide. He stood up and allowed Grayson to see inside. There were three shelves, and on the center shelf were three glass jars filled with red liquid. He couldn't smell the blood; the jars looked airtight. He just knew the color by now. The cabinet must have had a vapor compression system. Each jar was covered in a swirling pattern of frost.

"I've been drawing Ingrid's blood every three or four days for about a month," Vander said before further explaining about the blood-separating machine the Daicrypta had developed and how he and Nolan were creating something similar here in a room on the fourth floor.

Grayson eyed the contained blood with dawning realization. "You have angel blood in those jars."

Vander closed the cabinet doors and replaced the padlock. "The Directorate has ordered us to hand Ingrid's blood over when the troops and their representative arrive."

He twisted the key and then dropped it back into the pocket of his baize-green waistcoat.

"Why do they want it?" Grayson asked, though he could think of a few reasons on his own. Power, for example. Ingrid had been able to push gargoyles into submission a couple of times, and Grayson had heard about the Alliance's recent proposed gargoyle regulations.

"I imagine they plan to use the machine Nolan and I have been building to separate it and draw out the angelic blood. Maybe they have another machine in Rome that already works. I don't know, but after that assassin, I don't trust the Directorate," Vander answered, hushing his voice and glancing toward the closed door.

"You could waste it. Pour it into the Seine or down a drain, into the sewers, even."

Vander was shaking his head before Grayson had stopped suggesting methods of destruction.

"It's *angel* blood," he said, perking up as footsteps approached the medical-room door. "There has to be some good we can do with it."

The doorknob turned, cutting off Grayson's chance to argue.

Monsieur Constantine let himself in and immediately dropped into a graceful bow.

"Messieurs," he greeted them, his charcoal derby in hand. His usual gray palette matched the mood in the room perfectly.

"What are you doing here?" Vander asked, absent his usual good manners.

"I've informed Monsieur Hans that lessons at Clos du Vie have been suspended. My home is being watched, the comings and goings of my students observed. I think it would be wise for all Dusters to maintain low visibility for the time being. Lord Fairfax," Constantine said, addressing Grayson by the courtesy title that his place in the British peerage afforded him. He loathed it, and wished Constantine would simply call him Grayson or Mr. Waverly. "I am very sorry about our friend Léon."

Grayson wanted to rewind the days, go back to when he and Léon had parted on the Champs-Élysées. He would change things. He'd invite Léon to go with him to see Chelle. Let their friends wait for them in one of the cafés near the flat, he'd say.

Grayson wasn't sure his voice would remain steady if he tried to say anything about Léon. Instead, he tapped into a resource that was always plentiful: anger.

"Does your gargoyle know who's doing this to us?" he asked.

Constantine surprised him with a ready answer. "Members of the Chimera caste."

So Gaston did know. And if he knew, then so did Luc and Marco and all the others.

"Well, then we have to do something," Grayson said. Vander and Constantine exchanged glances, but neither of them spoke. "We know who to stop," Grayson insisted. "So let's go. Let's do it."

"Do what?" Vander asked. "Track down every Chimera we have a file on and ask if he's killed a Duster recently? They won't speak to us. We have no sway over them, not with Lennier, our one link to the Dispossessed, gone."

Grayson usually appreciated cool logic, but right then it was hard to stomach.

"We don't ask, then," Grayson said. "We make them talk to us. We make them stop."

"Mr. Burke is correct," Constantine said. The words only spiked Grayson's temperature. "To attack a gargoyle would be to incite a war. It is more important right now to focus on Axia and what her first move might be."

The room was too hot, the air too thick. Grayson knew better than to utter another word, to shout that they clearly had more than one enemy to concern themselves with. He grabbed his coat from the steel examination table and pushed past Constantine. Vander might have called his name, but Grayson's pulse had started beating loud in his ears, like it usually did before a shift.

He bolted from the room so fast, eyes down, that he barreled straight into someone. A smaller someone. A girl.

He grabbed Chelle's arms to keep from knocking her flat onto the floor. She bucked off his hands as if he'd insulted her by thinking she needed assistance. Before he could say a word, she held a finger to her lips to hush him. Chelle pointed over his shoulder and then proceeded around him, past the half-closed door to the medical room. She didn't wait to see if Grayson was coming. The girl was smart. She knew he'd follow her anywhere.

As he fell into step behind her, Grayson took stock of himself. He'd never come down from an urge to shift so quickly. Seeing Chelle had doused the anger and the heat better than any of Constantine's mind tricks. Or perhaps it was the mersian blood already taking effect.

They ascended a spiraling staircase. The metal clanged under his feet, but not hers. She stepped quietly, as if she wore slippers instead of army boots. He let himself smile, thankful she wasn't peering over her shoulder to see it. He wasn't foolish enough to believe that Chelle had actually missed him this past month. She wasn't a girl to pine. But having her trim waist and the flare of her trousers right in front of his face as they climbed the steps made him happy.

"Where are we going?" he whispered as they came to the top of the stairwell.

Chelle glanced over her shoulder. "I was listening to your conversation with the old man and Vander."

"Eavesdropping seems rather sneaky for someone as frank as you," he replied.

Chelle stopped at a pair of double pocket doors. His heart thundered when she shot him a playful scowl.

"I prefer to call it being pragmatic," she said, rolling the pocket doors aside.

Automatically, the overhead lightbulbs inside the room—which was about the size of the rectory's front sitting room and dining room combined—flickered on. They clicked and hummed, growing brighter as Grayson followed Chelle inside. For a moment, he forgot the pretty girl standing in front of him, blinded as he was by all the silver hanging upon the walls.

Swords, daggers, blades of every shape and size and purpose, all fastened to the room's four walls in orderly rows. The silver, polished to perfection, reflected the electric light as well as a mirror would have.

"I'm willing to bet this is a demon hunter's favorite room," Grayson said, turning his gaze back on Chelle. He'd never seen her with any weapons other than her *hira-shuriken*—flat silver disks edged with sharp, curved teeth. She never failed to send those throwing stars through the air with unbelievable dexterity and precision. As if he needed any more reasons to adore her.

Chelle rolled back onto her heels and crossed her arms over her chest, gazing upon the displays of weaponry. She wasn't well endowed, but Grayson never gave that part of her much thought. He liked how small she was, and more than once had imagined how her body might fit against his.

"It is an essential room," she replied.

"And why are you showing it to me?" he asked. There was no point in trying to charm Chelle. Better to be direct.

She responded by walking toward a waist-high shelf running along the wall to the right. The shelf, enclosed by locked glass lids, resembled a jeweler's display case. Grayson followed her. The case held another assortment of weapons. Daggers, swords, crossbow bolts, and even a few *hira-shuriken*. He noticed the sheen—dull pewter instead of reflective silver—and knew what they were.

"These are mercurite dipped," Grayson said. He'd learned from Léon and Monsieur Constantine that the Alliance had these weapons. First dipped in mercurite and then heated over flames to seal and harden the coating, a weapon like any of these would be able to debilitate a gargoyle. Kill it, if need be.

"The Chimera caste is behind the Duster murders," Chelle said. She'd overheard Constantine.

"Why just one caste?" Grayson asked. He hadn't thought of the question before now.

She leaned a hip against the shelf, a real scowl set upon her lips this time. "One of the Chimeras wants to be elder, and this is his show of power and leadership."

It wasn't speculation. Chelle's answer sounded confident.

"How do you know?"

She lifted one shoulder, feigning nonchalance. "I have been called sneaky."

He started to smile, until he lowered his eyes and saw the case of mercurite-dipped weapons. Because he now knew why Chelle had brought him to this room.

"You were right down there," she said. "We need to stop the Chimeras."

He met Chelle's hazel eyes, each iris flecked with gold. "By killing them?"

She set her jaw, and Grayson knew she was mentally rolling up her sleeves, preparing for a fight.

"Would you rather wait for more Dusters to die? Who will be next? Ingrid? Perhaps even you?" she said, her French accent growing stronger with her anger. "And do you believe Dusters will be their only target? Once they've taken care of your kind, they will come after mine."

Your kind. Grayson dragged in a breath and tried not to let it bother him. Chelle hadn't meant it as an insult. At least, he didn't think she had. Still, it was as if she'd drawn a line between them and shoved his chest, pushing him away. Humans on this side, Dusters on that side.

"Word is spreading that Axia has reclaimed her blood from your sister. The gargoyles will be out in droves hunting Dusters, trying to destroy Axia's little seedlings before she can use them for whatever it is she plans to do," Chelle went on, her cheeks beginning to pink.

"Maybe they should," Grayson heard himself say. Chelle squinted up at him, her lips parting in surprise.

"You think Dusters should die?" she asked.

Now he felt like an idiot. Of course he didn't think all Dusters should die.

"Some of us deserve it," he answered.

Chelle gathered a breath and walked around him, toward the opposite wall of blessed silver weapons. An unwieldy battle-axe hung at knee level, the buffed blade head so wide it showed the reflection of Chelle's legs.

"I don't know what happened in London. I mean, I do know, but I wasn't there and I don't know what happened to you, or what it must be to have something like that on your conscience. But, Grayson—" Chelle paused to face him. She didn't usually tangle up her words, and she started to blush for having done so.

Grayson saw the prickles of red wash over her creamy skin

and stopped breathing. He didn't want to smell her blood. He didn't want to feel that disgusting clench of desire lock up his stomach and throat.

"You don't deserve to die," she continued as his lungs started to beg for air.

He gave up and let his body have what it needed. Though it wasn't strong—Vander's blood must have been working its magic—the air tasted sweet. Grayson moved toward her.

"You want to know what happened to me in London?"

Chelle's soft expression turned wary. He was glad of it. She was smart and fast and trusted her gut.

"I caught the eye of a girl in a tavern. A working girl," he clarified. Chelle didn't bat an eye. "She blushed when I smiled at her, and the blood rising to her cheeks like that, it set something off inside me. I didn't understand it. I felt drugged, like I'd had too much whiskey, only I hadn't."

Chelle betrayed her thoughts when her palm came up to touch her own cheek, still rosy.

"Do you want to know the rest?" he asked.

She shook her head. "I can piece it together on my own."

Grayson took another step closer. "I promised I wouldn't hurt you, and I won't. But the truth is, when I scent your blood like this, I can't think of anything other than what it would taste like on my tongue. Sliding down my throat."

Chelle lowered her hand, revealing an even brighter flush than before. It was too dangerous. He had to leave.

"The only thing your tongue would taste is the cool silver of my *hira-shuriken*," she whispered, so softly Grayson needed a moment to understand what she'd said. And then he laughed.

"That's good to know," he said, still laughing.

Chelle's expression remained serious. "But you don't deserve to die, Grayson Waverly. Neither did Léon, or the other Dusters the Chimeras have hunted down."

His laughter subsided. No. Léon hadn't deserved to die, even with his own bloody and horrible past sins.

"You heard Vander and Constantine. The Alliance can't make a move against the gargoyles without starting a war," he said.

Chelle waited a few moments in silence before Grayson understood.

"But I'm not Alliance," he said for her.

Chelle then did something to surprise him. She touched him. Her hands settled on his arms, which he'd crossed at his chest.

"I'll be with you," she said.

He was lost for words, from her touch, from her closeness. From her blood. He knew, without having to ask, that Chelle would leave with those mercurite weapons, with or without him. She was determined, and there was nothing he could say to dissuade her.

Perhaps she was right. If the Chimeras were the ones doing this, they did need to be stopped. The next Duster target could very well be Ingrid. His sister wasn't some nameless Duster walking along a street somewhere. She was well known. If the Chimera vying for elder wanted to prove his strength and authority, killing her would be a fine demonstration for all the Dispossessed.

"All right," Grayson said, pushing back the weight of indecision. "I'm in."

CHAPTER TEN

The voices grew louder the closer she got to the entrance. Ingrid stopped a good twenty paces from the vine-swathed stone arcades that led into the courtyard at gargoyle common grounds. She'd approached them through the Luxembourg Gardens at an angle, shielding her arrival from any Dispossessed who might be lurking about Luc's new territory. It was late afternoon, but the sun still had another hour or so before it slid beneath the western horizon completely. Ingrid had hoped no other gargoyles would be about during the daylight hours. In vain, it seemed.

The voices drifting from the courtyard were harsh and insistent, just shy of shouting. The words weren't clear, however, and she wasn't sure she should move any closer to make them out.

An arm wrapped around her from behind, bracing her chest, and a hand clapped over her mouth to stifle her scream. A hot mouth pressed against her ear.

"You shouldn't walk into a lion's den without a pair of claws, Lady Ingrid."

Marco released her, and she threw an elbow back to jab him in the stomach. It was like elbowing a brick wall.

"You didn't have to creep up behind me," she hissed.

"And you didn't have to be so predictable," he replied, grasping her arm and dragging her toward the arcades.

She stumbled through the patchy snow and kept her voice a grating whisper. "But we can't go in—there are others inside the courtyard!"

"They have already felt my arrival, though not yours." Marco jerked her to a halt at the first of several stone columns forming the arcades. "I'll show myself and then make some excuse to leave."

He pushed her backward until her spine was against the column. "If you move from this spot before then, I will be forced to take you back to the rectory and chain you to your bed for the rest of your life."

Ingrid would have rolled her eyes had Marco not looked completely serious.

He stepped away and through the arcades, into the courtyard. A moment later, he was greeted by someone with a slick, sarcastic tone. She knew the owner of the voice at once: Vincent, the Notre Dame gargoyle who had threatened to attack her the last time she had been in Hôtel du Maurier's ramshackle courtyard.

"Ah, the protector of an abomination graces us with his presence at last," Vincent said.

Ingrid turned her shoulder into the column and pressed a palm against the cold stone.

"You should really improve the company you've been keeping lately, Luc," Marco replied, ignoring Vincent entirely.

Ingrid's heart beat faster. Luc was right there, on the other side of the arcades. Her fingers dug into the stone and she closed her eyes, forcing herself to remember Marco's black glare. Remembering Vincent's unveiled hatred the last time he had looked at her helped as well.

"Because of your demonic human, the fallen angel Axia has what she needs to come here, to our city." Ingrid opened her eyes. This voice didn't belong to Vincent. It belonged to Yann, the Chimera that guarded a bridge over the Seine.

"She will reap her abominations, using them to gain control of our territories," Vincent chimed in. "Unless we act together to put an end to them."

Arguments burst out, though none of the voices was familiar to Ingrid.

"Dusters are still human."

"We cannot touch them."

"Human? They are diseased with demon blood."

"The Order would wish them destroyed."

"And if a Duster belongs to one of us? What then?"

This last comment raised a valid point. Marco couldn't be the only gargoyle protecting a human Duster.

"We've already started." Yann's words came through the din. "They've been simple to kill. We could wipe out Axia's army within days if we had the Seer or Constantine on our side."

As if Vander or Constantine would ever give these monsters aid. At least it seemed as if Yann and the majority of the other gargoyles were still in the dark about Vander. That he was a Duster as well as a Seer appeared to be something only Luc, Marco, and Gaston, Constantine's guardian, knew.

"You will stay away from my human." Gaston's command and the unspoken threat attached to it lifted the hairs on Ingrid's arms. She wondered how many gargoyles were actually inside the courtyard. All of them?

Ingrid shifted her weight, her feet growing cold.

"Unprotected, these abominations are weak." Vincent again. "They barely know how to use their powers. I'm calling on all of you here to join me and my brothers to end them. Let us take back this city."

A round of quarrelling followed but was yet again silenced by a single voice.

"We are here to protect humans, Vincent. Not kill them."

The sound of his silvery voice, smooth yet brutal, spread warmth through her legs and arms and coiled inside her chest.

"And we have agreed Dusters do not qualify as humans," Vincent returned.

"*We* have not agreed on anything," Luc growled.

Ingrid was tired of standing still, of not being able to see what was happening. Holding her breath, she shuffled as quietly as she could around the column. A sliver of the courtyard came into view. She saw the backs of a few Dispossessed, but none she recognized.

"My fellow Dispossessed," Vincent bellowed, speaking to all who had gathered. "Is this the gargoyle you desire as your elder?"

Ingrid parted her lips in awe as she realized what was happening. *Luc* was Vincent's opposition for the role of elder. The Alliance had been saying everything was chaos among the ranks of Dispossessed, and this was why.

"Make no mistake," Vincent went on. "There are those among us who enjoy their precious humans too much."

Ingrid eased over another step and finally saw Vincent. He wore the cumbersome, faded black cloak she remembered. He stood with his profile to her, his narrowed glare presumably set upon Luc, still unfortunately out of view.

"This Dog took his human charge and made her his own," Vincent spit.

A murmur rumbled through the courtyard. Ingrid's heart stuttered and her mind raced ahead to what might happen next. She'd seen at least ten gargoyles so far. A group large enough to attack Luc and overpower him.

An electrical shiver combed her arms.

"The girl is a Duster," Vincent went on, blatantly shifting

the fear and loathing he'd just nurtured for Axia's seedlings toward Luc.

The electrical current fed on Ingrid's anger, on her desperation. It rolled along the slender bones in her hands, and she lassoed it, envisioning a sparking whirlpool at each fingertip.

She would not allow this wretched gargoyle and his supporters to harm Luc. She would not allow *anyone* to harm him.

"Irindi was mocking the Dispossessed by giving a human-lover an elder's territory," Vincent said. "I have waited too long to take it from you."

He threw off his heavy cloak and his body cleaved through his clothes, tearing out of his human skin. Vincent fell forward, transforming into a creature with the sleek black body of a panther topped by a pair of snow white–feathered wings, and with the head of a large, grotesque pelican. Its wickedly sharp beak was nearly as long and broad as its panther body.

Vincent raked his hooked beak to the side and bounded forward, out of Ingrid's view. Senseless of any fear, she raced out from behind the column, into the arcades. She ripped off her gloves, her fingertips sizzling with contained energy. Ingrid spotted Luc on the other side of the water fountain. He was still in human form, Marco and Gaston at his sides, and they, along with a handful of other Dispossessed, were staring down Vincent's advance—until they saw her and the lightning crackling from her fingertips.

Bold blue branches of electricity snaked across the courtyard and wrapped Vincent's gargoyle form in a paralyzing embrace. His snowy white pelican wings shook and shivered as the electricity pulsed through his body, until Ingrid drew the current back in, closing her fists tightly as she had learned to do, and he collapsed.

She had made it to the fountain's empty basin and, as she held her electricity in check, realized there were gargoyles on either side of her. *Vincent's* gargoyles.

Vincent himself, lying on the gravel, had melted back into his human form. Ingrid turned away from his naked body and found herself face to face with Yann. The Chimera sneered down at her, his black hair, lightly streaked with white, forming half-drawn curtains around his eyes. He'd never been warm or kind, but he had helped her in the past. After spending a few seconds on the receiving end of his hateful glare, she knew he would not help her again.

Luc slid between her and Yann. "She is a human on my territory. You will not touch her."

Marco appeared at her side and glared at her as murderously as Yann had. He tugged Ingrid behind him, shielding her from the restless group of gargoyles, every last one of them looking ravenous for revenge.

"If you stand with Vincent, leave my territory. *Now!*" Luc shouted. "I will not follow a gargoyle hell-bent on executing humans. We might have been murderers once." He slowly stood aside so Yann could pass. "But we aren't any longer."

Yann and a few others hovered over Vincent as the Notre Dame gargoyle pushed himself up on shaky arms. They wrapped him in his cloak; his other clothes were in pieces on the ground. Marco continued to shield Ingrid, backing up a few paces as gargoyles began to come toward them, heading for the exit into the gardens. Vincent shook off Yann's steadying arm and pinned Ingrid with his small black eyes.

"You will be difficult to destroy, but I will see it done."

She felt childish and weak, hidden as she was. She stepped out as far as Marco's unyielding grip on her arm would allow.

"Funny," she replied. "You were rather easy to electrocute."

Vincent thinned his lips until they were hardly visible and, without another word, left the courtyard for the Luxembourg Gardens.

The moment he had gone, Marco pushed Ingrid away and stormed to the arcades, muttering under his breath. She stumbled, her legs suddenly weak. Her cheeks were hot, as were the tips of her ears. There were still Dispossessed present, staring at her. And, of course, there was Luc.

She turned, spotting Gaston first. Constantine's gargoyle wore an unreadable expression. He was neither happy to see her nor angry. He nodded toward the few remaining Dispossessed, and they left through the arcades as well.

Marco shouldered past them as they went, coming back toward her, his fury carrying him like a tempest.

"Put these back on." He forced her hand out and slapped her gloves into her palm. "And stop trying to get yourself killed."

Ingrid fiddled with the gloves, her hands dampening the soft kid. Marco lifted his eyes and looked into the space over her shoulder. She knew Luc was right behind her.

"I'll wait in the gardens. Five minutes," Marco said, before vaulting his thick, dark brow. "And then it's to bed with you."

She recalled his threat to chain her to her bed and groaned inwardly. He wouldn't do such a barbaric thing, of course, but she knew he would punish her in some way.

Ingrid waited until Marco had disappeared before slowly turning around. She realized that she was afraid. It was ridiculous. She had nothing to fear from Luc, yet her pulse leaped and her breath caught in her throat when she saw him. He was as close as Yann had been, less than an arm's length away. He'd raked back his obsidian hair, and while Ingrid stood speechless, he allowed his eyes to rove over her. They coasted hungrily from her messy chignon to her lips to her neck and bodice and then up again.

"You should have told me where you were," she whispered.

Luc abruptly moved back, toward the open ballroom doors. "And now you know why I tried to keep you away."

Ingrid followed, her body shivering uncontrollably. "I'm not afraid of Vincent."

She knew Luc wouldn't believe the lie, but it felt good to say it anyway. Of course she was afraid of him. He was an angry, powerful gargoyle, and he'd just made a public vow to kill her.

Luc stopped in the center of the ballroom, underneath the giant chandelier hanging crookedly from the ceiling. He stood motionless on the dance floor, the cracked and stained tiles covered in filth, debris, and mouse droppings. The rotted piano had lost one of its legs and crashed into a tilt; yellowed sheet music lay scattered around it like leaves.

"He wants you dead," Luc said, his back to her. He wore the same clothes he always had, the loose alabaster linen shirt and tan canvas trousers. He looked the same and sounded the same, and yet there was something different about him. Ingrid didn't know what it was.

He turned to face her, the fading sun gilding the ballroom in a hazy golden light.

"And he wants me out of the way so he can be elder, unchallenged. What better way to do that than to prove to all of the Dispossessed that I've taken a human?"

Ingrid's stomach bottomed out as she realized what she'd done.

"Oh," she whispered, pulling back a step. "Oh, no. Luc—"

She'd entered gargoyle common grounds and defended Luc, attacking his opposition with her demon gift. And just moments after Vincent had accused Luc of falling in love with a human. With *her*.

"I gave him what he wanted." She buried her face into her palms. "I'm so sorry, Luc. I wasn't thinking. I heard him firing up the other gargoyles, and I knew they'd try to attack you and rip you apart like what happened to René, and I—"

Tears stung her eyes, and she was glad she'd covered her face. She hated when her lips and chin quivered in the effort to fight off a sob.

"Ingrid." Luc had come to stand directly in front of her. He pulled her hands from her face, but she turned her head, not wanting to see how disappointed he was.

He brought their entwined hands down between them, level with his hips, and tugged her forward. With his lips at her ear, Luc whispered, "It's not that I wasn't impressed."

She felt the brush of his lips against her earlobe and forgot her embarrassment. She forgot the run-down ballroom and her dwindling time before Marco came to fetch her.

"But don't risk yourself for me again," Luc said, his breath hot against her ear. She angled her head toward him, wanting nothing more than his warmth.

"You risked yourself for me," she said. "By finding me in the park. Coming for me when Vincent could have been watching your every move."

He sighed, nuzzling her temple before letting one of her hands go. He stepped back.

"Have you healed?" he asked, rubbing his thumb along the center of her palm. "I wish I could know without asking."

That was what was different about him. He couldn't sense her. She felt the loss of that connection, too.

"I'm fine now," she assured him.

He kept hold of her hand as he started walking, avoiding a pile of old sheets in the middle of the dance floor. He kept on toward the grand, Rococo-style double doors that led to the building's main corridor. She didn't know where he thought they could go with the few minutes they had left together. Ingrid wanted to follow Luc through the house anyway, perhaps up the stairs to Lennier's rooms. She wanted to stay with Luc in this decrepit, timeless place while the rest of Paris dealt with Axia's imminent return.

"What if Vincent is right?" she asked. Luc stopped on the threshold and she continued. "What if Dusters are dangerous? What if we end up belonging to Axia in the end, doing her bidding, the same way Grayson did after she released him from the Underneath?"

Her brother had had moments of clarity when he'd been under Axia's control. He hadn't wanted to harm her or Gabby, but he also hadn't been able to stop himself. What if the same thing happened to her? To all the Dusters?

"You don't belong to anyone," Luc said. He seemed to abandon his plan to take her somewhere within the town home and instead stood with her between the open ballroom doors, one of which hung perilously loose on a single hinge.

"Ingrid, you have more power than you give yourself credit for. I saw it just now; we all did. Axia is evil. You . . . you're good. She will not win. She will not take you away. You won't let her, and neither will I."

Ingrid felt the muscles in his hand and arm go rigid when she tried to get closer to him. He held her back, even though the low burn in his eyes said he wanted something different.

"Marco is coming," he whispered.

It couldn't have been five minutes already.

"I need to know something," Ingrid said, hating that she felt rushed now.

Luc furrowed his dark brow and waited for her to ask her question.

"Vincent accused you of taking a human." She forced her gaze on Luc to stay steady and not drift away with nerves. "Have you?"

Luc held still. He didn't smile; he didn't tilt his head in consideration. He didn't do anything but hold her gaze and her hand with absolute security. She felt the heat of a blush staining her cheeks, and she didn't know if it was from the intensity of his emerald stare, the humiliation of having been so forward, or the sudden fear that he was going to break her heart once and for all.

Luc lifted her hand to his mouth and pressed his lips gently against the back of it, as a gentleman might.

"I have," he answered softly.

She could only part her lips and whisper his name before Marco's heavy steps echoed through the ballroom. Luc released her hand and drew away, sending one thoroughly annoyed glance in Marco's direction. *See her home safely,* Luc's silent bidding seemed to say, and then he was gone, retreating through the ballroom doors and into the dim corridor.

Ingrid remained where she was until Marco cleared his throat. He said something sarcastic, she was sure, but the effect was lost on her. She could think of nothing, hear nothing, other than Luc's voice: *I have.* He'd taken a human. He'd chosen her. Luc loved her still, even without the gargoyle-human bond.

As Ingrid followed Marco from the courtyard and through the arcades, into the quickly purpling twilight, she could not smile, not even with her heart so gloriously full. Because what Luc had just said—what she had just asked of him—could very well get them both killed.

CHAPTER ELEVEN

London Daicrypta headquarters was nowhere near as impressive as the Parisian Daicrypta seat, a Montmartre mansion that must have once been home to royalty. The simple whitewashed Georgian home rested snugly in the heart of Belgravia, between Turk's Row and Sloan Square. The place looked like every other building along the street: a clean stone façade and four stories of tall, polished windows. There was no indication at all, from where Gabby stood on the well-swept front steps, that the people inside were demonologists with a penchant for controversial experiments involving both humans and creatures from the Underneath.

As she reached for the bronzed pineapple knocker, her gaze lifted and stuck on the triangular frieze above the door. A man's face had been carved into the stone, his mouth wide with horror. A small, clownish-looking gargoyle protruding from the stone frieze was nibbling on the man's ear with razor teeth. Gabby sighed and brought the knocker down hard, twice.

The other night, on their way back to Waverly House, Rory had been muttering a slew of crude epithets for Hugh Dupuis and the Daicrypta, while Gabby had been considering how to get her hands on some information. Namely, Hugh Dupuis's home address.

The following morning she'd quietly asked the butler, Reeves, and with a stiff bow, he'd set off to fulfill her request. He'd returned with an address in less than an hour. Meanwhile, Rory had received a second coded telegram from Nolan, this one saying that Ingrid had been taken into the Underworld and drained of her angel blood. Gabby had immediately known two things: Axia would now be able to come here, into their realm, and so far, the Alliance had no weapon with which to fight her. Gabby's mind had gone directly to the diffuser net. The Alliance had nothing like it in their weapons cache, but it could bond to a demon and seal it into place. What if the nets could work on other creatures that weren't of this world? What if they could capture an angel?

The door to the London Daicrypta swung open on soundless hinges and Gabby's eyes went wide.

"You!" She was looking up into the face of the gargoyle that had interrupted her and Rory's sparring at the dry docks and delivered a message from Marco.

The man smirked down at her, his ginger beard and mustache appearing redder than they had in the sheltered light of the dry docks.

"Me," he replied, a thumb pointing up over their heads, toward the frieze.

Gabby didn't need to see it again. "You're a *clown* gargoyle?"

His goading smirk fell off quickly.

"There ain't no clown gargoyles," he said with an irritated sniff. "I'm of the Primate caste."

She raised her chin, suddenly amused. "You mean monkey."

The gargoyle squared his shoulders. "I mean Primate. Now what's your business here?"

Gabby bit her lip to stop herself from laughing. The poor man. She could only imagine what he looked like in true form.

"I am here to call on Hugh Dupuis," she managed to say without cracking a smile.

The monkey man—oh, good heavens, it was too ridiculous, she thought—stood aside and allowed Gabby to step into the foyer. Though small, the interior was stylish, with mint-green walls and creamy trim, potted palms at the base of the curved stairwell, and a mahogany porter's chair, where the gargoyle likely sat waiting for the door knocker to sound.

The increasingly put-out gargoyle led her from the foyer and down the hallway directly ahead. Underneath a section of ceiling that had been outfitted with a skylight—for there was an odd shaft that cut through the center of the home—he stopped and rapped on a door. A muffled reply came from within, and the gargoyle, with one last glower, opened the door and stood aside.

Gabby, having been distracted by seeing this gargoyle again, had temporarily forgotten her nerves. She knew what the Daicrypta was and remembered all too well fighting off the disciples who had been studying under Robert Dupuis. Paying Dupuis's son a call without more than her short sword in her cape for protection was a risk. Rory would be furious. After the second telegram's arrival, she had told him she wasn't feeling well and wanted to take a long bath and rest for the day. He likely still thought her sleeping in her darkened room at Waverly House.

She stepped inside what appeared to be Hugh Dupuis's study. Through the slanted crimson veil of her hat she saw bookshelves lining the walls, all of them stuffed with texts. Brown leather sofas and club chairs sat before a hearth, and there was a large desk in front of a bay window that jutted out over the slim lane between this home and the neighboring house. Hugh Dupuis was lounging in a chair behind the desk, his raised brows revealing his surprise at seeing her. Her brow lifted as well, for on his right arm was a leather falconry gauntlet, and perched upon it was a massive, oily black corvite demon.

"Thank you, Carver. That will be all," Hugh said. The gargoyle grunted before slipping back into the hall and shutting the door loudly.

Gabby kept her eyes fastened on the Daicrypta doyen, who was dangling something that looked like an earthworm in front of the corvite's sharp beak. She watched in horror, prepared to see the demon bird snip off Hugh's fingers as it snatched the bait. Instead, it gently nibbled the squirming end of the worm before taking it from Hugh's hand. He stroked the bird's breast while it finished its snack.

"It's your pet," Gabby said, incredulous.

"I have many of them here. Practically a rookery," he replied, standing up. He appeared even shorter than he had at the docks, especially with the giant bird perched on his arm for comparison. "Although, at my last count, the number had dropped by one." He shot her an accusatory glare.

Gabby remembered Rory hurling his dagger at the corvite on her windowsill.

"You sent them?" she asked. "You've been spying on me?"

Hugh touched the side of his nose and then pointed his index finger at her. "Ah, Miss Waverly, that is my limitation with these birds. They can't exactly spy for me. They can, however, answer simple yes-or-no questions."

He came out from behind his desk, which was much lower than most. Should Gabby have stood beside it, the tabletop would have been level with her thighs instead of her hips or waist.

"So you had them answering questions about me," she said. "And your gargoyle. You had him follow me to the Battersea docks."

The gargoyle, Carver, had not accompanied Hugh to the London docks the night before. Not in plain sight, anyway.

Hugh approached an iron perching stand and, with a soft nudge and whispered instruction, transferred the corvite from his leather gauntlet to the long arm of the stand.

"You cannot blame me for wanting to keep an eye on you, Miss Waverly. Things got rather messy in Paris, did they not?" He gave the bird another loving rub on its domed skull and then turned to Gabby fully. "However, Carver must have come to you of his own accord. He has free rein, of course."

Hugh busied himself with the laces on the leather gauntlet. The crown of his head reached Gabby's well-corseted chest and no farther. His torso appeared to be the longest part of him, his legs and arms curiously stunted. His appearance, other than his height, held no other malformations.

"You may ask," he murmured, finally removing the gauntlet and hanging it on another arm of the perching stand.

"Ask?" she repeated.

"Whether I am a dwarf."

She felt her cheeks go warm. "It isn't polite to ask such things."

He peered up at her, his sandy-blond hair falling rakishly over his forehead. "It's also not polite to kill other people's pets."

Gabby turned away from him and moved toward the hearth. "I am afraid that general rule cannot apply to demon pets, Mr. Dupuis. And I didn't kill it. Rory did—the man who was with me on the docks."

Though there was no fire in the hearth, it was warm in the study. She felt a few beads of sweat gathering under her veil and wished to push back the tulle, but she didn't want to expose her scars just yet.

"Your Alliance muscle is not with you this morning."

Hugh leaned against his low desk and crossed his arms, appraising her silently. He wasn't overtly handsome, but he had distinctive features that might have been considered charming. Like full lips and wide, dark brown eyes. The most intriguing thing about him wasn't any physical feature, however. It was the keen intelligence that glowed behind those wide eyes of his.

"You are Daicrypta." Her statement required no further explanation.

Hugh didn't appear offended. "Most Alliance would not knock upon my door."

"I am not Alliance," Gabby retorted, but then added, "Not yet, at least."

He remained quiet, his inspection of her seeming to probe even deeper.

"I would like to know more about the diffuser nets," she said, uncomfortable with the stretch of silence. "You said your father invented them?"

He clenched his jaw with what looked like displeasure. "He did."

The thought of Robert Dupuis soured her expression as well. "Your father was a madman. If he hadn't been stopped, he would have bled my sister dry for her angel blood."

Gabby had plenty more to say on the subject of Hugh's father, but she forced her mouth shut. She wanted information on the diffuser nets too badly to risk being tossed out.

To her surprise, after a moment, Hugh laughed. "I see we aren't very different in our esteem of him, then. He *was* a madman, Miss Waverly. I left the Paris seat many years ago to put distance between us."

He walked away from the perch, toward where Gabby stood in front of the sofa.

"You see, my father was a genius, but his moral compass was no more evolved than those of the demons he studied. What he wanted rose above all else, and what he wanted was power."

"And you wouldn't have done the same as your father? You

wouldn't have tried to drain my sister's blood so you could sell it to the Alliance?"

He huffed, as if offended. "It is not power and influence I seek, Miss Waverly. What I want is to understand the demons that come from that other realm. What do they want here? What are their patterns and desires? What are their limitations, their powers, and even their bodily compositions? The more we know, the better able we are to protect humankind."

He sounded as passionate about his research as Nolan and other Alliance fighters did about the skill of demon hunting. Gabby was wary, though. He could have just been saying these things to appeal to her.

"You don't perform *experiments,* as your father did?" she asked, stressing the word so that he knew exactly what sort of experiments she referred to.

"None that harm human beings," he answered evenly. "I don't believe Carver would take very kindly to such goings-on under his roof here, do you?"

The gargoyle protector at the Paris Daicrypta mansion, Dimitrie, had suffered endlessly for the things done to human test subjects under his roof. Both the victim and the villain were his human charges, putting Dimitrie between a rock and a hard place. He'd failed to protect his human charges—Robert Dupuis's test subjects—so many times that the angel's burns he'd received as punishment had scarred his back.

"If you're so humane, why don't the Alliance and Daicrypta work together in a much more visible fashion? It seems you both want the same things," she said.

Instead of joining forces, though, the two underground societies held such contempt for one another that the only communication and partnerships seemed to happen behind closed doors.

Hugh continued around the sofa, toward the fireless hearth. "My father's madness tainted the Daicrypta as a whole, and unfortunately, his power extended all over Europe. Except here," he said, reaching for a small iron knob set into the wood paneling beside the hearth. She hadn't noticed it before he'd brought her attention to it.

"Why?" she asked.

Hugh puckered his brow as he opened the door. "The dynamics of our father-son relationship were, suffice it to say, strained. In short—pardon the pun—I was not his ideal heir."

"Because of your height?" She only felt bold enough to mention it because he had done so first with that pun.

"No," Hugh said, stepping through the door and into another room. "Because we could not see eye to eye—whoops, I've done it again—on what it meant to be Daicrypta."

Gabby thought carefully about Hugh's revelations as she followed him into the connected room, this one windowless, lit by electric wall sconces and glass-domed ceiling fixtures.

"And what does it mean to you?" she asked.

Hugh approached a long worktable in the center of the room, outfitted with a series of wide drawers underneath the zinc top.

"That is something I can only demonstrate over time. Now tell me: what about the diffuser nets are you interested in knowing more about?"

He rolled one drawer open and removed from it the familiar crossbow and the tucked-up net dart. He set them on the long table.

"I want to know how they work," Gabby answered, no longer nervous. "I know they are meant to capture demons, and I've seen them hold gargoyles as well. But can these nets also detain other creatures?"

Hugh processed her request with another stretch of silence. He reminded her of Ingrid in that way. Thinking before reacting. Weighing words as carefully as a jeweler might weigh the value of a mound of gold dust.

He left the long table and turned to a tall metal filing cabinet against the wall behind him. The six-drawer cabinet was covered in scraps of sketches and newspaper clippings, all fastened with thick, round magnets. Hugh pulled two magnets, currently out of use, free.

"Here, I want you to hold this," he instructed, quickly walking back to the table and extending his hand over the zinc top. Gabby frowned at the circular magnet but did as he asked. The magnet was smooth and flat as a river stone.

He kept the second magnet and held it out in front of him. "Now hold yours out to mine."

She kept her lips sealed and did as asked. Her magnet was less than an inch from his when she felt her magnet rear back and waver off to the side.

"Do you feel the magnetic field?" Hugh asked, their arms hovering over the table. "The way it balloons between your magnet and mine, rejecting their union even though they are made of the same material?"

Gabby felt her patience beginning to slip. "Yes, I know how magnets work. What does it have to do with the nets?"

Hugh gave his magnet a small push, forcing his way through the magnetic field and snapping the two black circles together.

"It's lodestone," he said. "A natural-forming magnet."

He took the joined magnets and rolled them around in his palm. "When I was a boy, my science tutor brought me a nugget of lodestone one day. After he left, I was in my father's laboratory, tossing the nugget from one hand to the next." He did so now, tossing the joined magnets to his other palm and closing them in his fingers, which were also slightly stunted, she noted. "I neared one of the tables to peer at a beaker of demon blood—a substance that was not as easy to come by twenty years ago as it is today.

"I took a step closer to the table and the beaker flew toward me, smashing against the same hand I had fisted around the lodestone nugget. The shattered beaker glass fell to my feet, but the demon blood"—Hugh held up a finger, as if this would be quite important—"the demon blood had congealed around my closed fist, sealing itself to my skin. The blood continued to move, pushing to slip through the gaps of my fingers and reach the lodestone. Frightened, of course, I opened my hand and dropped the stone. The blood followed, every last drop, and a moment later it had formed as a tumorlike mass around the lodestone on the floor."

He told the story so well, Gabby could almost feel the same shock he must have experienced as a boy.

"Demon blood will seal itself to lodestone," she said, and with a nod from Hugh, continued. "And the nets are made of lodestone? So the nets will . . . will seal to the demons they capture?"

She recalled how the net had closed around the mollug demon and the creature had not been able to move.

Hugh placed the magnets on the zinc tabletop. He lifted the net bolt by the longest of the four rods running through it, then pushed the steel-cap button on the tip of the bolt. The three other rods immediately lifted and spun, unraveling the tightly tucked net.

"The netting is crafted of hollow, transparent Parkesine," Hugh explained, touching the tubular crosshatched net. "It's flexible, easy to bend and twist. We inject a liquefied compound of lodestone into the Parkesine tubes. The same bond that happens between two magnets forced together also happens to the demon and the net. And on top of that, my father soon discovered that the lodestone also diffused whatever powers or energy the demon possessed. Their blood is simply no match for the magnetic force of the lodestone."

The smaller slugs skittering away from the trapped mollug demon made sense now, as did the hellhound in the Daicrypta courtyard in Paris that had avoided the net tented around Ingrid. They would have felt the pull of the lodestone and known to avoid it.

"The nets don't seal to Dusters," Gabby said. Ingrid had been able to move beneath her netted prison, and Vander as well.

Hugh nodded while admiring the silvery net. "Not enough demon blood in their bloodstream, perhaps?"

And then Luc, Gabby remembered. He had screeched in pain as he'd pried the net's stakes out of the ground to free Ingrid. "But what about gargoyles? It seems to hurt them."

"That I can explain. The nets are dipped in a thin wash of mercurite." He then whispered conspiratorially, "While I trust Carver, not all gargoyles are our friends."

Gabby reached across the worktable and fingered the netting. This net . . . it held such promise. She licked her lips before glancing back up at Hugh, who still stood on the opposite side of the table.

"You know of Axia?"

Hugh lifted his chin and nodded. "I have my connections."

"These nets," she said, holding the handful of netting in her palm. "Could the lodestone seal itself to an angel?"

"I would have to have some angel blood to test that theory on. Unfortunately, from what I hear, Axia has recently depleted the only known source of angel blood on the planet."

Gabby let her breath go and dropped the netting. Why couldn't she have discovered these diffuser nets *before*? Frustrated, she backed away from the table, hopes dashed. Her time here had been wasted.

"Thank you for answering my questions, Mr. Dupuis," she said, and began toward the door to his study.

"Miss Waverly—"

He was interrupted by a clamor outside the laboratory. Two raised voices, sharp and harsh. Hugh rushed past Gabby and out into the study, where the voices became clearer. They were right outside the study, in the hallway. Gabby groaned as she realized what was happening.

The door to the study crashed open and Rory and Carver

spilled into the room, each one shouting over the other. The corvite, still perched upon its stand, fluttered its wings and growled at the intrusion. Rory saw the bird and puzzled at it a moment before turning his attention to Gabby. He went quiet. Darkly and frighteningly quiet.

She knew excuses and apologies would only make things worse. Her tongue was sticking to the roof of her mouth anyhow.

Rory crossed the study with measured steps, his eyes briefly catching on Hugh Dupuis as he passed him. The look he sent the Daicrypta doyen was as cold and sharp as one of his blessed daggers.

"Miss Waverly has done nothing wrong," Hugh said, surprising Gabby with his show of support.

Rory ignored him and stopped within inches of Gabby. He pulsed with so much barely contained fury that the space between them felt like the force field between the two magnets she and Hugh had held up against one another.

"Ye shouldna be here alone wi' him," Rory said softly, though not so softly that Hugh and Carver could not hear.

"I pose no threat to her—romantically or otherwise," Hugh said, and Gabby knew what he said was true. He wouldn't harm her, and he had not shown a glimmer of interest in her the way other men might have. Well, *before* her accident, at least.

Rory took a tentative glance over his broad shoulder, toward Hugh. The two locked stares, neither of them speaking. They seemed to be reaching some sort of silent understanding, Gabby observed, though she wasn't sure what it was. She just knew it was time to leave. Before Rory or Carver, who remained in the doorway, his face pinched in disgust at the demon hunter, lost his temper.

"Good day, Mr. Dupuis," Gabby said, her breath rushed. She hadn't removed her cloak or gloves to begin with, so all she had to do was head for the door.

She heard Rory fall into step behind her, and with a brief

look up at Carver, she darted into the hallway, toward the foyer, and outside into the brisk Belgravia air.

"That was foolish, *laoch*," Rory said as soon as the front door had shut behind them. "Ye should ha' told me where ye were goin'."

"You would have never allowed me to go," she replied.

He stopped her from taking another step down the sidewalk with a hand on her elbow. Then he tugged her to face him.

"I ain't yer keeper, Gabby. If ye wanted to go, all ye had to do was tell me."

She didn't quite know what to say. All of a sudden she felt incurably childish and embarrassed.

"Oh."

He crinkled his forehead and grinned. "No more sneakin' about, then?"

She shook her head. "No more sneaking about." They walked side by side for another few moments before Gabby asked, "How did you know where to find me?"

Rory ducked under the overreaching branches of a holly hedge. "Nolan told me that if ye went off and did somethin' reckless, to think of the one place I knew ye shouldna be."

Imagining Nolan advising Rory like this made her slightly giddy. However, the feeling crashed before it could buoy her up. She didn't want to talk of Nolan, or even think of him. She didn't want to think of the nets, either, and how her one hope for them had, after just a quarter hour, been snuffed out.

Perhaps she truly was too far away to be of any use after all.

CHAPTER TWELVE

The abbey vaults were the only part of the church that had not yet undergone drastic changes. As Grayson led Chelle into one of the larger spaces in the underground level, he smelled the cold stone of the walls and columns, which split the vaults into domed rooms, much like a piece of honeycomb. He scented the musty air, long trapped beneath the abbey, and the faint tang of rotting wood. But that was it. For the first time, he couldn't scent Chelle's blood.

The mersian blood injection had worked. Vander's blood had somehow rubbed out everything: the ability to smell blood, the disgusting thirst for it. The aching, itching urge to shift into hellhound form. It was better even than dust reduction. He felt like himself again. He felt happy. So happy, in fact, that he was actually looking forward to Chelle's teaching him how to wield a blessed silver sword.

Grayson stopped within a large domed space. There was a solid wall of stone behind him, and three arches in front and on either side, leading out into the maze of vaults. He set the glass lantern in a beehive-shaped niche in the wall and then turned to Chelle. He spread out his arms.

"I am yours to command," he quipped, earning from her a suspicious—yet good-humored—glare.

"You sound strange," she said, setting the lantern she had been carrying in another one of the alcoves.

"I feel strange. Strangely wonderful," he replied.

This time, Chelle actually smiled wide enough that he saw the slim gap between her two front teeth.

"Should I ask why?" She shook her head. "Never mind. We have work to do."

She had arrived with a long, hard-sided case. She placed it carefully on the floor now and undid the latch.

Meeting at Hôtel Bastian would not have been too risky—the idea of Chelle's teaching Grayson how to protect himself with a sword wouldn't have been far-fetched, especially with the sense of subdued panic and focused preparation among the Alliance fighters now that the Roman troops and Directorate representatives were en route to Paris. However, Grayson had thought it wiser to avoid Alliance headquarters altogether. He imagined that if Chelle's plan to attack and destroy offending Chimeras was discovered, the consequences would be severe.

Grayson had suggested the vaults, which were quiet, private, and safe. And he didn't mind having Chelle all to himself for a little while, either.

From the case she removed two rapiers of equal length and size and handed one to him. His palm grasped the handle inside the intricate silver hand guard, a feature meant to protect his hand from an opponent's blade.

"I'm suddenly wishing I'd taken up fencing back in England," he said, the leather-wrapped handle slipping around inside his sweaty palm.

"These are dull, and only for practice. You will require a sharpened sword to pierce a gargoyle's scales," Chelle said.

Grayson tried to catch her eye to see if the words she'd just uttered had bothered her at all. They had bothered him. He couldn't imagine using any weapon to pierce a gargoyle's scales.

For he and Chelle to go out on their own and kill gargoyles bordered on insane. It wasn't that Grayson didn't want revenge for what those Chimeras had done—they'd taken Léon's life and the lives of other Dusters. But Chelle's passion for this plan, her insistence that it happen, still felt unsubstantiated. It seemed to Grayson that she must have had more than just one reason to put it into action.

Chelle stepped away and rolled her wrist, cutting her rapier through the air at angles. Grayson removed his jacket, shifting his rapier from one hand to the other before tossing the jacket to the dusty floor.

"Are you truly ready to kill a gargoyle in cold blood?" he asked.

She used his distraction to cut her blade up through the air and lunge toward him. He swung his rapier like a cricket bat and knocked the oncoming blade aside.

"Yes," she answered. The lack of hesitation or doubt unsettled him.

"If you really think killing them is the way to solve the problem, what makes us any better than the Chimeras?" he asked.

Chelle hardened her gaze at being likened to the Dispossessed.

"The gargoyles don't care about stopping Axia. They are doing this to prove their power and strength." She swung her blade again, this time in a downward, diagonal slice.

Grayson clashed his blade into hers and held it level.

"They are doing it because they will take any opportunity of unrest to lash out at humans," Chelle continued, her teeth gritted with the effort of throwing off the pressure of Grayson's rapier.

He loosened the tension in his arm and their blades swung toward the floor. Chelle breathed heavily, her nostrils flaring, and not just from physical exertion. His accusing the Alliance of being no better than the ruthless Chimeras had upset her more than he'd intended.

"What is it?" he asked, surprising her with a lunge and thrust of his own. Chelle intercepted the point of his blade, but not before it came dangerously close to her throat. "Why do you despise the Dispossessed the way you do?"

She'd never tried to hide how she felt about the gargoyles. She didn't trust them, and was definitely in favor of the proposed regulations to put the Dispossessed on shorter leashes.

The fire in Chelle's expression sputtered, and though it was only for a moment, Grayson thought he saw a touch of sad vulnerability. She glazed it back over with indignation before knocking Grayson's blade aside. She moved swiftly, the point of her rapier now nudging his pectorals.

"Something happened," he wagered, knowing full well Chelle might nick him for it.

She didn't. Instead, she let the tip glide down the front of his waistcoat. The distant sadness came back.

"My father was a hunter. One of the best," she said, her voice no longer gruff or defensive. The changing light of the two lanterns cast fingers of shadows across her face. "He was on patrol in the Marais one night when a gargoyle . . . it just attacked. No warning. No reason. The gargoyle's talons ripped through his arms, shearing muscle and breaking bone."

Chelle squeezed her eyes shut against the unbearable drain of memories. Grayson knew what it felt like to remember awful things and experience them again and again.

"There was too much damage. Even after he'd healed he wasn't able to hold a sword without it trembling and then clattering to the ground. His hands just couldn't stay closed around the handle. After that, they stuck him in the weapons room. His new duty was to polish and sharpen the blades he'd once wielded with such grace and skill."

Grayson watched as Chelle's face, screwed up like a prune, began to soften.

"What happened to him?" he asked.

Eyes still closed, Chelle swiped at a tear before Grayson could see it fall past her lashes.

"What do you think happened to him?" she bit off, the return of her defensive style oddly comforting.

Chelle's father was dead. If he had been alive, he would have still been in the weapons room at Hôtel Bastian polishing silver. How he'd died wasn't much of a mystery, either.

"And the gargoyle? What was done about him?" Grayson asked.

Chelle, though diminutive in height and weight, seemed to grow larger with the return of her anger.

"Lennier assured us that he was dealt with," she replied tartly enough to express her doubt.

This was the key, he realized. He didn't know how old she'd been when her father had been attacked, but from that moment on it had changed her. She didn't want to go out there now and stop the Chimeras just to protect Dusters. She was doing it because of what had happened to her father.

Grayson, still holding the rapier slack at his side, gently knocked his blade against hers. The joined silver sang out and lifted some of the weight in the air.

"You miss him." Saying anything else, like *I'm sorry*, would have been too empty a response for what she'd just shared.

Her rapier caught his and shoved. The unexpected attack threw his arm up high to the side, leaving his whole front unprotected. The tip of her rapier landed on the underside of his chin, the point pressing against his skin.

"More than you miss your father, I'm sure," she said, a victorious smile tugging at her lips.

"You're right," he answered, the motion of his jaw pushing the tip of her blade more firmly against his skin. He didn't miss his father one bit.

"But, Chelle," he started to say, unwilling to walk away from all she'd revealed just yet. "Not all gargoyles are like the one who hurt your father. Or the ones who have killed Dusters. Think about Luc. He's trustworthy, and there have to be others like him."

She kept her blade at his chin but eased off a bit. "Perhaps. However, the majority of them are simply criminals being punished for their sins."

Her eyes quickly darted to view Grayson's mouth, and in that moment her carefully composed guard faltered. She parted her lips, unable to shield her interest in the shape of his mouth.

"I'm a criminal," Grayson said, his heart gaining speed and his body growing warm from the way Chelle was looking at him. "I took a life, just as brutally as any rogue gargoyle. Why trust me?"

She knew what he'd done in London, and yet here she stood with him in the abbey vaults, wanting him at her side. Standing so close.

Grayson acted before he could think, and before Chelle's unusual vulnerability disappeared. He leaned forward and kissed her, fast and hard. He pulled back almost immediately, certain he would see her closed fist coming toward his nose. It wasn't. Her lips were soft and parted in surprise, her eyes fixed on his.

So he kissed her again, more gently this time, his hand hitching up her chin so he had a better angle. Chelle tasted like tea and sugar, like the fresh snap of spearmint leaf. He wanted to kiss her forever. He couldn't believe he'd actually found the courage to do it.

They dropped their rapiers, which fell to the floor with a clatter that echoed through the vaults. Her fingers, small but fierce, pressed against his stomach and curled into his waistcoat. She pulled her mouth away from his, but, to his continued surprise, she didn't appear angry.

"Who says I trust you?" she asked before rising onto her toes and kissing him again.

Hôtel Bastian was nearly as tense as gargoyle common grounds had been the afternoon before. Ingrid had been summoned there with a blood-red square of thick cardstock that required no signature—it was the color of the Alliance, and the few words in black ink were in Vander's script: *Come to rue de Sèvres as soon as you can. It's important.*

Mama had been busy in the abbey, and so, before Ingrid had needed to explain another outing, Marco had whisked her away in the landau.

Alliance headquarters practically throbbed with apprehension. Whether from Axia's impending Harvest or the anticipated arrival of the group from Rome as early as the next day, Ingrid wasn't sure. Vander had shown her quickly to the medical room, which provided an escape from the hum of unrest throughout the town home.

"*This* was important?" Ingrid now asked, seated on one of the metal tables with her legs stretched out before her. The hem of her dress and petticoats were bunched up around her knee, exposing her calf. She had reluctantly rolled her silk stocking to her ankle so that Vander could inspect the fang marks that had punctured the two strawberry ovals.

"See? I told you they had healed," she said, as Vander's spectacled eyes ran over her calf one last time. The demon mark was still there, as plain as ever, but the wounds inflicted by Axia's demonic fangs were gone.

Ingrid tugged up the stocking while Vander watched. Her face grew warm.

"Good," Vander replied. "I was hoping you were well enough, because I need you to leave Paris. Tonight, if possible."

Her hand stalled out and she stared at him. "Vander, what is it?"

He stood in front of her, his arms crossed over the brass buttons of his waistcoat. He looked a little green around the gills.

"The Directorate wants every dossier Nolan and I have on the Dusters here in Paris. The files we've been gathering on every demon-marked human, every stranger I've spotted with dust."

She finished quickly with her stocking and slid to the edge of the table. "How many files do you have?"

"Nearly fifty," he answered. "Nolan keeps them in his room here. Some have just addresses and physical descriptions; others have names. Many are Constantine's students, but there are many more who aren't. We've been keeping an eye on them when we can."

The old Ingrid would have accepted her first, optimistic theory right away: that the Directorate must plan to protect these Dusters somehow, either from Axia or from the gargoyles' picking them off one by one. Her time with the Alliance and the Dispossessed had made her skeptical, however, and a second, far less optimistic theory chilled her.

"They're afraid of the Dusters," she said. The Directorate had wanted Ingrid dead so that Axia couldn't reclaim her blood and come here, to Earth. Now that she'd succeeded, the only way to cut off Axia's power was to take away her army.

"I think the Directorate's idea of securing Paris is to get rid of the Dusters, yes. And I think the troops arriving tomorrow have orders to do just that." Vander uncrossed his arms and braced himself against the table. His arms bracketed Ingrid's body.

"I don't trust them, not after what Carrick confessed, and especially not after that assassin."

"But they wouldn't kill us," Ingrid said, then immediately felt naïve. "I mean, they tried to kill me, but they wouldn't kill *all* of us. Would they?"

Vander hung his head. His back and ribs expanded with a deep breath.

"When we take our Alliance oaths, we vow to protect the human race against the Underneath despite personal risk, and to accept the necessity for small sacrifices in favor of the greater good." Vander lifted his head, looking as if he wanted to say something more. Give her some further explanation. Ingrid didn't require it.

"Sacrificing Axia's seedlings would protect humankind," she said. Like thinning out a garden row of vegetable sprouts. Leave all the seedlings in and the row will grow wild and unmanageable, the plants stunted. Pull out half of the seedlings and the other half will have room to thrive.

Vander pushed off the table and stood straight, tall enough for Ingrid to have to crane her neck to watch his reaction. She wanted him to deny her theory, but he didn't.

He cupped her cheek, his fingers pressing against her skin with urgent determination. "They already know where to find you, so you can't be at the rectory when they arrive in Paris."

Ingrid tried to shake her head, but he took hold of her other cheek and stilled her.

"I could send you to my uncle's home in Vichy, or you could join Gabby in London—"

"I won't leave. I can't. What about Grayson?"

"I'll find him tonight and let him know what's happening."

And what about Luc? Ingrid closed her eyes. She didn't want to leave Paris, not even to save her own skin. She felt as tied to the city as Luc was. If he couldn't leave, neither should she.

"I know you only want to protect me," she said, looking up at Vander again. "But I won't run."

He didn't appear surprised by her defiance, only thoroughly vexed.

Just then the door to the medical room swung in on its hinges and Hans, the new Paris faction leader, rushed in. He took in the sight of Vander, whose hands were belatedly coming away from Ingrid's face, with only mild interest. He shifted his intense, searching glare behind them, toward the corner of the room.

"Where is it?" Hans barked, and started toward the back corner.

Ingrid hoisted herself from the table and turned to follow Hans's rigid figure.

"Where is what?" Vander asked.

"Enough, Burke. I want the blood."

Hans stopped at the squat refrigerated cabinet set in the corner. Ingrid stared at the padlocked zinc doors. She'd completely forgotten about the blood samples that Vander and Nolan had been storing.

"I'm handing it over to the Directorate representative tomorrow," Vander replied, plainly discontented to be doing so.

They wanted the Duster files *and* the leftover angel blood?

"Show it to me," Hans demanded, still strung tight as an acrobat's wire. "I want to see it."

Vander took slow steps toward the cabinet, which only seemed to grate on Hans's nerves. Ingrid followed him, just as curious.

"What's going on, Hans?" he asked, even more slowly reaching into his waistcoat pocket for the key Ingrid knew he kept there.

Hans didn't reply. He stood aside and waited while Vander crouched to unlock the zinc doors, which opened to a plume of cold white vapor.

The blood stores, the three frosted glass containers, were gone.

Vander leaped up and stepped back, nearly treading on Ingrid's toes. He caught her arm and kept a firm grasp, as if preparing for Hans to draw a weapon. But the faction leader only read her and Vander's shocked expressions.

"I've already been through the file cabinets in Nolan's room," Hans said. "The Duster dossiers were missing. But we found them."

Hans glanced toward the door, and Ingrid saw that two more Alliance members had joined them.

"They're a pile of scraps and ash in the kitchen stove," Hans finished.

Vander's grip on Ingrid's arm went slack.

"When did you last see Nolan Quinn?" Hans asked.

Nolan. He'd had a key to the cabinet as well. Ingrid had seen him lock and unlock it time and again.

"Yesterday," Vander said, muttering a curse under his breath. "Yesterday morning. After the Directorate's telegram arrived."

Nolan had *taken* the blood? He'd destroyed the Duster dossiers? He'd defied direct orders from the Directorate and what . . . gone into hiding?

"The blood was still there, at least until noon," Vander added.

"So he's had over twenty-four hours on the run," Hans said, kicking back into action and heading toward the door.

Vander's voice bellowed after Hans, stopping the faction leader in his tracks. "Whatever Nolan is doing, it's for the Alliance."

Hans swiveled back around. "Nolan Quinn is a traitor, and he'll be dealt with. We have our orders. The Directorate expects those orders to be obeyed. Follow them, Burke, and you, even with your demon blood, might find yourself on the right side of things when all is said and done. But they want the rest of the Dusters." His steely gaze landed on Ingrid, then shifted back to Vander. "And we will deliver."

Hans left the room, the other two Alliance members following in his wake. Ingrid stepped forward and touched Vander's wrist, his hand propped on his hip. He looked down at her fingers and stared at them as if they might offer answers.

"Nolan's protecting us," she whispered. "He burned the files and took the blood because he knew something was wrong. But, Vander, what will they do to him?"

He'll be dealt with, Hans had said. The Alliance had thrown Tomas, a traitorous member, into prison for the rest of his life. Nolan's freedom could be on the line.

Vander covered Ingrid's hand. "I don't know. But I do know that I won't give them a single Duster."

And then he'd likely wind up charged with treason as well. It made her grip his wrist tighter. How had the Alliance gone from something good to something so corrupt and wrong?

Or perhaps, Ingrid reasoned, it had never been completely good in the first place.

CHAPTER THIRTEEN

The London Daicrypta headquarters had been two or three steps down in grandeur compared to its Parisian counterpart, but the London Alliance headquarters, compared to Hôtel Bastian, was more like what awaited at the bottom of a refuse-laden gutter pipe.

The faction had set up shop in a century-old brick mill near Fleet Ditch, with a working front for the public as a storage facility for mechanical wares. They had even filled the first floor with all sorts of gears and engines, cogs and wheels, and other contraptions that were surely, Gabby thought, the iron and steel innards of some machinery, in order to make the building appear legitimate.

However, the next two floors of the building, which covered nearly an entire block, was the residence of some thirty Alliance members. It was, Gabby had noted in the few times she and Rory had visited, a much more organized and well-outfitted Alliance faction than what she'd witnessed in Paris. She had been welcomed earlier that month by their leader, Benjamin, a lean yet muscular man in his midforties who looked like he could still move and fight with the strength and agility of a fighter half his age. He'd assured her that the incident with Lennier would not be held against her here in London, and that she would be considered a friend of the Alliance. He'd stirred her hope that perhaps, with the right training, she could be more than a friend.

However, as Gabby sat with Benjamin and a few other upper-rank fighters in the second floor of the warehouse, discussing the demon trapping diffuser nets, she wondered if she was a fit for the Alliance at all.

"You don't seem to understand what these nets can do," she said, pushing herself up from the uncomfortable sofa Benjamin kept in the convening room, a glassed-in office that had perhaps once been used by a foreman. The office sat up a short flight of steps that looked over the open second-floor loft.

"They stop a demon in its tracks and diffuse its power, rendering it completely defenseless," Gabby explained for what felt like the tenth time. She and Rory had been summoned to the Fleet Ditch warehouse to explain their visit to Hugh Dupuis's home. Gabby wasn't certain how Benjamin had learned of it, but she figured Hugh and his corvites weren't the only ones keeping their eyes on her.

"Dupuis told you all this?" Benjamin asked, leaning against the wavy glass, his back to the activity below.

Portions of the loft had been sectioned off as meeting spaces, open training areas, even a kitchen and dining hall, and there were probably a dozen or more people milling about. Each one had glanced up toward the glass-faced office every now and then during the past fifteen minutes.

"Yes, but Rory and I saw it on our own as well," she answered. They'd already explained how they'd met Hugh Dupuis on the London docks. "Mr. Dupuis simply explained the nets in more detail to me yesterday during my visit."

Nadia, a middle-aged woman with close-cropped, mostly gray hair, lifted her booted foot onto the seat of a low stool and leaned forward. "And you thought nothing of going inside a Daicrypta doyen's home alone?"

She, like Chelle, dressed as a man, in trousers and a jacket, but unlike Chelle, Nadia truly had no feminine features and, Gabby had learned, went by the name of Ned outside these warehouse walls.

"I was never in any danger," Gabby said with a sigh. "I truly don't believe Hugh Dupuis is a threat."

"He's Daicrypta," Nadia threw back, as if the single word were enough of an argument. To the Alliance, perhaps it was.

"Yes, but he goes about things much differently than his father did."

Nadia put her foot back down and mumbled "Or so he says" under her breath. Gabby ignored it. There was no way to convince Nadia or Benjamin or the handful of others in the room of what Gabby had felt while in Hugh's presence: that he wanted to help.

"I think he would share these nets with the Alliance if you expressed an interest," Gabby said. "They could be useful in demon hunting."

Benjamin stood free of the window and paced the creaky cork floor. "We don't have a use for nets," he said. "We hunt and destroy demons. We don't trap them or experiment on them."

She looked at Rory, who stood beside the door, working the tip of one of his daggers underneath his nails and doing a smashing job of ignoring the conversation.

"But you *do* hold demons for experimentation," she argued. "There's a whole room in Paris at Hôtel Bastian dedicated to it!"

"Well, there isn't one here," Benjamin said, flashing her the universal expression for *don't argue with me*.

He was the leader in London, but perhaps he was still in the dark about the Directorate's dealings with the Daicrypta. Or perhaps he did know about them but wasn't authorized to say so. Really, the Alliance was starting to give Gabby a headache.

"I expect you both to show consideration for the way we do things here. Neither of you is part of my faction, but you're still Alliance." Benjamin tilted his head toward Gabby. "*Almost,* as far as you're concerned. And we do not work in tandem with the Daicrypta. Especially a Daicrypta with the name Dupuis."

Gabby wasn't sure whom she was more frustrated with: Benjamin, for his unwavering shortsightedness, or Rory, for keeping his mouth shut and his head down for the entire meeting. She told Rory as much as soon as they'd been escorted out through the side door.

"There's no arguin' wi' the leader of another faction," Rory explained as he helped her into the enclosed carriage that had been waiting for them outside the warehouse. They settled in, and the driver didn't waste a moment directing the horses onward, out of this part of the city.

"He's right, Gabby, we should stay away from the Daicrypta."

There was no arguing with Rory, either. He was as stubborn as his cousin. If Gabby told him exactly what was going through her mind—that she had found herself liking Hugh Dupuis's company infinitely more than Benjamin's or Nadia's—he might have guessed that she had no intention of staying away from the Daicrypta simply because someone had told her to. If she wanted to pay another visit, then she would.

It made her wish she actually had a reason to go back.

The nets were only proven to capture full-blooded demons, though. Who knew how much demon blood Axia had developed while in the Underneath? It might not be enough for the nets to seal to her, the same way they hadn't sealed to Ingrid or Vander.

Gabby leaned against the cushioned wall, which jostled her even more now that the carriage traveled along a road that felt like it had been pockmarked by a rain of meteorites. She wished for one useful thing to do. How had she suffered through her days before Paris? Teas and parties and dress fittings and dancing lessons and nothing but luxurious ridiculousness.

"I see I've got to do something drastic to keep ye from trouble, don't I, *laoch*?"

The words sounded playful, but Rory gave too much worry away with his watchful eyes. To her body's relief, the carriage stopped. The grumblings of their driver, raised voices from other nearby carriages, and a chorus of braying, agitated horses all pointed to a cluster of traffic.

"I don't require handling," she replied.

"I'll take ye out again tonight. We'll find plenty of demons to dispatch in Whitechapel—"

Gabby's interest had just been hooked when the door to the carriage swung open and then closed again, and suddenly there was a person on the seat next to Rory. Her right hand went to her boot and the dagger she kept there, but she was slower than Rory. The tip of his blade was already pricking the stranger's throat.

The stranger's hands went up in a gesture of surrender, the square case he'd been holding clunking to the floor at his feet. He wore a hat with a wide, floppy front brim, pulled low to obscure his face. As soon as Gabby's heart had slowed a notch, her eyes noticed details again—like the broad shape of the man's shoulders and the calluses on his palms. She knew those hands.

"Nothing like a warm Alliance welcome," he said, one hand slowly moving to push up the brim of his cap.

Nolan Quinn paid no attention to the knife falling away from his throat or to the curses Rory threw at him. He held Gabby's shocked gaze, his lips pressed into an uncertain frown. Waiting, she thought, to see how she would react. There were too many thoughts all at once. So many that Gabby, floundering in Nolan's blue stare, found that there was nothing at all she could say or do. So she sat back against the cushions, folded her hands in her lap, lifted her chin imperiously, and said nothing.

"Ye look like hell," Rory said to break the tension.

He most certainly did. Nolan hadn't shaved in days. Gabby had never seen him with so much dark stubble. His clothing wasn't dirty but definitely looked as if it had been slept in. Well, perhaps just traveled hard in, for the shadows beneath his eyes hinted that he'd slept little.

Even with these defects, plus the scent of sweat and burnt coal that clung to him, Nolan looked so deliciously handsome that Gabby had to remind herself to breathe. And that he had spurned her.

"Listen," Nolan said, too tense for a witty rejoinder. "I probably shouldn't have come here, but there was nowhere else I could think to go. I had to act fast."

Rory sheathed his knife and pulled his coat closed. "What's happened?"

The traffic must have cleared up, for their driver slapped the reins and the carriage started rocking again.

Gabby attempted to keep her expression cool. Nolan flicked his gaze toward her a few times as he explained how the Directorate had wanted Ingrid's leftover angel blood and the Duster files, and how his instinct had started tolling like a bell, telling him to avoid giving either to the arriving representative at all costs. When Nolan told them of tossing the files into the burning stove and then taking the blood stores, Gabby's mask of disinterest cracked and finally fell apart.

"You took the blood?" she asked, even though the answer was quite clear. Here Nolan sat, inside her carriage in London, and at his feet was a square leather case, about the size of one of Gabby's hatboxes.

"Jesus, Cousin," Rory breathed. "Ye defied Directorate orders. Have ye gone mad?"

Nolan ripped off his hat and his black hair fell around his forehead. He raked it back.

"It was instinct, Rory," he said. "I had to follow it. We're hunters. We *survive* on instinct. Mine screamed at me to take that blood and run, and so I did. I'll worry about the consequences later, all right?"

At that word—*consequences*—Gabby's stomach slipped into a knot. What would they do to Nolan when they found him?

"You think the Directorate means to harm the Dusters," she said, the vision of Nolan tossing file after file into the stove at Hôtel Bastian playing through her mind.

He leaned his head back and closed his eyes. "They're Axia's pawns. Who knows what she's going to use them for, but it won't be good." He opened his eyes and fixed them on hers. "Yes. I think they plan to harm the Dusters. If only to cut Axia's plans off at the knees."

Gabby sprang forward, sliding to the edge of her seat. "What about my sister? And Grayson? Why didn't you bring them with you?"

"Your sister has the best protection the universe has to offer, lass. And do you really believe your brother would have gone sneaking off with *me* anywhere?"

No. Not after their last encounter, when Nolan had threatened Grayson's life for leading a hellhound into the Daicrypta courtyard.

"Ye could have burned the blood with the files," Rory said, all calmness and logic, whereas Gabby's head swam with the confusing muddle of deceit and politics.

"No," Nolan replied. He tapped the case with the side of his foot. "Just as instinct told me to keep it out of the Directorate's hands, it also told me to keep it safe. I don't know why or how, but . . ." He sighed, sounding exhausted. "It's got to help us."

Gabby peered down at the locked case, and this time, comprehension struck. Angel blood. Nolan had brought them *angel* blood.

"Hugh," she whispered, suddenly so restless she wanted to get up and pace. "Hugh!"

Nolan peered at her from the sleepy position into which he'd begun to slouch.

"Hugh who?" he asked, frowning.

Rory groaned. "Daicrypta."

That got Nolan out of his slouch. He sat forward and opened his mouth, but Gabby waved her hands to hush him.

"He needs angel blood to test something." She couldn't stop her gloved hands from clapping. "Oh, this is perfect!"

Nolan's confusion turned into a solid glower. "You want to hand angel blood over to a disciple named Hugh?"

"He's a doyen, actually," she corrected him, and Nolan's mouth went wider with disbelief, his throat making little hoarse clicking noises when words failed.

"It's all right, cousin," Rory soothed with an elbow to Nolan's shoulder. "He seems moderately trustworthy."

Nolan's stare of disbelief shifted toward Rory. "I honestly have no idea what's happening right now."

Why would he? He'd been absent for weeks, and in more ways than one. He'd hurt Gabby with his silence, of course. She'd been reminded of that every night when she'd lain down to sleep, only to be haunted by questions like *Why?* and *Am I that easy to fall out of love with?* But until that moment, she hadn't known how *angry* his silence had made her. The knowledge surged inside her so quickly that she was certain the temperature in the carriage had jumped.

Well, good. Let Nolan be in the dark. Let him try to find a footing here, the same way she'd had to. And let him do it without her.

"You are not required to come with me, Mr. Quinn; however, I am taking that blood to the Daicrypta," Gabby said, the steel in her voice bringing both Nolan and Rory to attention. "Please give my thanks to your instincts."

* * *

Grayson paced in front of the locked vendors' stalls along a corner of the Quai d'Orsay and a bridge spanning the Seine. Only a few of Paris's many bridges were protected by the Dispossessed. This was one of them. Grayson stopped and stared through the darkness. There were precious few lamps along this pedestrian bridge, and the weak light made it difficult for him to see Chelle from where he stood. Others would have a difficult time as well. That was a good thing, considering Chelle had just climbed onto the bridge's thick stone parapet and was gazing down into the black water of the Seine.

Chelle didn't want any passing humans to help her. That wasn't the plan. The plan, Grayson had started to realize with that cold, greasy feeling that came with knowing he'd made a horrible decision, was wrong. Wrong and dangerous, and he couldn't just stand there waiting for his moment to leap in, the way Chelle had instructed. He had to move. Now.

Grayson clenched his hands into fists and stepped onto the bridge, walking fast. Chelle braced her weight confidently against the stone griffin. They hadn't talked about her father after their kiss in the abbey vaults earlier that afternoon. When Chelle had finally pulled away from him, a gorgeous pink blush on her cheeks, Grayson hadn't been able to think about anything besides her mouth and when he would be able to kiss her again. If she'd let him. She'd left the abbey with a promise to pick him up at ten o'clock.

He'd thought that he could do it. He'd listed off all the reasons why he *should* do it. Yann had tried to kill Grayson before; he was a Chimera, and next to Vincent, he was the most influential of his caste; he was likely the one killing Dusters, too. But he was still a man. A gargoyle, but also a man, and that was what stuck in Grayson's throat like a wad of dry crackers. Chelle wanted to kill a *man,* not just a gargoyle, and she wanted Grayson's help.

He couldn't do it. He couldn't kill again, not even someone who deserved it.

Grayson had just parted his mouth to call her name when another person came through the vaporous shadows, toward Chelle's perched figure.

Too late.

Grayson reached for the hilt of his sword, hidden at his waist under his long frock coat.

"I would ask you to step down to safety, boy," Yann entreated in French, his tone bored rather than concerned.

Chelle stood still and unresponsive. Yann took a step closer to the bridge.

"I will remove you if need be," he said, switching to English and probably growing irritated at the threat of an angel's burn.

Grayson knew Chelle's next move, and he dreaded it. She spun around and sank into a crouch, taking Yann by surprise when she aimed a primed crossbow at his chest. But Chelle had allowed him to get too close, and he'd moved quickly. He grabbed her ankle and swiped her off her feet. She landed hard on her side, momentum rolling her backward, toward the drop-off into the river below.

"No!" Grayson shouted, distracting Yann long enough for Chelle to regain the advantage.

She fired the crossbow from her downed position, her body still teetering. The mercurite-dipped bolt ripped into Yann's shoulder. He roared in pain, staggering back as Grayson ran forward. He stopped breathing as Chelle's body disappeared over the edge of the bridge—then began again when he saw her fingers digging into the stone edge.

Grayson grabbed her slim wrists, which shook with effort.

"Now, Grayson!" Chelle screamed. "I can pull myself up, but you have to do it now!"

Grayson let go of her wrists and spun around, his hand going to his sword; he expected Yann to be behind him, talons slashing. The Chimera was a few paces away, down on one knee. His hand hovered around the mercurite bolt, unable to touch it in order to remove it from his flesh.

He stared up at Grayson, a smirk lifting the corner of his lips. Yann's long black hair, streaked with silver, had fallen forward, half covering his amused grin.

"Yes, do it now, Duster." He echoed Chelle's order and then broke off into a dry, mocking laugh. "I'd like to see you try."

Grayson hadn't drawn his sword. His hand still rested on the hilt, his palm sweating, arms frozen. He wouldn't do it. He couldn't. His mind tumbled backward, toward the memories of the girl in London and the blood on his teeth.

"Grayson! Now!" Chelle's voice no longer came from below the bridge. She'd hauled herself up, elbows on the parapet.

Yann laughed one more time, and then, before Chelle could climb over completely and unleash her *hira-shuriken,* burst out of his clothing and his human form. He took flight, his great, razor-feathered wings unaffected by the mercurite bolt in his shoulder. He hurtled out of view and range before Chelle's feet hit the bridge.

"He was injured! You had the advantage!" she raged.

"No, Chelle," he said, his own voice strangely calm. "There is no advantage in murder. And that's what it would have been."

"What do you mean?" She stepped away from him. "We agreed it had to be done. They're animals, Grayson. They killed Léon. They'll kill *you!*"

"This wasn't about me." He followed Chelle as she took a few more steps away from him. "It was never about me or the Dusters. I'm not a complete idiot. What happened to your father was awful. It was wrong and sadistic and I don't blame you for hating the gargoyle that destroyed him. But killing Yann or any of the other Chimeras out there isn't going to make it right."

Chelle kept her body turned away from him.

"You're not a murderer," he said, remembering the softness of her lips, her small hands tentatively exploring the breadth of his chest. "Trust me, you don't want to be one."

He reached for her shoulder, but Chelle sensed his intent and darted to the side. She whipped around to spear him with an expression of pure disgust.

"You should have never agreed to this if you didn't have the stomach for it," she said, and Grayson knew she was right. He should have stopped her before it had gotten this far. He had no excuse.

Chelle pointed wildly up into the starless night sky. "Yann's gone to warn the others, and by dawn every last gargoyle in Paris will know that I tried to kill him."

She shoved Grayson hard in the chest and then stormed past him, toward the Left Bank, shouting over her shoulder, "Congratulations, Grayson Waverly. You've just signed my death warrant."

CHAPTER FOURTEEN

Lord Brickton quit Waverly House with less than a few hours' notice. Gabby and Rory had returned from Fleet Street, Nolan having jumped from the carriage before it turned into Grosvenor Square, to find her father's trunk being loaded into the family's second carriage, the one they reserved for trips to their country estate.

"Mitchard is expecting me," her father had said, referring to his land steward. Apparently he was off to Fairfax Downs, their estate in Cumberland, to make the annual tour of his lands. Papa had donned his greatcoat and taken up his walking stick in the entrance foyer, completely ignoring Rory and stopping only to peck Gabby on the cheek—her unblemished side.

She'd hated the feeling of relief when Reeves had closed the door behind him. Her father had left her to her own devices all month, tiptoeing around her and Rory, finding a reason to leave a room if she entered, eating in his study instead of at the dinner table. Gabby should have missed him more. Before, when she and Mama and Ingrid and Grayson were all living in London together with him, she would have. Before, she would have begged him to take her with him to Fairfax Downs. It bothered her how drastically things had changed.

That evening, she and Rory sat at the long dinner table, their cutlery scraping at their plates and their eyes drifting to the wall of windows that overlooked the lawns. Perched on the ledge of the window closest to Gabby was a raven-winged corvite. It stared into the dining room, its red-ringed pupils darting between Rory and Gabby. She wondered why Hugh would send another demon bird to sit outside her windows. Was it there to spy yet again? Or had it been sent as a pictorial invitation for her to return to Belgrave Square? She hoped for the latter.

"What will happen to Nolan?" she whispered.

"I wouldna worry." Rory speared his Cornish hen with his fork and carved it using one of his own blades instead of the one laid on the table before him. "He's a fox when he needs to be."

Nolan *was* a fox, sly and cunning and quick. But he'd still appeared shaken that afternoon in the carriage. Not being able to trust the Alliance must have felt like the earth giving way underneath his feet.

"You don't trust Hugh Dupuis," she said, thinking of the angel blood and her plan to take it to him. Nolan had left the carriage with the blood, saying he'd see her soon; she hoped it would be by tomorrow. There was simply no time to waste.

"I don't trust any man till he's saved my skin at least once," Rory replied, laying down his fork without finishing his hen. She hadn't touched anything since the soup course. Cook Edna would be vexed.

Rory wiped the blade of his dagger with one of the dinner napkins. "I don't trust Hugh Dupuis, but I do trust ye, *laoch*." He pushed back his chair and stood. "If ye trust him enough to bring him angel blood, I won't stop ye."

Rory bid her a good night and left the dining room. Gabby

sat back in her chair, her eyes drifting toward the corvite demon at the window. She didn't know if she trusted Hugh, but she did know that there was only one way to find out.

Gabby stuck her tongue out at the corvite and made her way up to her room. She passed a number of guest chambers and was equal parts glad and frustrated that Nolan wasn't able to occupy one of them. She was proud of how she'd acted in the carriage earlier, refusing to melt into a puddle at his feet. She wasn't so pigheaded as to deny that she'd missed him, or that she had wanted to crawl into his lap and kiss him until they were both gasping for air. But Gabby's pride had been akin to iron, easily crushing the urges.

She entered her room and found that her maid had prepared it for her. The lamps were on and the fire was going, her night-gown draped over the duvet.

"Kendall?" Gabby shut the door and moved toward the bed. Her maid wasn't in sight, but Gabby's senses were humming.

Someone else was in her room. And she knew exactly who it was.

Nolan stepped out from behind her four-panel silk changing screen. He'd shaved and changed his clothes, but his shoulders still looked like they were winched tight with a line of rope.

Gabby drew to a stop to stare at him and quickly realized that she'd drained every last ounce of her steely pride that afternoon. Tears welled up swiftly and unexpectedly. She didn't even have time to be mortified by them. She didn't see Nolan crossing the room, but then he was there, his arms closing around her, his lips in her hair. "I'm sorry, Gabby. God, I'm so sorry, lass."

She couldn't speak, her throat swollen with a suppressed sob, so instead, she wiggled her arm free and punched him in the stomach.

He answered by tucking her closer against him. She made another fist but only thumped it against his shoulder. How could he so quickly, so effortlessly, undo her like this?

"I know I did everything wrong," he said, clinging to her, his lips trailing kisses through her hair and over her forehead. "I know I hurt you. I know I should have fixed things."

Gabby found enough strength to untangle herself, but she couldn't look up into his eyes. If she did that, she knew she'd just fall right back against him.

"But you chose to ignore me instead," she said, busying herself by blotting the tears on her cheeks with as much dignity as possible.

"I couldn't apologize on paper, not for the things I said to you. Not for the way I treated you that night," he said.

He'd been cold the night his father had been killed, not allowing her even to touch him. Telling her she had to leave Paris and then acting as if he couldn't have cared less.

"It would have been better than silence," she said.

Nolan hung his head, his hands on his hips. He didn't have any more excuses. He wasn't the type of person to throw them out ahead of himself to clear a path anyway.

"I thought that you—" She took a breath, preparing to humiliate herself. "You told me you loved me."

He clutched her arm and tipped her chin up so she couldn't avoid looking into his eyes any longer.

"Did you really believe I'd stopped?"

Gabby itched to punch him again. "What was I supposed to believe when I didn't hear from you for a month?"

"I was wrong, Gabby, and I'll apologize for it forever if you want me to. But the truth is I couldn't face you. If I came to you and you sent me away, if I knew for certain that you didn't want me anymore ... God in heaven, Gabriella Waverly, I've never been so bloody afraid of a lass before."

Nolan's mouth hovered over hers and she could see the fear bright in his eyes. She wanted to laugh. Nolan Quinn, a fierce swordsman who picked battles with Underneath demons on a regular basis, was afraid of *her*? But she couldn't laugh. He was being completely serious, and for the first time Gabby felt the weight of what that meant. He was real and he made mistakes, but he loved her.

"Please forgive me," he said, still worried she wouldn't. He traced her scars with his thumb with such tenderness it made her ache.

Gabby was certain she kissed him first, but after a moment, it didn't matter who had started it. Nolan had her against his chest and he was kissing her as if she were his air source.

She had the urge to pull him closer even though there wasn't a single gap between their bodies. His hands were everywhere; raking through her hair and uncoiling her chignon, coasting down the curve of her spine and fanning out over her hips, his fingertips brushing dangerously lower. He murmured her name as he drew her hair aside and nuzzled her neck. He lifted her from the floor, spun around, and set her down again, this time on the edge of her bed.

He stood in front of her, breathing hard. His eyes traveled from her loose curls down the front of her dress, to her legs, and then back up again. He must have noticed the heat in her cheeks, but he didn't tease her the way he normally would have. Nolan had gone acutely sober. Predatory. Gabby had seen something close to it in his eyes before, in her rectory bedroom when he had climbed through her window and asked her to lie beside him for a while. Nolan had promised to be a gentleman then. However, as he took a step closer to the bed and tilted her chin up, she understood that he no longer wished to be a gentleman.

Gabby couldn't breathe. The room was too hot, the fire in the grate roaring. She closed her eyes when Nolan's fingertips brushed down the curve of her throat. He leaned forward to trail kisses in their wake, and Gabby honestly believed her body might combust. Her back met the forgiving plush of the duvet and she opened her eyes to Nolan, holding himself on one elbow over her, the palm of his free hand flat against her stomach.

He said nothing as his hand grazed over her ribs, tightly cinched in a corset that Gabby suddenly despised more than ever. She hitched her breath when he continued his exploration, allowing his palm to shape around her breast. Nolan then took her mouth in the sort of kiss that said things. Things that would sound graceless if bound by words.

She twined her fingers through the silk of his hair, arching her back in an attempt to be closer to him. When he pulled away, Nolan stared down at her with an unexpected hint of trepidation in his eyes. He put on one of his half smiles.

"This isn't very gentlemanlike, is it, lass?"

No witty comeback surfaced, and after a moment of simply staring up at him, her fingers running over his lips, she watched as Nolan pushed himself off of the bed.

She sat up, suddenly realizing with stark clarity what had just nearly happened.

"I have to go," Nolan said, buttoning the top buttons of his shirt. Gabby blushed furiously. Had she undone them?

"Of course." She averted her eyes and touched the side of her head and the mess of loose curls.

"I don't *want* to go," Nolan said, his husky voice rich with disappointment. "Someday I won't."

Gabby forgot her untidy hair. She fixed her eyes on his, heat coursing into her cheeks yet again.

"I love you, Gabby."

Air. There wasn't enough of it. Nolan stood a moment while Gabby stared up at him, stunned speechless, just as she'd been the first time he'd said the words to her.

He gestured to the silk screen. "The case with your sister's blood is over there."

Gabby blinked. He was just giving it to her?

"Will you come with me?" she asked.

"I thought you didn't require my presence," he said, quirking one brow.

Gabby smiled but looked down, thinking how haughty she must have sounded.

"I don't require it," she said. "But I want it. So will you come?"

He stayed back from the bed, though she knew he wanted to come closer. Instead, he cleared his throat and went to her door. She had no doubt he'd be able to sneak out of the house the same way he'd sneaked in.

"I'm at your service, as always, Miss Waverly," he said, and with a playful bow, disappeared into the corridor.

CHAPTER FIFTEEN

Ingrid had seen a number of maps of Paris. The layout of the city had always reminded her of an inked thumbprint. The roads all seemed to swirl inward, crossing, merging, and growing tighter together until they reached the two islands in the Seine. Ingrid knew the city was large and sprawling, that there were over a million people living here and going about their daily lives without fear of the Underneath or of a vengeful fallen angel. For those people, it was life as usual.

But for the past handful of days, it had seemed to Ingrid as if the thumbprint of the city had started to smudge and disappear, as if those other people didn't exist and the only things that were real had to do with the Alliance and Dispossessed and the scattered Dusters, driven into hiding.

Ingrid didn't want to hide. She'd had the intense urge to leave her arrondissement for some other part of the city she didn't normally see. To experience something that reminded her that that thumbprint was still there. That those other people were real.

Marco was at the reins of the landau, directing the horses down rue de Berri. She wasn't certain Vander would be in his apartment, but she knew better than to go to Hôtel Bastian again. Marco would have refused to bring her there anyhow. He must have trusted Vander; he'd only put up a mild stink about acting the part of lowly driver.

Ingrid was restless. She couldn't go to Hôtel Bastian, she shouldn't go to gargoyle common grounds, and she definitely couldn't stay at the rectory or abbey any longer. If Vander wasn't at his apartment, she would direct Marco to Clos du Vie next, despite Constantine's message that lessons had been suspended.

The landau drew to a stop, and a moment later, Marco handed her down to the curb. Ingrid saw Vander's wagonette parked in front of them, the traces at rest on the pavement and his black mare likely put away in the stable behind the church.

"The Seer is beneath your station, Lady Ingrid," Marco said, scowling up at the building that shared a wall with the apartments next door.

"It's not like that," she said. "He's my friend."

Marco gave her a look of pity. "And does the Seer know that is all he is?"

Ingrid gathered her cloak around her and pushed past Marco, heading toward the door. She'd only been to Vander's apartment once, but she remembered the way in.

"I'll be back in an hour," Marco called as he climbed into the box.

Ingrid turned around. "You're not waiting here?"

"You do realize I'm not truly your servant, don't you?" He released the brake and guided the horses away from the curb. "I'm going to Yann's bridge. If you need me, I will know."

Marco merged into traffic, and with a groan of annoyance, Ingrid entered the apartment building. *And does the Seer know that is all he is?* Marco's question poked at her as she ascended the stairwell. Saying Vander was just her friend had been a lie, though Ingrid wished it hadn't been. Everything would be so much simpler if they hadn't kissed those few times. If he hadn't told her how much he wanted her in his life. Vander hadn't yet told her that he loved her, but at this point the words weren't necessary.

He knew how she felt about Luc. Didn't he? Words weren't necessary for that, either. Were they? Ingrid turned onto the third-floor landing and a quiver of nervousness weakened her legs. She had to tell him. Perhaps that was what she'd come here to do. She suddenly felt sick to her stomach. As soon as she told Vander about Luc, she would lose him—and she didn't *want* to lose him. The idea of it sent her heart into a flutter of panic, and then a sharp twinge ignited at each shoulder.

The current leaked from her fingers before she could rein it back in. It sparked off the metal discs in her gloves, sparing the electric bulbs strung along the short hallway. Vander's door was just ahead. She would tell him. She'd get it over with.

Ingrid reached his flat and was about to knock when a familiar voice sounded from within.

"Is it working?" the muffled voice asked.

Ingrid leaned closer to the door. What on earth was *Grayson* doing here?

Vander's voice followed. "Well, how do you feel?"

"Amazing," Grayson answered. Ingrid could hear his excitement. "I only started feeling the itch to shift this morning. I can smell blood now, but it's been two days."

Ingrid pressed her ear against the wood, unable to believe she'd just heard her brother correctly. He'd gone *two days* without scenting blood?

"That's . . . I don't know what to say," Vander replied. "I think we should tell Ingrid. I'd already tested our compatibility before Nolan took the blood stores, and it didn't clot."

Grayson: "Do you think she'd go for it?"

Vander: "What Duster wouldn't?"

Enough. Ingrid had to know what they were talking about.

She opened the door without knocking and entered the small room, which somehow appeared even more cramped than it had the first time she'd seen it. Her brother sat in a chair at Vander's desk, his arm propped on the top and his sleeve rolled above his elbow. Vander stood beside him, piercing his skin with a needle.

"What are you doing?" She slammed the door behind her, her eyes on the needle. "And what is that?"

They both straightened at the sight of her, Grayson swearing loudly as Vander fumbled with the needle and syringe. Grayson swore again, regaining Vander's attention. He pushed the plunger and the contents of the glass barrel disappeared into Grayson's vein. He extracted the needle and set it aside on the desk roughly before turning toward Ingrid, hands up in surrender.

"Let me explain."

"What did you just inject into my brother?"

Grayson stood up. "Mersian blood. Ingrid, it's okay. You don't have to look like that."

She frowned. "Like what?"

"Like you want to electrocute the good reverend," her brother answered.

"She wouldn't electrocute me." Vander peered at Ingrid. "I hope."

"Why would you inject Grayson with your blood?" she asked, not in the mood for humor. "And, Grayson, how do you know where Vander lives?"

The two men looked at one another and, with a few raised eyebrows and hand gestures, silently discussed who would be the one to explain things. Grayson bowed to the pressure first.

He stepped toward Ingrid. "I've been coming to Vander for a little while. Don't be angry, Ingrid. I asked him to keep it a secret," he said quickly, as if knowing how she would react. "He's been taking some of my dust, making things easier for me. And this experiment, mixing his blood with mine, is actually working."

"My mersian blood seems to have cancelled out his hellhound symptoms," Vander explained.

She remembered what Grayson had said behind the closed door. That he hadn't itched to shift in days.

"I didn't want to be around you or Mama until I could trust myself," Grayson added. He stood in front of Ingrid, slightly taller than she was. He cocked his head to meet her eyes.

"I can do it now. With Vander's help," Grayson said, and then, running both hands through his hair, went on, "I think his blood is our answer, Ingrid. Not just us, but all Dusters."

She peered over Grayson's shoulder to where Vander stood at his desk, taking apart the needle and syringe, one ear on their conversation but clearly trying to stay out of it. He'd been helping her brother this whole time? Ingrid had been desperate to know where Grayson was, and Vander had known. He'd known and kept quiet.

Her brother pinched her arm, jerking her attention back to him. She swatted his shoulder.

"Would you give me a minute?" she asked. "I'm trying to catch up."

Grayson laughed and took his jacket from where he'd tossed it on Vander's bed.

"All right, I'll give you more than a minute, okay? I have to go. But, Ingrid, get the injection. See for yourself."

He started for the door but doubled back, as if he'd forgotten something. He took her by the shoulders. "We can be us again. We can be a normal family doing normal things. Normal, boring, mundane things."

He lifted her off the floor and twirled her once before she kicked and demanded he put her down. He did, but by then she was laughing.

"I should say that sounds awful," she said.

"But it doesn't, does it?" Grayson asked. He nodded his thanks to Vander and left.

Ingrid's head still spun, her laughter fading. Vander closed the needle kit and stood at his desk. After a long pause, he leaped in with an explanation.

"I know how worried you were about him, and I wanted to tell you, Ingrid, I did. But if I had and you had come here, forcing him to see you when he wasn't ready, he might not have come back."

She stood in the center of his room, her hands feeling warm. No current now. She wasn't upset. And yet tears were pricking at her eyes.

"I thought if I could help him, even a little, that it would be at least something."

It was more than just something. It was good and selfless and earnest. So very Vander.

"Did he find you?" she asked.

Vander hesitated. "I found him."

"How?"

"I tracked him."

He'd found her brother. He'd helped him. Given him hope. And because of that, Grayson had just picked her up and spun her around the way he'd always done before, whenever he'd been too happy to hold still. Her brother hadn't been happy like that in ages.

Ingrid crossed the room to the desk where Vander still stood and, without a word, threw her arms around his shoulders and clung to him. He stiffened briefly before his arms encircled her in return.

"This doesn't feel like you're angry," he said.

She laughed, her cheeks wet with tears. "How could I be angry? You went out of your way to track down my brother, and you helped him. He needed someone to care for him, and I couldn't, but you did," she said, her voice muffled by Vander's shoulder.

She pulled away, wanting to say thank you. Vander's mouth

caught hers, stunning her long enough for him to ease her forward, against his chest. Ingrid's lips had already been parted to speak and Vander had deftly stolen inside. The touch of his tongue and the way his fingers worked underneath her coiled braid, rubbing against her scalp, stunned her for a second time. But when he wrapped one arm around her waist and whirled her around, lifting her to sit upon the desktop, Ingrid laid her palms flat against Vander's chest and pushed. Hard.

"No. Stop," she gasped as she slid off the desk and stumbled away from him.

Vander stared after her, heaving for air. She covered her mouth with a trembling hand, unable to meet Vander's gaze.

"Ingrid—"

"I can't," she whispered. "I'm sorry, I can't."

She hadn't expected him to kiss her. And she hadn't expected to have to remember how good kissing him felt.

"Because of Luc," he said.

She dropped her hand and dared to meet Vander's eyes. He narrowed them at her. "What has he done?"

Ingrid hesitated. "Nothing."

Vander raised his voice and came toward her. "Do you know how much danger he's put you in if the other Dispossessed find out?"

"I'm already in danger," she said, though she immediately knew it was a poor retort. It only made Vander more furious.

"That's right, Ingrid. Gargoyles are *already* hungry to destroy you, and now Luc would give them one more reason."

It was tempting to be a coward and allow Vander to heap all his anger on Luc. She couldn't do it, though. She was British. Cowardice simply wasn't acceptable.

"You're acting as if I didn't have a say in any of this. I did, Vander. I *do*."

He shook his head and, since there was not enough room to pace, turned in a tight circle. "He's manipulating you. Making you confuse gratitude with affection. I can guarantee you wouldn't feel anything for him if he hadn't saved your life so many times, or been bound to you the way he was."

Did Vander truly think her so susceptible? Or shallow? Ingrid stopped shrinking from him and stood her ground.

"They are my feelings, Vander Burke, not yours to pick apart and evaluate. And if you believe Luc would manipulate me, then you don't know him at all."

Vander took two strides across the room and stood directly before her, using every inch of his height to bear down on her.

"You're right, I don't know him. I know you, though, and I know what we have is real." He took her hand in his and pressed it against his chest. "I know you feel the same things I do when we kiss. When we touch. And it's not just our dust. It goes deeper than that."

He'd inclined his head as he'd been speaking, his voice growing fainter though his lips had come closer. Ingrid didn't know what to do. She *did* feel something when they kissed. She *did* like it. But she didn't long for Vander's kisses when they were apart the same way she did Luc's. She longed for Vander's company. His friendship. The comfort that came from being with him.

Ingrid wrenched her hand from his and stepped away. She couldn't bear to look at him. The last thing she wanted to do was hurt him. But she had to.

"Vander . . . ," she said, her next words still undecided.

They remained that way. For right then, the floor gave a violent shake. Or perhaps her legs had curiously lost their strength. Either way, Ingrid tumbled forward. The lights started to wink, and a voice rose from somewhere within the apartment building. The voice was getting louder, and even as blackness swirled thick and stole away Ingrid's sight, the words became distinguishable: *"Come, my seedlings. It is time."*

CHAPTER SIXTEEN

Grayson had hailed a hackney as soon as he'd left Vander's flat. Just past the Arc de Triomphe, however, he'd pounded on the roof and asked to be let out. The air was crisp, there wasn't a single cloud over Paris, and he wanted to keep his body moving instead of cooped up in the back of a stale cab.

The coil of tension along his shoulders and spine had returned that morning after two days of being absent, along with a riptide beneath his skin, swirling and sucking at him. His nose had become more sensitive as well. His mother had crossed the street to his new flat to see if he'd like to join them for breakfast, and he'd traced the barest scent of her blood as she'd knocked at his door. He'd accepted, though reluctantly, and he hadn't had much more than a croissant and coffee before excusing himself. Being inside the rectory when the mersian blood wore off completely would not have been wise.

Grayson crossed the Pont des Invalides with his hands deep in his pockets, the collar of his coat up to block the wind. The elevated body temperature was the only thing he missed about having hellhound blood.

There was a minor problem in all of this: he would be dependent upon Vander Burke from here on out. He didn't like it, but he'd manage it, if it meant keeping his demon side at bay. And who knew, perhaps the old boy would be Grayson's brother-in-law soon. He and his sisters had a weakness for the Alliance, it seemed.

But he didn't want to think about Chelle just then, or about the night before on Yann's bridge. He'd done everything wrong. The only things he consistently felt with regard to Chelle were admiration and frustration.

A woman's scream made him look up. Ahead, a Bohemian-looking man tugged on the sleeve of his companion before breaking into a sprint toward the Right Bank. The other man followed, his long, artfully patched and frayed coattails rippling in the wind. Grayson searched for the woman who had screamed, his rational mind suggesting that those two men had done some nefarious thing to her. He pivoted to look behind him and saw two more people—a woman and a man—also running, these two toward the Left Bank. No one ran in Paris. They walked gracefully and slowly, carrying themselves as if time revolved around their needs, able to stretch or stop if required.

Grayson continued toward the Right Bank, his senses alert. He wasn't sure what made him go to the bridge's stone barrier and peer down. Instinct, perhaps. When he saw the giant, shaggy, black-furred hellhound stalking along the quay in broad daylight, he didn't startle. The demon wasn't the creature that caused his breath to turn to syrup in his throat.

It was the smaller furred creature behind it, the one wearing the remains of a purple skirt and white shirtwaist. A Duster. A hellhound Duster, transformed. And the fur around its maw was plastered with blood.

"Christ," Grayson whispered as another scream broke from the direction of the Right Bank.

He followed the sound. A second scream joined in, then a third, and then a chorus sounded from the head of the bridge. When he reached the street, people were tumbling through the doors of a corner café. A man surged through, knocking over a coal-filled brazier. His hoarse cries drowned out the others, and for good reason—a demon serpent had its fangs jammed deep into his ankle, its pale yellow body trailing behind in the spill of sparking coals. The man kicked his leg and fell, and he disappeared underneath another surge of screaming patrons.

Grayson rushed forward, reaching for the sword he'd had at his waist the night before. His fingers slid along his hip, grasping fabric and air. He'd left it at the rectory. Time seemed to slow for the next few seconds under the roar of panic. He forced his eyes shut and exhaled. *Focus.* He wasn't Alliance, but unlike the people scattering frantically in every direction, he knew how to fight demons.

He was closer to Hôtel Bastian than he was to home. He had to tell the others—had to tell Chelle. And he had to arm himself.

Time kicked back into motion, and with it came the piercing screams of women, the wild bleating of horses, and the grating wails of a baby from some open balcony door above him. Grayson ran as if his legs were a gargoyle's wings, carrying him with effortless speed and power. He swerved into the road to avoid an awning that had collapsed over an outdoor market, and then jumped over the ravaged carcass of a poodle, its jewel-encrusted leash still attached. Windmilling his arms, he came to a halt as a carriage teetered onto two wheels just ahead of him. The horse was bucking and braying as something that looked like a gigantic fly straddled its neck, tearing the flesh to bloody ribbons. The fly was wearing trousers.

It was the Harvest. It had to be.

Grayson bounded out of the way of the crazed horse and started to run again. The Dusters had to be under Axia's control, or perhaps demon control. He didn't know. He just knew that he hadn't been affected. Because of Vander's blood?

Grayson flung himself to the pavement as a black bird sheared through the sky toward him. *Corvite.* It growled when it cut through the air overhead, missing its target by inches. Grayson ignored the flare of pain on his skinned palms and scrambled up, craning his neck to see where the demon bird had flown.

It had spun around, its wingspan easily the length of his own arms outstretched, and was making a dive for him yet again. Grayson's legs hit a metal trash can and he bowled over it, striking the ground and working more grit into the raw skin on his palms. The lid of the trash can spun on the pavement beside him. Grayson grabbed the lid and swung it through the air, connecting with the corvite. The bird thumped to the ground in a shower of black feathers. It was only stunned, so Grayson found his feet and darted away.

If he'd had his hellhound blood, he wouldn't have needed to run to Hôtel Bastian for a blessed silver blade. Then again, if he'd had his hellhound blood, would he even be thinking for himself? Or would he be like that Duster on the quay and the blood-sucking fly feasting on the horse?

Grayson hooked around a corner, onto a street that appeared calm and demon-free. He skidded to a halt and thought of Ingrid. What had happened to his sister?

From where Grayson stood, Vander's apartment was farther away than Hôtel Bastian. He had to get to Chelle and the others. If Ingrid had succumbed to whatever spell Axia had laid down over her seedlings, at least she would be the predator and not the prey. And what of Vander? If his mersian blood was keeping Grayson immune, would he be immune as well? There were too many questions. He'd have to find answers for them later.

Grayson began to jog down the side street. Up ahead, a

woman ran from one side of the street to the other, a child in her arms. They disappeared into a building, and the slam of a door followed. It was the only sign that the chaos had traveled this far. No street would be spared if demons and Dusters were out together.

Grayson broke into a run, his mind laying out the streets, charting a course to rue de Sèvres. At this pace, he'd be there in ten minutes.

Ahead, the road bent into the narrow warren of medieval streets that hadn't been razed and widened, the way the boulevards Saint-Germain and Saint-Michel had been decades before. These roads had been ignored and left to accommodate local foot traffic and perhaps a horse or two astride.

Grayson rounded the corner, where a small bistro, currently empty, had set out tables and chairs. He ground to a stop so quickly his heels kept slipping forward, his body falling sideways. He caught himself on a chair, propelling himself back up and into a wolf's direct line of sight. Not a meaty, greasy-furred hellhound, but a lean, lanky wolf. The only thing that set it apart from the wolves Grayson had seen before were its pitch-black eyes—no iris, no white, just fathomless black—and a maw filled with fangs that sawed back and forth in its bloody gums.

Grayson's stomach churned. Rose-tinted saliva dripped from the demon's mouth, and clumps of long, blond human hair were caught in its teeth. The demon wolf snarled, its black eyes fixed on Grayson. He gripped the lacy iron back of the bistro chair and held it before him as he might a shield. The wolf surged forward, and its teeth crushed one of the curled chair legs as if it were made of papier-mâché. The wolf jerked its head and tore the chair from Grayson's clenched fingers.

He slammed into one of the tables and swiped up a glass ashtray to defend himself with. As if it would to do more than give the wolf something to pick its teeth with. The demon wolf lunged for Grayson—and then combusted into green sparks.

Grayson stared at two, six-pointed silver throwing stars clattering to the ground at his feet. And then Chelle was in front of him where the demon wolf had been, retrieving her *hira-shuriken* and stowing them back in her red sash.

She stared at Grayson with marked disbelief. "You are you."

"Chelle," he said dumbly, releasing his death grip on the ashtray and taking hold of her arms instead. They were thin and muscular beneath the billowy white sleeves of her shirt, and they also threw him off fast.

"The Dusters," she said harshly, avoiding his eyes. "They're attacking humans with the demons. Why haven't you changed?"

A grating shriek thundered overhead. A jade-winged gargoyle hurtled over the rooftops and collided with another winged creature, this one a skeletal horse with a forked tail and featherless wings. Fire streamed from its snout.

"It's difficult to explain," Grayson said. There wasn't time to tell her about the mersian blood or Vander's experiments. The sight of the gargoyle's talons punching through the wings of the demon gave him hope. Wherever she was, Ingrid had Marco to protect her.

"Come on," Chelle said, and she started in the direction Grayson had been heading, into the labyrinth of medieval streets. He followed, his heart thrashing.

"I was in the Tuileries when I saw a hellhound leading two Dusters on a rampage," she said, glancing over her shoulder. "We'll go to Hôtel Bastian. The Roman troops might already be—"

Chelle was cut off by a woman jumping through the smashed display window of a *boulangerie*. The woman landed on the sidewalk in front of Chelle. Grayson reached out to pull Chelle back, but again she wrested her arm free. She spared him a glance of irritation—and that was when the long, razor-edged tail protruding from underneath the woman's dress swiped through the air and sawed into Chelle's thigh.

She screamed and her knees buckled. Grayson dove forward, catching her before she could hit the sidewalk. He moved quickly, pulling a *hira-shuriken* from her red sash. He sliced his palm before whirling the star toward the female Duster. The star missed, and the Duster sprinted away.

Chelle clawed at her thigh and gasped for air, her face contorted in agony.

"Let me see it." Grayson peeled her hand back, but the wound wasn't gushing blood. It wasn't even that deep. Nothing someone as fierce as Chelle would lose every last ounce of coloring over.

Her lips pressed together and her eyes fluttered shut. "P-poison."

Grayson swore. That thing had been a Duster, not a demon, and yet it had still injected poison?

"Tell me what to do." He took her head in his hands to keep her from rolling it side to side, and made her look into his eyes. "Chelle, what do I do?"

Her hand clutched at her trouser pocket and Grayson rifled through it, his fingers closing around a glass vial the size of his pinky finger. Mercurite. He uncorked the vial with his teeth and spat it out. The viscous silver liquid ran like honey over Chelle's blood-smeared wound. It beaded into wide globules and seeped into the torn flesh. Chelle grunted and tensed, her back arching off Grayson's thighs. But a few moments later she was still squirming and panting in agony.

"Not . . . working," she gasped.

He chucked the vial, shattering the glass on the ground. The few drops of remaining mercurite balled together on the pavement, creating a miniature silver dome. Mercurite was supposed to destroy all demon poison.

But a demon hadn't attacked Chelle.

"It's Duster poison," Grayson said, staring at her wound. "We have poison, too."

Why hadn't he thought of that before? They were half demon—why *wouldn't* they have poison?

Chelle began to seize. Grayson stood up, cradling her against his chest and pinning her arms and shoulders. The only other thing that cured demon poison was gargoyle blood. He had no idea if it would prove as useless as the mercurite had, but there was nothing else he could think of. The only gargoyle he could approach—the only gargoyle he trusted—was Luc.

"You're going to be fine," he whispered as he started to run, Chelle's body shivering and twitching.

Her voice came through as a whine. "Common . . . grounds."

Good. Even locked in anguish, Chelle was present enough to know his plan. For once, Grayson didn't feel inadequate. He'd take care of her. He'd make her safe. And then he'd let himself think about Ingrid.

She smelled the acrid bite of smoke. Heard the muffled blare of screams. Ingrid woke with her face cheek-down on something soft. *Grass. The Champs de Mars.* The two thoughts were so clear that when Ingrid opened her eyes she expected to see the exhibition buildings surrounding her. Instead, she saw the curved brass legs of an upholstered theater seat. She wasn't lying on grass, either, but on a floor of red velvet carpet.

She tried to push herself up, collapsing twice before succeeding. Her arms were stiff, and her hands stung with the fiercest case of pins and needles she'd ever had. As she struggled to sit back upon her knees, her head spinning like a dervish, Ingrid saw she was most definitely not on the Champs de Mars. Why had she thought such a thing? She wasn't in Vander's room, either. She had found consciousness on the carpeted floor of a theater balcony box. How on earth had she gotten *here*?

She wobbled to her feet, clutching the edge of one burgundy upholstered seat with her numb hand, and looked out over the theater in horror. It wasn't just any theater, but l'Opéra Garnier, and below, flames had consumed the stage.

An echoing crack ripped through the theater, and Ingrid shrieked as the stage collapsed in a ball of fire. More screams sounded from the other side of the balcony box door, and suddenly Ingrid was back in her friend Anna Bettinger's ballroom, the curtains going up in flames, guests tripping over one another to flee the fire that Ingrid had accidentally set.

She held up her numbed hands before her. Her gloves. They were gone.

Had she done this?

She coughed as the box filled with smoke. She staggered toward the door and pushed it open, only to be met with another gray wall of smoke. Ingrid fell to her hands and knees. The air was easier to breathe near the floor, though barely. She coughed and choked and crawled, not knowing where she was going.

She remembered being in Vander's flat, and the darkness that had overcome her. The voice tunneling into her head: *Come, my seedlings.* It had been Axia.

She had come for the Dusters. She was here. This was *her* bedlam.

Ingrid crawled toward the sounds of screaming, the blare of whistles and bells. The smoke seemed to lift a little, and she saw that she'd crawled into an enormous room. Light streamed through the billows of smoke. There were windows ahead. A whole wall of them. Her eyes stung and her vision blurred, but she still spotted a door on the far right-hand side of the ballroom. Hope that it might lead to a terrace drove her to her feet. She hurried to the door and clutched the handle but had to sink back down to the floor to drag in a breath.

Ingrid fumbled with the handle, pushing and pulling and then falling out onto the terrace when the door at last gave way. She collapsed, gasping fresh air, hearing the wails of sirens and bells, and panicked shouting from the street below.

A pair of talons landed on the terrace beside her. Marco sank into a crouch by her side, his cinnamon-red scales and amber wings fiery in the afternoon sunlight. He'd flown in daylight? Exposed his gargoyle form to humans all over Paris?

Things were bad. Cataclysmically bad.

His arm, bricked with muscle, scooped Ingrid up off the cold stone.

"It's Axia," Ingrid croaked as Marco tucked her close to the plates of his chest. Her throat and eyes burned from all the smoke. "She's here."

He lunged off the edge of the terrace and Ingrid caught an unsteady, tear-hazed sight of the street below. Rue de l'Opéra in flames; fire leaping from windows and punching through roofs; carriages overturned in the middle of the street, their hitched horses bucking as hellhounds feasted on their flesh. A gunshot cracked through the pandemonium and Marco rose higher into the air, his wings beating through the black curls of smoke, taking them away from the maelstrom below. But there was no escaping it, she knew. No safe place. Axia's Harvest had begun.

CHAPTER SEVENTEEN

Luc darted higher into the sky in an attempt to get the demon stink out of his nose. They were everywhere, out in full view of humans, laying down a path of destruction and blood. Luc had spent the last hour on the roof of his territory watching and listening with rising dread as the city erupted into turmoil street by street. He'd stayed in human form, even though no fewer than twenty Dispossessed had soared over common grounds in broad daylight.

Their passing shrieks had conveyed the news that fissures had turned into geysers spewing Underneath demons. When more than one gargoyle had screeched down at Luc, reporting that Duster abominations were banding with the demons, Luc had risen to his feet. The worn clay tiles had shifted under his weight as he'd undressed.

Their world, their boundaries, their time living in the dark, had reached an end. Luc had shed his clothes and then his skin while humans on the street below watched and screamed. He'd launched himself from the roof, leaving his territory, thankfully vacant of any humans taking refuge from the waking nightmare unfolding in the streets. He had to find Ingrid. If she'd somehow turned into Axia's pawn and joined the demons roaming Paris . . . Luc didn't know what he would find, but whatever it was, Ingrid would need him.

When he'd reached the abbey and rectory, it had been completely quiet. The chime at the base of Luc's skull had not come. If Marco wasn't there, neither was Ingrid. Lady Brickton, if home, would at least be safe from demons, Luc thought as he'd wheeled in the air and headed for the only other place he knew Ingrid might flee: Hôtel Bastian.

He flew through a cloud of black smoke, a fire having engulfed a row of homes along rue Saint-Sulpice. He felt the heat of the flames and flew faster, clearing the smoke cloud and angling toward the ground. Though rank, the air there would be easier to breathe.

The streets had started to empty. He figured the panicked humans were seeking shelter indoors, and as he flew at rooftop level, he saw that most windows and balcony doors had been closed and shuttered. If only those shutters had been made of blessed silver.

He skewed left and turned onto rue de Sèvres. Except for a handful of people a quarter mile down, the wide boulevard had been abandoned. Four uniformed *gendarmes* were skirmishing with an appendius demon, and closer, a lone man was brandishing his sword at a hellhound, its fangs painted crimson. Luc could only see the man's back, but he knew who it was. He never forgot a human charge.

Grayson Waverly swung the sword at the hellhound's front paw as it swiped at his head. The blade bit into the hound, the wound spitting green sparks. It was a novice stroke of a blade that was clearly not his own—Grayson would have been better off hurling books at the beast.

Luc darted lower, tucking in his wings to gain speed, and rushed over Grayson's head. The talons of his feet punctured the fibrous skin and dense muscle of the hound's neck. He then grabbed hold of the two protruding slanted fangs and broke them off at the base. It was the first thing to do when fighting a hellhound; the wicked points were the hound's most dangerous weapon. Luc kept the fangs in his hands and, with a shriek, plunged them into the hellhound's fire-lit eyes.

He landed deftly on the pavement as the demon's death sparks fizzled, then turned to face Ingrid's brother, who still held the sword aloft. Luc released the trigger inside him and let his true form go. Within seconds, he stood on the cold pavement in human form.

"Where is Ingrid?" he immediately asked.

Grayson let the sword down. He kept his eyes level with Luc's. "I don't know. I was coming to find you."

"Why haven't you become a hellhound?" Luc asked. "The Dusters—"

"I know, they've joined the Underneath demons. I can't explain it all right now. Luc, I need your help."

If Grayson hadn't become one of the crazed Dusters, perhaps Ingrid hadn't, either. Luc realized Grayson was still talking to him.

"I brought her to Hôtel Bastian. She's burning up and needs gargoyle blood. I didn't know who else to ask."

Luc stared at him. "Who?"

"*Chelle,*" Grayson answered. "Mercurite is useless against Duster poison."

Luc glanced behind them, toward Paris Alliance faction headquarters. He could see the building from where they stood.

"Ingrid isn't there?"

"Damn it, Luc, no! I told you, I don't know where she is. But Chelle needs your help!" Grayson took a steadying breath. "Please, Luc. I can't let her die."

Luc turned back to Grayson. He understood Grayson's desperation; he himself felt the same intense need to find Ingrid and protect her.

He nodded, realizing that Grayson must be in love with this Alliance girl. "Fast. I have to find your sister."

Grayson narrowed his eyes at Luc but said nothing. He kept the blessed blade out and began to jog back toward Hôtel Bastian. Luc followed, thinking that a naked man walking down rue de Sèvres was but a slight disturbance compared to the bloodbath up ahead, where the appendius had mopped the ground with the bodies of the four police officers who had been attempting to kill it.

If Ingrid was out there, letting her electricity flow freely, possessed by whatever spell Axia had cast over the Dusters, she was in danger. Not just from uninformed humans, who would see her as a monster, but from other gargoyles. Without Marco to protect her, she would be at their mercy. And if she woke from this spell—if she woke from it at all—and saw what she'd done . . . if she'd hurt people . . . it would devastate her.

Itching to leave, Luc stormed up the flights of stairs to the third floor, where the normally closed and bolted door to faction headquarters had been left wide open. Grayson entered, and Luc hesitantly followed.

Grayson noticed his uncertainty. "The Roman troops aren't here yet. They were due this morning and could be out there right now with the rest of the demon hunters. The place is deserted. Come on."

Luc passed through the open loft, following Grayson to the row of curtained makeshift rooms. Grayson shoved one curtain back on the rods and revealed the Alliance girl lain out on a cot, and Vander Burke crouched beside her.

"Vander?" Grayson said, entering the room. "Where is Ingrid?"

The Seer stood up, his eyes landing on Luc, then looking away. "I don't know. We got separated after she electrocuted me."

He took off his glasses. "I don't know if it's my mersian blood, but I don't seem to be affected by Axia. Neither do you," he said to Grayson. He turned back to the cot. "But what happened to Chelle?"

The right leg on her trousers had been torn up and bloodied; her face was covered with a sheen of sweat. She rolled her head side to side, murmuring nonsense. Grayson knelt by her side, grasping her hand and lifting it to his lips.

"Duster poison," he answered. "And mercurite is useless on it." He looked back at Luc expectantly.

"Hold out your sword," Luc ordered, and Grayson did so. Luc clasped the tip and pulled hard, slicing open his palm. He let the blood well up before reaching inside the ragged rip in the girl's trousers and pressing his hand against her wound.

"You're going to be all right," Grayson whispered into her ear, bending his head against hers.

Luc felt a pang of sympathy for him. The girl—Chelle— looked mostly dead already. Her lips were dry and the color of bleached bone. Her eyes were screwed up tight in agony. The skin beneath Luc's hand was searing hot, and the wound . . . he still felt the gash in her leg. It wasn't healing.

"Grayson." There was no easy way to tell him, so he just came out with it. "It's not working."

Grayson kept his head against Chelle's. "No. It *has* to work. Try again, goddamn it!"

Luc removed his hand from Chelle's leg. He stayed crouched by the cot.

"I'm sorry," he whispered. He really was.

Grayson said nothing. He only squeezed Chelle's hand, his cheeks wet against her temple. Vander stood silently behind them.

Luc turned to him. "Where did you last see her?"

Vander put his spectacles back on. Luc noticed that his clothing was torn and blackened in spots. Probably from where Ingrid had electrocuted him.

"My room on rue de Berri," he answered.

Luc grew cold, then scorching hot with the urge to destroy something. He swallowed the question of what Ingrid had been doing there.

"And Marco?" Luc asked.

The Seer glared at Luc. "He wasn't with us," he said slowly, each word stretched tight by frustration.

Voices entered the open loft outside the room. The telling chime pounded at the base of Luc's skull.

"Hello? Is anyone here?"

Luc closed his eyes and exhaled at the sound of Ingrid's voice.

"You might want to put something on," Vander muttered before shouldering past Luc into the loft.

He dressed himself in jet scales before exiting through the curtains, his wings catching on the fabric as he entered the hallway. Seeing Ingrid in the Seer's arms wasn't ideal, but at least she was here and alive, and flanked by another massive gargoyle. Marco had kept his true form as well. He saw Luc and nodded his wolfish snout in greeting.

Then Ingrid, her cheek pressed against Vander's shoulder, saw Luc. Her eyes went wide. Soot had streaked her cheeks and darkened her thick tumble of blond locks. Her mint-green dress had been dirtied to a deep myrtle, torn at one shoulder, and frayed at the hem. She had never looked more beautiful.

Ingrid pushed herself out of the Seer's arms and ran down the short hallway toward Luc. Her face crumpled with a sob in the instant before she threw herself against the plated muscles of his chest. He caught her with his corded arms, trying to soften the collision before she bruised herself. She clung to him, her arms so slight he hardly felt them around his waist. Luc tensed his wings to bring them forward, and then he crossed them, folding Ingrid into a double embrace.

"I think I've hurt people," she said, her voice small and muffled by the cage of his wings. "I don't remember anything. There was a fire, and I think . . . I think it was me who set it."

He wanted to grip her tighter, but he didn't trust his talons. He wanted to tell her that it wasn't her fault. That it didn't matter. That she was safe now and that he'd keep her that way. She wouldn't have understood any of it, though. He could hold her, but the wall between them was still there. It would always be there.

He let his wings down, revealing their embrace. Vander skewered Luc with a glare as he came back toward them and turned into the room where Chelle lay. Marco grunted and spoke, his screech making perfect sense, if only to Luc: *You're making things worse for yourself, brother. And for her.*

His reply startled Ingrid, who flinched when his answering shrieks rumbled in his chest: *Come what may, I've made my choice and she's made hers.*

He loosened his wings and arms, and Ingrid stepped back. She held Luc's eyes. It was the only way to communicate right then.

"My God." Vander's voice drew her attention away. She pulled away from Luc and entered the curtained room, rushing to her brother's side. He was still kneeling by the cot and had turned to Vander, who was staring at Chelle. She lay immobile, no longer thrashing and moaning. If not for the slight rise of her chest every few moments, Luc would have assumed she was dead.

"What is it?" Grayson asked.

Vander continued to stare at her. He reached out over Grayson's head and combed his hand through the air above Chelle. "It's dust. She's started to give off dust."

*   *   *

179

Gabby hadn't returned to Waverly House after bringing Hugh Dupuis the case of angel blood. She, Nolan, and Rory had arrived on the Daicrypta's Belgravia doorstep that morning and had made themselves comfortable in Hugh's study. He had offered them refreshments while he and his assistants—he'd scoffed at calling them disciples the way his father had, as if they were simply followers of a godlike doyen—had accepted one pint of Ingrid's blood and disappeared into his laboratory to commence work separating the blood and then testing it against the lodestone mixture used in his diffuser nets.

Gabby had paced endless circuits around the study, had sipped tea and nibbled on biscuits and cold sandwiches, and had even taken to inspecting Hugh's bookshelves—a true testament to how deliriously bored she was. Rory and Nolan had spent the passing hours happily reclined in club chairs before the fire, or actually reading books, when Gabby had only enough interest to look at the cover and title page. Neither of them seemed at all anxious or pressed for time. She supposed they knew to reserve their energy for when it would truly be needed.

The noon hour waxed and waned, and later, when Gabby's feet and back finally ached enough from pacing the room all day, she collapsed onto the sofa. The leather was fire-warmed and plush, and with the first golden-rum rays of sunset bleeding through the windows, she'd felt her eyes growing heavy. Nolan left his chair to ease himself down beside her. He'd spread a velvety blanket over her lap and Gabby had ignored propriety and relaxed against his side. She must have drifted off, for when she opened her eyes again, it was to darkness. The fire was the only light in the room, and Gabby was snuggling a pillow instead of Nolan.

Disorientated, she sat up and glanced about the study. The hidden door to the laboratory was cracked open, as was the door to the corridor. She was alone, and though a little bit of light spilled from the laboratory, it was quiet enough for the sparks and crackles from the logs in the hearth to sound like pistol shots. As Gabby swung her legs to the floor, she fought the puerile anger that something important had happened and no one had woken her.

She got up and had taken a step toward the laboratory door when a cold gust of wind blew against her ankles. She stopped. It had blown in from the corridor. She changed direction and went to the study door, where the chill increased. Wind licked at her shoulders and the crown of her head as she stepped into the corridor. Craning her neck, she saw that the skylight shaft, which cut through all three stories of Hugh's home, had been levered open to a smoggy night sky. Air barreled down the shaft and snapped at Gabby's cheeks and nose. The moonlight was just barely starting to cut through the brume when a pair of wings eclipsed the rectangular opening. Gabby leaped backward as a gargoyle shot down the wide shaft. She deserted her space on the checkered marble floor a heartbeat before a gargoyle like none she'd seen before landed in a crouch in front of her.

A mantle of amber fur covered its wings and body, though the coat wasn't like anything she'd wish to pet. While Luc's scales were flat against his body, this gargoyle's fur stood up and out as spikes. Its arms, legs, and chest were brawny and intimidating, it talons long and hooked, just as any other gargoyle's would be. Its face was what frightened her. This was no clownish chimpanzee face. This was the face of a vicious, angry ape: round, flaring nostrils; a dark, pronounced brow; and a grimace that exposed a mouthful of broad teeth and canines. This was *Carver*.

"I'm sorry I laughed at you earlier," Gabby whispered to the enormous gargoyle, who was still staring down at her. "You're not a monkey at all, are you?"

She expected him to reverse his shift right there in the corridor—Luc or Marco would have held no reservations about such a bodily display. However, Carver blew air out of his crumpled nostrils and stalked farther down the corridor in his true form, disappearing around a bend in the hallway.

Gabby let out her breath and decided against searching the rest of the dark house for Nolan or Rory. She returned to the study and headed for the papered-over door to the laboratory. She nudged the open door wider and slipped inside.

The room was brightly lit from the many bulbs dangling from the ceiling. Hugh Dupuis and Rory were speaking in hushed tones at the long center table. Neither of them had noticed her quiet entrance. They were occupied with a microscope and were sharing the eyepiece. The position had their ears brushing up against one another. While Rory needed to lean down to peer through the microscope, Hugh needed to use a stepstool.

Gabby parted her mouth to announce herself but stopped when Hugh shifted his head slightly, just enough for him to look sideways at Rory. The demon hunter's shoulders stiffened, though he didn't step away from the lens. He didn't bark at Hugh for holding himself too close. Gabby's head was still muddled from her nap, from finding herself alone, and then from the sight of Carver's gargoyle form. This quiet scene with Rory and Hugh was also peculiar. It ended as quickly as a dream upon waking.

Rory noticed Gabby standing behind them and straightened his back. He moved away from the microscope.

"Feeling refreshed, Miss Waverly?" Hugh asked easily.

"Not exactly," she said, unable to ignore the way Rory was looking over her head instead of at her.

"Well, you've joined us just in time," Hugh replied.

"You've finished?" she asked. Hugh gestured for her to step forward and look through the eyepiece.

She approached the microscope. The knobs and dials were far too complex for her to instinctively know how to use them.

"Not quite. However, we have successfully magnetized any atypical blood cells from the sample," Hugh said, guiding Gabby's fingers to a knob. "Adjust the focus for your eyesight. There. Now, we studied the atypical cells and determined that they vary in structure and size. Using a lodestone composite, we were then able to divide the cells a second time. The demon cells attached themselves to the lodestone composite, while the other cells remained immobile."

Gabby straightened her back and faced Hugh. "Other cells? You mean the angel blood? It *didn't* work? Lodestone doesn't magnetize it?"

Hugh cocked his head and again gestured for her to look through the microscope. Gabby did, but her stomach was already sinking, her hope growing cold. The focus came clear.

The magnification rendered the drop of blood in a Petri dish into hundreds of red, round pillows, all of which had a single indentation in the center. They bounced off one another, moving and shifting like they'd been caught in a current of water.

"These are human erythrocytes. Red blood cells," Hugh explained before sliding out the Petri dish and replacing it with another. She tapped the focusing knob once more, and another sample of round red pillows came into focus. These did not have the indented centers; they had a silver dot in the center, like a pearl in the mouth of an oyster.

"And these?" she asked.

"That angels have cell structure amazes me," Hugh said in answer. "That angels have the capacity to bleed amazes me further."

So this was what angel blood looked like. They didn't move about as the human cells had. The cells clung together in a single glob. Gabby wished to reach in and poke at the pillows of cells.

Something did enter the magnification field just then: Hugh inserted a long, thin needle, driving apart the glob of cells.

"Watch," he instructed, then removed the needle. The cells that had been driven apart slapped back together instantly.

He forced the cells apart again with the thin needle, and then pulled the needle back once more. The cells rushed back into the glob, crashing into one another and staying put, as though they were huddling together against yet another invasion of the needle.

"Lodestone doesn't attract angel cells," Hugh said. "However . . ."

Gabby's hand fell from the focus knob. "Angel cells attract to other angel cells."

"Like draws to like," Hugh said with a nod.

Gabby had nearly forgotten Rory's presence behind them until he spoke. "Can ye make a net filled wi' angel blood, then?"

"My assistants are already at the task," Hugh answered.

It had worked. It had actually worked! They would have a weapon against Axia. They would have a way to stop her.

Gabby hopped in excitement, throwing her arms around Rory's neck. He caught her and returned the embrace, her feet dangling in the air as he kicked up his feet and turned in a jig, swinging Gabby as she laughed.

"I go out for a walk, leaving the pair of you snoring, and I come back to revelry."

Nolan stood in the doorway to the laboratory, his frock coat unbuttoned, his bowler hat in his hand.

Rory ceased his jig immediately and set Gabby back down.

"What have I missed?" Nolan asked.

"Only that Miss Waverly's idea for a new diffuser net will be a reality within, oh"—Hugh took out his pocket watch—"twelve hours or so."

Nolan shrugged out of his coat. "That's a relief. I'm glad I won't spend the rest of my life in an Alliance prison for nothing."

The reminder of Nolan's actions and the gravity of what his punishment for defying Directorate orders might be removed the smile from Gabby's lips.

"Once the Directorate sees what this net can do, they'll forgive you," she said.

A wistful grin touched the corner of Nolan's lips. He said nothing, though she could tell he thought her statement naïve.

"You heard Hugh," she said. "It will be finished in twelve hours. We can return to Paris with it—"

"*You* are not going to Paris," Nolan said, a finger pointed in her direction.

As if being interrupted weren't enough to send a jolt of irritation through Gabby, Nolan had told her what to do. Her pulse jumped with a hot surge of defiance.

"*I* will do as I please, Nolan Quinn."

He squared his shoulders and placed his hands on his hips, battle ready.

"A month's time is about as significant as an hour for the Dispossessed. Do you really think they'll have moved on from what you did to Lennier?"

Gabby clenched her fists, remembering her first encounter with this arrogant Scot. The way he'd challenged her had driven her mad. Despite the fact that she'd fallen in love with him, it seemed little else had changed.

"The gargoyles must know Axia's return is imminent. Given the choice between two targets, I'm quite certain the gargoyles would focus on her and not me," she said.

"You're underestimating their world and their rules, Gabby. If you're going to be Alliance, you have to start thinking like a hunter and not like prey."

"I *am* thinking like a hunter, and my prey is Axia. You want me to be afraid. Tell me something—are good Alliance hunters afraid?"

"There's a difference between bravery and stupidity."

Gabby widened her eyes at the slap of insult just as Carver, in his human form, entered the laboratory. He looked pointedly at Hugh.

"I need to speak to you," Carver said. The doyen made a short bow and followed his gargoyle into the study without question.

"Gabby's got a point," Rory said, continuing the argument

once Carver and Hugh had exited the room. "And she isnae as defenseless as ye might think. She's got decent skill wi' a sword."

The compliment buoyed Gabby, if only for a moment. Nolan turned toward his cousin and crossed his arms over his chest. He took his time assessing Rory. He lifted his chin and tipped his head just so.

"You've been training her."

"Aye," Rory answered, that one syllable drenched with challenge.

Nolan took a step forward. "Without my consent."

I wanted to be the one to train you. Gabby recalled what Nolan had said to her after he'd figured out that Chelle had also given her a few lessons in demon hunting. He hadn't been upset with Chelle, but right now he looked ready to draw the sword resting in his waist scabbard.

"She can fight," Rory said, glossing over Nolan's last statement. No, he hadn't asked for his *consent*. That word refueled Gabby's ire, and fast.

"And now, after a month of unauthorized training and her so-called decent skill, you're all for tossing her to the gargoyles. What entertainment. We'll just go along and see how well she does. I'll pack the picnic," Nolan bit off.

He'd closed in on Rory and now stood so close he had to look up in order to meet his cousin's stony glare.

"Are you quite finished insulting me?" Gabby asked. "I don't need your consent to train, Nolan, and while I'm certainly not under any illusion that I'm skilled enough to fight a gargoyle, I'd appreciate a little more faith."

Nolan looked over his shoulder, then lowered his eyes to the floor. "I'm not trying to insult you. I'm trying to keep you safe."

Safe as a porcelain bowl wrapped in cotton linen and boxed up. It would be a lie to say she didn't want to feel safe, or that Nolan's worry didn't leave her feeling warm and even a bit precious.

But it also left her feeling trapped, like an ornamental bird kept in a cage, its wings clipped.

"I can't stay in London," she said. "I should be in Paris. I should be with Ingrid and Grayson and Mama, and—" She stopped short of saying *and you*. Hugh and Carver had reentered the laboratory, and besides, Nolan was making her so furious she couldn't bring herself to pay him a compliment.

Nolan ran a hand through his hair, scrubbing at his scalp. "I'm leaving."

Hugh held up his hand. "If I might take a moment to—"

Nolan brushed past him, through the laboratory door and out of sight.

Hugh cleared his throat before turning toward Gabby and Rory instead. "Carver's been out this evening. He brings a rumor that something is happening in Paris."

Gabby tried to listen to Hugh, but her ears kept hold of the sound of Nolan's steps fading through the study.

"In Paris?" she repeated, distracted by Nolan's retreat into the hallway.

"What is it?" Rory asked.

"One of the Dispossessed here received a telegram," Hugh began to explain, but Gabby got too bungled up in the comedic image of a gargoyle tapping at a telegraph with its talons and then the sound of the front door slamming to hear what Hugh said next.

He'll come back, she told herself. *He was just going out for another walk.*

It was only then that she realized he might *not* come back. Was he leaving Hugh's home—or leaving London altogether?

Without a word, Gabby started for the laboratory door. She'd been walking at first, but in the study she picked up her pace, driven by the sharp fear of losing Nolan again. Perhaps for good. He couldn't go back to Paris. He was on the run from the Alliance. He could so easily slip away and stay away, and that thought had Gabby all-out running down the corridor toward the foyer. She couldn't let him go. Gabby reached for the front door, her breath stuck in her lungs, and flung it wide with every intention of shouting Nolan's name from the front steps for all of Belgrave Square to hear, if necessary.

It wasn't.

Nolan hadn't gone farther than the bottom step. By the steaming light of a gas lamppost, Gabby saw two burly men flanking Nolan with menacing closeness. Benjamin and Nadia, of the London Alliance, stood on the sidewalk in front of the steps.

"Miss Waverly," Benjamin said, his greeting accompanied by an arched brow. It somehow managed to chastise her.

"What is going on?" she asked. Nolan turned and started to climb the few steps toward her. One of the burly men restrained him. Nolan glanced down at the sausage-link fingers clamped around his forearm.

"Release my arm immediately or you'll be nursing five bloody stumps," Nolan said, his voice soft yet murderous.

The man let him go and Nolan continued up the steps to Gabby's side.

"We had a communication from the Paris faction yesterday," Benjamin said. "Hans suspected Mr. Quinn might have fled to our city with something that doesn't belong to him. Said if he did come here, he'd start by looking for you, Miss Waverly."

Her breath came back to her, but only in little gasps. She stayed quiet, uncertain about what she should and should not say. Nolan was in trouble here. *Real* trouble. However, flicking her eyes up to see his face, she wouldn't have known it. He wore his arrogant smirk as comfortably as he might an old hat.

"Where is the blood?" Nadia asked, her voice gruff. It went well with the men's clothing she wore.

"What blood?" Nolan returned. He startled Gabby by taking her hand and threading his fingers through hers. "I've only come to London to make amends with my lady love." He raised Gabby's hand to his lips. She wasn't wearing gloves, or one of her veiled hats, allowing Benjamin and Nadia and their two muscled goons to look fully upon her scars. Right then, for the first time, she realized she didn't care. The scars were insignificant compared to what was at stake. Nolan had risked everything to come here: his name, his safety, his future. He'd followed his instinct and it had led him true. As he lowered her hand from his mouth, she had never admired him more.

"You choose to kiss and make up at the Daicrypta?" Nadia asked. "How romantic."

"It's private, at least. And protected," Nolan replied, his fingers still twined with Gabby's. He flashed one of his easy, charming smiles. "Just try to get inside. I don't think you'll have much success."

Gabby had left the front door open, but looking back now, she saw Rory and Carver blocking the entrance.

"I'll ask you one last time for the blood," Benjamin said.

"And I'll tell you one last time that I don't know what you're talking about."

Hugh appeared in the doorway, between Carver and Rory, and to Gabby's surprise, his diminutive stature didn't make him any less intimidating. Even his false smile appeared ominous.

"So many Alliance on my doorstep." He clapped his hands and rubbed them together. "Why, this is even more enjoyable than carolers at Christmastime." Hugh pouted. "However, I'm afraid I cannot extend you an invitation inside at the moment."

Benjamin and Nadia's men both started up the steps. Nolan released Gabby's hand and took a step down.

"I doubt you came here solely for this blood you keep insisting I have." Nolan held up a hand and extended it behind him, motioning for Carver and Rory to halt. They had come forward, ready to meet the two bruisers.

Benjamin shifted his weight, as if bored rather than irritated.

"You're coming with us, Mr. Quinn. Hans wants you back in Paris. Draw your weapon and I assure you, I'll bypass Paris and take you straight to Rome instead."

"No," Gabby said. It slipped out like a plea. She descended to the same step as Nolan and took his arm. "Come back inside. Carver won't let them in."

She hadn't wanted him to leave, and she certainly didn't want him leaving like this. Not when she knew there was a very real chance—more real than even before—that she wouldn't see him again.

Nolan pulled her into an embrace. He wrapped his arms around her waist, his mouth buried in her hair. She felt his breath warm her scalp when he spoke.

"I won't hide behind a gargoyle."

"Then I'm coming with you," she said, even though she knew it might return them to their earlier argument about Paris and vengeful gargoyles.

It didn't, however. Nolan only nuzzled her closer, dipping his mouth close to her ear and whispering so low that no one else would be able to make out his words.

"The net is more important, Gabby. Have Rory bring it to Paris as soon as it's finished." He pressed his lips to the skin just south of her earlobe and gripped her arms. "Stay with Hugh and Carver. I don't want you in Paris. Do you hear me, lass?"

He pulled back until his morning-glory eyes found hers. He was waiting for a nod. She gave him one because she had heard him. She just didn't plan to obey.

Nolan tugged her forward, kissing her forehead the same way he had the night in the rectory kitchen before she'd left for London. Only this wasn't a cold, angry, or obligatory kiss. His hands came up to cup her cheeks, and as he let her go, he looked pained. Perhaps a little scared. He shook off the hand of one of the Alliance men and fell into step behind Benjamin and beside Nadia.

Nolan didn't look back.

CHAPTER EIGHTEEN

Outside, the city had gone quiet. Too quiet, Ingrid thought as she pulled the heavy velvet drape in the medical room aside and peered down rue de Sèvres. There was no traffic, foot or wheeled. No activity at all. The only signs of life along the horizon of rooftops were the plumes of smoke from scattered fires. The smoke blocked out the light of the setting sun and washed a burnt-orange haze over the city.

Chelle was still alive but unconscious, and Grayson had carried her to the medical room so Vander could stitch up the gash on her thigh. Demon poison, left untreated, would have killed her by now. Apparently, Duster poison was an entirely different beast. That didn't make it any less frightening or confusing. Chelle was giving off dust, and if Vander had the color right—pale amethyst—it was rattilus dust.

"The Duster had a long, scorpion tail, spiked with teeth like a saw," Grayson said, hovering over Chelle's unmoving form on one of the examination tables. He hadn't let go of her hand or stopped smoothing her short black hair away from her face.

"A rattilus," Luc confirmed from where he stood sentry at the door. He'd borrowed some of Nolan's clothes and a pair of boots.

Marco had left a little while before, but only when Ingrid's mother's tension had not abated. He'd growled in frustration, unable to trace any of the servants, even Margaret, Mama's lady's maid. They hadn't been harmed. They had simply disappeared from his senses, suggesting they had quit the rectory, leaving Mama alone. Ingrid wouldn't have believed Margaret could be so cowardly. She supposed desperate times showed a person's true mettle. Marco had left, saying he would be back after he relieved Lady Brickton's worry.

Demons couldn't set foot on hallowed ground, Ingrid knew, and felt better about her mother's being holed up in the rectory. It was the Dusters that worried her. However, if she had been released from the spell, the others had to have been as well. She hoped.

"So a rattilus Duster cut into Chelle, injected its poison, and, what . . . *created* another Duster?" Grayson asked.

No one needed to answer. Chelle wasn't awake yet, but she was alive. And she was a new Duster.

"Axia is creating more Dusters," Ingrid said, letting the drape swing back into place. If there were demons out there, she didn't want them to see the lights and get curious. "She's building an army, and she's using Dusters to do it."

Ingrid didn't want to contemplate how many humans had been injected with Duster poison during the single hour Axia had compelled her seedlings to ravage Paris. Her throat was still raw from the smoke she'd breathed in at the opera house. Her fingers and hands had regained feeling, but they still tingled. She didn't remember anything, but she knew she'd thrown a lot of lightning. One of her targets had been Vander. He'd told her not to worry, that he had recovered just fine, but she'd still cried. Still felt like a monster.

"Only certain Dusters would have the capacity to inject poison," Vander said, his eyes landing briefly on Grayson. "There are others who don't. Like you, Ingrid."

She flexed her fingers, trying to dispel the last of the tingling. Demon poison was used to debilitate prey. Lectrux demons used electricity to do that, not poison. She kept quiet but inside shuddered with relief.

"And you," she said to Vander, who had turned toward one of the long counters. He was busying himself with a microscope and a sample of Chelle's blood. "Mersians aren't dangerous to humans. You didn't even fall under Axia's spell."

Vander had given Ingrid an injection of his blood immediately after he'd sutured Chelle's wound. They hoped it would work the way it had for Grayson.

"I don't know why she would have given me the blood of a mersian if it meant she wasn't going to be able to command me. If she even knew," Vander said, peering through the microscope. He swore and slammed his hand onto the table. "It's clotting. Chelle's blood and mine."

Grayson dug his palms into his temples and raked his fingers roughly through his hair.

Out in the street, a rise of noise broke the unnatural silence. Vander crossed the room to the window and lifted the drape just enough to peek out.

"You need to leave. All of you. Now."

Ingrid joined Vander at the window. She peered out just as stealthily, feeling Luc press up behind her for a glance as well. Four stories below, three conveyances had pulled to a stop directly in front of Hôtel Bastian's entrance. The carriages were surrounded by Alliance members, all of them armed. She spotted Hans among them. They were guarding the carriages, it seemed, and the dozen or more men climbing out of them and onto the curb.

"The Roman troops?" she guessed. A man wearing a bright red cape and hat appeared among those below.

"And the Directorate representative," Vander said. He stepped away from the window and, crouching, pulled up the hem of his right trouser leg. He gripped the hilt of a knife strapped inside his boot and held it out to Ingrid. "You're not safe here."

Ingrid didn't take the proffered blade. She'd had one in her reticule, but she'd lost the purse, along with one pair of her custom-made gloves and Luc's stone talisman, when the hellhound had dragged her to the Underneath.

"All we have to do is tell them about your demon blood being able to subdue ours," she said.

Vander stood up. "And if they don't care? If they don't listen or understand? They're hunters, Ingrid, and they've got their orders. You need to go."

"He's right. Take the knife," Luc told her, still at her back.

She didn't want the knife! "Where are we supposed to go? We can't keep running. There has to be something we can do."

"We find Axia," Grayson said. He'd gone back to Chelle's side.

A low rumbling of feet and voices drifted from a few stories below.

"If she's started her Harvest, that means she's here. In human form. That's why she consumed the blood of those girls back in December, right? To give herself a corporeal form," Grayson explained as the bottom floors of Hôtel Bastian came to life.

"One that can be harmed," Ingrid said. Or better still, killed.

Vander's patience snapped. He grasped her hand and forced the handle of the knife into her palm. He closed her fingers around it.

"Go. Go with Luc and Grayson and stay away from any Alliance, understand? There's more mersian blood in my room on rue de Berri. Get to it in at least another day or so."

She frowned at him. "You can't stay here. You're a Duster!"

"I'm Alliance," Vander replied, then nodded toward the table where Chelle was lain out. "Besides, I can't leave her."

"Neither will I," Grayson said. Ingrid spun toward him to protest, but he already had his poker face on and his hands up. "I'm not leaving her, Ingrid."

She pursed her lips. Ingrid knew her brother, and she knew when he'd made up his mind to see something through. Besides, she had a strong feeling that her brother had fallen in love.

More voices, the scraping of furniture, the slam of a door.

"What will they do to you?" she asked Vander.

"Get her out of here, Luc," he said, ignoring her question. "Avoid the roof. There will already be a few fighters stationed there. Go down the hall, to the last room on the right. There's a balcony."

Luc took her elbow and dragged her from the room, Ingrid craning her neck to see her brother and Vander before the door shut. They ran down the hall to the room with the balcony, just as Vander had instructed. Luc threw open the doors and tugged Ingrid against his chest. He swung one leg over the wrought-iron rail.

She froze, staring down at the four-story drop. "Wait—aren't you going to shift?"

He lifted her to sit on the rail, her legs dangling over the edge. He held her steady, and she didn't even consider being afraid.

"I'm not planning on flying anywhere," he said as he hooked her legs with his arm and cradled her against his chest. He brought his anchoring leg over and then they were falling. The wind rushed up her nostrils and through her hair; a scream lodged like a stone in her throat. Luc hit the pavement below. His legs, like oiled springs, sank into a smooth, graceful crouch before bounding back up again. Ingrid's stomach swam somewhere around her ankles.

"We'll be less visible on foot," Luc said, inclining his head toward hers. "Are you able to walk?"

She licked her lips and nodded. He let her down, but she continued to gaze up at him.

"How did you do that?"

His lopsided smile made her forget the ground beneath her feet. "Not human, remember?"

He kept her hand in his as they ran along the alleyway, away from the main road. They reached the next block and Luc turned right. Ingrid looked left, toward the abbey and rectory.

"We're not going home?" she asked, forgetting for the moment that he no longer called it that.

"It will be the first place the Roman troops go," he answered.

She thought of Marco and what he would do to any Alliance fighters who showed up searching for her.

"Don't worry about Marco. He'll know where we are," Luc said, his read on her unsettlingly accurate.

"To your territory, then?" she asked as Luc slowed their pace to a jog.

"Not with Vincent and the others likely massing there right now to discuss the demon invasion," he answered quickly.

She yanked her hand from his and came to a stop. This side street was as deserted as rue de Sèvres had been, but she still kept her voice low.

"Why did we even bother leaving if we had nowhere to go? Why am I running from the Roman troops if Vander and Grayson aren't?"

Luc expelled a long breath. His hands were on his hips, his alert gaze coasting along the empty road for a moment before settling on her.

"Because the first Alliance fool to touch you would have died." Luc took the three steps back to her side. "I would have killed him, and then maybe a few more, but eventually they would have overtaken me. I'd be dead—for good, this time—and the Alliance and Dispossessed would be at war."

A gust of wind barreling down the street caught the last traces of her anger and stole them away. She hadn't thought that far ahead. She closed her eyes, knowing she had to start or they weren't going to make it through the night.

"Marco's old territory," she said, opening her eyes. "He said it was deserted."

Luc held out his hand. She slipped her fingers through his.

"I know where it is," he said.

The stately town home covered nearly half a block of a street directly off rue de Vaugirard. The windows were dark when Luc and Ingrid approached, as were most of the windows surrounding Marco's old territory. Shutters drawn, drapes thrown closed, awnings over storefronts secured. There were few people milling about as the last rays of sun streaked through the dust and smoke drifting through Montparnasse. A group of young men, loud and cocky, were making a racket farther down Vaugirard; two policemen on horses trotted toward them; a brave girl in one of the buildings had her window open, her elbows propped on the sill, her eyes pinned on Luc and Ingrid.

Luc led Ingrid toward the back door of the town home, where deliveries and servants had come and gone. His hand loosened around hers.

"No gargoyles, at least," he whispered, reaching for the knob. He twisted it, breaking the lock and reminding Ingrid once again that even his human form couldn't mask what he truly was.

The glass-paned door glided inward and Luc and Ingrid stepped inside a dark, cold room. Ingrid couldn't see anything beyond black shapes, a glint of copper or glass, and the hulking shadow of a stove. Luc, however, had reclaimed her hand and easily guided her through the dark. The last vestiges of dried herbs and vinegar, of burned coal and wood, hinted that this was the kitchen.

She stayed behind Luc, her hand closed in his. He led her deeper into the pockets of darkness, treading up stairs to the second floor. With every step she felt as if they were ascending farther and farther from the mad world outside, into a safe haven of their very own.

He brought her into a room and closed the door behind them before leading her across the bare floor. Her skirts brushed along a piece of furniture, and Luc guided her to sit upon a sofa. The cushion was soft with use, and Ingrid sank down into it.

"There's a fireplace," Luc announced before releasing her hand.

Ingrid was still shaking, but she didn't think it was from the cold, musty air of the closed-up town home. She couldn't stop wondering what had happened when the Roman troops had walked into the medical room. How had they treated Grayson? And what if Vander refused to point out other Dusters? Ingrid buried her face in her hands. It was a nightmare. Not just Axia and the hellish realm she'd unleashed, but the Alliance and how they'd undergone a sea change.

A small flame ignited in the hearth. It revealed the black outline of Luc's crouched figure. He wasn't as broad or as tall as Marco, but he was powerfully built. Nolan's borrowed clothes fit snugly, defining the able muscles of Luc's arms, shoulders, and back. He blew into the flames and added a few small pieces of firewood.

"I'll have to search for things to burn," he said as he straightened his legs and came toward the sofa. He stopped in front of her. The firelight revealed furrowed brows and an expression of concern.

"Get up," he said. Ingrid shot to her feet, panicking for a moment that they weren't alone. That they would have to start running again. But Luc only grabbed the arm of the sofa and dragged it closer to the fireplace.

"There. You'll be warmer."

She ignored the sofa and buried herself in his arms instead. He held her, his breath fanning out over her scalp as he let out a long sigh.

"What if you need to return to your territory?" she asked. If a human sought shelter from this madness at gargoyle common grounds, Luc would have to go.

"People won't hide away in a drafty, run-down building," he answered. "They'll want shuttered, intact windows and doors that lock."

It made sense, and she supposed it was at least one blessing. Still, if he had to leave, then he had to leave. There wasn't anything either of them could do to stop the force of an angel's order. Ingrid pulled back at the thought.

"Irindi," she said. Luc peered down at her.

"What about her?"

"We need help." She slid from his hold as an idea took her. "We need help stopping Axia, and Axia is part angel. What if Irindi and the other angels could stop her again? Banish her, like they did the first time?"

Luc didn't react. He stayed still as a statue. Contemplating the merits of her idea, she hoped.

"Irindi and the other angels of the Order don't concern themselves with human problems," he finally said.

"But this isn't just a human problem! It involves one of their own."

Luc turned toward the growing fire.

"I've never summoned her," he said into the flames. The light played off his bright eyes, turning them into glittering gems.

He would try. Ingrid didn't need to ask him to do so, and he didn't need to say that he would. He drew her back to his chest, tucking the crown of her head under his chin. The fire was already warming her legs, and she'd stopped shivering.

"I know it was difficult," he whispered. "Leaving Grayson back there. And the Seer."

He said the last bit quickly, spitting out the word as he might a chunk of gristle.

"He loves you," Luc added, even more quickly.

Vander, he meant, not her brother. Ingrid raised her eyes, though she couldn't see Luc's expression from where she was, underneath his jaw.

"I think you love him, too," he went on.

She gathered her breath. He didn't say it angrily or pose it as a question. He'd simply stated it.

"You could have a life with him, Ingrid. A real life, and I think you want the things he could give you. Things like a family."

A family? She already had one, and she wasn't ready for anything more than that, not yet. She wasn't even eighteen. Luc was older. Much, much older. He'd had plenty of time to consider all the things he wasn't capable of having.

Silence yawned before them. She knew he wanted some sort of reaction. He would know a lie if she attempted one, and she would only end up disappointing him with anything less than the truth.

"I do love Vander," she whispered into Luc's shoulder. She felt his intake of air, the way it inflated and hardened his chest. She forced her way out of his hold so she could look up at him.

"But what I feel for you burns brighter. I may eventually want things you can't give me," she continued. "And I know I'll grow old and you might stop loving me—"

He shook his head and growled, "No. This is not about how you look, Ingrid."

"But right now," she went on as if he hadn't spoken. "Right now I choose *you*. I give myself to you."

She didn't have a moment to take a breath before his lips had crushed against hers. He wound his arms around her waist and sealed her body flush against his. She felt him everywhere, their bodies joined from ankles to lips, all soft curves and hard muscle. He formed himself around her, reaching in to take what he could before he inevitably had to stop. Before he transformed into something Ingrid couldn't kiss. Couldn't touch, not the way her hands were touching him now, gliding up the soft skin of his neck and into his hair.

Luc peeled her hands from where they were, lost in his short curls, and with a long, husky groan, moved her quickly, though gently, away from him. He held her at arm's length before letting go of her hands completely, then stepped from the fireplace and turned his back on her.

Ingrid stayed quiet, her pulse loud, her lips throbbing. She knew what was happening to his body, and she slid farther back to give him more room. The bunching and heaving of muscles underneath the borrowed dove-gray linen shirt was more than a trick of the firelight, as were the broadening of his shoulders and the shortening of his hair as it started to pull back into his scalp.

But in the next moment, it all stopped. Luc stood still for another minute before he faced her again, looking faintly uncomfortable.

"Is that all?" she asked, amazed. He had stopped the shift. He'd actually fought it off.

He cleared his throat, his eyes only flashing to hers for a split second. "That was my fault. I lost control. Next time, if we go slowly . . . I might be able to last longer."

Ingrid flushed and found it difficult to breathe.

Luc backed out of the room, saying he was going to search for more firewood. He closed the door behind him and Ingrid sank down onto the shabby sofa. She could still feel his hands on her skin, his lips against hers. *Next time.*

In this small sitting room, closed behind heavy, light-blocking drapes, with only an old sofa and a few other pieces of unloved furniture left behind by Marco's former human charges, it was easy to believe that she and Luc were safe. It wouldn't last. Ingrid wasn't a fool. She knew that the fire would go out and the sun would rise and that at any moment, the demons could come crashing through the windows. She would take this reprieve from reality, however, and happily. A part of her knew she would not be offered another one.

CHAPTER NINETEEN

The fire had grown cold again. Luc had torn apart a Biedermeier desk and chair, a wooden table from the kitchen, the frames of a few portraits left hanging in the dining room, and stacks of slatted crates hauled up from the cellar, and yet the fire continued to crumble. Ingrid was freezing. It had been over a day since they'd arrived at Marco's old territory, and this was their second night in the sitting room, the sofa pulled as close to the weak flames as was safe.

Luc reclined lengthwise on the sofa, one leg on the floor, the other propped against the cushioned backrest. Ingrid lay half on top of him, half beside him, sleeping fitfully. He stroked her hair, hanging loose and gorgeous down her back.

Though Luc had left earlier to find something for Ingrid to eat and to discover the state of things outside, he'd wound up returning within minutes. The demons hadn't left. They were still stinking up the streets, and to Luc's unease, corvites were everywhere. They lined the roofs of buildings, sat atop lamp-posts, curbs, benches, and balcony railings. They perched on the sinewy bones of ravaged horses and dogs and, Luc had noted with a roll of his stomach, even a human carcass splayed out in the street.

They watched. Corvites were annoying that way. Luc had waited until he was sure no corvite was paying him any attention before slipping back to the town home. The other unsettling thing was that he hadn't heard or felt the presence of another gargoyle in more than twenty-four hours. Not knowing what was happening out there made him tense.

Not that time alone with Ingrid was something to wish away. She'd chosen him. Given herself to him, and even though he couldn't claim her in the human way, she was still his. Passing the day and night in the quiet town home was giving him a taste of his fantasy, sweet as meringue and just as easily dissolved.

Luc hadn't been successful summoning Irindi earlier that morning. Never in the last three centuries had he called the angel to him—her presence was not something a gargoyle would actually request. He'd gone to the kitchen, out of Ingrid's view and earshot, and whispered Irindi's name. He'd closed his eyes and asked her to come to him. But the kitchen had remained cold and dark. It hadn't surprised him—the angels held no love for humans or gargoyles—though he did regret having to tell Ingrid it hadn't worked. He'd said he'd try again, but the pull of her corn-silk brows told him she'd already given up hope.

Ingrid's arm, tucked against Luc's ribs, twitched. A small whine preceded a more violent shudder, this one seizing her whole body. Luc shushed her, bringing her higher onto his chest, but she was already awake, gaping at the fireplace and marble mantel with bewilderment.

"It's just me, Ingrid. You're with me."

She blinked up at him, lips parted. "I—I saw flames. I heard screaming, and Grayson, he was . . . he was somewhere dark and cold," she choked out, trying to lift herself up, off Luc. He held her firmly, not wanting her to go anywhere.

"A nightmare," he said. "That's all."

Ingrid allowed him to guide her back to his side. She lifted her hand from his chest and flexed her fingers once, twice.

"Is it back?" he asked.

He didn't want to leave her here alone, but if he had to fly to rue de Berri for more of Vander's mersian blood, he'd do it. He'd do whatever was needed to keep Ingrid from falling under Axia's spell again—if and when another one befell the Dusters.

Ingrid put her hand on Luc's stomach and fiddled with one of the metal buttons on his shirt. "No. I haven't felt a single spark since we left Hôtel Bastian."

Her chin rubbed into his pectoral muscle as she looked up at him. "Luc, we can't stay here much longer. My mother must be mad with worry, and Marco—"

"He knows where you are, and he's being smart to stay away. Those corvites are Axia's eyes, and I get the feeling she wants to know where to find you."

"I'm just another Duster now."

Though he disagreed, Luc didn't argue. "Your mother is safe with Marco."

"Still, we can't stay here forever," she said as her fingers accidentally popped open the button she'd been playing with. She apologized bashfully and started to button it again. Luc stilled her hand.

"I wish we could," he heard himself saying.

After a moment's hesitation, Ingrid slipped her fingers through the gap of his shirt. Her cool touch met his hot skin. His abdominal muscles hardened in reaction.

"Wishes aren't practical," she replied.

He smiled. "Says the voice of reason."

The base of Luc's skull throbbed to life, pulsing out the signal of another gargoyle's presence. He tightened his grip on Ingrid's wrist and sat up.

"What is it?" she asked.

"Gargoyle."

She craned her neck to see into the dark corner of the room. The door was shut, insulating them from the rest of the cold house.

"Marco?" she guessed.

"Possibly." Luc stood and tucked the tails of his shirt into his trouser waist. "Just in case it isn't, stay here. And stay quiet."

Luc left the weak firelight and let his night vision take over. The hallway and stairwell were bright shades of gray and white as he walked toward the kitchen, his whole body on alert. He was certain the intruding gargoyle would be in there, and it was. Only it wasn't Marco.

"Gaston," Luc said, as he entered the kitchen and saw the familiar grayed features of Constantine's valet. Night vision didn't allow much detail, but Gaston's receding hairline and wiry build were unmistakable.

"We've been looking for you," Gaston said. Luc heard the frustration in his voice and swallowed a pang of guilt.

"I haven't wanted to be found."

Gaston paid Luc's reply no regard. "It's Vincent. Something has to be done about him."

"I agree." Luc glanced around the kitchen impatiently. The cupboard doors. He could use them as firewood.

"During yesterday's disorder he and his supporters killed a dozen Dusters, perhaps more."

That didn't sound anything out of the ordinary. It was Vincent, after all, and he abhorred the Dusters.

"They've flown by day," Gaston continued. "Coalescing within sight of humans, causing the Dispossessed to appear as nothing more than another kind of demon that the humans now desire to kill."

Luc had done the same during the attacks, though he hadn't acted as Vincent and his Chimeras seemed to have done.

He approached one of the tall cupboards and, with a fast jerk, ripped the wooden door from its hinges.

"You believe it's time to stop him," Luc said, reaching for another cupboard door.

"It's time for you to stop him," Gaston corrected him. "I've spent the last day bringing together the Wolves, Dogs, and Snakes, and we're ready. We can strike en masse and end this."

Luc wrenched down the second cupboard door and set it on top of the other. "You're the leader here, Gaston, not me."

What Luc wanted was to go back upstairs and throw the cupboard doors on the fire so Ingrid could stay warm. So her fingers wouldn't be so cold.

"They want you, Luc," Gaston said. "They want you *because* of the reasons you don't want the role of elder."

Luc turned from the next tall cupboard and looked at Gaston. "What is that supposed to mean?"

Despite his next blasphemous words, Gaston's expression stayed just as wooden as it always was. "You want to be human. Believe it or not, many of us do. You're the only one who's been brave enough to show it openly, and to do so without shame or fear. You've brought about a change, Luc. And to everyone's wonder—my wonder, even—it's a change we're ready for."

Luc forgot the cabinets. He forgot the cold and his swirling night vision. "That's impossible."

"Lennier changed our world hundreds of years ago, but he never let go of the old ways and the old rules. The next elder has every right to change what he sees fit. Vincent would take us in one direction, and you in another. Claim the role of elder and no one will question you. We'll gladly follow."

Luc felt as though he'd been backed up to the edge of a cliff and, with one touch, sent over. What Gaston was saying—if it was true, if it was how the Wolves and Dogs and Snakes he'd banded with really felt—could alter the Dispossessed entirely. The line between feeling human and being a gargoyle was thin, and difficult to tread. However, if Gaston could be trusted—and yes, Luc did trust him—there were many Dispossessed willing to follow Luc along that thin line.

He met Gaston's impervious gaze. "Organize everyone and be at common grounds within the hour."

Gaston gave a curt nod and was gone.

Vander had prepared Grayson for the worst in the moments before the Roman Alliance troops found their way into the fourth-floor medical room. They would know Grayson on sight, Vander had said—the Directorate would have acquired likenesses of the Waverly twins long ago—and their orders could very well be for immediate elimination.

Grayson had stowed one of Chelle's *hira-shuriken* in his coat pocket and kept his hand closed lightly around it, ready, as the barrage of feet approached the surgery. Not that the six-pointed star would have done more than buy Grayson an extra breath or two before what Vander had so delightfully called "elimination."

Three Alliance, wearing identical black coats buttoned to the chin, black tight-fitting trousers, tall polished black Hessians, and crimson caps, had come through the door with their weapons in hand but had not moved against either Vander or Grayson. They'd simply waited until two more fighters arrived behind them before taking Grayson by the arm and escorting him into the basement of Hôtel Bastian. Which was where he sat now, nearly twenty-four hours later.

The basement stretched the length and width of the town house, but it wasn't a spacious place. Grayson had already smacked his forehead against a few hewn beams along the ceiling, shaking ancient dirt and coarse plaster into his eyes. There was no light at night and precious little during the day. What light there was filtered in from two small, arched-brow windows cut out of the foundation bricks. He'd already considered the windows as avenues for escape, though neither would have accommodated his head, let alone his shoulders.

And heat? Forget about heat. His fingers had gone stiff, and they ached, even when he cupped them against his mouth and blew hot air. His feet were ungainly blocks of ice. And to make matters worse, the Roman Alliance fighters had seen Chelle's wounded leg. Even though Vander had said nothing about her having dust, they had known.

It was happening all over Paris, Hans had explained. They'd seen people falling insensible with fevers after being wounded by a possessed human. They were taking no chances. So Grayson was not alone in the basement. Chelle was with him, as were four other unfamiliar Dusters Hans and the others had rounded up.

Grayson crouched before her shivering figure. "Still toasty warm?"

She'd risen from her stupor an hour after they had been locked in the basement. When the fog of unconsciousness had cleared, she'd shrugged out of the coat Grayson had draped over her shoulders. She was fine, she'd told him. Then, upon hearing the reason for why she had been imprisoned, she'd screamed at Grayson to leave her alone. She'd gone off into a dark corner and stayed there until past dawn. Grayson had heard her soft sobs, the rattles of tear-soaked breaths, but had left her alone, as ordered.

Chelle had eventually come over to his spot beneath one of the windows, but she had still refused his coat.

She combed her short black hair behind an ear now, lifting her chin with her usual display of stony dignity. "They are treating us like animals."

Behind him, deeper in the basement darkness, one of the other Dusters, newly made like Chelle, moaned. They'd already exchanged names and fears and theories regarding how long they were going to be kept caged like this. With nothing remaining for them to discuss, they had all retreated into their own corners to brood.

"You aren't an animal," Grayson said, the pale blue light that trumpeted dawn coming in through the window. "You're one of them, Chelle. That will count for something."

The truth was, he wasn't so sure it would.

"If they were going to kill us, they would have done it already," he added, still attempting to ease her worry.

Chelle continued to shiver. Grayson slid his hand underneath her short, straight bangs and pressed his palm to her forehead. Scorching hot.

He brought his hand back and started to remove his coat.

"Keep it on, Grayson. We are both freezing," she hissed.

"You have a fever," he argued. She sat forward and grabbed his arms to stop him from shedding his coat. She made a little growl in her throat and tugged him toward her. He shifted his fall at the last moment so that he landed on the hard-packed dirt beside her.

"What are you—"

She cut off his question, though not with words. She did it with her body. Chelle swung both of her legs over Grayson's thighs and wriggled herself onto his lap. He sat rigid as a scarecrow as Chelle's arms traveled inside his coat, under his arms, and circled around his back. She leaned against him, her head resting on his shoulder.

A hot tide rolled out from someplace low in his stomach. No. Lower than that. Grayson let his arms enclose Chelle and shifted her weight on his lap.

"I can move back to the floor—" she started to say.

"Don't you dare."

Chelle let out a warm breath against his neck.

"What do you think they have done with Vander?" she asked.

Grayson brought up his knees, cradling Chelle closer.

"They need his sight," he answered.

She rocked her head along Grayson's collarbone. "He'll never give the Dusters up."

If that was the case, Grayson expected Vander would be joining them in the basement shortly.

"You know," Grayson said, wanting to lighten the subject to something more suitable for lap snuggling, "if someone unlocked the basement door right now, I'm not sure I'd be willing to leave."

Chelle's head popped up from his shoulder, and in the hazy blue light, he saw a smile transform her usual grimace. The gap between her top front teeth had seemed adorable to him the first time he'd seen her allow herself a smile. Now, however, it struck him in the gut as alluring.

"You should have left with Luc and your sister," she said.

Grayson feathered her bangs back from her forehead with a careful brush of his fingers. He had taken a risk, allowing himself to be captured. The mersian blood could wear off while he was locked up in this cellar hole, and he could fall under Axia's command or just start to scent and crave Chelle's blood. But he couldn't have run.

"I wasn't going to leave you," he said. "I failed you on the bridge with Yann. I don't regret stopping you from killing him." He needed to be clear about where he stood. "I just regret making you a promise I couldn't keep."

Chelle turned her head away from Grayson's fingers as they threaded through her hair once again. "So you stayed, you allowed the Roman troops to take you, because you felt guilty?"

He filled the basement with a sound that didn't belong there: laughter.

"No," he said, still smiling. Feeling bold. What more did he have to lose? "I stayed because I'm mad about you."

She stared up at him, eyes narrowed, the scowl settling back into place. He waited for a string of harsh words. He waited for rejection. It was all right. It was Chelle. She wasn't the sort of girl to melt into a puddle from a confession of ardent admiration. She was the sort of girl who *challenged* such confessions.

So when Chelle leaned her head against his shoulder once more and let out a shaky breath, Grayson wondered which parallel dimension he'd been plunged into.

"I don't want to be this way," she said, gasping on the last word as she fell apart into a sob. "I don't want to be a Duster."

Chelle crying seemed so foreign a notion that for a moment, he sat stiffly. He recovered, however, and pulled her tighter against him.

"I don't want to be this way, either," he said instead. They were locked in a basement with strangers most likely hanging on every word of their private conversation. But why shy away from honesty now?

"I killed someone. I murdered her. And I'm relatively sure I enjoyed it. It doesn't matter how many days pass; the guilt keeps digging in. It keeps carving away. I've reached the point where it feels as if I'm walking around with a gaping hole in my stomach."

Chelle hadn't hurt anyone. Yet.

"Your blood can't mix with Vander's, but he can still help you. He can take away some of your dust and make things easier for you. Provided we get out of here," he added.

Chelle lifted her head and pressed her lips against Grayson's cheek. They were wet with tears. He turned toward her, instinctively, and her lips brushed against his. She kissed him, her fingers inching up his neck, running through his hair, against his scalp. Grayson shifted her closer, not caring if she felt his reaction to her. He didn't care about the cold floor or the other Dusters listening. He didn't care about much of anything beyond the salty taste of Chelle's lips, the feel of her hands as they departed his scalp to stroke his neck, then the front of his shirt, and then—oh God—low against his stomach.

He tensed. Chelle must have felt it, for she stopped kissing him long enough to laugh.

"Am I making you uncomfortable, Lord Fairfax?"

Usually, hearing someone address him by his proper title annoyed him to no end. When Chelle said it, though, with her voice purposefully seductive, it made him catch his breath.

"Yes. And I've decided I never want to be comfortable again."

Chelle tipped her lips to his. Of course, that was when the basement door gave a shuddering rattle.

She tore her mouth away and leaped to her feet. Grayson followed, albeit a bit more slowly. His body didn't quite want to shed its reaction to Chelle so swiftly.

"Qui est là?" one of the other Dusters shouted, and approached the short set of steep stairs that led to the basement door.

Two more of the other Dusters followed. The door opened.

"Move away from the bottom of the stairs," a man with a deep, cavernous voice ordered. He spoke in English, but his words had a strong Italian accent. This was one of the Roman Alliance members.

"Why have you imprisoned us?" the same Duster asked, this time in English.

"Let us go! You cannot keep us here!" another shouted.

"Move back into the cellar, or you will not receive your rations for the day," the Alliance member repeated.

Grayson's stomach cinched at the memory of the rations from the morning before. Bread, water, thin soup. Not nearly enough to carry them through a long, frozen day.

The Dusters, cowed by the idea of not receiving their food and water, slunk away from the stairs, back into their shadowy corners. The Alliance member took the steps down, slowed by vigilance. He held a large tray, and Grayson could hear the contents rattling upon it.

He crouched to set the tray on the basement floor. Chelle, still standing, suddenly arched her back and screamed. She crashed to her knees. From other parts of the basement came more groans and cries of pain. Grayson sank to Chelle's side, his hand hovering over her back.

"Chelle?"

The Alliance member dropped the tray. "What is it?"

A second fighter came down the first few steps and repeated the question.

"I don't know," Grayson answered, grasping Chelle's shoulders. "Chelle? What's wrong?"

She was facedown on the floor, and he was about to turn her up when he heard a rasping sound coming from behind him. He glanced over his shoulder and saw a pair of bright green eyes cutting through the dark.

Grayson got to his feet and stumbled backward as a Duster emerged from the shadows and into the spill of light. His chin had lengthened to a sharp point, the skin along his neck had blown out like a frilled lizard, and his forehead and hairless scalp shimmered with pearly scales. A long, forked tongue darted through his lips, then retracted.

The Duster lunged at Grayson, fangs first. A broadsword cut through the air between them, the long, sharpened edge burying into the Duster's stomach.

"No!" Grayson shouted as a dark stain seeped into the fibers of the Duster's shirt. "He's human!"

"He is a monster!" the Alliance fighter returned, pulling the blade back with a wet squelching sound.

The other fighter now vacillated on the last step and shouted for his comrade to hurry.

The serpent Duster fell to his knees. And then Chelle's prostrate form began to move. The fighter's sword swung toward her. Grayson grabbed his arm and twisted him away, pushing him from Chelle's side, toward the stairs.

"Do not. Touch. Her."

The man shoved Grayson off, propelling him into the chest

of the other Alliance member. The second man flung Grayson to the dirt floor.

"She is not human any—" The first man's mouth stretched wide, his eyes bugging out. His next words dissolved into a hoarse scream. He collapsed to his knees. Chelle stood behind him, and with a twist of her torso, she yanked the long, curled tail that had punched through the seat of her trousers out of the fighter's back.

The second Alliance fighter staggered, tripping over the tray of food, but Chelle snapped her tail like a whip. The quill-like spikes running the length of it rippled and clicked together in the second before they guillotined him.

The second fighter's head and body parted and dropped limply to the floor. Grayson stared, revolted and on the verge of being ill.

Chelle's eyes snapped to him, showing the same ferocity her tail had shown these fighters.

"It's me," he said, but her eyes were empty of any recognition. He hoisted himself upright using the bottom of the stairwell's railing, his eyes still locked with Chelle's. There were more noises coming from within the basement as well.

Grayson took the stairs three at a time, bounding toward the door, hoping he was out of her tail's reach. The steps shook behind him, and he could feel Chelle closing in.

He barreled through and slammed the door, throwing his shoulder against it and jamming the heavy deadbolt into place. Through the thick slab of wood Grayson heard Chelle roar with anger. The door shuddered, and long ruby-colored spikes stabbed through the wood, less than an inch from his shoulder.

Grayson leaped back, staring at the quills. Chelle drew them out, leaving behind a dozen holes. Grayson backed down the short hall, toward a side-entrance servants' door.

"I'm sorry, Chelle." She could neither hear nor understand

him, but he had to say it. He'd promised he wouldn't leave her, but if he stayed he'd wind up as dead as those two Alliance fighters.

"I'll be back for you," he said, knowing what he had to do. None of this would end until Axia had been destroyed. She was here, controlling her seedlings and the newly created Dusters, and she would be in a mortal form. Grayson was sure of it. She *had* to be here. She *had* to be fallible. Grayson couldn't allow himself to imagine what would happen if she wasn't.

He opened the ground-level door that emptied into the narrow lane between buildings, elated to be free from the cellar but feeling guilty as well. There was a waxing roar outside: screams and raised voices, sirens and bells and whistles and breaking glass. It was starting again. Grayson stepped out, shut the door behind him, and walked toward the noise.

CHAPTER TWENTY

Ingrid could tell that Luc hadn't wanted to leave. His expression had remained cool and unconcerned when he'd explained to her about Gaston's visit and how something important regarding Vincent and the Chimeras was under way. It had to be now, he'd said, and would she please stay here, in front of the fire with the curtains drawn, until he returned?

"I'm not invited," she'd stated.

Luc had given her a relaxed smile. "You're safer here."

When he'd taken her into his arms, however, she'd felt tension turning his muscles into steel rods. He'd kissed her forehead, breathing a long, warm sigh against her skin. Then he had pulled away and left in a rush, shutting her inside the second-floor sitting room.

He'd stacked wooden cabinet doors on the fire before leaving, so at least she'd have light and heat. No food, however, and Ingrid's stomach complained. She paced before the fire and, after a quarter hour or so had passed, grew bored. There was nothing for her to do except worry and wonder. What was happening out there? What exactly did Luc and Gaston mean to do about Vincent and the Chimeras? Where were Grayson and Vander? Was Marco going to be with Luc and Gaston? If so, then her mother would be left unprotected at the rectory. The thoughts and doubts spiraled on and on as she paced, the first blue hints of dawn seeping through the gaps in the curtains.

She felt trapped and restless, and not having even a lick of a spark in her arms or hands for the last day and a half was not as welcome as Ingrid had imagined it would be. Not that she wanted to black out again and wake up in some strange place consumed by flames, but it would have been nice to know that she could protect herself.

She spent the next half hour trying to conjure up a current, the same way she had during lessons at Constantine's home before she'd figured out her electricity could be fueled by other electric pulses. Fast-flowing water had electricity, as did dark, brooding thunderheads in the sky. Fire, too. Ingrid was staring into the flames eating away at the charred cupboard doors when she heard noises coming from outside. After the uneasy silence of the day before, when Paris itself had seemed to curl into a protective ball, the racket outside seemed unnaturally shrill.

She moved away from the fire and toward the windows overlooking the street. She widened the gap between two curtains. Dawn was much closer than she'd realized. The building across the street, with its terraces and tin smokestacks unevenly placed along the roof, was visible. The silhouettes of at least a dozen corvites lined the roof, a few more scattered along the balcony railings.

Something black, fast, and huge raced by the window. Ingrid jerked back and swallowed a scream. It hadn't been one winged creature, but many. A whole flock of corvites, growling through the air, black and thick as a cloud of midnight. Ingrid went back to the window and looked out again, this time down toward the street. There were people out. More people than she and Luc had seen the afternoon before, when they'd last peered outside. One courageous shopkeeper had even opened his awning and set out a few baskets of bread. The shopkeeper and the people who had ventured from their homes had likely grown restless hiding away from something they most certainly could not understand. And if they didn't understand it, they could not properly fear it.

A few mounted police officers trotted by, but the horses they were riding were shifting and snuffling loudly. Ingrid was just about to step away from the window when a carriage, pulled by two horses, clattered past, the horses whinnying and jumping, their bodies smacking into one another in panic. There was no driver at the reins, just a pale, nearly translucent crypsis serpent coiled on the roof of the carriage. Half of its body hung over the roof's canvas edge and inside the window. The driverless carriage cut from one side of the road to the other in a deranged zigzag.

Ingrid tugged the curtains together and closed her eyes. The demons hadn't left, and now people were chancing going out among them. It would be another bloodbath.

A tinkle of breaking glass sounded from above. Ingrid looked up at the ceiling, the white plaster moldings of vines and fruits cast in orange by the firelight. A second crash from upstairs had her backing toward the door. Someone—or something—was in the house with her. She couldn't stay. Yes, if she left she would be in danger, but she couldn't just sit and wait for whatever it was— demon or human or gargoyle—to sniff her out.

Ingrid left the sitting room and stumbled through the inky-blue corridor. She didn't have Luc's hand to hold this time, but a set of stairs appeared on her left and she flew down them, the clumsy thudding of her boot heels padded by carpet. She heard the sound of cracking wood upstairs as she came into the foyer instead of the kitchens. Ingrid unlocked the bolt on the front door and raced into the cold dawn. She stopped on the sidewalk and craned her neck to see the windows of the town house. Sure enough, there were two on the third floor that had been smashed.

Digging into her skirt pocket, her fingers found Vander's dagger. The tip grazed her palm before her fumbling hand got a grip on the handle. She started for rue de Vaugirard. As a main road it promised more people; perhaps there would be strength in numbers. Besides, it would be a more direct route toward boulevard Saint-Michel and eventually the abbey and rectory. The Alliance members searching for her would have already gone there and left, she hoped, and she had to let Mama know that she was well. Besides, when Luc returned to Marco's old territory and realized she was gone, the first place he'd look for her would be the rectory.

Ingrid kept her pace at a fast clip; she didn't want to run and draw attention to herself, from people or demons. There were few others about. A kitchen maid quickly filling a basket of bakery goods at another open shop; two old men in some sort of military costumes standing on a corner, each of them wearing a brace of highly polished pistols; a fast-moving hackney, this one with a driver, coming down rue de Vaugirard.

She'd never felt more exposed. The hackney was bearing down on her, the horses' heavy breaths panting out steamy clouds. She had a little money and considered hailing the hack. The crypsis rooting around through the window of that other carriage gave her pause, but it was a long walk to the rectory from here. Ingrid put up her arm and waved to the driver. He clattered by without sparing her more than a glance. Ingrid cursed beneath her breath and walked on, allowing her pace to advance to a half jog. Wherever he was, Marco was likely pitching a fit right then. She was attempting to keep her fear under control, but she knew he would be able to sense something amiss. She kept glancing up, expecting to see his winged form at any moment.

Two streets ahead, an enormous black beetle scuttled into

the road, its body easily the size and girth of an Irish wolfhound. Ingrid stopped moving and stared at the beetle's antennae. Two black rods as thick as her arms passed a blue electric current from one tip to the other. The tips sparked and spit, and barbs of electricity shivered down each long feeler, encasing them in spirals of blue.

A lectrux demon, it had to be. The demon she shared blood with. Ingrid felt a fast, and odd, sense of understanding and, even more fleetingly, kinship as the lectrux paused in the middle of the road. It lowered its feelers to the pavement and swept them side to side. Her arms were her antennae, she realized. They projected the current the same way the lectrux's feelers projected it. The demon perked up and its giant beetle body shifted in Ingrid's direction.

The connection she'd felt severed instantly. Ingrid took the immediate right up ahead. Without her own electric pulses at her command, she would be nothing more than prey. Ingrid threw caution to the wind and ran, her lungs tight and her legs burning with exertion. The street meandered to the left, cutting around a raised square set in front of a church. Narrow stone steps, crafted of pale yellow marble to match the façade of the church, led to the square. There were no trees or gardens, just a matching yellow marble fountain and scattered benches. The square was empty, so Ingrid took the steps, keeping her pace just as quick.

Her boots scraped to a stop as someone stepped out from behind the fountain and into her path. The cloaked and hooded figure remained still. There was nothing more than a dark, cavernous hole where the face should have been. Ingrid stared, unable to breathe.

Axia's robes undulated. "I have been searching for you, Ingrid Waverly."

* * *

The orangery glowed with electric light, casting a flood over the snow-crusted shrubs that trimmed the glass-and-iron walls. Luc stood among the trellised rows of Clos du Vie's vineyard with Gaston and Marco and the rest of the Dogs, Wolves, and Snakes, watching the chateau from afar. They were all in true form, and quieted by somber determination. Luc had not cobbled this plan together with any sense of levity, and he did not stand here now, waiting for the Chimeras to arrive, with a featherlight conscience. None of them did. The decision to attack fellow Dispossessed was not an easy one to make. It had to be done, though. Vincent could not keep killing humans, and the sooner he was stopped, the sooner the rest of the Chimeras would see they had been led astray.

Luc hoped for this result, at least.

Constantine had unwittingly helped their plans. Gaston's human had taken in at least a dozen dazed and frightened Dusters under his roof at Clos du Vie. Without a doubt the Chimeras knew about this as well. So many Dusters in one place made for an irresistible target, Gaston had reckoned. Luc had agreed and called all of the gargoyles standing with him to surround the chateau. He'd also ordered the others to leave Vincent to him.

Their monotonous wait came to an unexpected end as a clamor resounded from the chateau. It pierced the stillness of the morning, and to Luc's right, Gaston's wings sprang open. A second later the gargoyle shuttled into the air. He raced low to the ground toward the glass orangery while Luc held his arm aloft—a signal for everyone else to stay where they were. There must have been trouble within the chateau. Something having to do with Gaston's humans.

Over the next minute or two, the clamor grew to a discordant mélange of screams, clipped shouts, and breaking glass. It wasn't until Marco sank into a crouch, grunting as though he'd been punched in the abdomen, that Luc began to suspect the problem stretched beyond the walls of Constantine's chateau.

"What is it?" Luc asked, his high-pitched shriek shattering over the quiet slopes of the vineyard.

Marco stayed in his crouch, but his scaled wings cracked open.

"You are needed here, brother," Marco gargled low in his throat. He rocketed into the sky, and his wings melted into the coming dawn.

Ingrid. Something was happening to her, and like before, when Axia had succeeded in dragging her into the Underneath, Luc was completely blind as to what. He had followed Marco that time, but he couldn't now. He was leading this attack. If he were to go after Marco, he would forfeit his bid for elder. A bid he hadn't made for himself, and yet it was his all the same.

Finally, after not wanting it for so long, a position of such power made sense. *No one will challenge you,* Gaston had said. And if Vincent were to claim the position, no one would challenge him, either. He'd plunge the Dispossessed and all of Paris into days darker than the ones Lennier had lifted them out of centuries ago.

No. Luc had to stay here, and he had to trust in Marco. He filled his lungs, his plated chest expanding, and realized that putting his faith in the Wolf was easier than he'd expected.

The racket at the chateau had died down, but there was still something off. In the distance, the blare of whistles and the tolling of church bells were waking the city. There was something else, too. It appeared to be a dense black cloud racing toward the chateau from the direction of the city. The cloud split, created gaps, and then merged again. It swayed through the sky, and when it reached the space above the front lawns of Clos du Vie, Luc saw that the cloud was as wide as the chateau itself.

Luc hadn't expected this many Chimeras. They circled the roof, a tornado of wings and tails, paws and talons, fur and scales. Luc searched the rotating horde of gargoyles for Vincent's long, pointed pelican's beak, while the gargoyles beside and behind him shook their wings with nervous anticipation. He understood his brothers' sense of urgency but wanted to sight Vincent before moving them up and out of the vineyards. The Chimeras were swarming and spinning too quickly for that, though. The frenzy of wings spun toward the orangery, and a Chimera bashed through the slanted glass roof.

Luc was the first one into the air and fleeting across the lawns. Chimera after Chimera smashed through glass panels and poured into the orangery. Luc plunged after them, nicking his wings on the jagged entrance. He dropped through a green bower of moss and his talons cracked the terra-cotta tiles below. The electric lights in the orangery, still shining, exposed a swarm of Chimeras overhead, circling two Dusters like vultures. One of the Dusters still looked human, though his teeth had lengthened into fangs and no longer fit within the confines of his mouth. Strings of saliva dripped past the boy's jaw. The other Duster had shifted into a ginger-furred hellhound, its clothing in tatters around its shoulders and waist.

They hissed and spat at the circling Chimeras—Vincent not among them. A snake-headed goat, its scales bright green, made the first dive. Its tail swiped the fanged Duster off of his feet.

"Stop!" Luc's shriek blared through the orangery. It distracted the snake Chimera long enough for Luc to swoop low and wrap his talons around the tapered, fur-tipped end of its tail. He pivoted fast, slinging the Chimera into a stand of bamboo.

Above him, an eagle-winged, double-headed antelope with curled horns made a dive. A Dog gargoyle slammed into it, driving the Chimera off course and straight into a glass garden table and set of wicker chairs. Dogs, Wolves, and Snakes clashed overhead with the Chimeras, and the orangery throbbed with high-pitched caterwauls.

"Vincent!" Luc strained to be heard above the pandemonium.

The Chimera had to be here. This was his army, his orders. Vincent would want to see his bidding done.

Something thudded against Luc's back and knocked him off balance. He swung out of his fall and hurdled into the air, barely evading the swipe of the hellhound Duster's fangs. He resisted the urge to sink his talons into the greasy ginger fur. The Duster was just a spellbound girl, the stretched and ripped amethyst silk gown speckled by dried blood.

A silver gleam parted the air and the hellhound girl went down, howling, a dagger embedded in her flank. A throng of well-armed and red-capped Roman Alliance wearing crisp black suits had entered the orangery. Interspersed among them were nonuniformed and more familiar Alliance members, including Vander Burke.

The Seer saw the injured Duster and jammed his hand crossbow into the chest of one red-capped soldier. "Only the Chimeras, you idiot!"

"We came here for the Dusters!" the red-capped fighter bellowed, and then with a flash of silver, raked a dagger along Vander's shirtfront. The blade flayed the fabric and sprang blood.

Luc flew over the mewling hellhound Duster with every intention of bowling into the Roman fighter, talons out. Constantine's short gray form sidled up next to the fighter first, however, and Luc threw out his wings to avoid colliding with the old man. Constantine twisted the round knob of his cane and pulled a thin rapier from within. He raised it to the fighter's throat and said something lost to Luc's ears. With a quick nod to Constantine, Vander set his spectacled eyes on Luc and started toward him.

"Where is Ingrid?" Vander shouted, his hand testing the shallow wounds on his chest. What did the fool think? That Luc was going to change back into human form so he could hold a conversation?

Gaston flew between Vander and Luc, his black pennant wings completely blocking the Seer from view.

"Yann isn't here," Gaston announced, his vocal cords grinding through three shrill keys.

"I haven't seen Vincent, either, but he'll be close," Luc replied. "I'm leaving to find him."

Luc surged into the air, his wings brushing against the heavy limbs of a lemon tree and rustling up a bright citrus scent. He'd thought to use one of the gargoyle-sized holes in the glass and iron roof as an exit but met with an impenetrable barrier of gargoyles above the bower of Constantine's jungle. Neither side seemed to be dealing deadly blows, and Luc felt a twinge of relief. They needed to end Vincent, not his followers.

The orangery's ground-level door would have to serve. Luc dove back through the maze of shrubbery and trees, which was thinning out now as wings bent and snapped limbs and stalks and as swords hacked into the greenery. The sweet odor of crushed berries, citrus, and tropical blooms being mashed under boots and shredded by talons hit him as he dipped under the dome of a pink flowering tree and then plowed through to the other side. Luc reeled to a stop. The Seer had made his way deeper into the orangery, and now, less than ten yards from Luc, he staggered away from a Chimera—part pelican, part panther. *Vincent.*

Luc's mind went blank. His body seized with indecision. He knew what he had to do. It wasn't as if he hadn't killed another gargoyle before. But this gargoyle wouldn't stand still and allow death to come, as Dimitrie had.

Vander clutched his stomach with one hand while holding a short silver sword in the other. The blade dripped with an oily black substance—gargoyle blood—and Vincent's pickax of a beak wore a thin wash of crimson. It took another vicious stroke toward Vander's body. The Seer deflected the strike with his sword, but the beak's rugged cartilage barely received a nick. Vincent's long, fleshy orange bill came back and slammed into Vander's sword hand. The blade disappeared into a white-berried shrub. The Seer grappled with his hand crossbow, attempting to load a bolt, while Vincent's front paw drew back, his black claws extended and hooked for the kill.

Luc moved without thought. Without plan. He hurtled into the slim gap between the Seer and Vincent and planted his foot on Vander's chest. He shoved him away, perhaps with more force than necessary, and turned to face Vincent head-on—a move he should have made first.

Fire tore down Luc's left wing, rending through leathery membrane and thin cartilage. Vincent's claws sheared into Luc's wing, wrenching him down onto the terra-cotta tiles. The agony was worse than the white-hot scorch of an angel's burn, but what turned Luc's stomach and brought on a pulse of panic was the sudden featherlight weight of his left wing. Luc rolled to his right and stole a glance, but he looked away and faced Vincent before he could fully understand what he'd seen: his wing, still attached to the thick bone base in his back, but except for the first peaked gable, it had been almost completely sheared off. The wing drooped, lifeless, on the floor, hanging by only a finger's length of scaled membrane.

"This is an unexpected windfall," Vincent snarled. He shook his claws and spattered Luc's obsidian blood onto the fronds of a palm tree. "Destroying you should be much easier now."

He used his beak to slash at Luc—a predictable advance Luc easily avoided, even while in agony. He caught the ungainly beak around its wider center, hooking it tight between his forearm and bicep while swinging himself onto Vincent's white-feathered head. The Chimera bucked and squawked, but Luc held on, giving up a fraction of his hold in order to rake his talons across Vincent's down-covered neck.

Vincent's paws crashed onto Luc's hanging wing. He felt it catch and twist, and with another crack of pain, the final few inches of scales and membrane severed. Vincent threw Luc off, pinwheeling him through the air, into the stand of palms.

"Luc!"

The Seer. Coming back. The idiot. A grating shriek followed the Seer's shout. Vincent loped to the side, a gleaming silver crossbow bolt lodged in the muscle of his front left leg. Vincent roared at the Seer but, instead of resuming his earlier attack, shot upward, through the combatants above, and out through one of the shattered roof panes.

Luc clambered from the destroyed palms, slick with his own blood, and attempted to lift off after the Chimera. His remaining wing propelled him into a drastic slant, and unable to sustain flight, he thudded back down into the palms.

"Luc—" Vander approached the palms, his eyes riveted to the mangled remains of his wing.

"No pity," Luc growled. Vander didn't need to understand the words. He nodded and backed away.

Luc plunged through the broken palms on foot toward the orangery door. Once outside, he'd try to fly again. By fleeing, Vincent had showed the true coward he was. Hopefully his followers had been witnesses to his retreat.

A brassy ridge of light pushed up over the bare trees beyond Constantine's vineyards, the lawns and trellised rows of pruned vines deserted. Luc fluttered his one wing and the bony base of the one he'd lost. The motion jolted pain through his back. It reached into his arms and legs, and he stumbled, his heart pumping out a panicked rhythm. He'd had scratches along his wings before, and a mercurite-dipped rod jammed through both, but never anything this grave. Wings could heal and regenerate, but Luc didn't know how long it would take.

Movement to the right of the orangery walls attracted his attention. Vincent was there, on the frosted brown grass, the Seer's dagger gone from his leg. Luc fought the urge to close his eyes, to sink to his knees and breathe through the agony. He had to pay attention. Had to fight. Giving in now would mean losing everything, including his life.

It's only pain, he told himself. Luc blinked away the fogged corners of his vision and focused on Vincent with new determination. The sleek curves of his panther's body began just below the bloody gouges Luc had made in his lithe pelican neck. Luc had seen some horrid Chimera blends, and Vincent's was one of them.

"Do you actually believe you can have her?" Vincent said, his meaty black paws gliding over the grass toward Luc. The tip of his tail rolled with the suppressed excitement a real panther would show while stalking its prey.

"When you are dead and I am elder," Vincent began as he herded Luc backward, "I will enjoy making an example of your beloved abomination. However ... I may stop to investigate what the bother is all about first."

Luc's snout crinkled back, but he kept his teeth ground together. He wasn't game for the distraction of a verbal fracas, which seemed to be exactly what Vincent was attempting to incite. He believed he had a leg up on Luc. Luc, with one wing and one bloody stump. Wings were as important to gargoyles as air and blood. Wings were strength and majesty. They were feared. What use was a gargoyle without them?

The ground beneath his feet dropped into a stepped slope, and Luc stumbled into the sunken garden sited beside the orangery. Vincent laughed, and with the sound, an icy spike hammered through Luc's stomach. Was he too wounded to fight?

Vincent bounded into the garden. The winter had claimed whatever flowers the garden usually had, but there were still carefully pruned boxwoods, and stone and marble statuary was scattered along the crosshatched brick walkways. Constantine had a penchant for armless Italian women, or so it appeared. Luc stopped beside one statue, raised upon a stone pillar.

"Ingrid is more powerful than both of us. Touch her and she'll bake your insides."

Vincent sprang forward and spread his wings, his speed lifting him into the air. Luc wrapped his arm around the stone pillar and heaved it down into Vincent's path. The Chimera reared back to avoid the falling statue while Luc planted his foot on the overturned pillar and launched himself into the air. He didn't need to fly. He just needed to level the playing field.

Luc caught Vincent's wing as he fell back to the earth and with a swipe of his talons carved through tough skin and flexible cartilage. White feathers speckled with black blood clouded the air as Vincent and Luc thudded onto the upended Italian statue, cracking it into several pieces. Vincent's bottom bill ballooned as he screamed, his black paws pummeling Luc in the chest. Luc's steely plates protected him, but he still sailed backward, his talons ripping free of Vincent's wing. It hung, useless and bloodied, but Vincent came at Luc again, swinging his beak side to side like a scythe. Luc dodged it once, twice, but on the third swing, the pointed tip raked into his abdomen, tearing a long gash through his scales.

His heel slammed into something and he lost his balance. He fell backward into a fountain, the stump of his wing grinding into the stone of the dry basin. Vincent placed his paws on the rim of the fountain, and his garish pelican's head, his small black eyes ringed by yellow feathers, loomed over Luc.

He screeched as he drew back, preparing, Luc knew, to impale him with his beak. When he lunged, Luc rolled to the side and Vincent's bill hammered into the stone basin instead. The Chimera's paws slid out from underneath him, as if he were a cat on ice. He slipped forward, momentarily stunned.

Luc knew he wouldn't get another chance like this.

He hooked the talons on one hand and drove them through Vincent's chest. He clasped the Chimera around the neck and gritted his teeth as he punctured skin, tendon, muscle, and finally, bone. Vincent went rigid. With a twist of his wrist, Luc's talons sheared through a defiant swath of gristly sinew and ligaments, enlarging the wound. Grunting with resolve, his throat tight with disgust, Luc plunged the rest of his hand into the cavity of Vincent's rib cage. The Chimera's black eyes went wide as Luc's palm filled with what he'd gone in for. He didn't know if it was pity for Vincent or for himself that made his own chest feel as if it were being torn apart.

"We were human once," Luc whispered, his hand hot and wet and throbbing with every thrash of Vincent's heart. "You forgot that. I didn't."

He pulled his hand free. Vincent's body drooped and Luc shoved him to the side with an easy thrust. His Chimera form flopped over the rim of the fountain, his pelican half draped inside the basin. Luc heaved himself to his feet and climbed out of the fountain, his muscles strung tight and bile rising high into his throat. Vincent's true form deteriorated rapidly; ivory down and black fur pulled back into his skin, leaving him pale and naked; his vicious beak shrank into his face, reshaping into a mouth, chin, and nose; his eyes were still black, but they were human once again. They stared blankly into the basin.

The heart had gone still in Luc's hand. He backed away, toward the slope of the sunken garden. Inside the orangery he could hear chaos, and when he walked in, Luc found he didn't have the slightest urge to do more than stand and watch. Alliance fighters were quarreling among themselves on the floor of the orangery, while the gargoyles were still brawling in the air, though no longer physically. They screeched back and forth, arguing about Dusters and Axia and the fate of the city. They all just wanted answers, Luc knew, and no one had them, human or Dispossessed.

Vander saw Luc first. He held his hand up to a Roman, red-faced and shouting, and stepped away from him. That Roman fighter followed Vander's attention, and then another one beside him did, and so on and so on. Within a minute, the rest of the Alliance had gone quiet. All of them stared at what Luc held in his hand. Gaston dropped from the bowers of the orangery jungle and landed on the tiles in front of Luc.

Constantine's gargoyle pinned his eyes on Luc's dripping

hand, his expression as inscrutable as ever. Luc stayed where he was as one by one, every last gargoyle dropped to the floor and stared. The silence stretched on, but it wasn't an expectant kind of quiet. No one waited for Luc to speak or explain.

Luc opened his talons, and the oil-black heart made a wet slap on the tiles.

Gaston lowered himself to one knee and bowed, his clipped ears pointed toward Luc's feet. The rustle of wings and the scratch of talons echoed off the glass walls as the rest of the Dogs followed their leader's show of fealty; then the Snakes did the same. Luc searched for Marco as the Wolves dropped to their knees next. Their leader was still gone. How long had it been? Luc wondered, his mind racing toward Ingrid even as the first Chimera got down onto one knee as well. Two more Chimeras knelt, then three more, then five, and then every last one of the Dispossessed had bent in bows of recognition. It was a significant moment, one that would change Luc's existence forever, but it was weighted by a creeping unease.

The Seer came through the rows of kneeling gargoyles, taking deft steps to avoid brushing against any of them. As he passed, however, the gargoyles straightened. Luc sighed and began to shift back into his human form. The broken ridge of his injured wing sank into his back with such pain it made his vision swim.

"I'm glad it's you," Vander said a moment later, his eyes flickering away from Luc. He nodded toward Vincent's heart. "I'm sure that was necessary in some ancient and ritualistic way."

Luc shook his head. "Not really."

Vander huffed a laugh and adjusted his spectacles. "You saved my life," he mumbled, unable to meet Luc's eyes. "Thank you."

Luc looked over Vander's shoulder. "I hope you savored the experience. It won't happen again."

Vander shook his head and started to speak. Luc cut him off.

"I can't fly and I need to find Marco."

Constantine's cane preceded him through the lines of gargoyles. He cleared a space to step out between two Dogs, then coughed and straightened his hat.

"You may have one of my horses," he said to Luc, and with another small cough, added, "as well as some clothing."

"Is it Ingrid?" Vander kept his voice low so the Roman troops wouldn't hear.

Luc followed Constantine, who had started to thread his way back through the Dispossessed.

"That's what I'm going to find out," he answered.

CHAPTER TWENTY-ONE

Ingrid had not believed anything could be more frightening than coming face to face with Axia in the Underneath. That was before. As the fallen angel, covered as usual in an all-encompassing dark blue robe, glided across the stone square toward Ingrid, she knew she had been wrong. Coming face to face with Axia here, on earth, was absolutely terrifying.

"You were with me the day before last." Axia's voice tolled through the square. The vibrations tickled up through Ingrid's feet. "However, now, you are absent."

Ingrid gripped the handle of the dagger hidden within her skirt pocket so hard her knuckles ached. "How do you mean?"

"I can feel all of my seedlings," Axia replied, her figure now gliding to the left.

The arms of her robes were crossed over her abdomen, the panels tied tightly with golden brocade. She had no notable shape underneath all those folds, and Ingrid worried that Grayson's theory about Axia's having taken on a corporeal form was wrong.

"You should not be able to ignore the call of the one who has created you," Axia said. The writhing shudder of her robe ceased. "I do not understand. How do you defy me? Do traces of my blood linger within you, Ingrid Waverly? Have they magnified just enough to obstruct my will?"

Her deep voice turned shrill, and Ingrid winced. Axia's robes began to ripple with blustery rolls. Her robes reflected her emotions, and right then they seemed to thrash with unharnessed anger.

"I thought I had reclaimed every drop, leaving none to mature within you," Axia continued.

Ingrid parted her lips, uncertain what to say. She stammered through the beginnings of an appeal before feeling a rush of air whisper against her shoulder. She turned instinctively and startled backward. Axia stood beside her, her cavernous black hood an arm's length away. Ingrid looked back to where Axia had just been standing and saw nothing but an evaporating blue mist, a few shades darker than the coming dawn.

"How did you—" she started.

"I will have all of my blood, Ingrid Waverly."

The robed arm struck out and a pale hand emerged from within the sleeve. It grasped Ingrid's arm with strength of a machine. Ingrid fumbled the dagger out of her pocket with her free hand and, what felt like a decade later, sliced the blade across Axia's forearm. The blade never slowed, never met resistance, and then Axia's robed sleeve was evaporating into another cloud of mist.

Ingrid staggered to the side as phantom laughter rumbled through the square. She swiveled around, her eyes catching on Axia, who was once again by the fountain.

"I cannot be ensnared," the fallen angel said.

"But you just took hold of my arm. I felt you," Ingrid said, her fingers clamped around the dagger's handle. "You have a human body."

More laughter resounded, and Axia's robes rippled in harmony. Ingrid was still watching the sway of them when something pummeled into her side and knocked her to the ground. Axia was now hovering over her instead of standing by the fountain. She'd simply *appeared* at Ingrid's side, with the same fading blue mist marking where she'd been a moment ago.

Axia started to laugh again. Ingrid found a new grip on the blade's handle and plunged it through the bottom of her robes. The knife struck something definite—Axia's leg. Her caterwaul stabbed at Ingrid's eardrums, but the angel disappeared once more, the dagger no longer rooted in flesh.

So she *could* be caught if taken by surprise. Ingrid got to her feet as another scream filled the abandoned square. This one came from above. Its familiarity made her lightheaded with relief. A shadow raced overhead, and as it passed, a Herculean arm took her with it. Ingrid's feet were torn from the ground, the single gasp of air in her lungs driven out.

She angled herself toward Marco's body and clung to him, expecting him to soar up and over the buildings, away from the square. But his wings stopped, his body seized, and the ground rushed at them. Marco flipped midair, so that when they crashed, the prominent ridge of his spine cracked the yellow stone. He shoved her from his chest, propelling her toward the narrow steps leading down to the street that meandered around the raised square.

Marco rolled over and crouched against the stone, his wings sinking into his back, his body reversing into his human form.

Ingrid climbed the steps. "Marco!"

Axia's hooded form still presided over the square, as if she, and not the church, were its centerpiece.

"Go," he growled, his vocal cords not quite shifted yet.

Ingrid had seen him like this before, when she'd used her angelic blood to control him.

"You cannot fight me, gargoyle," Axia said. Ingrid noticed

the difference in her voice when she spoke to him. There was no humor, no honey. There was only steel.

"And you cannot subdue me and chase my human at the same time," Marco groaned, his face buried in the rubble of stone beneath him.

Axia said nothing, but almost immediately, a strident cry climbed up and out of Marco's throat. His arms shook; his fingers curled into the fragments of stone as a line opened across his broad back. An invisible scalpel drew apart his skin, flaying him from shoulder blade to shoulder blade, directly underneath three similar white lines. Axia was inflicting an angel's burn.

Marco grunted out a slew of curses as that burn ceased, black blood welled, and below it, another immediately began.

"Stop!" Ingrid screamed, but Axia was no longer focused on her.

Marco groaned and swore as the burn dragged slowly through his skin.

Ingrid backed down the steps toward the street, not wanting to leave him, and yet knowing she could do nothing if she stayed. Marco was buying her precious time to escape. She wouldn't let it be for nothing.

Ingrid ran from the square, toward boulevard Saint-Michel, with the echoes of Marco's screams knotting around her heart.

The reports of a Paris under siege had reached Gabby on the docks for the Dover–Calais ferry. The rumor Carver had relayed to Hugh about an incident in Paris had bothered her the eighty or so miles from London to the Dover docks. When Rory had placed a hand on the small of her back to usher her forward through a bottleneck of men and women at the end of the boarding ramp, however, she knew it was more than just a rumor.

"I don't know what they were!" a woman had exclaimed in English while a French gentleman spouted off about enormous *chiens crocs,* or fanged dogs, and *monstres ailés,* or winged monsters. The clash of English and French had grown to a dull roar as Rory had shouldered their portmanteau, containing the finished angelic diffuser net, Ingrid's blood stores, and a few common demon diffuser nets onto the ferry. Hugh, who had elected to bring his pet corvite in an enormous birdcage draped in black broadcloth, had led Gabby to seats far away from the excitement. The ferry had emptied as if it were going up in flames, the travelers for Paris converging around the ticketing office with demands of refunds. It had to be something else, something less absurd, people murmured as they moved away from the ferry—and yet they did not turn around and repurchase passage.

When, after a full day and night of hard travel without a single stop to rest, their train had pulled into Gare du Nord, Gabby could feel only relief that those people had decided to stay behind. The reports had not been exaggerated in the least.

Plumes of smoke chugged up from the city's skyline, and the clouds above Paris were tinged a deep umber from the fires below. They'd fought through a riotous bevy of people at the station, all of them attempting to flee the city, and all of them wearing the same pale mask of panic and fear. On the curb outside the station, the price for a hack had risen to an absurd two francs per mile—if the drivers were going to die driving through a war zone, they at least wanted to die with a full purse.

Hugh had shelled out a small fortune to a cabriolet driver to transport him, their valuable portmanteau, and his pet corvite to Clos du Vie, while Gabby and Rory had headed for Hôtel Bastian. By the time they'd hit rue de Sèvres, Gabby had shrunk back from the window and welcomed the formidable steadiness of Rory's arm against her own. They had both drawn their silver blades and sat with them at the ready. Outside, uniformed police and French military, fully outfitted with their own, ineffective weapons, had been trolling the streets from rue La Fayette to the Sorbonne. There had been a startling lack of citizens, however, and even more eerily, a lack of noise. It was as if the smog clouding above the city had somehow muffled all sound, making the clap of hooves and the jangle of the hackney carriage's tack louder than it should have been. It filled Gabby's head and grated on her nerves.

She leaped from the hack as soon as it stopped. She and Rory dashed inside, up the curving stairwell, to the third-floor door. Gabby itched to go to the rectory—she wanted to see Ingrid and Mama and make sure nothing had happened to them. But right then, there was nothing more important than finding Nolan.

As a red-capped Roman Alliance saw them into the open loft, she thought her stomach might cast up what little food she'd consumed over the past day. What if they'd taken Nolan directly to Rome? What if he'd attempted something stupid—it was Nolan, after all—and they'd harmed him?

Benjamin stood from the sofa and faced them, temporarily allaying her worries. The London faction leader wouldn't still be in Paris if Nolan had escaped, would he? Nadia was there as well, though she remained on her cushion, her arms crossed and legs relaxed. Vander was seated beside her, his shirtfront torn and bloodied.

"Gabby?" He stood up, a tender hand against his wounded side. "What are you doing here?"

She searched the room. "Is Ingrid with you?"

"What's happened?" Rory asked before Vander could answer. Gabby didn't see her sister. She did notice, however, that the dozen or more Alliance members present, both Roman and Parisian, looked ragged and drawn, and were just as blood-spattered as Vander.

"Axia happened. Her demons. The Dusters, fallen under her spell. The damned gargoyles," a Paris Alliance member spat out as he crossed the loft toward them. He had intense gray eyes, silver-dusted black hair, and a rugged set to his chin.

"The Dispossessed are with us, Hans," Vander replied, his voice hard. His flash of anger surprised Gabby.

Hans snorted and muttered something indecipherable. Behind him, in the hallway of curtained-off rooms, stood a willowy man in a crimson cape and matching crimson beret, his hair white as powder underneath. He would have resembled a Vatican cardinal had it not been for the brace of swords he wore at his hip.

"Where is Ingrid?" she asked again. If the Dusters were under Axia's command, what did that mean for Ingrid and Grayson? Or Vander, for that matter?

Vander pursed his lips. "I don't know."

Gabby closed her eyes and forced her breathing to steady. Her sister would be fine. She had Marco. She would have Luc, even if the gargoyle was no longer her protector. Gabby had to remain focused, just as Ingrid would do.

"We're here for Nolan," she said, opening her eyes again.

"Quinn is a traitor and will be punished accordingly," Hans replied.

"I wish you would stop slandering me," came Nolan's voice from the curtained hallway. Gabby and the others in the loft swung their heads in that direction.

"Nolan!" she called, starting toward the hallway. Hans held up his hand and two red-capped Romans slid into her path.

"I'm all right, lass. They've just got me tied up in my room," he answered, his voice bouncing off the beamed ceiling. "You told me you'd stay in London."

Gabby pitched her voice to meet his. "I said no such words. Besides, we've finished the net!"

"What net?" Hans asked.

Benjamin stepped forward, his blocky shoulders widening as his eyes narrowed on her. "Does this have to do with the Daicrypta diffuser net you came to us about?"

"Yes," she answered, but then pulled back. "And, well . . . no."

Rory pushed his way in front of Gabby and bore down on the two red-capped Alliance. "My cousin isnae a traitor. He took the angel blood, but wi' it, we made a net that can stop Axia."

Hans snorted on a laugh. "A *net* to stop an angel? Spare us, Quinn. You'll be going to Rome with your cousin for your part in this." Hans made a rolling gesture with his hand and the two Roman Alliance advanced on Rory.

Gabby could have sworn that his hands had been empty a moment before, but silver now glinted in Rory's closed fists. "Keep yer distance or lose important appendages."

The two Alliance stopped, though they didn't retreat.

"But what he says is true," Gabby said. "The net is hollow tubing filled with angel blood, and angel blood bonds to itself like two magnets." It was a poor rendition of the calm and convincing explanation Hugh had supplied her. "If the net comes into contact with Axia, it will seal to her and trap her, and for heaven's sake, look out the window! She's here, and you need this net. It can stop her!"

Even as the words left her mouth, Gabby heard them for what they were: desperate and fantastic. She didn't blame Hans for scoffing, or the other Alliance members for slanting their brows. None of them looked in any way impressed by what she'd said. In the curtained hallway, the red-caped man continued to stare evenly at her, his hands resting on the handles of his swords at each hip.

"Did you exhaust all of the angelic blood on this . . . *net* of yours?" the man asked. His rich baritone carried well.

"All of it? No," she answered. "But that's not the point—"

"Where are the reserves?" he interjected.

"She isn't going to tell you, Hathaway!" Nolan shouted from his room.

Was this the Directorate representative? One of the men who had declared her sister's life inconsequential? If so, then no, she wouldn't tell him—not unless it could buy her something in return.

"Wait," she said.

"Gabby . . ." Nolan drew out the last syllable of her name as if in warning.

She disregarded him. "I'll tell you."

Rory looked sharply at her. She kept her gaze on Hathaway.

"No, you won't," Nolan called.

"I'll take you to the angel blood myself," she went on.

"No. You. *Won't.*"

Gabby ignored him. "I'll take you to the blood *after* I take you to the net and you see it for yourself."

"Burke, do something useful and gag her," Nolan commanded. His disembodied voice earned a bored sigh from Vander, who was checking the bandage underneath his shredded shirt.

"Sorry. One claw wound per day is my limit," Vander replied, wincing.

"Very well," Hathaway said to her. "Take us."

He stepped forward. Gabby crossed her arms. "Release Nolan first."

"Yes," Nolan called. "Release Nolan. His hands were bound too tightly and he can no longer feel them."

Hathaway stopped, his expression unreadable. "Simply seeing the net will not prove its worth."

Gabby snatched at the opening. "Then help us find Axia so we can prove that it works."

"And then the angel blood?" Hathaway prompted.

Gabby thought of the two pints of her sister's blood left over from the making of the net. She wished there had been time for Hugh and his assistants to create more angelic diffuser nets. She trusted him with the remainder of the blood, though. Hugh hadn't had the covetous gleam in his eyes this Directorate representative had. She didn't know what the highest-ranking officials within the Alliance wanted the blood for—to control the

Dispossessed, the way Vander and Nolan had theorized? She couldn't see that far into the future. She could only see that it was her sole leverage.

"Is yours," she answered Hathaway.

"Betray me, Miss Waverly, and the fact that you are not Alliance won't impede me from tossing you into our reformatory."

He snapped his fingers and a Roman Alliance member disappeared inside Nolan's curtained room. Neither Rory nor Vander showed or said what they thought of her bargain. However, when Nolan stepped through the curtains and stalked down the hallway, nudging past Hathaway with an intentional shove into his shoulder, she saw his thoughts clearly.

If a glare could have strangled someone, his would have wrapped around Gabby's throat and squeezed. He rubbed his wrists where the binding rope had left red lines. He came to a stop directly in front of her.

"We'll discuss your bargaining skills later," he muttered.

"I just had you freed, Nolan Quinn. You could at least thank me."

His mouth twisted with what was no doubt a suppressed sarcastic retort. Nolan stepped closer, the tips of his boots coming toe to toe with hers. He inclined his head and lowered his voice.

"Some things should be done in private," he said, allowing a moment for Gabby's cheeks to heat before dashing her with a bucket of cold water. "Murder, for example."

Gabby narrowed her eyes on him as Nadia rose from her relaxed position on the sofa.

"How do we get Axia to show herself to us?"

"We're hunters," Vander answered before a moment's deliberation had passed. "We use bait."

It was purely logical, which made Gabby think of her sister again. She had to get to the rectory and find Mama and Ingrid, and hopefully Grayson.

"How, exactly, do we bait an angel?" Rory asked, keeping his threatening glare fixed on the two Roman Alliance boys as he sheathed his daggers.

Nolan drew alongside Gabby, and though he didn't reach for her hand or grip her arm, the closeness of his body gave her an inexplicable sense of accomplishment. Let him be cross. She had freed him, poor bargaining skills or no.

"We bait her with her mistake," Vander answered, reaching for his threadbare tweed overcoat on the arm of the sofa. "Me."

CHAPTER TWENTY-TWO

Luc hadn't expected Ingrid to still be at Hôtel Dugray. It was the last place he'd seen her, however, and considering rue de Vaugirard was closer to Constantine's end of the Bois du Boulogne than St. Germain-des-Prés, he'd gone to Marco's former territory first.

The front door to Marco's old territory had been left open, a couple of windows along the third floor shattered. Luc felt no presence of another Dispossessed and quickly led Constantine's horse northeast, toward the Luxembourg Gardens. The borrowed black gelding complained and shivered beneath Luc's legs. Animals didn't like him, and it had been a long time since he'd sat upon the back of a horse. Flying was faster and more efficient, and honestly, it smelled better. A deep, throbbing ache pulsed under his left shoulder blade, subduing his urge to shift and fly. His wing would regenerate. It *had* to regenerate. But thoughts of his wing would have to wait.

A hard push through the fifteenth and sixteenth arrondissements had lathered the horse's flanks in sweat, and now its nostrils flared and snorted with exertion. As Luc approached an intersecting street, he caught a thready chime at the base of his skull. He followed its lead, turning up a narrow side street. The chime grew stronger as he neared the raised square in front of a yellow marble church. Luc drew the reins back and brought the horse to a stop when he saw two uniformed *gendarmes* and five citizens standing in a circle around an unclothed body.

"No," Luc breathed, jumping from the saddle.

He tore his way through the small crowd, heaving one of the military policemen aside when the man tried to block Luc. The others had enough sense of self-preservation to step back a few paces.

"Marco." Luc crouched beside the Wolf's naked human form, which was facedown on the stone square. He fought back a swell of bile as he took in the state of Marco's back.

From the nape of his neck to the base of his tailbone, angel's burns had carved into his skin. There wasn't a strip of spared flesh. It was just a canvas of raw meat, with ribbons of white sinew, pink muscle, and red flesh. Oily black blood trickled to the cracked stone underneath, pooling in viscous puddles.

"Do you know this man?" one of the *gendarmes* demanded.

"I know that you want to be gone when he wakes up," Luc answered.

The two policemen were the first to back away. The citizens quickly followed, deserting the square with whispers about the black blood.

Luc touched Marco's shoulder. *"Marco."*

His eyes were closed, but he wasn't dead. His ribs still expanded with shallow breaths every few seconds.

Luc shook Marco's shoulder, not caring if it inflicted pain. "Goddamn it, Marco, wake up! Where is Ingrid?"

The Wolf's eyes opened to slits. "Ouch."

"Where is she?" Luc asked again.

Marco pushed himself to his hands and knees, and a rasp of pain whistled out of his throat. Luc had endured only one angel's burn at a time. To receive dozens . . . he wasn't surprised Marco had lost consciousness. Irindi wouldn't have done this.

"You're elder," Marco groaned, and before Luc could ask how he knew this, he continued, "I feel it. Every gargoyle will feel it. Congratulations, brother."

"I don't want congratulations. I want to know where Ingrid is."

"The rectory," Marco answered. "In her room."

Luc stood up, his eyes going to Marco's back once again. "It was Axia, wasn't it?"

The Wolf held out his hand for assistance. "And we thought Irindi was a bitch."

Luc gripped his hand and pulled him to his feet. A shot rang out and a chunk of stone from the nearby fountain exploded in a rain of dust. Luc dropped into a crouch. He scanned the square until his eyes came to rest on one of the *gendarmes* who had retreated earlier. He was behind one of the church's arcade columns now, his rifle aimed at them.

"No one likes it when you're naked, Marco," Luc said, positioning himself behind the shelter of the fountain. Marco remained upright, his hands on his hips.

"Everyone likes it when I'm naked," he replied as another shot cracked off and hit the smooth yellow marble less than a yard from his bare feet. "I imagine he objects to the color of my blood. Let's fly."

Luc swore under his breath. "I can't."

Marco stared at him.

"Vincent," Luc said, hoping it was enough of an explanation for now.

"I've helped you fly before," Marco said. He rolled his head and shoulders and then, wincing from the pain of the angel's burns, shuddered into his cinnamon scales. The policeman opened up a volley of shots, and a second rifle joined in from another corner of the square. Luc didn't have time to undress. His true form burst through the borrowed livery, though with only half of its usual grandeur. Marco surged into the air, the talons of one foot clamped tight around the bony stump of Luc's lost wing. He beat the air with his one wing, his speed slower than Marco's, making their rhythm choppy, but at least Luc didn't spin into a dive.

The reports of the rifles faded as the two gargoyles glided into the thick orange smog. To be elder, Luc thought, and yet be dragged through the air like this, like some useless, decrepit invalid, was pathetic. By the time the abbey's bell towers came into sight, Luc was certain he'd never been more humiliated. Marco released the remains of Luc's wing as they crossed over the flat hedgerow top; then he veered toward the carriage house loft, presumably to search for clothes. Scores of weeping black ridges ribbed his back between his wings, mirroring his flayed human skin.

Luc coasted toward Ingrid's bedroom window, where the gauzy white curtains had been tied back. He'd just started to dip into a slanted fall when his talons caught the wooden ledge. He lost his balance, overcorrected, and splintered off a piece of pulpy wood. The casement windows flew inward, revealing Ingrid, her mouth open in alarm. Luc fell inside, his humiliation complete.

"Luc!"

Her hands wrapped around his arm and tugged in a fruitless attempt to lift his bulky form from the floor.

"Oh, Luc, what happ—"

She let out a shriek and he guessed she had noticed his destroyed wing.

Luc pushed himself to his feet and angled his back away from her. He didn't want her to see him struggle, or to stare at the pitiful stump. She'd covered her mouth with her hands, and her eyes burned with unshed tears. He shook his head, trying to tell her not to cry. She took her hands from her mouth and laid them flat against the plates of his chest.

"Will you be all right?" She fanned her hands over his chest, down the hard swells of muscle over his abdomen, and then dragged them to his arms. She touched him as though inspecting him for damage, her fingers light as a breeze against the thickness of his scales.

Luc nodded. He had to shift back—he had to tell her about the battle, about becoming elder. He wanted to know what had happened to her out there with Axia as well. The painful memory of his torn wing sinking back into his body on a reverse shift was still fresh enough to make him hesitate.

Ingrid's fingertips came to Luc's mouth. Her thumb brushed across the leather of his bottom lip, and then her satiny palms cupped the lines of his jaw. She was so soft. So fragile, and yet here she stood making contact with a beast.

Ingrid had touched his mouth before—in the underground shopping arcade after the mimic demon attack. Luc had jerked away, ashamed of how ugly he was. But he knew now that she wasn't touching him to explore something grotesque. She loved him. She loved all of him, every scale, every monstrous detail, right down to his hard leather lips. Still, he wasn't prepared for her to stand on the tips of her toes and press her mouth to them.

Her kiss was just a whisper. Nothing more than a promise. A reassurance. He faced the pain of his wing and shed his scales, trimming down into his human form while Ingrid's hands were still against him. She sucked in a breath as his steel plates dissolved under her palms, to be replaced with the smooth, pale skin of his chest.

Once his talons had formed into blunt fingers, with no danger of shearing through her skin, Luc curled them around her waist and brought her against his body. Her dress, the same wilted silk she'd worn for more than two days now, brushed his bare skin.

Nothing had ever felt so fine. She kissed the shallow canyon running between his pectorals and let her lips linger.

"I'm elder," he told her. Saying it made it real, so he said it again. "I'm elder. Ingrid, you can be mine again. Come to common grounds with me."

The tip of her nose drew a line across his chest as she shook her head. "I can't. It's still forbidden to take a human. Being elder doesn't change that." Her eyes lifted to his. "Does it?"

Gaston had likely only been telling Luc what he'd wanted to hear, to get him motivated to move against Vincent. But it had lit something within him, a hope that refused to burn out.

"Lennier changed everything for the Dispossessed hundreds of years ago. We went from being hunted by the Alliance to being their ally. I have the chance now to change things between us and the rest of the humans." He raked his fingers through her loose golden tresses. "I can't believe I'm the only one who's ever felt like this. There have to be others . . . others who want the same things I do."

Ingrid closed her eyes and tilted her head into his hand. "But the Angelic Order—"

"Punished me for having an affinity—a preference for one human over another. If you were to be my only human . . ." He let his thought trail off. He knew it was selfish, asking her to be his and to live with him alone, without another human under his roof at Hôtel du Maurier. It wouldn't last. It couldn't last. But he also couldn't give her up to reality just yet.

"My body is cursed. I can't be with you, but I can love you. I can love you for as long as you'll have me."

Luc kissed her temple and buried his nose in her hair. He breathed her in, smelling salt and faint rosewater, sweat and woodsmoke. It wasn't the sweet spring grass and dark, fertile soil he'd known, and it didn't matter. It was *her*. Just her.

"I don't want what happened to René to happen to you," she whispered, her breath stirring against his bare skin.

"I can't promise any—"

The door to Ingrid's bedroom burst open. Luc heard the scream before his eyes registered Lady Brickton standing within the doorway, her hands slapping over her mouth. With his arms still around Ingrid's body, Luc quaked into his reptilian scales. Too late. Vander Burke had already pushed past Ingrid's mother and into the room.

Vander raged across Ingrid's bedroom, his brutal gaze locked on Luc. Ingrid threw out her arms, as if they could actually block Luc's gigantic form behind her.

"Stop!"

If Vander got any closer she didn't know what Luc might do. She didn't know what *Vander* might do.

"What in God's name is going on in here?" Mama demanded.

Vander pulled up just short of slamming into Ingrid, his glare still fixed on Luc. "You know what happens to humans caught up with gargoyles. You know and you don't care, you selfish bastard." He took Ingrid's arm and jerked her aside, his other hand reaching into his coat and closing around the handle of his sword.

"Vander, no!" Ingrid screamed.

Luc swatted down Vander's sword hand with what looked and sounded like enough force to break bone.

"Luc, stop!" she screamed again. She would have stunned them both had her lectrux blood not been subdued.

The room became smaller as Nolan darted inside. He grabbed Vander's arm and heaved him back to a safe distance. "Use that brain of yours, Burke. He is elder. You *do not* challenge him."

Ingrid slipped back in front of Luc and put her palms flat against his chest.

"You should go," she whispered.

His phosphorescent green eyes met hers for a moment before something over her shoulder drew his attention. She followed his gaze, but only until she saw her mother in her side vision. Oh God. Mama. And what she'd *seen*.

"Our former driver is one of them?" Lady Brickton asked, painfully shrill this time. Ingrid winced.

"Mama—"

Ingrid had no idea how to continue. The usual excuses—*It wasn't what it looked like* or *I can explain*—would be pathetic. It was exactly as it had looked, and no, truly, she could not explain. Not without sounding like a complete lunatic.

Ingrid was saved by a voice calling her name from the hallway.

"Griddy?"

No. It couldn't be.

"Gabby?" Ingrid turned to face the door, resisting the magnetic pull of her mother's ferocious glare.

And there her sister was, entering the bedroom with her rum-colored hair falling out of combs and pins, a bright, rosy flush upon her cheeks, and no slanted veil to mask her scars.

Gabby's smile trembled as she skirted their mother, Nolan, and Vander, and rushed into Ingrid's arms. Her smile fell away completely as she backed out of their brief embrace and looked between Luc's true form and Mama.

Gabby angled her head so no one could read her lips. *Why is he in your room?* she mouthed. Ingrid shook her head stiffly.

"Yann is still out there," Vander boomed. "He and a few Chimeras who haven't bowed down to the great and mighty elder just yet. You should be out there finding them, Luc, not in here where you don't belong."

"I won't pretend to understand who and what Mr. Burke is referring to. However," Mama began, her tone now calm, yet no less severe, "I agree with him. You do not belong in my daughter's room, Mr. Rousseau, and most certainly not in the state in which I found you."

Gabby gasped, likely deducing in what state Luc had been found. It was all going to pieces. Ingrid felt Luc's talons against the small of her back. He nodded once and backed toward the open casement window.

"But you can't fly like this," Ingrid said, her stomach coiling again as she looked at the tattered remains of his wing, which had been shorn neatly to the curved-in arch along the bottom. There, it looked like the stringy bands of a celery stalk, pulled and stretched and finally ripped off. Black blood crusted the stump.

Luc snorted a low *hufft* in answer, and she presumed he was telling her not to worry. He tucked his long black talons into his calloused palm and gently swept his knuckles down Ingrid's cheek. He then lifted himself onto the windowsill, furled his remaining wing, and jumped.

Ingrid watched his landing and the heavy, locomotive strides he took toward the carriage house. He was such a beast. So inhuman and impossible, and she knew from the silence behind her that every last stomach in the room was tight with disgust, every tongue numbed by mystification.

Ingrid turned around and met a host of different reactions. Gabby's jaw hung loose, her brows pressed together the way they were whenever she was fighting tears. Nolan had his hands on his hips, his eyes on the floor. Mama's pallor had gone ghostly white. And Vander . . . well, he glared at her with barely contained fire. The only person missing from this display was her brother.

"Where is Grayson?" Ingrid asked. She wanted to know, but she also couldn't think of anything else to end the insufferable silence.

Gabby blinked and cleared her throat. "Vander said he'd been in the basement of Hôtel Bastian but that he escaped."

Ingrid had too many questions. About Grayson and Chelle and why Vander's shirt was torn and bloody, and where Nolan had been for so long, and what on earth Gabby was thinking coming back to Paris in the middle of this insanity. Nolan didn't allow her time to ask questions, however.

"We're going to Clos du Vie. We think we have a way to stop Axia." He glanced over at Vander and hooked his arm again. "Come on."

Vander's hot glare never wavered from Ingrid's face. "I'll be there in a minute."

Ingrid shrank back a step. Oh no.

Nolan sighed. "Remember your vows," he murmured, and then released Vander's arm.

Gabby spun on her heel and touched Mama's hand. "Let's get your coat."

Mama inhaled deeply but didn't object. She let Gabby lead her into the hallway, and Nolan followed. He shut the door behind him, and almost immediately the air turned dry and suffocating.

"Vander—"

"You're choosing him. A gargoyle."

It was the disappointment in his voice that crushed her, a palm on her heart, pressing and twisting.

"I . . ." Ingrid took a breath and it became a cracking sob. "I love him."

He lowered his head and turned it sharply to the side, as if it had just been slapped. "And you feel nothing for me."

"No, that's not true," she insisted. "You know it isn't true."

He belted out a grim laugh. "I see. You want us to be *friends*." He started toward the door.

"No! I mean . . . well, yes, but no, it's not like that, either," she stammered. "You mean more to me than that. The few times we've kissed, Vander, you've made me feel . . . I don't know how to explain it."

Vander stormed back to the bedpost where he'd been standing. "It's not something that requires explanation. It only requires two mouths, two bodies, and two people who want one another." He left the bedpost and took the last strides toward her. "My mouth wants you. My body wants you. *I* want you."

There was nothing left inside her when he stopped speaking. No hot guilt roiling in her chest and stomach, no anxiety shivering along her arms and legs. There was only a tranquil sort of weightlessness. Those precious few seconds when your mind and body haven't quite realized the peril of gravity. When you can see with utter clarity and be brutally honest and you have to act before you plummet toward the ground.

"I want you, too." She closed her eyes when his hand cupped her cheek and his thumb brushed along her lower lip. "But I want Luc more."

His hand froze. Ingrid, her eyes still shut, jerked her cheek out of his palm and slid past him, accidentally ramming into his side. She opened her eyes and stumbled around the bed, toward the door. Away. She couldn't look at him, not after driving in that dagger. She'd had to do it, though. She'd put it off for far too long.

Ingrid was halfway down the stairwell when she saw Marco, wearing fresh livery, on the step below her.

"Lady Ingrid—"

She grabbed two fistfuls of his dark gray merino jacket and, before he could say anything more, buried her forehead against his crisp white, buttoned shirt. His chest muffled her sob. Her outburst caught them both off guard. He stood stiffly while she took a shuddering breath. His hand clunked down onto her shoulder and he gave it an awkward pat. Ingrid eased herself back.

"I'm sorry," she said, stepping away. "Are you injured?"

Marco frowned and smoothed the merino where she'd clutched it. "A sniffling human does little more than fray my nerves."

"I meant did Axia hurt you very much?" Ingrid said, listening to the landing above for Vander's approach. How was she going to face him?

"She's caused a bit of a problem for me," Marco conceded as they stepped into the foyer.

Ingrid allowed Marco to drape her cloak over her shoulders. "For all of us. Are you coming to Clos du Vie?" she asked.

"Do I have a choice?" he retorted.

He didn't. None of them did. Axia held sway over them all, or so it seemed. Ingrid could only hope that Nolan had been right: that they had a way to stop her.

CHAPTER TWENTY-THREE

Getting to Vander's flat on rue de Berri hadn't been easy. Grayson had gone on foot, preferring to have the freedom of ducking into a building or the mouth of an alleyway whenever he might require it. The only demons he'd crossed paths with had been corvites. There had been one on every street he'd traversed so far, and he had started to wonder if it was in fact only one bird, following him, landing atop a fence or hitching post or standing in the center of the street. Its red-rimmed pupils would watch him intently as he moved past, toward his next turn.

He hoped this was the case. They were Axia's messengers, and he wanted a specific message delivered. Grayson had forced himself to maintain eye contact with the demon bird, even though the corvite's stare left an oily feeling in his stomach.

Demons weren't the only danger on the streets, either. Grayson had encountered three different gangs of looters, smashing storefront windows, swinging off lampposts, climbing to upper-story balconies to wrench shutters open and kick in doors. For the last year or so he'd been hearing nervous chatter about some priest's prophecy that the new century would bring on a doomsday event. The end of the world, an apocalypse. Religious fanatics everywhere had latched on to the idea. Perhaps the prediction had been on the mark after all, Grayson had considered as he'd jogged up the Champs Élysées, the wide boulevard eerily empty and quiet. Perhaps people had the right to go a little mad now that hellish demons had started feeding on humans in plain sight.

Grayson had found the vials of mersian blood, labeled in Vander's precise, slanted script, and the injection kit in his room. He'd filled the glass barrel with a dose of blood and emptied it into his own vein. He couldn't risk Axia's next beckoning. She'd sent out two waves of attacks thus far, each one lasting just about an hour. Axia had told him that her hellhounds couldn't remain on the Earth's surface for long stretches of time—Earth being as toxic to them as demon poison was to a human. Perhaps that was the reason behind the short bursts of attacks. The actual duration didn't matter; the hounds had still had enough time to cause damage and instill fear.

Grayson had filled the barrel again and then pocketed the needle and syringe and five eight-milliliter vials of blood. If only Chelle's blood had been compatible with Vander's. It would have been nice to have her here, at his side. If it was weak of him to admit that Chelle's skill set gave him a certain peace of mind, well then, so be it. But he would have to do this on his own, and another part of him was glad she was locked in a cellar on rue de Sèvres.

He left Vander's apartment building, his mind focused on the contents of his pockets: the blood and one of Vander's blessed silver daggers. His entire weapons cache to take down the most powerful being on the planet fit in his two trouser pockets. Grayson laughed. This plan of his was crazy and desperate and far too malleable. He needed to find Axia, and yet if he succeeded, he would place himself within her reach. It could work. Or he could wind up dead.

Another gang of looters caught his attention across rue de Berri. They were looking directly at him. Grayson held up his hands as he walked, as if to say *Go on about your business*. They followed him, though, and their quiet procession sent the hairs along the back of his neck prickling. A glance over his shoulder showed that there weren't just men. Two girls, oddly enough in fashionable tea gowns, were part of the group as well. They were all young, no older than twenty, and they looked terrified.

Grayson stopped walking, one foot off the curb and in the street. He kept his hands in the deep coves of his pockets, his fingers rubbing the smooth curves of the needle's plunger and the handle of the dagger. The others stopped walking as well. He knew what they were.

"You're Dusters," he said.

One of them, a tall boy with a flop of curry-red hair, stepped forward. "Mistress is waiting for you."

Mistress? Grayson swallowed hard and stared at the boy. Their clothing was torn, the seams stretched to show white thread, and there was blood. Rusty red stains ran along the girls' hems. But these Dusters didn't appear to be under any kind of spell right now.

"Why do you call her that?" Grayson asked.

One of the tea gown girls combed her dirty fingers through her hair, which was loose around her shoulders in a style that no proper young lady would be caught wearing beyond her own bedroom. "You are supposed to lead us," she said, her English heavily accented.

Grayson turned fully toward the group. "You've seen her? Spoken to her?"

The red-haired boy and the girl exchanged an uncertain glance.

"She speaks to us," he said, palming the hair out of his eyes before touching his temple. "In here."

Grayson nodded, remembering what Ingrid had said about Axia's voice calling to her Dusters.

"Right now?" he asked.

The group slowly shook their heads, eyes coasting toward one another to be sure they were all in agreement.

"Do you know where she is?" Grayson pushed.

The girl spoke again. "The Champs de Mars. It is where we are all gathering." Her chin quivered and dimpled. "She commanded us to find you. We have to take you to her."

The girl's quivering chin explained that there had been a promise of punishment should they not succeed. Grayson understood how she must have felt. He knew just how terrifying Axia was firsthand.

"I'll come," he said, knees trembling as he spoke. "But you don't need to follow her. There is someone . . . someone who lives in that building, over by the church." Grayson pointed out Vander's place. "He might have a way to help you escape, the same way I have."

The red-haired boy pushed back his hair again, and two other boys straightened their backs and shoulders.

"Escape how?" one asked.

Grayson started to pull one of the vials from his pocket, when a strong scent of decay tickled up his nostrils. The other Dusters must have smelled and recognized it as well; they stood at attention and drew themselves into a huddle.

Two hellhounds—real hellhounds—emerged from an intersecting street. Grayson doubted he would have been successful in convincing these Dusters to leave Axia anyway. There was no chance at all now. The hellhounds stalked forward, curling up around the group of Dusters so closely that one beast's greasy tail swished the seat of a girl's tea gown.

"Mistress is in the nest," the red-haired boy said, his voice strangled. "Follow us."

Grayson rolled the glass vial of blood in his palm, still concealed in his pocket. He let out a breath. "I can do this," he whispered, and he fell into step behind the other Dusters.

The orangery at Clos du Vie was a complete disaster zone when Gabby and the others arrived. The Bois du Boulogne, usually a peaceful spot for strolling, had been graveyard quiet as their caravan had wound through on the way to Constantine's home. Vander and Rory had led the way in Vander's wagonette, followed by the Waverlys' landau, Gabby, Ingrid, Mama, and Nolan inside. The Roman and Paris Alliance, joined by Benjamin and Nadia, had brought up the rear of the caravan with their few carriages.

The silence inside the landau had been nearly as fragile as that outside in the parkland. Something had broken between Vander and Ingrid back at the rectory, and all of them were feeling it. And then there was Nolan to worry about. What would Gabby do if none of this worked? What if the Alliance took him back to Rome and charged him with treason? What if the net did work and they took him anyway?

Since the glass walls and ceilings of the orangery had been riddled with gargoyle-sized gaps and the vegetation had been hit with what looked like hurricane-force winds, Constantine's butler had led their party to the largest room that could accommodate them: the library. The musty scent of aged paper and oiled leather hit Gabby as soon as she stepped into the room, where ceiling-to-floor shelves of dark mahogany paneled walls and forest-green upholstered furniture seemed to muffle all sound.

Monsieur Constantine and Hugh Dupuis sat upon one of

three sofas arranged in a bracket in front of a marble fireplace. Each man held a teacup and saucer and was in the process of sipping when the heavy black boots of the Roman Alliance slapped against the parquet floor.

Constantine set down his cup and saucer and leaped to his feet. "Lady Brickton, it is an exquisite pleasure to see you once again." He strode across the library floor, completely ignoring the Alliance members spreading out around the room, and reached for Mama's hand. He kissed the back of her black lace glove.

"Monsieur, I don't know what to say. All of this is beyond my comprehension," Mama replied.

"You are not alone, madame, I am sure." Constantine released Mama's hand and shifted his gaze to Hans and Hathaway, who stood to her left. "I am not as ecstatic about your return to my home, gentlemen. However, I believe I know why you have come."

He turned slightly to indicate Hugh, who was still sipping his tea on the sofa. His short legs were crossed and about six inches or so from the floor. Gabby also noticed the familiar weapon flat on the sofa cushion at Hugh's side.

"There it is," Benjamin said. "The weapon Miss Waverly described."

"*That* is the net?" Hans asked. His brusque manner was unable to ruffle Hugh's composure. He set his cup and saucer on his lap without a tremor.

"It is a crossbow, actually," he said. "The net is the bow's projectile."

"Don't get smart with me, halfling," Hans retorted.

"Would you prefer me to be stupid? Perhaps then we might have more in common."

Hans took a step toward the sofa, a move that finally caused a reaction. Hugh slid forward, tea splashing onto the china saucer as he got to his feet.

Rory shouldered his way in front of Hans and barred him from taking another step. "Easy."

The word was a warning, not counsel. Hans looked too stunned by Rory's intrusion to do more than blink and part his lips.

Hugh cleared his throat. "This is one of our original diffuser crossbows, not the latest one we've crafted using angelic blood," he said quickly in an obvious attempt to draw attention away from Rory and Hans. It wasn't working. "Would you like to see it?"

"I do not hold much confidence in this net of yours," Hathaway said, moving around Rory and Hans as if the two men were not even there. "However, I have given my word to Miss Waverly that I shall assist her in her attempt to use it against Axia. Immediately following, whether the attempt succeeds or fails, the remainder of the angelic blood will come into my possession."

Hugh looked to Gabby, who nodded. Ingrid latched on to Gabby's arm. "You promised him the blood?"

Gabby and Ingrid had tried to catch up on the ride from the rectory to Clos du Vie, exchanging all that had happened to each of them over the past few days. Gabby, however, hadn't admitted what the cost for the Alliance's help would be.

Nolan leaned forward until his mouth was near Gabby's ear. "Bargaining skills," he sang in a whisper.

She huffed and started toward Hugh's birdcage, set upon the portmanteau, behind the sofa. Nolan shadowed her.

"Vander wants Axia to know he's using his mersian blood as a sort of cure against her," she said, reaching the cage and tugging off the black cloth draped over the sleeping corvite. It startled, ruffling its slick feathers and letting out a growl.

"We need to use your bird," she said to Hugh.

He sighed. "It is a demon, not a bird."

"But it *can* carry a message to Axia, correct?" Gabby persisted. "You said the corvite can only answer yes-or-no questions for you, but to Axia, the bird can relay more?"

Hugh approached the cage, and the corvite hopped closer to the bars near where he stood. He stuck his fingers through a gap and stroked the corvite's long black beak.

"It can," he said.

"What is it?" Rory asked, reacting to the unspoken caveat weighing down Hugh's words.

Hugh retracted his hand. "It may also deliver the message that we are attempting to lure her out for capture."

There was a commotion near the entrance to the library. The Roman Alliance parted their meticulous line of troops along the wall to allow two more guests. Luc and Constantine's gargoyle, Gaston, both in human form and clothed, entered. Marco, who had been standing quiet and disinterested in the far corner of the room, gravitated toward them.

Gabby noticed Ingrid's cheeks betraying her embarrassment over the earlier unfortunate incident in her bedroom; however, her sister remained focused.

"Axia might be confident enough to allow us to try," Ingrid said. "She told me she cannot be ensnared, and she might be telling the truth. She moved so quickly it was almost as if my eyes couldn't keep up with her. I kept seeing a sort of mist dissolving in the spot where she'd last been."

This seemed to pique the interest of both Constantine and Hugh.

"A mist, you say?" Hugh repeated. At Ingrid's nod, Constantine rubbed the dart of a beard he wore on his chin.

"And in the Underneath, you say she had fangs? She drank from you with her mouth?"

"Like a serpent," Ingrid said. "A crypsis demon."

"No crypsis moves as fast as that," Luc interjected from the back of the library, which only inspired daggered glares from both Mama and Vander. Luc at least had the decency to appear slightly uncomfortable.

"Luc is correct," Constantine said. "This mist you speak of, Lady Ingrid, and the forked tongue and fangs . . . it sounds as if Axia has taken the blood of a severix demon."

A grumbling broke out among the Alliance.

"Oh dear," Mama could be heard saying above the din. "That doesn't sound very good at all."

She accepted Constantine's proffered hand and eased herself onto one of the sofas.

"It is not," Hugh confirmed. "A severix can split itself from its actual form so quickly that it leaves an ethereal 'fade' behind."

A rise of panic blocked Gabby's throat. "Axia told you she couldn't be captured?"

Ingrid held out her hands. "That's what she said, but I did stab her. I caught her by surprise."

Gabby swallowed, this revelation about Axia sticking hard.

"Their fades aren't powerful in the least, but when a severix casts multiple fades in a short handful of seconds, it can be nearly impossible to keep up with. Severix demons use their fades to confuse their prey," Constantine added.

This was not what Gabby wanted to hear. Even if Axia was lured out into the open, she very well might be too fast to be caught by a net of any sort.

"Good. So we can abandon this ridiculous plan," Hans said, turning his back on Rory and rejoining Hathaway.

"No." Vander hadn't said a word since leaving the rectory. The muscles in his jaw flexed now as he walked toward the corvite in its cage. "It's flawed, but it's the only plan we have."

"Burke, you're hardly in a position to make decisions," Hans said. "Your refusal to bring in Dusters as the Directorate has ordered is about to land you in the basement at Hôtel Bastian."

"Don't be an imbecile," Vander spit. "There are exponential numbers of Dusters being created with every attack. Bringing them all in is an impossible task."

"Then we'll have no choice but to treat them as demons!" Hans shouted.

Gabby threw up her hands. "Enough! Hugh, please give the corvite its message for Axia."

Hugh unlocked the cage door and swung it open. "There is no need. It has been listening to this entire conversation, Miss Waverly."

The corvite's twiggy black claws closed around Hugh's forearm and he drew it from the cage. Rory crossed the library to the double glass-paned doors leading onto the grounds and opened them.

Hugh ran his index finger along the bird's beak and whispered something against its domed skull before thrusting his arm up. The corvite flapped its wings and beat its way into the sky.

Constantine punctured the silence. "And now?"

Hugh shut the doors and returned to the fireplace, his shirt-sleeve torn and spotted with blood from the demon's claws. He hadn't been wearing the leather falconry gauntlet this time.

"I've instructed the corvite to return once the message has been delivered. Until then . . . we simply wait." He clapped his hands together. "Who fancies a game of whist?"

Not surprisingly, there were no takers.

Hans belted out orders to his fighters while Hathaway did the same to his men.

"There is still the rest of the city to protect," Hans explained as a third of the Alliance fighters began filing out of the library. "The fewer able bodies left here to be inactive, the better."

It was clear that he didn't believe Axia would come. This was nothing but a waste of time to him. Perhaps it was, Gabby thought, allowing her own conviction to flag.

She felt a hand touch her shoulder. Nolan again whispered in her ear, but not with a sarcastic remark.

"Come with me."

How does a moth resist a flame? Gabby stole a glance at Mama and Constantine on the sofa, whispering in conversation as other chatter built within the library. Gabby followed Nolan as he weaved his way toward the door and out of the room.

He didn't take them very far—just across the hallway and into Constantine's formal dining room. The long table had a crisp yellow linen runner topped with an enormous vase of hot-house flowers that looked freshly cut. Gabby wouldn't put it past the old man to have a hothouse on his property somewhere. The world was going to pieces and yet the French aristocracy still required fresh jonquils, lilies, and white roses.

She was shaking her head at the bouquet when she heard the door shut.

"Don't pretend that you wouldn't have done something equally stupid had I been the one tied up in your room," she said, unable to turn and meet his eyes. She touched one silky petal of an over-bloomed rose.

"Had you been tied up in my room . . . ," Nolan began, and Gabby instantly regretted her choice of words. He surprised her, however. "I would have used my sword against anyone who stood between us."

She peered over her shoulder. Nolan hadn't shaved in days, and the new black scruff covering his chin, cheeks, and upper lip had a funny effect on Gabby's stomach. She wanted to rub her hand along his cheek and then work her fingers through the waves of his hair.

"You see? Stupid," she said.

A smile pulled on the corner of his mouth, but he fought it and stayed where he was, four chairs down the long table from her.

"I know you want to come with us when we use the net against Axia," he said, visibly steeling his body for her reaction.

"Don't start this again, Nolan."

"What is it you're trying to prove?" he asked.

"Nothing!" Gabby heard the transparency of her lie and

leaned against the table. Had she not been wearing a corset, she would have slumped. "It's only . . . I know I can be useful. I don't have special powers like my sister and brother, and maybe I won't ever be as good with a sword as you are, but I *can* be useful."

Nolan made his way to her side. He made no attempt to touch her. "For what it's worth, I trust Rory when he says you're a damn fine swordswoman for the amount of time you've been training. I'm not saying you'll never be ready. I'm just saying you're not ready right now."

She was watching his legs and his dirt-smeared tall boots rather than looking him in the eye. He scuffed his feet closer to hers.

"And hell, lass, whoever said you had to be useful to be necessary?" He traced her jaw and, hooking his finger under her chin, guided her gaze up to meet his. "You're necessary to me, Gabby."

For some reason, those words left her more breathless than when he'd told her he loved her.

"Maybe I worry about you more than the others," he conceded.

"I worry about you, too," she said. "If they take you to Rome and put you in that . . . that *reformatory* or whatever it is they call it . . . Nolan, what will we do?"

He held both of her cheeks now, his thumb passing over her scars as if they were not even there. Even she had forgotten about them until then.

"Don't worry about that yet," he said. "I'm not. We still have the end of human civilization to focus on. And then next in line is keeping that angel blood out of Hathaway's hands."

His attempt at humor to lighten the moment didn't hit its mark. Gabby shook her head, dislodging his hands.

"I don't know if I want to be Alliance, not if it's led by people who would order assassinations, or force gargoyles into submission, or use angel blood to make themselves powerful."

Other than Nolan, Vander, Rory, and Chelle, she didn't trust the Alliance at all. She held more trust for Hugh Dupuis and his gargoyle, Carver, than she did for the Directorate.

"I know. They're not what I thought, either," Nolan admitted. "But the Alliance isn't broken, Gabby, not yet. We can make it better. Together."

She didn't know what to say. Being together with Nolan sounded wonderful, though it was dampened by the idea of the Directorate being a kind of horrible extended family they would need to invite to holiday dinners.

Nolan stood so close she could feel the rise of his chest when he breathed.

"We haven't been alone since your bedroom in London," he said, bringing forward a rush of blush-inducing memories and images. He smiled when she squirmed against the table.

"We aren't alone at all. There are at least twenty dangerous men across the hall, not to mention my mother and sister and a trio of very protective gargoyles."

"Don't try to dissuade me from kissing you, Lady Gabriella Waverly."

"Fine. I give up."

"It's your resolve that really won me over, you know," Nolan said, shushing her ready reply with the hard press of his mouth.

The fact that they were in Constantine's dining room and could, at any moment, be interrupted by any one of a host of intimidating people—Mama topped the list, of course—did not stop Gabby from turning to hot liquid underneath Nolan's lips and hands. She thought of the last bleak month in London and pulled herself closer, clinging tighter to his shoulders.

He lifted her feet from the thick carpet and set her down atop the polished oak table. Nolan rubbed his open palms down Gabby's corseted waist and then along the round flare of her thighs.

He groaned and shifted his mouth to the curve of her neck. "You make it difficult to be a gentleman."

Gabby threaded her fingers through his hair as she'd longed to do earlier. "I thought you enjoyed challenges."

He laughed, his hot breath waving out over her skin.

At that unfortunate moment, the door to the dining room clicked open. Gabby froze and Nolan turned his face out of her neck, but he didn't release her from her tabletop seat.

Rory took in the scene he'd interrupted with a brief twitch of his brow, as if he was an expert in such displays.

"Your timing is horrible, cousin," Nolan said as Gabby wriggled off the table and smoothed her skirts.

"At least I'm not her mother," Rory replied. "Ye should come back to the library. Quick."

Nolan started forward, reaching for his broadsword. "Demons?"

Rory shook his head. "Angels."

CHAPTER TWENTY-FOUR

The perfection of the library floor reflected Luc's face with disconcerting mirrorlike quality. He closed his eyes, loath to see himself in the humiliating bow Irindi's sudden presence had thrown him into. Marco and Gaston had also crashed forward when her burning light had daggered through the room. Lady Brickton had screamed in alarm, and a confused murmur had gone up among the rest of the humans as the three gargoyles had grunted and fallen. The humans couldn't see or feel the angel's presence, though the fire in the hearth had guttered and no doubt they each felt an unexplainable density in the room, like a storm about to break near the top shelves of Constantine's library.

"What's happening? Luc?" he heard Ingrid say.

"Stay back," Vander cut in. "They only bow before an angel of the Order."

Smart bastard.

Irindi's hollow voice bellowed. "Why have you summoned me, Luc Rousseau?"

He took a moment to understand. He'd tried to summon her the day before, when he and Ingrid had still been hiding out at Hôtel Dugray. She was showing up *now*? Here? In front of all these humans? Not for the first time, Luc questioned whether the Order understood or adhered to any sort of plane of time at all.

"We need your help." Luc spoke into the floor. "The fallen angel, Axia, is leading demons of the Underneath against the humans and possessing the minds of demon-blooded humans—"

"We are aware of our fallen sister's actions," Irindi intoned. Luc waited for her to continue, to assure him that they were going to stop her.

No such assurances came.

Luc turned his cheek as far as it would go, attempting to see the silvery contours of her glow. "You are the only ones powerful enough to stop her."

He felt a nudge against his head and found himself staring into his reflection once more.

"We cannot interfere with human dealings. It is not God's way," she said, compassionless and cold. No wonder her presence sucked the heat straight out of the fire in the grate. "The paths humans take are their own to traverse."

Marco spoke from Luc's immediate left. "If that is the case, what the hell are we doing here?"

She ignored him. "This Eden has been slowly crumbling since mankind discovered the ability to sin. Every new plague feels as if it is the end of the world. It is not. Humans adapt. Let this plague pass and allow God's children to evolve."

Luc gritted his teeth. "Allow countless humans to die? Be enslaved? Made into demons?" He pushed against the solid block of light and heat pushing him toward the floor. "How are we to protect them?"

A hushed murmur swept through those behind Luc. The humans only heard one side of the conversation, but Luc was certain they were easily inferring the rest.

Until Irindi's reply came. No one, least of all Luc, could have expected it.

"It is not your duty any longer to protect, Luc Rousseau. You have atoned for your sin."

He stared at his reflection, unable to speak. Unable to think. Luc peered out the corner of his eye toward Marco, who had turned his face toward him. Gaston, on his right, was also looking his way, limited as their movements were.

"I . . . I don't understand," Luc said.

"You, by your own free will, chose to save the life of one of God's devoted servants, a human who was not under your divine protection. A human for whom you feel nothing but the shameful sin of envy."

Luc blinked at his reflection and swallowed his confusion, trying to comprehend what she was saying.

"And yet, you chose to protect this man from harm," Irindi continued. "It was a decision born of the one thing God holds most dear: forgiveness."

Luc still couldn't make sense of it. Whom had he saved? Whom had he forgiven?

"Luc Rousseau, you have earned our Lord God's forgiveness. Stand," Irindi commanded.

Stand. He couldn't *stand*. What was she talking about?

He heard Lady Brickton's voice from somewhere behind all the noise in his head. "What is going on? Why have they gone quiet?" Then Gabby's voice saying, "Shhh, Mama."

Luc sucked in a breath as the invisible block pressing between his shoulders and locking him into a reverent bow slowly lifted. Stone by stone, the weight lightened, and Luc's knees began to straighten. He kept his eyes on the floor, his chin tucked into his neck, even when his back became a long, straight line again. He was standing. Luc was standing in an angel's presence and yet he couldn't look at her. Wouldn't look at her. He wasn't ready.

There were many sounds coming from behind him—gasps, mutters, questions—but it was Marco's and Gaston's stooped figures Luc could not ignore. They were still bowing. They had not been forgiven. *He* had. Luc raised his eyes and nearly crashed back down onto his knees.

She was beautiful.

Luc didn't know how, but Irindi had changed. Her entire presence had shifted. Her light, something that had always been harsh and blinding, had become a soft, golden embrace. The once-searing heat that accompanied that light, a reminder of the punishing burns Irindi had lashed him with, now felt like a warm bath.

Luc stared, transfixed, at the flickering silver glow of Irindi's form. She was like the center of a flame, trembling and impossible to touch. He held out his hand to try anyway.

"Luc?" Ingrid's strangled voice pierced him. He dropped his hand.

Looking around, he saw that he'd taken at least five or more strides away from Marco and Gaston. He didn't recall moving.

"Luc, what's happening?" Ingrid asked, her voice cleaving through what remained of his trancelike state.

"Come." Irindi beckoned.

Luc took a step back. "I can't."

He couldn't leave. Not now. Not when Ingrid needed him most. He couldn't leave her ever.

"Don't be a fool," Marco grunted where he remained prone.

"I'm not," Luc said, his mind clearing as Irindi's summoning warmth began to cool.

He couldn't leave Ingrid. He couldn't leave the Dispossessed, not when Axia and her demons were sharpening their teeth on the human world. The gargoyles had chosen him to lead. He was *elder*.

"You wish to remain cursed?" Irindi asked. She hadn't needed to. She knew every thought streaming through Luc's mind. Every emotion.

Remain cursed, or finally, after centuries of denial, be allowed entry into God's kingdom. A place he had once dreamed of constantly, wondering what it looked like and who might be there. His parents? His sister, Suzette? And then he'd met Ingrid and he hadn't given God's kingdom another envious thought.

"I do," Luc answered.

He felt the cold clench of his stomach and the sensation of falling as Irindi's glow sputtered.

"Very well," she said, and then her light flickered out completely.

Ingrid watched, unblinking, as Luc spoke to the angel that no one else—at least no one else standing—could see. The air was humid and thick within the library, and a sudden wind outdoors had started gusting against the tall, mullioned windows. Ingrid's skirts hung like wet canvas around her legs. She'd noticed the fire's flames shorten to cautious licks as well. Was this what it felt like to be in the presence of something holy?

Ingrid didn't like it.

Nor did she like it when Marco and Gaston both leaped to their feet, each of them immediately rounding on Luc.

"What were you thinking?" Marco snarled.

Luc remained composed, though he swiftly glanced Ingrid's way. Marco followed the direction of Luc's gaze and laughed. The sound was harsh and mocking, and without his having to say a word, Ingrid knew Marco believed Luc had made a horrible mistake.

"I am all curiosity," Gabby's Daicrypta friend, Hugh, said from where he stood at the empty birdcage. That he was Robert Dupuis's son had stunned and frightened Ingrid at first, but now that she'd met him, she understood why her sister had placed her trust in the man.

"Has the angel gone, then?" Mama asked from her spot on the sofa. Poor Mama. Angels and demons and gargoyles, all on the same day.

Gaston crossed a meaningful glance with his human before nodding. Constantine patted Mama's hand, while his valet and protector returned to glaring at Luc.

"I don't know what to say, so I'll say nothing," Gaston murmured, and promptly left the library.

Ingrid stared at Luc and Marco in turn and thought she might scream. "Will one of you please tell us all what has happened?"

Marco's false grin fell away. He followed Gaston out of the library without bothering to meet Ingrid's pointed stare.

"Irindi can't help us," Luc finally said, his words clipped by some emotion Ingrid had trouble reading. Anger? Sadness?

There had been more to the angel's visit. Everyone in the library knew as much.

"Won't be attending Sunday services after this," the husky London Alliance leader, Benjamin, said before gesturing to the woman dressed as a man. Nadia was her name, and she and Benjamin slipped off to seclude themselves near a row of encyclopedias.

Only one red-capped Roman and one Parisian member had been ordered to remain at Clos du Vie. They slowly cut their eyes away from Luc and reentered their own conversations.

Gabby and Nolan came forward. "She isn't going to help at all?" Gabby was fuming. "What use is God if he turns his back on us?"

"He hasn't turned his back on us," Vander replied softly.

"Stick up for him all you like, Mr. Burke. I, however, am not convinced." Ingrid's sister walked away, toward the sofa where

Mama still sat. Nolan clapped Vander on the shoulder in tacit support before trailing Gabby.

A second passed before Ingrid realized she, Luc, and Vander had been left alone.

"Seer, I saved your life this morning," Luc stated with unnecessary intensity.

"You won't hear another thank-you from me," Vander replied and started to follow Nolan. Luc held up his arm.

"Have you been ordained yet?"

Vander pulled back. The question seemed completely irrelevant to the situation at hand, and yet Luc looked desperate to know.

"He isn't being ordained until . . ." Ingrid paused, trying to remember. It seemed like years since the afternoon they'd strolled the Champs de Mars and Vander had asked her to attend the ceremony. "Until Sunday. Isn't that right, Vander?"

He wouldn't want her there now.

Vander frowned, his attention still on Luc. "Today is Wednesday, Ingrid."

"What? It is?" Ingrid shook her head. She couldn't believe she'd lost track of the days.

"You'd just returned from the Underneath," Vander said as Ingrid tried to calculate where she had been and how she could have forgotten. "I didn't want to bother you about the ceremony."

Vander had been ordained. He was officially a reverend.

Luc rubbed his cheek before scratching his fingers over his scalp. "Of course it was you."

"You know what, Luc? I won't pretend to care what you're talking about." With a short, icy nod toward Ingrid, Vander excused himself.

Until that moment, Ingrid had never felt relieved to part from his company. She watched him disappear behind Hans and Hathaway. Both men had their eyes trained on her and Luc. She knew Hathaway had voted for her death once, and there was little question that Hans, had he been a Directorate member, would have agreed.

She turned her back on them and navigated her way toward the glass doors where Hugh Dupuis had released the corvite. The afternoon light had taken on a jaundiced tint, painting the shingled roof of Constantine's stables a light honey. The day was winding down, and once again she had no idea where her brother was.

It had been quite a while since Ingrid had felt ordinary, without the lashes of a sparking electric whip beneath her skin. Vander's mersian blood had rid her of that, and even now on this second day since her injection, Ingrid felt nothing. But the mersian cure couldn't subdue the twitching of the line that had always tethered her to Grayson. Perhaps he no longer felt it, and perhaps for her, the line had grown slack. It was still there, though, and she could feel the incessant thrum of the connection, as though someone were bouncing upon it.

"Where are you?" she whispered against the cold glass. A circle of fog bloomed.

"I wish I could tell you," Luc said as he came up behind her. He'd read her mind yet again.

She drew an infinity symbol in the circle of fog, her finger dipping and curving again and again. "I hate to think of him out there alone. What if his mersian dose has worn off?"

"He knows where Vander keeps the vials," Luc answered. His solid reasoning was exactly what she needed. "Speaking of which, Vander should give you another dose."

"I'm doing fine," she insisted, though mostly she just didn't want to have to sit with Vander and take his cure now that she'd made it clear she could give him absolutely nothing in return.

Ingrid turned to look over her shoulder at Luc. "You're not going to tell me what happened just now with Irindi."

"No." The reply was quick and hoarse—and final.

She resumed gazing at the well-kept stables, the wide barn

boards meticulously trimmed and nailed, the Pegasus weather-vane cast in polished copper.

"I saw her, Luc. No net is going to be able to take Axia down, especially not if she knows it's coming." She kept her voice hushed, not wanting to upset Gabby. Her sister had already looked panicked when Constantine and Hugh had explained the elements of a severix demon.

"Then we need to find another way."

"We need to surprise her," Ingrid said, remembering the sickening tremor that had gone through her when the dagger had sunk into Axia's flesh and muscle.

"She knows we're sitting here, waiting for Hugh's corvite to return. She knows we have a net. She knows everything." The flaw in their hasty plan gaped open before Ingrid. "Why should she come when she could send her demons and Dusters? We aren't going to have a chance at her."

Luc's fingers closed around her elbow. "I think you're right. We need to leave."

Ingrid faced him, casting off his gentle grip. "Run? Where to this time, Luc? No. No, we must face her. We must . . . we must go to *her*. She won't expect it."

Luc bit back his instant retort and settled, Ingrid was sure, for something kinder. "Ingrid, none of us are strong enough to fight her. You saw what she did to Marco. The only hope we had rested with the Order."

Ingrid recalled Axia's laughter, the way it had ricocheted around the stone courtyard. She imagined Axia laughing now, at ease with her strength. Not nervous in the least that she might be thwarted.

The only thing Axia had appeared upset about that morning had been the question of why Ingrid had not fallen under her spell. Believing Ingrid still had angel blood in her body had whipped Axia into a bubbling rage.

Or had it been something other than anger?

Ingrid caught Luc's arms and squeezed. "What if she was afraid?"

Ingrid left the doors and made her way to the sofa and the corvite's birdcage. Hugh Dupuis was in conference with Rory, but his keen eyes saw Ingrid's approach and he detached himself from the Scot.

"Miss Waverly?" Hugh greeted her with such elegance she half expected him to be holding a whiskey and a cigar.

"Mr. Dupuis," she replied, her mind at a gallop. "I have an awful idea and I require your help."

He slanted a brow at her as Luc caught up. "What is it?" Luc asked.

"Apparently it's awful," Hugh replied.

"It is," she said. "It's probably insane, but I think it may be our only hope."

She was trying to keep her voice down, but curious eyes had already started to drift in their direction.

"We're using the wrong bait," Ingrid started to explain, her thoughts and ideas buzzing about her head like an angry swarm of bees. "Axia has no equal here. No human or gargoyle can match her. Only another angel could be a true opponent. This morning, she found me. She came *looking* for me, believing I still had some of her blood. Axia was convinced it was the reason I wasn't falling under her sway. Even without intending to, I lured her out. I can do it again."

Hugh's expression lit with understanding.

"No, Ingrid," Luc said.

Hugh held up his palm. "Wait. The idea has merit."

"I said no." Luc's bark secured the attention of everyone else within the library.

"It isn't your decision," Ingrid said to him, firmly enough to forestall a third refusal. Luc clenched his jaw and speared her with a look of fury and defeat. He pivoted on his heel and put a few strides between them.

"What's this about?" Nolan asked, approaching Ingrid and Hugh at the birdcage.

She kept her eyes on the Daicrypta doyen. "I go to her. I bring a vial of her blood and let her have it, and then tell her that there is more. That I want to strike a bargain."

Hathaway pushed his way to Ingrid's side. "That blood belongs to the Alliance now, Miss Waverly. Reneging on the agreement your sister and I made would not be wise."

"Our agreement hinges upon your witnessing the net's ability," Gabby said. "You haven't yet done so, and so the blood is not yet yours."

Hathaway lost his careful composure "Do not split hairs with me, young woman. If you think you can play me for a fool, you will be sorely disappointed."

"So many threats, Hathaway," Nolan cut in, angling his body toward the representative with a clear threat of his own. "Is that all the Directorate is good for?"

"We're giving her one vial," Ingrid said. "I have no intention of handing over the rest. All I mean to do is distract her attention while drawing her out into the open long enough for Gabby's net to capture her."

Long enough for Axia to let her guard down a bit, and perhaps feel a bit greedy. Wasn't that what they needed?

"And how do you plan to find her? By wandering through Paris alone?" This time it wasn't Luc but Vander who'd chosen to argue.

Constantine raised his hand to interrupt. "Many of the Dusters I housed here before the Chimera attack this morning mentioned the Champs de Mars as a hotbed of demon activity. Perhaps Axia's new hive here on earth."

The exposition buildings surrounding the esplanade, and the commanding view from the tower would definitely give Axia a protected central headquarters of sorts.

"While that sounds like a truly delightful place to visit,"

Marco began, having returned to the library, "someone else will have to take the blood and lure her out. You, Lady Ingrid, will be staying here."

Ingrid tightened her hands into fists. "Axia would sic her demons on anyone else. I'm the only person she will stop to listen to, especially if she still believes I have some of her blood in my veins."

Mama pushed forward to the edge of the sofa cushion. "And what is to stop this Axia woman from harming you straight out?"

Her smoky quartz eyes watched Ingrid with uncut doubt and fear. That she'd referred to Axia as a woman only underscored how little she understood about the situation. However, she was far from fainting dead away at the idea of evil angels and blood-thirsty demons. Ingrid was surprised at how similar her mother's fortitude was to Gabby's. Perhaps even to her own.

"She wasn't going to kill me this morning," Ingrid answered, feeling more and more confident. "She was only going to draw out the angel blood she believed I had."

Luc had been brooding behind Nolan and Gabby until then. "If the net fails or if it misses its mark, we can't protect you. We can't fight an angel."

Vander took a sidelong glance at Luc. "It won't miss its mark," he said. "Not if I'm shooting it."

Knowing Vander would be aiming the crossbow reassured Ingrid like nothing else could have.

Rory, who had remained silent and watchful, finally spoke. "Ye can't approach her alone. She'd be suspicious of that."

"I will not assign any of my men to guide you into this suicide mission," Hans said to her. "Entering a boxed-in space such as the Champs de Mars with those buildings built up around it now would be like walking into a gladiators' arena."

Benjamin and Nadia ignored Hans's declaration and made one of their own.

"We can stay out of sight but within earshot," Nadia said, with Benjamin adding, "Should you require it."

Ingrid nodded her gratitude while trying not to look at Luc and the muscles clenching along his jaw. His disapproval burned.

"I do not want you to do this, Ingrid," Mama said. Soft lines fanned her eyes and lips as she frowned. "However, I trust your instinct. If you think this will work . . ."

Ingrid wished she could say something different to reassure her, but she didn't like to lie. "I don't know if it will."

Mama absently patted her skirts and found Marco with her steady gaze. "You will keep her safe."

Marco looked at Ingrid's mother as if he'd never seen her before. Two vertical lines creased the skin between his brows as he frowned. "I will," he said, and with a glance at the gargoyle at his side, added, "As will Luc."

Mama pursed her lips, her hands stilling over her dark plum lace overlay. "Mr. Rousseau is not my daughter's gargoyle."

Ingrid crossed a look with Luc. His grimace was enough to pierce her. She was certain that her mother's disdain hurt him as much as it did her.

"Let's just say he's self-appointed," Marco replied.

Hathaway rested his hands on the handles of his swords, sheathed at his hips. "One vial, Miss Waverly. Hans will accompany your outing to the Champs de Mars and bear witness to the diffuser net display."

Hans, utterly galled, speared the Directorate leader with a mutinous glare as Hathaway went on. "I don't wish failure upon this harebrained scheme of yours. I just think it very unlikely to succeed."

What to say to that? Hathaway was a cold man, but he was probably correct.

Hugh coughed to break the clouding tension and extended his hand to Ingrid. "Then it's settled. Come, Miss Waverly. I believe you have some blood to collect."

CHAPTER TWENTY-FIVE

The blue-white-and-red-uniformed French Imperial Guard officers surrounded the Champs de Mars. As Grayson and the other Dusters approached the main exhibition halls from avenue de la Bourdonnais, the police did not open fire or attempt in any fashion to stop their small group from passing through the arched entryways that led to the enclosed esplanade. They simply backed up, staring at them while clutching their issued rifles and sabers. Grayson figured the enormous hellhounds flanking them were the primary reason for that.

The police had most likely already discovered that their bullets did not stop the beasts. If only they had known about blessed silver, Grayson thought as they traversed the long entryway. The seams the Alliance had sewn so tightly around their secret world had finally split. The mess wasn't something Grayson could wrap his mind around just then. The only thing he could allow himself to think about was Axia and his plan to bring her to her knees.

He'd wanted this confrontation, he reminded himself upon

entering the esplanade. He had cleared the line of trees, their limbs barely budding, and could now view the entire length of the Champs de Mars. To the left were the ornate fountains of the Château d'Eau and the glass ceilings of the Palace of Electricity, visible just behind the chateau. To the right, farther down the esplanade, stood the Eiffel Tower. Everywhere in between, along the wide gravel walk and the thin strips of snow-dusted grass, were swarms of demons and Dusters. The Dusters stood in tight clusters, the demons circling them. And not just hellhounds. Close to him, a thick, squat black beetle the size of a miniature pony scuttled back and forth in front of a group of six or so Dusters. The beetle's long antennae crackled with blue spits of electricity. Bands of it reached from one antenna to the other, licking back and forth in constant bursts of light. It was a lectrux, he assumed, and the Dusters it was fencing in were a mixture of boys and girls. They were filthy and haggard, and their fear was so real Grayson could practically taste it.

The boy with the mop of red hair who had approached Grayson with the others on rue de Berri nudged him.

"Mistress is there," he whispered, his chin jerking in the direction of the Eiffel Tower.

It was time. Grayson's pulse throbbed in his ears as he started along the gravel esplanade toward the tower. When he had entered, there had been a low, breathy roar within the exhibition space—Axia's nest. There had to be at least a hundred or more Dusters here, and just as many creatures scraped up from the Underneath, to guard them. Crowds like that made noise. Yet as Grayson took measured steps toward the iron behemoth, a silence settled in. He kept his chin lifted and his sights on the tower. Of all the demons present—from rattilus demons and crypsis serpents to corvites and the flylike beings Luc had once called Drainers—hellhounds were the most prominent. They stopped pacing as Grayson walked past. Their ember-red eyes watched him intently.

He still had his hands in his pockets, his right hand closed around the warm glass barrel of the syringe. The glass was slippery; his palms were damp. Suddenly every last nerve in his body jumped to attention.

"You have come to me at last."

The Dusters and demons in Grayson's side vision pressed themselves toward the ground. He saw her then, emerging from behind two of her hounds. Her hooded figure was the only one that did not stoop. Axia glided toward him. A black corvite swooped overhead, its growling call echoing off the façades of the surrounding buildings.

For a moment, he forgot that he had been the one to design this meeting, and felt trapped again, a prisoner inside her Underneath hive. His skin itched along his arms and legs with the memory of the fanged man—one of these beastly hounds, he realized—and how he'd punctured Grayson's skin again and again, injecting him with black demon poison.

Axia lifted her arm, the sleeve of her robe long enough to cover her fingers, and pushed back the cavernous hood. He tensed, remembering how in the Underneath she'd been bald, her skin stretched tight over the sharp bones of her face, emphasizing her unnaturally round black eyes and her lipless mouth. He prepared himself to be struck by her hideous visage again.

But when her hood fell around her shoulders, that wasn't what Grayson saw at all. She wasn't the decrepit creature she'd been in the Underneath. She had lips, full and pink. She had dark brown eyes instead of all-black, fathomless pupils. And her hair cascaded around her shoulders in wild golden ringlets. It wasn't just her hair that was golden—*she* was. Axia had a luminescent glow that seemed to leak out of her very skin.

"Do you bring a weapon into my nest, Grayson Waverly?" she asked.

He froze under a sweep of panic.

"Lay it down," Axia commanded after his beat of guilty silence.

He cautiously removed both hands from his pockets, though only one extracted a weapon. He let the dagger drop to the ground, where it thudded dully. Grayson damn well hoped she didn't have him turn out his other pocket. Thankfully, she seemed appeased.

"I wish you had come of your own accord." She spoke in the same honey-sweet voice he remembered from before. It chimed through his ears, leaving behind something like the faint peal of bells.

I have, he thought, but instead replied, "I won't be your slave."

Axia's laugh tinkled through the air, wrongly bright within the solemn, fear-filled Champs de Mars. "You refer to the mersian blood cure. I admit my decision to bestow such a gift on Evander Burke was erroneous. Mersians are unto themselves in the Underneath, as I learned during my imprisonment there, and are indifferent to my influence. However, he is but one seedling. It seems Evander Burke will have to be weeded out."

So that was why Vander—or Evander, or whatever his full name was—had not fallen under Axia's spell. That only presented yet another pressing reason Grayson knew he must succeed: to protect Vander—and the mersian blood. He settled his hands back inside his trouser pockets, hoping the action appeared casual.

Axia's golden brows slanted and her lips puckered into a moue. "Do not worry so, Grayson Waverly. The mersian blood within you will soon fade, and you will give yourself over to me. You will become what you have always been meant to be."

He and Ingrid had never been the sort to speak without first weighing their choice of words. Gabby would have begun arguing with Axia immediately, and a part of Grayson longed to do the same. To assert that he would never give himself over to her, no matter how easy it would be. He'd felt the draw before, the overwhelming urge to shift and settle into the form that, if he allowed himself to admit it, felt more comfortable than the one he currently held.

He couldn't argue with Axia. It did seem, in many ways, that he was meant to be a hellhound, or at least part hound. But he also knew he would never allow himself to be owned.

"I'd rather die than become one of your pets." As soon as he'd spoken the words, he felt as though a door had slammed behind him. He'd crossed over some threshold. Some understanding within himself. There would be no turning back.

The black wings of another corvite circled over Axia's head, and then the demon bird's claws settled on the soft mound of golden curls draped over her shoulders. The bird growled. Axia canted her head just enough to hint that whatever the demon had said had been significant.

She twitched her shoulder and the corvite flew off.

"Grayson Waverly, while I am as dissatisfied with you as I am with my mersian seedling, I see no reason to weed you out yet."

She took a few steps to the left and angled herself toward him, as if to impart some confidence. "I can remove your demon blood just as easily as I bequeathed it."

Grayson stilled. The pure hatred he'd felt for Axia slipped. He felt something he hadn't since she'd taken him to her hive before: reliance. A knowledge that he was a prisoner, had always been a prisoner, and that she had always been the gatekeeper. She was telling him this for a reason. To Grayson, it sounded curiously like the beginning of a bargain.

"Why would you do that?" he asked. "Don't you need your seedlings for this war of yours?"

Her radiant skin was difficult to look at. It produced the same abrasive glare the surface of a pond did at sunset.

"I require obedient seedlings," she answered, and continued with a loose sweep of her hand. "As you can see, I have many here. Many more will come. You say you would rather die than become my pet?"

Axia tacked to the right and stepped directly in front of Grayson. He cradled the barrel of the needle in his pocket and slipped his fingers into the twin holes of the plunger. She was close. But close enough? He eyed the hellhounds on either side of her, knowing if he made his move now, the hounds would rip into him. The tremor of his wrist did nothing to inspire courage. He *would* rather die than become her pet, but that didn't exactly mean he wanted to die.

He stayed quiet, hoping she would continue without his answer. She did.

"Tell me, Grayson Waverly." Axia said. "Who else would you so willingly sacrifice?"

Gabby ran her hand down the velvety blaze of one of Constantine's bay mares. The stables were quiet and warm, drenched in late-afternoon sunlight. She hadn't been able to take pacing the library, or any other room in the chateau. Ingrid and the others had left for the Champs de Mars a half an hour before, and only Gabby, Constantine, Hathaway, and Lady Brickton remained at Clos du Vie. Mama had even formally accepted Clos du Vie as her home, absolving Marco from any need to leave Ingrid's side.

Nolan had pulled Gabby aside while the others had been loading into the carriages and Luc and Marco had been preparing behind one of the conveyances to coalesce into true form. He hadn't pleaded with her to stay at Constantine's. He hadn't reminded her how dangerous walking into Axia's new hive was going to be. Gabby had seen his request in his eyes, had felt it in the glide of his fingers along her scarred cheek. He'd kissed her in front of everyone—even Mama—before jumping into the driver's box of Vander's wagonette.

The bay mare in the warm stables snuffled and stomped one of its hind legs. Gabby nearly laughed. She felt like making the same complaint.

"It's not fun being left behind, is it?" she asked, rubbing the mare's snout once more before leaving her be.

Gabby had worn her cloak but had removed it, her Prussian blue day dress warm enough for the gathered heat in the stables. Her cloak hung on a peg driven into a beam near the doors, and as she ambled along the weathered floorboards, hands clasped behind her back, she saw a glint of silver from within the folds of the cloak. She always kept the pommel of the sword Nolan had given her at a high polish, though it had been some time since she and Rory had last sparred.

Gabby crossed to the cloak, withdrew the sword, and as usual, admired the craftsmanship. Nolan would not have given it to her had he not believed that she would one day wield it well. Perhaps he was too protective, too coddling, but she also knew he was right. When she and Rory had come across the mollug demon on the London docks and Rory had simply handed her the diffuser net, expecting her to figure it out on her own, she'd been furious. And scared. She wasn't ready yet. But she would be someday.

Gabby cut the sword through the air and sank into a defensive crouch. Rotating on one heel, she spun and slashed the blade in a clean stroke, then, taking hold of the handle with both hands, practiced one of the offensive moves Rory had shown her. The sword was the perfect size and weight for her, showing yet again just how well Nolan knew her. Gabby imagined him with her, circling her as she thrust and cut, calling out instructions or correcting a blunder, his eyes sharp and his lips turned up in a mischievous smirk. He would be thinking about kissing her, no doubt. And she would chastise him for distracting her.

Gabby heard a soft thump as she punctured the air in front of her with the tip of the sword. She held still, her heart beating fast and making her breathing loud. The noise had sounded as if it came from overhead. She stood tall, her sword falling until the tip brushed along the hay-strewn floor.

Another thump came, this one louder than before. Something had landed on the roof. Gabby's eyes drifted up. She stared at the beamed ceiling and the curved rafters and for a fleeting moment convinced herself it had only been a pair of birds.

Her throat felt unnaturally dry as she regripped the handle of her sword and eyed the doors. She'd shut them behind her to keep out the cold, but she hadn't thrown the heavy wooden bolt into place. Instinct, base and immediate, urged her to hide. To duck into one of the empty stalls or climb into the hayloft. She imagined Nolan issuing another piece of advice: *Trust your instinct, lass.*

Gabby swung herself into the nearest stall just seconds before the stable doors crashed inward. They sounded as if they'd been blown open by a black-powder explosion. The stall belonged to the chestnut she'd been petting. Gabby retreated to a rear corner of the stall, the mare whinnying and stomping.

"I know you're in here."

Gabby's stomach bottomed out at the sound of the canyon-deep voice that filled the stables.

"Did you believe I would forget?"

She squeezed her eyes shut and exhaled a tremulous breath. The total silence allowed her to hear the soft rush of a gargoyle coalescing.

Yann had come for her.

CHAPTER TWENTY-SIX

The Champs de Mars had been totally surrounded by armed citizens and the French Imperial Guard by the time Ingrid, Hugh, Nolan, and Rory had approached the exterior of the exhibition buildings. They'd come on foot, Luc having stopped the landau two blocks distant in an attempt to go unnoticed by Axia and her demons. He had argued, once again, against Ingrid's leaving his side. And Ingrid had been reluctant to, as well. She couldn't show her unease, however, considering the whole plan had been her idea.

Eventually, Luc and Marco had assented that they could not be part of Ingrid's small party when she entered the Champs de Mars. The demons there would only trigger their impulse to coalesce and to shield Ingrid from danger, when danger was exactly what Ingrid needed to find. She needed to get close to Axia and distract her long enough for Vander to sight a clear shot from where he would be hiding with an unenthusiastic Hans.

A trio of uniformed military policemen stepped into their path, just in front of an arched entrance to the Champs de Mars.

"Vous n'avez pas permission d'entrer," one of the policemen said, his eyes alighting on the vest of blades worn by Rory, who had left his coat purposely unbuttoned.

"Listen to me carefully," Nolan said, his attention fixed on the flat roofline of the exhibition halls. "Bullets are useless against these creatures. You need silver blades, and you need to have them blessed."

The trio of policemen glanced skeptically at one another, then back at Nolan and the broadsword he'd just drawn from his hip scabbard.

"Steel or iron won't work. It has to be silver."

The policeman switched to English. "And who are you?"

Nolan finished inspecting the roofline and met the man's eyes. "Someone who has fought these things before and won. Let us through. We're here to help."

The absence of his ever-present sarcasm made Ingrid feel the sheer magnitude of what was to come. She wished for more confidence. She wished for the sputter of electricity beneath her skin. Instead, all she had was the erratic thumping of her pulse, a knot in the pit of her stomach, and a curious light-headedness as the policemen parted to allow them to pass. As she followed Nolan closely, Rory and Hugh behind her, she heard a man giving orders to search for silver weapons. Another was muttering a prayer for the souls walking toward their own deaths. Ingrid wished she hadn't heard that part but praised herself for at least knowing more French than she used to.

The long, tunnel-like entrance took them past entrances to the exhibition halls and out into the esplanade, a rectangle closed in on three sides, the fourth capped by the Eiffel Tower. A fiery sunset glow, hazed by smoke and clouds of ash, pinked the white plaster façade of the opulent Château d'Eau. The smokestack on the far right end of the Palace of Electricity, directly behind the chateau's scalloped roofline, caught her attention. A gargoyle perched atop the stack. It was Marco, she realized, with a slight dip in her spirits. Luc would not have been able to fly up there without help. He couldn't fly at all, and not for the first time, she wondered how he would get to her if she needed him.

"Eyes down," Hugh whispered as he came up beside her.

Ingrid dragged her gaze back toward the ground and immediately took an unintentional step in reverse. Demons occupied nearly every patch of grass, every melting mound of snow. Hellhounds circled humans, who huddled together for what she assumed was both warmth and comfort. Corvites perched upon the crocodile- and goddess-shaped fountainheads of the Château d'Eau, and tiny, monkey-shaped creatures with curling horns swung from the swaths of red-and-white striped fabric shading each arcade directly across the esplanade.

A lectrux demon scuttled down the gravel walk toward them, its antennae sizzling with electric light. A wolf-shaped demon, half the size of a hellhound but with equally vicious fangs, slammed into the lectrux, knocking it off course. The lectrux spit more electricity and shocked the wolf but hung back. Nothing else approached, though Ingrid was certain every demon and Duster within the Champs de Mars was watching them stand underneath the domed colonnade entrance.

"Hugh," Rory said, his hands already holding the double swords he'd freed from his back sheath. "Ye canna stay."

Despite Rory's discontent, the London Daicrypta doyen had insisted upon entering the Champs de Mars with them. He was neither tall nor brawny, but he had training, he'd assured them, and he knew more about demons and their weaknesses than the Alliance did.

"It appears I cannot leave, either," Hugh replied.

Ingrid turned around and saw a giant black spider crawling along the ceiling of the entrance arcade. Its legs were easily the length of Ingrid's entire body, its hairy belly and head the size of a hansom cab. The arachnae demon ceased moving and clung, upside down, to the ceiling, blocking their escape.

"Do you see him?" Ingrid whispered, trying to keep her eyes lowered instead of up, searching along the roofline for Vander's creeping form.

"We won't see him," Nolan answered just as softly. She supposed that meant the demons and Axia wouldn't, either. If they did, all would be lost.

"I suppose we should wander out like the sacrificial lambs we are," Nolan said next, attempting nonchalance. Ingrid could still hear his underlying uncertainty.

Ingrid let her gaze bounce up toward the smokestack again. Marco was gone, but a half-dozen or more shadowy figures hunched on the cars of the giant Ferris wheel. Anyone seated within one of those passenger cars would have just as good a view of Paris as someone standing on the Eiffel Tower, though she was certain the winged creatures now atop them, with their night vision, had a far superior view than even that.

Ingrid stepped from the domed colonnade and matched Nolan's cautious pace. There were no lights along the esplanade, electric or gas, but within minutes they would be required. Ingrid and Nolan marched along the gravel walk toward the looming Iron Lady. The path cleared for them as they went, hellhounds slinking to the periphery, a bench-shaped appendius loping out of the way, though it kept its spiked teeth on menacing display.

Axia was the only being capable of ordering these beasts to refrain from attacking. She was here. And Ingrid had reached the point in her rather hastily thought-out plan where she officially became bait.

"Axia!" Ingrid's voice reverberated off the surrounding buildings. The utter stillness of the esplanade, and of Paris beyond the square of halls, made her voice sound as though it belonged to a giant. She cringed but called the angel's name again anyway.

"Axia, come out!" Nerves squeezed her vocal cords and made her words tremble. "You were right! I still have your blood in my veins, and you can have it back—on one condition!"

She took the clear glass vial from her skirt pocket and held it above her head.

"This is my blood! Take it and see for yourself!"

The esplanade remained dark and quiet. A chill worked its way up Ingrid's spine as the sun sank quickly behind the fire-kissed brume.

"She isn't coming," she murmured, lips barely moving, her arm still high in the air.

"Give her a moment," Hugh replied.

For the first time, Ingrid allowed herself to imagine what might happen should Axia call her bluff. Two demon hunters, one Daicrypta, and one human girl against an arena filled with demons and spellbound Dusters did not an even fight make. And Ingrid would be useless. At least Hugh had a sword and some training. If only she still had a fraction of her lectrux power. It had been two full days since her first mersian blood injection . . . . Shouldn't it have been wearing off by now? Shouldn't she have been feeling *something*?

This was more frustrating than before, when she'd had no control over the electric impulses. It wasn't until her nightmarish imprisonment in the Daicrypta draining room with Hugh's father that she had realized she could draw electricity from other sources around her—lightbulbs, rushing water, stormy skies . . . anything that generated electricity.

The incessant shivers skittering along Ingrid's back suddenly turned to steel. She stood taller, shoulders squared, afraid even to breathe for fear of losing hold of the realization that had just struck her. She spun around and looked toward the opposite end of the Champs de Mars, past the magnificent façade and fountains of the Château d'Eau, to the sloped glass ceilings of the building behind it. The Palace of Electricity.

The Exposition Universelle wasn't set to open for another week, but Ingrid knew the Palace of Electricity was in working order—she and Vander had heard the low hum of the machines inside less than a week before. Ingrid had felt the current of tremors rolling through the air. The air was still now, though, the building likely abandoned. But underneath that darkened glass roof were the generators that would power the entire fair. The Eiffel Tower would no longer be lit from the top with gaslights but with thousands of bulbs strung along its sides. She knew what it felt like to draw energy from a single powered bulb. But thousands of them? A whole building of generated power?

Her distraction had not gone unnoticed.

Hugh touched her arm lightly. "Lady Ingrid?"

"That building," she said, still dazed by her realization. "The Palace of Electricity."

Nolan stood close enough for Ingrid to feel his side knocking gently against hers. "What about it?"

She felt a cramp of desire, of pure need, close around her stomach. She'd never thought she'd long for her ability like this.

"I need it turned on."

Hugh cleared his throat and started to speak, when a high, keening wail spiraled up from somewhere within the Champs de Mars. Other sounds joined the single moan—grunting and hissing, rasps of pain. The huddled Dusters, penned in by demons, sank to the ground, clutching their heads, fists pounding against their ears.

"This is not a promising sign," Nolan said, his broadsword sweeping up into a defensive position.

The moans of the Dusters stopped in unison and the esplanade was silent once again. Only now, the hellhounds that had been slowly circling the Dusters stepped out of their rotations, allowing the humans freedom. They weren't free, though. Ingrid knew better. Axia had reached into their minds and taken up the puppet master's strings.

What she hadn't taken was the bait.

A rattilus came at them, whipping its serrated scorpion tail, the hooked quills looking as though they could saw through flesh and bone. The tail scythed once past Nolan's kneecaps, and on the second attempt, Nolan's sword connected. The blade sheared through, and before the lopped-off tail could even hit the ground, his sword speared the thick, crusty exoskeleton of the creature. The explosion of green death sparks hung in the air a pregnant moment. As the last one disappeared and no other demon or en-thralled Duster attacked, Ingrid began to wonder if Axia had changed her mind.

She hadn't.

Ingrid screamed as Rory pitched a dagger in her direction. The blade whistled past her shoulder and thudded into one of the wolf demons midleap, its paws less than a foot away from Ingrid's head.

"We could use our wings now!" Nolan screamed, though he hadn't needed to. The sky above the Champs de Mars darkened as scores of gargoyles swooped, dropping into the esplanade.

Their contingency plan wouldn't last, however; not if Axia forced the Dispossessed into submission the way she'd done with Marco that morning. It would only give them enough time to backtrack out of the esplanade.

And then they'd be at the beginning all over again. No ground gained. All hope dashed.

Rory and Nolan had widened their circle, their swords flash-ing in every direction as they attempted to beat back the demons coming for them. Hugh had his sword in hand, and though it was only the size of Gabby's short sword, it looked enormous and unwieldy in his grasp.

"Lady Ingrid, you should at least have a dagger," Hugh said, his eyes on the ever-shifting battle around them.

"I wouldn't know how to use it," she replied, searching the esplanade for the one-winged gargoyle she wanted to see more than anything else. It was too chaotic, though. and the fading light was tingeing every thrashing body—human, demon, and gargoyle—the color of mud. Any moment now she expected to see Marco's wings slicing toward her. He would seal her to his chest and twirl her up to safety, pulling her from her one plan to destroy Axia.

"Ingrid!"

The shout had come from a distance, but it had still hammered into her, clear and strong. Breath lodged in her chest, Ingrid searched the esplanade, where the path widened out to bracket the base of the Eiffel Tower.

She spotted him, his arm waving manically over his head to capture her attention. And this time, it wasn't a delusion demon.

"Grayson." She stood tall again and waved madly in return. "Grayson!"

He stood alone, just out from underneath the belly of the tower. He hadn't shifted into hellhound form, so she knew his mersian blood, like hers, was still holding strong.

"Mr. Dupuis!" Ingrid turned to the Daicrypta doyen and grasped his arm. "The Palace of Electricity—can you get inside? Can you work the machines?"

Hugh had yet to swing his sword, Rory and Nolan doing a fine job of caging the both of them off from approaching threats.

"Breaking in and working the machinery should be simple," he answered, the first hint of panic lacing his tone. "If I don't become a tasty hors d'oeuvre first."

"See that you don't," Ingrid said.

"Yes, well, I hope— Wait! Miss Waverly!" But Ingrid had already lifted the hem of her skirts and started dashing along the gravel esplanade to meet Grayson.

Her brother rushed forward, his arm outstretched and ready to hook hers as soon as he was close enough. She heard a sharp shriek behind her, near the Château d'Eau. It reached into her stomach and gave a ferocious tug. Somehow she knew it had been Luc, that he'd been calling to her, and yet she couldn't stop and turn back, not with her twin so close.

Grayson took her arm and immediately started hauling her

toward the tower pillars. The Champs de Mars ended on the other side of the tower, and unlike at the other end of the esplanade, there was no building to block their exit. They could keep running to the Seine if they liked.

"We can't leave!" Ingrid heard herself shouting, breathless. She could do nothing to help, either, but ducking out for safety would have been cowardly. And if Hugh got the generators going in the Palace of Electricity, she might actually have a weapon more powerful than any blessed silver blade out there.

"Grayson!" she shouted again, but he wasn't slowing. He also wasn't cutting straight underneath the tower. He'd veered toward one of the thick pillars.

His hand tightened around her upper arm. "Ingrid, I need you to trust me."

"Where are we going?" He didn't answer, but directed her onto the first step of the stairwell leading into the center of the pillar.

Their feet scuffed up a dozen or so iron steps before reaching a platform where the stairwell turned on itself. Ingrid tried to drag her feet, but Grayson tugged her along, up the next section of steps.

"Grayson, tell me what's happening." Ingrid was short of breath at the next twist in the stairwell, and by then, she'd had enough. "Grayson!"

He paused on the iron step above her, his chest heaving.

"I'm sorry, Ingrid. I promise you, this is the only way."

She gripped the cold metal handrail and took a wary glance down. They were already a good distance up.

"Where are we going?" she asked, wishing she'd heeded Luc's shriek and turned back.

"I'm sorry," her brother repeated, his grip on her arm unrelenting. "I'm taking you to Axia."

CHAPTER TWENTY-SEVEN

Gabby's wrists quivered like aspic as she braced her sword with both hands. The laces on her corset seemed to tighten with every shallow breath. She listened as Yann moved through the stables; his lion's paws scraped along the floorboards about two stalls to the left. The boards groaned under his immense weight.

He wasn't alone. There had been two thumps on the roof earlier. There were more gargoyles outside. Perhaps dozens. Gabby closed her eyes and tried to curb her fear. This was Gaston's territory. She was a guest on it, and Gaston would feel Yann's presence. He'd be here any moment.

As the drag of Yann's claws drew closer, the horse sharing Gabby's hiding place lashed its tail and bucked its powerful hind legs. They were intuitive creatures, and this one clearly knew something wicked was near. The animal was as large as Yann's true form, she wagered. It didn't have talons, but its wide body was pure muscle. A perfect shield.

Gabby slipped to the other side of the mare and crouched.

The stall door was still rolled open—she hadn't had time to close it.

Screwing up her courage, Gabby slapped the flat side of her sword against the mare's rear end. The horse bleated, but it didn't bolt forward as she'd hoped. She gave the animal another tap, but it still played coy with the open stall door. Gabby ground her teeth. If the horse wouldn't be her shield, then it would be her ride.

She climbed onto a half-tumbled stack of hay and threw herself, belly first, onto the mare's back. She kept low, swinging her left leg forward to straddle the mare, despite the scandalous rise of her watered silk dress. Who the devil cared if her knickers showed? Gripping the horse round its thick neck, she dug her heels in and the chestnut took off, skittering out of the stall and into the open stables.

The hopes that perhaps Yann had left or that the horse would provide adequate protection proved false. Gabby had nearly made it to the stable doors when a long, whiplike tail pounded into her right side, lifting her clean off the horse's back. The bay mare was gone before Gabby hit the floor. She lunged to her feet, weaving slightly, her sword out before her. Yann's lion-and-eagle amalgamation appeared in front of her. The long silver hair covering the lower, lion half of his Chimera form glistened like stardust. His black eagle eyes were cold and alert, his yellow beak hooked into a sharp tip.

His tail lashed out at Gabby and bit into her sword arm. She screamed and the sword clattered to her feet. She reached for a dagger sheathed inside her cape, but her hand only combed the air. Blast! Her cape still hung on a peg behind Yann. She had only one dagger left—the blade at her heel. Yann's wings snapped open, his starry-night feathers singing a metallic song as they bristled. Gabby had seen his feathers shear through a crypsis demon, the edge of each one as keen as any blessed silver blade.

The Chimera's tail lashed out at her again, aiming for her

shins. Gabby jumped as it cut underneath her heavy skirts. She landed, bent into a crouch, and extracted the blade at her heel. It left her palm, her aim hasty but precise. The dagger drove into the lion's meaty breast, though nowhere near its heart. Yann shrieked and lurched as his wings collapsed.

Gabby scooped up her dropped sword and bolted through the open stable doors, into the dusky blue sunset light. Her knees nearly gave out when she saw Gaston, still in human form, rushing across the gravel drive, toward the stables.

But then he stopped, his eyes on the space above her head, and in the next second, Gaston shattered out of his clothes and skin. His black leather wings, stretched tight over slender bones, unfolded and he launched himself into the air. Gabby swiveled around to follow his course, losing her balance as she did. She stumbled, her feet and ankles crossing over one another as if she were a baby giraffe taking its first steps.

Gabby's hip slammed into the gravel drive, but she was still looking up, so she could see a half-feline, half-stag Chimera with feathered wings swooping toward her. Gaston had already collided with a second Chimera, so this one was all hers. Gabby rolled to the left in the last second before the Chimera's calico legs, tipped with bulbous paws and wicked nails, could land and crush her skull. Still holding her sword, Gabby sliced the blade a few inches above the gravel and hacked into its front legs. Her blade stuck there; the blessed silver was crafted to melt through the flesh of a demon, not a gargoyle. She needed a mercurite-dipped weapon.

The Chimera thrashed and recoiled, and the handle of Gabby's light sword was ripped from her palm. The silver blade was still embedded in the creature's legs, but she wasn't about to try to get it back.

Gabby dug her hands into the cold gravel, heaved herself up, and stumbled toward the chateau. The doors to the library were open, and Constantine filled the entrance.

"Go! Inside!" she screamed, though she knew a gargoyle could easily crash through the glass door or windows of the library.

Constantine, however, didn't retreat into the relative safety of his library. He twisted the globe topper of his walking stick and withdrew a long, thin rapier. Gabby's pace faltered a moment as the older gentleman rushed from the doorway, looking for all the world like a soldier entering the fray of battle.

The telltale shriek of a Chimera closing in from behind made Gabby's legs pump harder.

"Inside! On the table!" Constantine shouted as their shoulders brushed past one another. Before Gabby could ask what on earth he'd meant, his coarse battle cry rent the air. Gabby kept running, her ears filled with the deafening crash of her own pulse and ragged gasping. She didn't stop as she came to the doors, or even when Constantine's war cry abruptly cut off.

She plowed into the library, the soles of her boots slipping along the polished parquet floors as she threw out her arms to slow her momentum. A pair of hands clamped around her arms and Gabby screamed before seeing the red-caped Directorate representative, Hathaway, at her side.

"What in Hades is happening?" he bellowed as Gabby tried to wrench her arm from his grip. The table. Constantine had said something about it being on a table.

And then she saw it. The low table in front of the sofa, where Constantine and Hugh had been seated earlier drinking tea. Resting forgotten, atop the lacquered mahogany wood, was the diffuser net. Vander had taken the one designed for Axia, but not this one, designed for demons—and mercurite-dipped for protection against gargoyles.

The tall, mullioned window behind them exploded. Hathaway dropped Gabby's arm to shield his body from the rain of glass. Jagged shards rained down on Gabby's neck and scalp as Yann's shaggy coat shook off the bits, like a dog casting off water. Hathaway came up out of his hunched stance with both swords drawn, and Gabby, ignoring the raw sting of her sliced skin, bounded across the room for the low table.

Yann's screeches and Hathaway's grunts of exertion were a tidal wave, pushing her forward. Gabby dove for the crossbow. Her heart sank. The bloody thing hadn't been loaded! In her haste, Gabby knocked the bolt, the net tightly wound and ready for loading, onto the floor. She lunged for it as Yann's next grating shriek thundered directly behind her. The Chimera had beaten his way past Hathaway and now stood at the arm of the sofa, the corvite's vacant birdcage directly underneath him, the dagger still embedded in his chest.

With unreasonable calm and unnatural strength, Gabby yanked the crossbow string into locking position. Yann's beak darted forward in a pecking jab, and Gabby braced herself, ready to smash the empty crossbow into his beak.

But another object smashed into Yann first. And then another. Books, Gabby realized as a third volume, this one thick as a dictionary, rammed into his neck.

"Stay away from her, you big ugly bird!"

Gabby gasped as Mama chucked another book at Yann, distracting the Chimera long enough for her to slam the wound-up net into place. She heard the satisfying click, raised the crossbow, and pulled the trigger. The kick of the release knocked Gabby off her feet, and as the net went sprawling through the air, she crashed backward onto the floor. The net spun open as Mama hurled one last book at Yann, striking him in the eye. The silvery mesh slapped down over Yann's head and back. Though the net didn't drape entirely over his outstretched wings, it didn't matter. He shrieked as the mercurite-dipped mesh flattened him, the rim of the net springing spikes that drove into Constantine's parquet floor. The tips of Yann's wings, left outside the perimeter, were pinned into place as well.

Gabby heard the bend and twist of metal as the birdcage

disappeared under Yann's thrashing body, and then another, sharper snap and the distinctive peal of shattering glass.

"Gabriella!" Mama dropped her next heavy text and rushed toward her.

"Mama," she breathed. "That was . . . that was *brilliant*!"

Mama reached for her arm and helped her to her feet.

"Well done, Lady Brickton," Hathaway groaned as he stumbled against the back of the sofa, clutching his bloodied arm to his stomach. The sleeve of his shirt had been flayed open, his skin underneath as well.

Gabby felt Mama stiffen. "I desire no compliments from you, sir."

Hathaway glowered before turning to see the Chimera, sealed beneath the net, a puddle of blood seeping out beneath the spiked rim. For the briefest moment, Gabby puzzled over the blood— she hadn't mortally injured him with the dagger, and the net wouldn't kill, only immobilize. And then the color of the blood registered. Cherry-red. Not black, as a gargoyle's blood would have been.

Hathaway's strangled outburst put everything into place. He started toward the captured Chimera with a look of pure shock but drew up short of actually reaching for the net. The blood streaming out from under Yann was neither gargoyle nor human. It was angel blood. The jars had been inside the portmanteau Hugh had perched his birdcage upon earlier.

"Oh dear," Gabby said, unable to hold back a smile. "That is quite unfortunate for you."

The Directorate representative made a low growl in his throat. He turned his back on her and stormed out of the library.

Grayson bypassed the exit to the tower's first level and continued up the stairwell, toward the second. It had been less than a five-minute climb to this point, but that was plenty of time for Marco to home in on Ingrid's peril.

The gargoyle was frantically flapping his wings as he circled the pillar, searching for a break in the iron that caged the stairwell. Grayson ignored him and took a glance back at his sister instead. His hand still shackled her elbow in an effort to keep her from running away and to help pull her up the steps.

Ingrid's deep blue eyes met his. She'd said nothing since he'd told her he was taking her to Axia. Rather than ask a slew of questions, his sister was apparently trying to determine his course of action on her own. He doubted she would ever succeed, and they only had another few minutes before reaching the second level, where Axia waited.

"I'm supposed to be convincing you to give up your angel blood willingly," Grayson said, more winded than he'd have liked.

Ingrid lifted her chin. Grayson saw a spark of understanding.

"Axia bought it?" she asked, taking the next few steps in a short burst of energy.

He slowed. "Bought what?"

Ingrid peered out at Marco, who continued his dizzying circuit around the pillar.

"That I still have some of her blood inside of me, and that there is more elsewhere," she said. "We just needed to get close to her, and then Vander was going to capture her with Gabby's net."

He narrowed his eyes. Gabby's net? What on earth was that?

Ingrid shook her head. "Never mind! It's not going to work up here. Vander can't get a clear shot, not with all this ironwork." She struggled against his grasp. "We can't go up, Grayson. We have to get Axia down onto the ground."

Grayson put more pressure in his fingers and Ingrid yelped. "She won't come down. She isn't a fool."

Ingrid huffed as they spun onto yet another section of steps. "Then what do we do? Why are you even here?"

Grayson loosened his grip. "I have a plan. And like I said, I need you to trust me."

Ingrid made a little annoyed growl while gasping for air. "You don't need to ask. Of course I trust you. I just want to know what you plan to do."

They had nearly made it to the thin waist of the Iron Lady. They'd be at the second level within moments.

"I can't tell you everything, there isn't time. And there are too many ears," he said. As if on cue, a corvite wheeled through the gaps in the iron pillar, most likely to tease Marco. "It's going to seem bad, Ingrid. But you know me." He wished he could stop and look her in the eye. There wasn't time. "You know that I'd do anything to make things right. To fix this."

He knew he wasn't making sense, but being vague was both deliberate and necessary. If this was going to work, Ingrid needed to react convincingly in front of Axia. She needed to appear horrified. And truth be told, she was an awful actress.

"Grayson, I'm afraid." Their feet slammed onto the metal steps, drumming up an echo that nearly drowned out her voice. "I don't know what you're planning, but you should know that Axia is faster than before. She has the blood of a severix demon—"

He hushed her when he saw the turnoff for the second level up the next flight of steps.

"Trust your big brother," he said.

"By a whole six minutes," she muttered as they turned onto the second level. He tugged gently on her hair, which was loose around her shoulders.

Their footsteps clanged against the iron platform. Grayson suppressed the amusement the old argument usually brought him—Ingrid had been griping about her status as the younger twin for ages. Had the situation been different, Grayson would have kept at it, asking her if it was six minutes to the hour, or if she thought that climb up the stairs had lasted less than six minutes.

But his wistful grin couldn't withstand the stench of Axia's hellhounds. They greeted Grayson and Ingrid in front of the stairwell.

Wind from the elevation whipped at Grayson's coat and trousers, batting his hair back and forth into his eyes. With one hand still clutching Ingrid's arm, he reached into his trouser pocket and closed his fingers around the needle and syringe. The glass barrel had gone cold.

Ingrid tensed under his hand. He felt her nerves and his as a bubbly sensation in his chest, heard the change in her breathing. When this was all over, Grayson intended to make up for lost time with his sister. Walking so close beside her as the hellhounds led them to the outer rim of the platform, along the promenade, felt natural. For the first time in a long time, he didn't feel so alone.

Marco appeared on the promenade railing, but the gargoyle made no attempt to rip into the hellhounds. Not yet, at least. That would change within a minute or two, Grayson figured.

"You have come to me to strike an accord, Ingrid Waverly?" Axia's silky voice preceded her hooded figure, which emerged from the curve along the gallery walkway ahead. The sun had slipped beneath the horizon, and the smoke from the fires raging unchecked around the city consumed whatever light dusk usually granted. Below, the spectacle continued, the esplanade having filled with more Alliance and gargoyles.

"I'll give you back your angel blood." Ingrid's hand opened to present a glass vial she must have been clutching the entire climb. Her arm trembled and her voice lacked confidence. Good. Axia would prefer it that way.

"Take it. There is more. If you cease these attacks, it's yours. If you do not, it will be used against you," Ingrid said.

Axia had not pushed back her hood, but if the lazy sway of her robes was any indication of her expression, she was not intimidated.

"I believe you do have my blood, though not within your

veins," the fallen angel said. Ingrid shifted uneasily under Grayson's hand.

"Of course it is in my veins."

Like Grayson had already considered: an awful actress.

"It is not. And since it is not and that small chalice you present to me now is but a token of your false greeting, I have but one last offer to make you," Axia said, finished playing the game Ingrid was so clearly losing.

He felt his sister shudder. "I want nothing from you."

"The world is going to burn, Ingrid Waverly. However, pledge your fealty to me here, now, and you will know only safety."

It was time.

Grayson released Ingrid's arm and stepped toward Axia. It was a carefully measured step, one that would not alarm the two hellhounds at the fallen angel's side. His twin, however, lurched forward, attempting to hold him back. He jerked his arm out of her feeble grasp and dropped to one knee before Axia's rippling blue robe.

"Your brother has already made his accord with me."

"No . . . no, he hasn't," Ingrid said, though Grayson detected her uncertainty as he bowed his head before Axia. A show of devotion. Of fealty.

His stomach in knots, Grayson waited. And then Axia gave him exactly what he needed. She extended her hand and touched him on the shoulder. He moved slowly, clasping his free hand over hers. Her hand was hidden, once again, within her robe, but the fabric was thin. It would be easy to pierce.

"Grayson, stop!" Ingrid shouted.

Axia began to laugh. She would be distracted, at least for a second. Grayson started to pull the syringe from his pocket. Marco, his talons scraping the high metal railing of the promenade as he grew restless, screeched. Damn it.

Grayson felt Axia's hand tense; start to pull away. The edges of her robe began to glow, golden light seeping out from the hem, from the two panels crossed and bound by a rope belt. The iron floor quaked as Marco slammed onto it, felled, Grayson knew, by Axia's power. He had to do it now.

Grayson moved fast. He clenched his fingers around Axia's hand, drew out the needle, and, holding her firm, stabbed at her arm. He felt resistance as the needle sank into her flesh. Grayson pressed the plunger hard, emptying as much of the mersian blood as he could before she, or her hounds, could stop him. But in the next second, Grayson toppled forward. Axia had vanished, the needle ripped out of his hand.

Marco roared as he surged up, freed by Axia's momentary loss of control. Grayson flattened himself to the grime-covered floor as the gargoyle skimmed overhead, his target now standing deeper within the tower. Grayson watched as a second Axia appeared to the left of Marco, then a third to his right; the one Marco had been going for was quickly fading. Ingrid had tried to warn him that Axia was fast, but not that she could make copies of herself.

"Grayson!" Ingrid shouted. He pushed himself to his feet and saw that a hellhound had backed Ingrid up against a support beam.

"Get away from her!" Grayson shouted as Axia's copies appeared in a dizzying circle around him.

Marco chased the fallen angel, his talons slicing through mist instead of flesh. The gargoyle roared his frustration, his wings cutting dangerously close to Grayson as he swerved after Axia.

The hellhound cornering Ingrid turned its head toward Grayson, its red lantern eyes narrowing. The beast turned its body and came at him. But then a black-scaled gargoyle with only one wing appeared out of nowhere, colliding with the hound and sending the beast off course. The hound recovered and pushed back at the one-winged gargoyle, blocking Grayson from reaching Ingrid's side once again. Behind him, Marco shrieked. As Grayson turned, he saw that one of the other hellhounds had raked its claws through his wing, snagging on one of the bony ridges.

Grayson was noticing that every last Axia had faded when the third hellhound rammed into him—and a shock of brutal pain tore through his stomach. He heard Ingrid's scream at the same second he saw the hellhound's fang protruding from his abdomen.

Grayson knew he was going to die before his feet left the floor. Before the hellhound, its hot breath gusting against his back, bounded toward the railing. And then they were over it, out into the air, falling, Grayson slipping off of the beast's long fang. Ingrid screamed his name as the wind took him, the ground rushing up at a mesmerizing speed. He had seconds, he knew. Seconds to say a final prayer that he'd made a difference tonight.

Grayson closed his eyes, ready.

CHAPTER TWENTY-EIGHT

Luc caught Ingrid around the waist as her frenzied screams for Grayson grated through his skull. He shrieked for Marco to follow, and with one last lash of his tail toward the hellhound he'd been battling, launched himself over the railing. His single wing hadn't been strong enough to beat his way up to the second level—he'd had to climb the stairwell set alongside the tracks for the lift—and it wasn't able to glide them safely to the ground now, either.

Marco's talons clamped around the bony wing stump and leveled out Luc's twirling fall. The Wolf guided them to the ground, Ingrid still screaming her brother's name.

Grayson had hit a few yards from where Luc and Marco touched down. Luc spun around and unfurled his wing, wanting to shield Ingrid from the sight that had just cleaved through Luc like a dull axe.

"Don't look," he said, though his vocal cords mangled the words. Had Ingrid understood them, she wouldn't have obeyed.

She writhed in Luc's grasp and he let her go, not wanting his talons to accidentally slide along her arms in his attempt to hold her still.

She jerked out to the side, beyond his wing—and saw.

Ingrid fell forward, one arm braced across her stomach as her face crumpled, her mouth opening to a silent scream. Luc couldn't protect her, not from this. He could do nothing more than stand beside her as she stumbled to her brother's broken body, his arms and legs splayed at odd angles, his head turned toward Ingrid's approach. His eyes were open and empty, and Ingrid crashed onto her knees at his side. She dug the heels of her palms into her temples, drew in a breath of air, and screamed.

Marco doubled over as her wail echoed across the Champs de Mars, her anguish cutting through the Wolf.

Luc knew this pain. He'd experienced it the wintry day Suzette's body had been delivered home, her soaked dress frozen stiff, her skin the color of ash. He'd clung to her rigid body as his parents had dissolved into shouts and sobs, the men who'd dragged her out of the Seine muttering useless apologies. Luc had rocked her, shook her, railed at her to wake up just as Ingrid was now screaming at Grayson to not be dead.

Her high, keening wail had paralyzed those in battle nearby on the esplanade, though only for a moment. The Dusters, having been released from Axia's spell, had merged back into their huddles. A new influx of Alliance fighters and Dispossessed continued to clash with the demons—gaining ground in their direction, Luc noted. They had to move, and he knew he'd have to drag Ingrid away from Grayson's side.

"Such a pity."

Axia's bellowing voice split through the battle, as clear and powerful as a bell. Luc couldn't see her, but in the next second, he felt her. The familiar weight of an angel's presence drove Luc and Marco and all gargoyles on the ground to their knees. The Dispossessed churning in the sky over the Champs de Mars plunged toward the earth.

Though the all-out battle slowed, the Alliance and demons continued to clash in intermittent bursts. A light started to brighten near the fountains of the Château d'Eau, and Luc heard a strange humming sound. The growls of hellhounds and the clicking of Drainer wings were closer, though. Stuck like this, Luc and the other gargoyles would be at the mercy of whatever demon wished to tear into them.

"I grow weary of this resistance," Axia said, and straining to crane his neck, Luc saw her gliding down the center of the esplanade. She had pushed back her hood, and though he couldn't look directly at her, he saw that she had changed from what she'd been in the Underneath. Her body had become more human. "You have all been so accommodating," she went on, "to come here and allow me to extinguish it."

She glowed, though not like Irindi, whose figure was always completely hidden within her shuddering ball of white light. Axia merely shimmered, as if she had conjured stage lights to hover over her. Her hellhound guards, still at her sides, enclosed her like two granite walls. Vander needed a better shot than that.

The strange humming sound had grown steadily louder, and Luc realized Ingrid had ceased screaming. She'd ceased sobbing. He curled around to see her. Ingrid no longer knelt beside Grayson's body. She stood beside it, facing up the esplanade. Her arms hung limply at her side, her chin tucked into her neck, her wrathful eyes locked on Axia.

Ingrid wasn't breathing. She didn't need air. She didn't need anything but vengeance, hot, ruthless, and swift. When she had seen her twin lying still on the cold ground, something deep inside her had splintered off. A part of her that she would never get back. It had belonged to Grayson, and he had taken it with him.

He was dead. He was *gone*. The pain was too much, too uncontrollable, to be real.

Ingrid glared up the esplanade, her gaze unwavering as Axia drew to a halt. Grayson had stuck Axia with one of Vander's needles, injected her with mersian blood. It had been his plan, the one he'd asked her to trust blindly. He'd meant to cancel out the angel's severix powers and failed. Ingrid felt the last echoes of his sorrow, his disappointment. One final shared emotion.

And then Ingrid started to shake. Her body trembled. Not with cold or fury or shock, but with something else. Something much more useful. Behind the fallen angel, the lights inside the Palace of Electricity had brightened. Hugh Dupuis had done it. The generators inside had hummed to life, and inside Ingrid, her lectrux blood flared.

"Your brother could have been magnificent," Axia said, her voice ringing out crisp and clear even as Alliance fighters and Underneath creatures continued to clash and the gargoyles, pinned to the ground, shrieked in frustration.

Ingrid moved forward, burning beneath her skin. The current rolled and twisted, licking down her arms and up again, curling past her shoulders. Whether because of natural depletion, grief, or the newly churning power underneath the Palace of Electricity's glass ceiling, Vander's mersian blood no longer held sway. The electricity fanned out into her chest, coursing down her spine into her legs. This was her fury, raw and untamed.

As Ingrid continued up the esplanade, lights began popping on inside the exhibition buildings. The electrical charge in the air notched, and Ingrid reached for it. She breathed it in. Gathered it close.

One of Axia's hounds grew restless and lunged. Ingrid didn't flinch. She simply held out her hand. Vines of electricity intercepted the beast and sent it sprawling backward. It had been so easy, so effortless, and Ingrid glided on toward Axia, her steps deliberate and controlled.

"You attempt to challenge *me*, Ingrid Waverly?" Axia threw her voice along the esplanade, where the subdued gargoyles all suddenly shot to their feet. No sooner had they lifted their wings for flight than they came crashing down again.

A weakness in Axia's control. A ripple in her concentration.

The electric current had dammed up in Ingrid's throat, and she couldn't speak. She knew that at any moment Axia could reinstate her control over the Dusters—and that she herself was no longer safe from it.

"You believe your demon blood can best my own?" The fallen angel threw her arms up, her palms facing out—a signal for the rest of her demons to hold off. "I accept the challenge. My blood against yours. When I am finished, I will weed you out."

Ingrid kept her concentration on the lights brightening the exhibition halls and on the fountainheads, now turned on and jetting water. Behind her, Ingrid felt the charge of thousands of lightbulbs as they winked on along the tower.

She held her arms out at her sides—*pulled*—and threw her arms forward. Lightning cracked from her fingertips with a blinding flash. But Axia had cast herself aside, leaving behind a fade, unscathed. The gargoyles rose and fell as the fallen angel's attention slipped, then strengthened. Her wild laughter came from a few yards to the left.

"I am faster than lightning," Axia trilled before severing herself yet again. She reappeared directly beside Ingrid, who unleashed another coil of lightning.

The Dispossessed surged up and crashed down yet again as the lightning burned through Axia's fade.

"Faster than your brother's fall," Axia whispered in Ingrid's ear.

Ingrid whipped around. The mention of her brother eviscerated her frustration and replenished her fury. Briars of electricity sizzled from her fingers, toward Axia, who predictably, cast a fade and vanished.

Ingrid was about to turn and search for her yet again when the fade did something different. It didn't evaporate like mist. It became solid again. It wasn't a fade. It was still Axia. Her smile wilted. Axia tried to sever herself once more, started to disappear—Ingrid saw the blurred lines of her form stretching out into another direction. But her body snapped right back, slamming into her fade, like an elastic band snapping back to its starting point.

Ingrid held Axia's confounded stare. Her demon power wouldn't work. *The mersian blood.* Grayson *hadn't* failed. He'd done it!

"Vander—now!"

She heard Nolan's shout and saw Luc and Marco pitch forward, released from Axia's hold, just as a howling wind whipped through the esplanade. It thrashed the branches of the trees and sprayed the fountain water in angled sheets, the icy mist flecking Ingrid's face.

No longer laughing, Axia threw down the full force of her angelic power, buckling Luc and Marco at the knees. Ingrid expected to feel the ground quaking, to see blackness seeping into the corners of her eyes as Axia dragged her under the Dusters' spell. But Ingrid could still see, still stand. And then she remembered what Axia had said: *I will weed you out.*

A hellhound, a Drainer, and a rattilus bore down on Ingrid, their orders to hold back terminated. She could attempt to stun them all, the way she'd done to that first hellhound. But they would just keep coming, one demon after another, while Axia held the gargoyles in submission. Ingrid knew she could not electrocute every last demon here.

They had come here for Axia. *Grayson* had come here for Axia.

Time in the Champs de Mars slowed, and though the demons were nearing, Ingrid didn't see them. She saw Grayson, the two of them as children. They were sitting in the grass, comparing their birthmarks; together in Hyde Park, Grayson playfully nudging her closer to the Serpentine River; in their father's library, building a domino line out of books; at Victoria Station before he left for Paris last fall, twirling her in a circle, trying to make her dizzy so she wouldn't see his anxiety; Grayson, in the Underneath, bite marks riddling his skin.

Grayson. Dead.

And there it was again. The sob that poured through her chest and into her throat, eddied through her head, going everywhere but out of her mouth. She dragged in air, gulping it, trying to release the scream. To release the pain.

The demons bearing down on her were obliterated by blessed silver before they could touch her, but there were more on their way. Ingrid paid them no attention. What she saw were the bulbs along the Eiffel Tower, brightening, straining, and then bursting. The lights within the exhibition halls flickered and went out. Behind her, the screeching wheels of the generators revved to a deafening whine before clanking and crashing to a halt.

Ingrid raised her arms and finally, *finally* screamed as fire raced over her palms. An orb of lightning slammed into Axia, throwing her back. Her body seized in the air, the ropes of electricity wrapping her, holding her in place while Ingrid continued to scream, continued to drain the current from every last corner of her body.

Released from the fallen angel's hold, Luc and Marco rose and collided with the hellhound and appendius that were seconds away from tearing into Ingrid. She watched everything unfolding as if she were merely an observer, untouchable. Lightning shivered from Axia to the iron tower and then back to the angel, who hurtled toward the ground as a net twined around her convulsing body. The spikes along the rim of the angelic diffuser net shot into the grass. The mesh netting sealed to Axia, who was still shivering in blue and white spits of electricity. Vander had hit his target. They'd captured her.

Ingrid's arms went limp, her ears rang, and a dark tunnel closed around her vision. She didn't feel anything as she hit the ground. The last thing she saw was the top of the tower, a gargoyle perched on its spire.

CHAPTER TWENTY-NINE

Paris was supposed to be beautiful in April. The city's greening had started to paint over the destruction left behind by Axia's Harvest. It had been one week. One week since the world had exploded with news of the madness in Paris, a near-apocalyptic event. The citizens who had fled had since returned, and tourists for the exposition had come early and in droves. Surviving an invasion of bloodthirsty demons had seemed to inspire a need to celebrate, and everyone wanted to join in, hear stories, relive the horror.

Some enterprising artist had started hawking papier-mâché hellhounds and gargoyles near the Champs de Mars, churches hadn't seen higher attendances in years, and there were even guided tours cropping up, highlighting the places where the most savage deaths had taken place. People weren't repulsed by the demon invasion at all. They were absolutely giddy.

It made Gabby ill. She'd purchased a hellhound from one such street vendor, dropped it on the pavement, and crushed it under her boot heel. She'd gotten stares and a cry of disappointment from the vendor, but she had kicked the paper hellhound into the gutter and stormed off.

The Harvest was over, but it had taken everything.

And no, as it turned out, Paris wasn't beautiful in April. The ground was just thawed enough for them to bury Grayson, however, and that was what they were doing that morning.

Clouds, platinum-lined with the hint of another spring rain, hung low above the rectory cemetery. Gabby stood on the soft grass, still damp from the rains that were melting the snow and exposing new, pale green grasses underneath. She and Ingrid had wound their arms together and laced their fingers tightly. A bracing wind buffeted their black silk mourning dresses and black velvet capes. Before coming out to the graveside burial, Gabby had put on one of her hats with a slanted veil. She'd tugged out the pins and chucked the thing across her bedroom before breaking down into gasping sobs.

Her brother wasn't supposed to be dead. He wasn't supposed to have left them, not now, not yet. Not like this.

Mama stood to Gabby's right, with Papa there to shore up Mama's other side. He'd arrived two nights after the Harvest ended, and though his eyes had been red-rimmed, Gabby hadn't yet seen him cry. She'd only heard him. That first night, and every night since, whenever Gabby passed the study door, she heard soft, muffled sobs. She pictured her stoic father, the man who had disowned Grayson, slouching in his chair, bawling into his monogrammed handkerchief. That was all any of them had been doing.

Ingrid had spent the week in her room. Mama and Papa had turned their heads when Luc arrived each morning and slipped up to Ingrid's bedroom to hold her the day through. Gabby had stayed with Mama during the day and Ingrid at night, when Luc left. As she listened to Vander, who was standing at the head of the dug grave, reading from the book of Psalms, she felt exhaustion weighting her.

Theirs was a small crowd of Alliance, Dispossessed, and those who knew their secrets standing around the casket, which had already been lowered into the freshly dug ground. Nolan stood behind her, his hand lifting every now and then to the small of her back. Rory was with him, his dagger vest replaced by a more respectful black waistcoat, jacket, and tie. Hugh Dupuis had delayed his departure for London until after the burial, and he kept beside Rory—a place in which Gabby, and a few others, had noticed he could usually be found.

And then there was Chelle. She stood between Rory and Nolan, trembling like a reed in a rushing stream. Nolan and Vander had broken her out of the basement at Hôtel Bastian, and when they'd told her about Grayson, she had done something neither of them had ever seen: she had collapsed. She'd cried in great, heaving sobs, and Nolan had later told Gabby that he'd needed to carry Chelle out of the basement. That she'd been inconsolable since.

So Grayson had gone and fallen in love. And yet he'd only known that first taste of it. Gabby had tried putting herself in Chelle's place, imagined Nolan being taken from her now, before they could even really begin. It had made Gabby cling to him when he'd next visited the rectory.

Finishing with the Psalms, Vander closed the Bible he'd been reading and adjusted his wire spectacles. He was a reverend now, though he wasn't wearing anything that would mark him as such. Just his usual threadbare tweed.

"I would like to say something more before we commit Grayson's body to the earth. Something not found in here," he said, lifting the Bible in explanation.

Ingrid's arm kept shaking, and Gabby wished Luc could be standing on her sister's other side. He, Marco, and Gaston, accompanied by Monsieur Constantine, stood across the open grave. Luc's eyes were fastened on Ingrid, watching her, ready. But the intimacy of standing so close would not have been borne here, in public view.

"I met Grayson when he first came to Paris. He was here alone, trying to prepare this old rectory for when his sisters and mother would arrive. He admitted to me that he was nervous, that perhaps he'd made a mistake listening to Constantine and purchasing the abbey." Vander paused and sent Constantine an apologetic glance. "Grayson told me about Waverly House, and the conditions his sisters and mother, whom I hadn't yet met, were used to. This place would be a change. A drastic change, and he worried it wouldn't be good enough."

Gabby listened, rapt. This was Grayson before the Underneath. Grayson before she'd known he'd changed. Nolan slid his hand against her back, a sturdy reminder that he was there.

"I asked him, half joking, if his sisters were really that spoiled." This time Vander sent Gabby and Ingrid the apologetic glances. "He looked at me, and more serious than I'd yet seen him to be, he said his sisters deserved to be happy here. He said he'd tear down this place and put up a new Waverly House if that was what it took."

Ingrid's fingers tightened around Gabby's. She knew Ingrid's chin was quivering just as violently as her own, the tears coursing freely down her cheeks.

"I knew right then," Vander continued, "that Grayson was the kind of man who would do whatever it took to take care of the people he loved. He walked into Axia's nest knowing he probably wouldn't leave it alive." Vander crouched before the grave, his toes crumbling a bit of dirt. The clumps landed on the varnished tiger-oak casket. "He went anyway. He went for all of us."

Gabby released Ingrid's hand as Luc threw caution aside and broke from his indomitable hold across the grave. He walked around Vander, to Ingrid, and brought her against his chest.

He began to lead Ingrid away, her broken sobs knifing through Gabby.

Nolan touched her shoulders and brought her closer to him. If Ingrid could seek solace in the arms of a gargoyle, then she could very well do the same with a demon hunter. She still snuck a glance up at her father as she allowed Nolan to guide her away from Grayson's grave.

Lord Brickton stared at his son's casket, his wife shuddering in his arms. The insignificance of everything else hit Gabby, and she sank into Nolan's warm side.

"Cousin," Rory whispered, tagging Nolan's elbow. He glanced toward Chelle, who had seated herself on the flat top of an old gravestone. Her shoulders and back heaved and shook. "Ye know yer the only one who can calm her."

Nolan took a deep breath, his arm taut around Gabby. "Rory . . . stay with Chelle for just a little while and I'll be there when—"

Gabby pressed her palm flat against Nolan's chest. "Go. It's all right."

Nolan would return to her side in a few minutes. Grayson would never return to Chelle's.

He kissed her forehead and ceded Gabby's arm to Rory. "Don't get into trouble."

He walked across the grass, between the scattered gravestones, toward Chelle. Gabby was grateful for Rory's muscular arm. There weren't many people here to say their goodbyes to Grayson, but those who were had proven their loyalty to one another.

"Are you going back to London?" Gabby asked, keeping her voice low.

Rory's bicep flexed underneath his black suit jacket. "Aye, *laoch*."

"I'm sure Carver will be thrilled to see you again," she said, remembering Hugh's gargoyle.

Rory smiled, confirming Gabby's speculation with his usual poise.

"Hugh'll have a time of it tryin' to keep Hathaway and the rest of the Directorate off his scent," Rory added, switching tracks.

In the craze and chaos following the battle in the Champs de Mars, the Daicrypta doyen, with Rory's help and a few gargoyles as well, had transported Axia's netted and incapacitated body to the abandoned Montmartre mansion owned by his father. He'd hooked Axia up to the ancient draining machinery housed in the little outbuilding behind the courtyard and drained every last drop of her blood. Had they allowed the Alliance to drag her body away, Hathaway would have had the same thing done, most likely on the machine Nolan and Vander had been building at Hôtel Bastian. Gabby didn't know what Hugh had done with the blood, but she trusted him. Whatever his plans, he had no designs against the Dispossessed, as Hathaway did.

According to Rory, Hugh had given Axia's desiccated remains to the horde of gargoyles waiting in the Daicrypta courtyard. The gargoyles had disposed of her, and with relish.

Hans and Hathaway had suspected Rory's deceit, but with no evidence, what could they do? They certainly couldn't charge him with treason, the way they'd threatened Nolan. Of course, the angelic net *had* worked, and there was no doubt that Nolan's actions had only helped bring Axia and her Harvest to an end. There would be no trial against him in Rome. When he'd told Gabby the news, she'd dissolved into new tears. Better tears. And they had felt good.

"I'm going to miss you," Gabby said, squeezing Rory's arm.

"Ah, *laoch,* I dinna think ye'll be missin' me long."

She released his arm and peered up at him. "Why do you say that?"

"Quinns have a way of stayin' close."

Gabby stepped away. "But I'm not a Quinn."

A little smile lifted the corner of Rory's lips. "I suspect Nolan'll take care of that in time."

Gabby, flushed and speechless, let her mouth hang open as Rory bowed and walked away. She didn't have a moment to think about what Rory had said before a hand settled on her waist. Nolan's forearm braced her back as he returned her to his side.

"What's my cousin smirking about?" he asked, looking after Rory. And then, upon seeing Gabby's shocked expression, added, "What did he say to you?"

Oh no. She wasn't about to divulge *that*. Gabby straightened her posture and searched for Chelle. Vander was leading her away, toward the abbey.

"Will she be all right?" she asked.

Nolan reached for the collar of Gabby's cape and drew the panels tighter together for her. "We're talking about Chelle."

"But she loved him," Gabby said, and then realized something. There were words—significant words—she hadn't yet said. Gabby lifted her gloved hand and caressed Nolan's freshly shaven cheek. "I love you."

He stared, gone still at her confession. He had to have already known, but he looked as if she'd just told him the location of the Holy Grail. Or, on second thought, he stared at her the way he had in London, in her room, when he'd confessed that he wouldn't leave her side.

"Gabriella," he whispered. If they had not been where they were, surrounded by sadness and gravestones, she knew he would have swept her up into one of his kisses. The ones she dreamed about at night. Instead, Nolan took a long breath and started walking her slowly back toward the rectory.

"Your oaths ceremony will be in Rome," he said softly. "As soon as you think we should leave."

Hathaway hadn't been able to save his precious angel blood

from underneath Yann—who had ultimately suffered the same fate as Axia—but the Directorate representative had witnessed Gabby's bravery and acknowledged her hand in capturing Axia. Though without genuine excitement in the request, Hathaway had asked her to Rome.

"I don't think I should leave Mama yet. Or Ingrid," she answered.

"Don't forget yourself, lass," Nolan said. "You lost him too."

She leaned her head against his shoulder as they walked. He nuzzled the crown of her head.

"I should probably stick around as well. For Chelle," Nolan said, then tacked on, "And Vander."

They were mourning Grayson, yes, but Vander had lost something else. It was no longer a secret, not within the Alliance or the Dispossessed, that Ingrid had fallen in love with Luc, and he with her. Things were still tense and uncertain, but so far, the Dispossessed had not acted against Luc in any way. It could have been because he was their new elder. Marco had confided in Gabby earlier that the majority of the gargoyles seemed willing and open to a new way. Or, Gabby considered, they could have been willing because of who Luc's chosen human was. After Ingrid had unleashed that electrical firestorm into Axia in the Champs de Mars, no gargoyle could believe it wise to cross her.

"Gabby." Nolan pulled up short of the rectory's front door. "I know you were having second thoughts about joining the Alliance, and if you decide not to . . . if you don't want to go through with it . . ." He cradled her scarred cheek in his palm. He always reached for that side of her face. Always ran his fingers along the track of scars. He loved every inch of her. Even her flaws.

"Whether you're Alliance or not, I'm staying with you, lass."

She leaned into his touch and sighed. "We are a good team, aren't we?"

"The finest. Although I think I'll have to be even more disciplined than I was before. I anticipate being more interested in kissing you than hunting demons."

Gabby laughed, and she imagined Grayson would like the sound of that more than he would all the sobbing. So she laughed again. "I don't think my father will approve of that."

Nolan scowled. "Your father and I will have to come to an understanding, then, because I intend to kiss you every day for the rest of my life. Starting now."

Without checking to see if they were alone, Nolan took her mouth in a fast, fervent kiss. After a week of feeling cold and lost, it made Gabby feel alive again. Grayson would want her to live— he'd died so that she might.

This was her life. The one she wanted. And for Grayson, for all he was and all he could have been, she would live it.

Ingrid shouldn't have been smiling. She shouldn't have been feeling so happy and proud. But as the abbey's fan-vaulted ceilings captured the animated voices of the gallery's first patrons and organ music breathed from the copper pipes, she couldn't stop.

The gallery was filled to overflowing. Opening night, so far, was a smashing success. There were oil portraits and bronze sculptures alongside woven tapestries and Impressionistic landscapes, and even works by that awful painter of women's dimpled backsides whom she and Gabby had so unfortunately met at a salon once.

Ingrid stood mostly to the side, avoiding conversation and waving away Marco when he came around in his crisp tuxedo offering champagne and colorful commentary on the well-heeled guests. His mood had improved in the days following an unexpected visit from Irindi. The angel had repaired Marco's back, erasing the burns that Axia had wrongly inflicted. The mending had been almost as agonizing as the initial burns, Marco had

said, and he'd gleefully shucked his shirt for Ingrid and Gabby—
and unfortunately Mama—to show off the return of his smooth,
bare skin. Mama had been quite flummoxed, which Ingrid imagined had been Marco's intent.

The gallery opening had been delayed by a week, for obvious
reasons, but more tourists for the exposition had begun flowing
into Paris. Mama had hired an entirely new staff to replace those
who had abandoned the rectory, and her energy had returned. As
brokenhearted as she was, she'd whisked into the dining room
one morning for breakfast, Papa seated at the head of the table
with his paper, and made an announcement.

"Grayson worked tirelessly to get this gallery under way for
me," she'd said, fighting back tears. "I will not disappoint him."

And that had been that.

Ingrid caught sight of her mother now, milling about the
nave, her black bombazine dress the only indication that she
was in mourning. Papa stood with her, and though he looked
as starchy as ever, at least he was there. The grin fixed on her
mother's lips as she spoke and laughed looked genuine to Ingrid,
and her own smile felt real, too.

"It's nice to see that."

Ingrid startled, stepping aside and brushing against the
carved wooden frieze of the twelve apostles near the transept
door. Vander had joined her, his gaze following hers.

"Mama's smile?" Ingrid guessed.

Vander cut his eyes to hers. "And yours."

She hadn't seen him since Grayson's funeral. She'd missed
him but understood why he'd stayed away.

"So, Reverend, are you enjoying the gallery?" she asked,
stressing his new title.

It earned her a groan.

"What? No clerical robes yet?" she asked, still teasing.

"I think I can follow my calling wearing my usual getup,"
he replied.

"What about your crossbow and sword?" Ingrid asked. "They're hardly reverend-like."

Vander patted the side of his long tweed coat. "They *are* blessed, remember."

Ingrid resisted the urge to laugh and flirt. Vander had always made it so easy for her. But that was over now, and Vander, seeming to sense her unease, took a step away.

"How are things going with Constantine?" she asked.

Her teacher had started taking in Dusters at Clos du Vie—both the original seedlings and the Dusters they had created when under Axia's spell. People like Chelle.

"We've got a regular laboratory going on over there," he answered.

He and Constantine, through correspondence with Hugh, were learning how to proliferate Vander's mersian blood. The draining machinery Nolan and Vander had been working on had been moved from Hôtel Bastian to Clos du Vie, and with Hugh's aid, it wouldn't be much longer until it was in full working order. For now, those who could safely take injections were receiving them, and those whose blood would clot when matched with Vander's, like Chelle, were learning to adapt to their new powers.

"So you're an ordained scientist," Ingrid said.

"I wouldn't want to be too conventional," he replied, and then, before she could respond, turned to face her. "Can we talk? Outside?"

Ingrid took a last glance into the crowd. She couldn't find her mother, but she did see Marco staring at her from beside a marble sculpture of a well-endowed Greek god. *How fitting,* she thought, as she turned and led Vander outside through the transept door.

The late April night was cool, a rain having just fallen. She smelled the spring-rich air as they walked toward the courtyard fountain, burbling for the first time since Ingrid had come to Paris.

The silence between them had started to grow awkward, when Vander finally spoke. And so like him, he swiftly cut to the heart of things.

"If a life with him is what you want, if it will make you happy, then I'll never say another word about it."

He wasn't roiling mad, as he'd been in her room the time he'd found her with Luc. He didn't corner her or rail at her the way he had then, teetering on the verge of losing control. He was just determined now.

"You know . . ." Vander gathered a breath. "You know that I love you."

Ingrid had been crying for weeks, and not just over losing Grayson. She was exhausted, though, and she didn't want to cry any more.

"And I love you," she whispered. "But I can't have you both."

Vander stuck his hands in his pockets and nodded. "And right now you choose him."

Right now. Right now and forever. "So long as he exists."

He nodded again, though to himself, as if conducting his own conversation in his mind. "Luc saved my life. I don't think he would have done that if you didn't love me." Vander met her eyes, which were rebelling against her will and filling with tears again. "That says something about him."

Vander leaned forward and kissed Ingrid on her forehead, his hands still in his pockets, unable to touch her. He then turned and walked away, toward the hedgerow. He didn't look back.

Ingrid stared after him. Being hurt was one thing. Doing the hurting was another. She didn't know which one felt worse.

The grass squeaked under someone's approaching feet.

"Griddy?" her sister called, using the awful nickname that she had graciously abandoned lately.

She must have seen Vander disappear through the hedgerow gap. She touched Ingrid's arm. "He understands. He's hurt, but he understands. He's a reverend, for goodness' sake."

Ingrid smiled and quickly wiped her tears away with the back of her hand. The black lace glove scratched at the tender skin. She turned toward Gabby and was pleased once more to notice that her sister had not pinned on one of her veiled hats. She was still reluctant about holding her head high and meeting a stranger's gaze, but she was determined, and Ingrid was proud of her.

"Do you think the pain will ever go away?" Ingrid asked after a moment.

She trusted her sister would know that she was speaking not of Vander, but of Grayson. Gabby did.

"No," she answered. "But if we feel the pain together, we can share it. We have each other, Ingrid. And we have people who love us."

When had her little sister become so wise? Ingrid held out her hand. Gabby took it.

"Would you understand if I said I had somewhere to go right now?" Ingrid asked.

Gabby squeezed her fingers. "I've covered for you before. I believe I could do it again." She smiled and Ingrid tugged her into an embrace.

"You'll crease my dress!" Gabby complained, laughing and swatting her away. "I'll fetch Marco."

They had a proper driver now, and Marco had been relegated to strict butler duties once more. But for this particular outing, only a gargoyle would suit.

CHAPTER THIRTY

The fire breathed low in the grate, casting weak light around the front room of Lennier's apartment. *Luc's* apartment. He had to get used to calling it that. A change in furniture might help. He'd hung up drapes, at least, to block the guttering light of the fire from the many tourists who had taken to wandering inside common grounds. Luc had also given the order for the Dispossessed to come on foot rather than by air, and to stay in their human skins as often as possible. To the ignorant humans, now awakened to the existence of otherworldly monsters, demons and gargoyles were one and the same. Vincent's campaign against the Dusters in plain sight hadn't helped things.

Lengthwise on the sofa—he might keep it, he thought; the thing was comfortable—Luc paged through one of the books that Chelle, the Alliance tomboy, had delivered to his door the week before. He had felt the presence of a human and had gone to meet whoever it was, to drive them off his private property. When he'd seen Chelle in the ramshackle ballroom carrying a crate of books as heavy as she was, Luc hadn't known what to say. The girl had stopped in her tracks, conveying only a glimmer of anxiety, before demanding to know why Luc had not yet offered to carry the bloody crate for her.

They were Alliance texts: personal journals, scholarly volumes, and histories, and there were many more back in the Alliance library at Hôtel Bastian. In his rooms, Luc had dropped the crate on the sofa and turned to Chelle, who he knew despised gargoyles. Without being asked, she had launched into an explanation.

"Grayson believed there were good gargoyles. He believed in you," she'd said. And then she'd asked for his help. Since Luc was eternal and was not responsible for any humans at the moment, perhaps he would be willing to change things between the Dispossessed and the Alliance.

"If we're going to work together, we should know more about one another, correct?" she'd asked.

Luc had taken the books. He still didn't know what to make of Chelle, or whether her reception would extend to Euro-Alliance headquarters in Rome, but he liked the idea of having a purpose beyond protecting.

He angled the book's pages toward the fire, though his night vision helped him make out the ancient typeface. It seemed that at one point, the Alliance had even used a secret language as a means of communication. Luc enjoyed the idea of learning it— and then teaching it to the Alliance once more. How satisfying would that be?

He felt the chime of another gargoyle's presence at the base of his skull and closed the text. He sighed and sat up, setting the volume atop one of the several towers of books scattered throughout the front room.

He approached the door and opened it to find his visitor on the other side of the threshold, her hand poised to knock. Ingrid dropped her hand and her lips bowed into a bashful grin.

"Marco brought me," she explained, and at that moment, Luc sensed the Wolf's departure as well.

"He'll be back later," she said, still standing in the corridor. Luc came to his senses and moved aside. She stepped into the front room and stared around at the towers of books.

"Do I want to know?" she asked.

Luc closed the door. "I'll explain later. Is something wrong?"

He hadn't expected Ingrid tonight. She'd only come to common grounds once—the day of her brother's funeral. Luc hadn't wanted to leave her at the rectory, and so he'd chanced bringing her here. He'd been ready to challenge any gargoyle that dared speak out against him. None had. The few Dispossessed lounging around the courtyard fountain when Luc and Ingrid had arrived had merely glanced from human to gargoyle and bowed their heads, as if in acceptance.

Luc still wasn't completely convinced, though. It would be a long while before he would be easy with Ingrid at common grounds.

"Nothing is wrong. I just needed to see you," she said, her hand running along the tops of a few stacks of books as she walked toward the sofa.

"Isn't your mother's gallery opening happening right now?" he asked.

Ingrid paused at one stack and lifted the top book. She then crouched and tilted her head to read the spines. "These are Alliance books."

She stood and faced him before pulling off her lace gloves and opening the book she'd snatched up.

"Are you working with the Alliance? How did you get these?"

Luc said nothing, only watched the sparkle of excitement in her aubergine eyes. He had a vision then, of the two of them on the sofa, each of them reading through the stacks of books, working with the Alliance in their own way. Together. He liked it, and when Ingrid looked up from the book she'd been scanning, she saw his grin.

"What?" she asked. Then, "You haven't answered me."

"I'll tell you later."

"Why not now?" she pressed.

"Because right now I want to know why you've left the gallery opening. If your mother finds out, she'll have even more of a reason to hate me."

Lord and Lady Brickton had looked the other way when Luc visited the rectory in the days following Grayson's death, but that was over now. He couldn't imagine that Lord or Lady Brickton would seriously entertain the idea of a gargoyle's coming to call on their daughter.

Ingrid closed the book and set it down, shaking her head. "Oh, she doesn't need any more of a reason to dislike you. Finding you in my room, unclothed, was quite enough."

Luc crossed his arms and walked through the path of books toward Ingrid. "Well, at least I'm clothed. For the moment."

He liked flirting with her and seeing her flush. He liked the mystery of trying to figure out what she was thinking and feeling.

When he'd held her on her bed those days after the Champs de Mars, he'd kissed her temple, her forehead; he'd been there to comfort her. Now, with Ingrid standing before him, her misery fading, he felt the draw of her. She held his gaze, her blush rising another moment before she looked away, toward the curtained windows.

"How is your wing?" she asked.

He'd been coalescing every few days, just to see how things were progressing. The bones had grown some, along with new membrane, but the truth was, regenerating an entire wing hurt like hell.

"It will be a while," he answered. There was no point in

telling her that his back ached constantly, or that coalescing felt like breaking and then setting a bone.

Ingrid perched herself on the edge of the sofa. "What do the other Dispossessed think?"

Luc neared the fire and, though he knew it would prove dangerous, lowered himself to sit beside her.

"About my wing?"

"No." She stared into the fire and worried the lace cuff of her dress. "What do they think about me? About us?"

Things had been peaceful the past few weeks as Paris recovered from the Harvest, but Luc—and apparently Ingrid as well—was far too realistic to believe things would always stay this calm.

Perhaps it was being elder, or that his turning down Irindi's invitation to enter Heaven had spread like all gossip did amongst the gargoyles, but Luc didn't sense any immediate danger from the Dispossessed.

"Don't worry about them," he told her, allowing his knee to brush against hers. "We'll take this day by day. And you'll be protected, Ingrid. You have Marco and the Alliance. You have me."

Her knee pressed against his more ardently. "You suggested a few weeks ago . . . you said something about my being your human again. You asked me to go with you to common grounds."

Luc leaned back and rested his head against the sofa's plush cushions. He remembered that overzealous proposition. "I still want that. But it's too soon. It will be some time before I trust the rest of the Dispossessed enough to have you here."

Ingrid shifted to face him, the curves of her bodice and the tempting lines of her bare neck a distraction.

"When I reach my majority, if I haven't yet married, I can do what I wish with my inheritance." She clutched a fistful of her black moiré skirt. "I want to buy Hôtel du Maurier."

He held still. Watched the jump of her pulse in her neck.

"You said Irindi disapproved of your preference for me, but if I'm your only human charge—"

Luc sat forward. "When?"

If she bought this wreck of a home, she would have every right to be here. His territory. Her property. It would give Luc one more layer of security against any gargoyles who objected.

Ingrid's shoulders softened and her posture rounded. "When I'm twenty-one."

She was seventeen now. Christ. Four years. Luc reached for her hand and cupped it against his cheek. He then kissed the center of her palm. What was four years? "I can wait."

Ingrid closed her eyes and sank against his chest. "I can still be your human, though? Like this?"

He wrapped his arms around her waist and pulled her closer. "Always."

He knew what she was thinking. That she would get old. That he would not.

"Day by day, Ingrid," he murmured in her ear.

She moved closer to him and tucked her legs up, over his lap.

"Will you tell me now what happened with Irindi?" Her breath fanned over his collarbone and against his neck. He'd thought about that meeting in Constantine's library numerous times, but he had not once regretted his decision.

"Marco and Gaston couldn't stand, but you could," she pointed out while drawing a scrolling line with her fingertip along his neck.

He had given up heaven. And by choosing him over Vander or some other human, Ingrid was giving up a part of life Luc couldn't give her—marriage, children. A family.

Luc didn't want to lie to her. So he told her the truth about saving Vander's newly ordained skin and being forgiven, and then turning down his welcome into heaven. When he finished explaining, Ingrid was sitting up, ramrod straight, her mouth agape. Marco had glared at him with disappointment; Gaston with incredulity. Ingrid's expression was a mixture of both.

"Why? Why would you say no? Luc . . ." She grasped for words. "You . . . you can't *want* to stay a gargoyle."

"My decision didn't have anything to do with being a gargoyle. I couldn't leave, not with Axia out there, coming for you and the other Dusters. Not with the Dispossessed having just declared me their elder. Staying was the right thing to do." He circled her wrist with his hand. "I spent over three hundred years just *existing*. Not living. Not until I met you. Nothing can tempt me away from you now, Ingrid. Not even heaven."

She eased back and settled her legs over his lap once again. "I don't know what to say," she whispered. Luc heard the catch in her throat. "You gave up what every gargoyle must dream of."

He let his hand glide over her knee, down the slope of her thigh. "I only know what I dream of." Luc hitched Ingrid's hip toward him but abstained from exploring farther. He liked sitting here with her, and coalescing would bring that to an end.

A saturating light brought it to an end anyway. Irindi's white-hot glow engulfed the front room, sucking Luc from his relaxed position on the sofa and flipping Ingrid from his lap. His knees and hands slammed onto the floor in front of the fireplace, razing two piles of Alliance texts. Ingrid uttered a short scream as she toppled onto the floor next him.

"I'm sorry—it's Irindi," he groaned to her.

There was no reason for the angel of heavenly law to visit him, nothing to punish. And yet here she was, her voice blowing through the room. The tremor sent a teetering pile of books into a collapse.

"Luc Rousseau," she bellowed. He waited for it: *You have erred.* However, Irindi surprised him. "The Order wishes to understand why you have chosen to remain dispossessed from God's kingdom."

Irindi's radiance rolled off her in relentless waves, buffeting him as he practically kissed the floor.

Ingrid's hand touched his back. "What's happening? What is she saying?"

The tension in his throat made it difficult to speak. When he did, it wasn't to answer Ingrid. When an angel was in the room, you paid attention to the angel.

"I'm not finished here yet," he rasped.

"God determines when you are finished." Irindi's voice flogged his eardrums and rattled his teeth.

"He sent me here to protect humans, and I . . ." Luc searched for a way to explain himself, fast. Irindi wouldn't give him much of her time. "I understand now. I *want* to now."

Ingrid stayed crouched at his side, quiet. He'd always despised being tossed down into a bow and held there. But he'd chosen this. So long as he could stay with Ingrid, he would continue to choose it. Her life would be short compared to the years he'd already known. Even if she were to live into old age, Ingrid's years would be over in the blink of a gargoyle's eye. He would take them and cherish them, and whatever came after, he'd deal with it.

"You would sacrifice your own salvation to pledge yourself to the protection of God's children?" Irindi asked. Had her monotone voice allowed it, he was certain he would have heard in it the same incredulity that Ingrid, Marco, and Gaston had shown at his decision.

"I do," Luc answered. "I'm sorry, but yes. I do."

As if sensing the weight of the conversation, even hearing just one side of it, Ingrid leaned her forehead against his back. "I love you," she whispered.

Luc closed his eyes and basked in those words. She hadn't said them before now. He expected a perfunctory dismissal from Irindi, the loss of her light, and that would be welcome. He wanted to turn to Ingrid and tell her he loved her. He hadn't. Not in some time.

"Then, Luc Rousseau," Irindi said, "stand before me now."

The room fell dark and cold. The pressure holding him to the floor vanished, along with the glaring light.

Like before, at Clos du Vie, Luc pushed himself to his feet. However, unlike before, there was no warm glow, no magnetic draw toward the angel forgiving him. There was only the wavering light in the hearth from a few logs and a mound of ash.

And a woman.

She stood directly in front of him, her hair a tumble of spun-gold ringlets. Her skin was flawless and pale, and she had a pair of wide, deep umber eyes that made Luc feel as if he were being swallowed whole. She wore a hooded, marine-blue robe. A robe nearly identical to the one Axia had always worn.

"Irindi," Luc breathed.

Ingrid's hand clutched his, her attention riveted to the robed woman as well. She could see her. Irindi was . . . well, she appeared . . . human, though her face remained an emotionless mask.

"You have pleased God and the Order," she said.

Luc lifted his free hand, the one not being crushed by Ingrid, and absently rubbed behind his ears. Her voice. It didn't bellow or chime. It didn't hurt to listen to her.

"I have?" he asked, feeling asinine.

"Surrender thyself, forgive thine enemy, and ye shall be cleansed and made anew." Irindi—this human-looking version of her—said this as though it were scripture, but despite his centuries at the abbey, Luc had never so much as cracked open a Bible. He didn't know what she meant.

"The angels of the Order are not without their gifts. I offer one to you. The opportunity to protect and guide God's children here, among men—*as* a man."

Luc wasn't given the chance to comprehend, or breathe, before Irindi continued speaking.

"You shall embody all that is forgiveness. All that is God's miracle."

His stomach and heart dove in a mad rush, dipping and spinning. He didn't understand what was happening or what Irindi was telling him.

"Until we meet again, Luc Rousseau."

He blinked, and Irindi had gone. Ingrid gasped beside him, her body adhered to his side. He was shaking as he spun around, searching the corners of the front room for Irindi. Everything had suddenly been swamped in shadow.

His night vision wasn't working.

"What just happened?" Ingrid whispered.

Luc was afraid to move. What had Irindi just done?

"Luc?" Ingrid pulled away, her lips parted in awe. "What did she mean . . . *as a man?*"

He stepped away from her, his heels treading on a couple of tumbled books. He stumbled but held out his hand to signal Ingrid to stay back. She stood still, and Luc felt a queasy churn in the pit of his stomach.

He hunted for the trigger inside his core, the one that had always given way to the command to coalesce. Whether he coalesced willfully or under compulsion, pulling that trigger, changing from man to monster, had become as natural as breathing.

It wasn't there.

The trigger, the catch inside of him that had never failed to mutate his body, was gone. He couldn't find it.

Luc's breathing came faster. An edge of panic crept in. He couldn't shift. He couldn't see in the dark.

"Say something, Luc," Ingrid pleaded in a small, uncertain voice.

"I think—" Another queasy growl churned his stomach, and he remembered a feeling like it. He'd felt it before, long, long ago. He was *hungry*.

"I'm human," he said, so soft the words barely reached Ingrid's ears. She turned her ear.

"What did you—"

"I think I'm human," he said louder than before, his confidence rising as he tried, and failed, once again to locate the trigger that had centered him.

"Coalesce." Disbelief lent urgency to Ingrid's demand.

A solid knot bound up his throat as he shook his head. "I can't."

A hand muffled her cry and then Ingrid surged toward him. His knees gave out as she reached his side and they fell together to the floor, a tangle of laps and legs and arms. She clung to him, her hands running wildly over his cheeks, through his hair, smoothing down the front of his shirt.

"Is this real?" she gasped.

"I don't know what else it could be."

It wasn't just his faultless sight or his ability to coalesce that had fled him. Hôtel du Maurier itself had gone mute. His connection to this territory had completely disappeared from his senses. Everything around him felt quiet and still, except for the rapid-fire beating of his heart.

Irindi had said it was a gift, but that word . . . it was too small, too insignificant, to describe what this was. Even *miracle* didn't measure up.

He didn't know what to think. Once again the angels had left him with more questions than answers. All he knew, as Ingrid lowered her lips to his, was that he wouldn't have to push her away. He'd been granted a second chance. A second life. Luc gathered Ingrid closer.

He wasn't going to waste a moment.

Acknowledgments

The idea for this series came from a picture of a Notre Dame gargoyle looking out over the city of Paris. It's amazing what can happen in just a handful of years. I feel incredibly lucky to have been given the chance to tell that gargoyle's story, and to write this trilogy. There are many people to thank for believing in these books and, ultimately, in me: my phenomenal agent, Ted Malawer, who was there with me every step of the way; the entire Random House team, including my editor, Krista Marino, and publisher, Beverly Horowitz, who have worked so hard for this series; my fabulously talented critique partners, Maurissa Guibord, Dawn Metcalf, Cindy Thomas, and Amalie Howard; Charley, my mother-in-law, who picked up my youngest daughter twice a week to give me some uninterrupted writing time; and of course, every reader who has followed this series from the beginning—your support and enthusiasm mean more than I can ever explain.

When I was growing up, my parents not only taught me to love books, they also encouraged me to go for my dreams. Writing has always been my dream. Thank you, Mom and Dad, for believing in me.

And finally, to my husband, Chad, and our three beautiful girls, Alex, Joslin, and Willa—there are a hundred different things you do every single day that bring me joy. I love you all so much.

About the Author

Page Morgan has been fascinated with *les grotesques* ever since she came across an old black-and-white photograph of a Notre Dame gargoyle keeping watch over the city of Paris. The gargoyle mythologies she went on to research fed her imagination, and she became inspired to piece together her own story and mythology for these remarkably complex stone figures. Page lives in New Hampshire with her husband and their three children.

Look for the first two books in the Dispossessed trilogy, *The Beautiful and the Cursed* and *The Lovely and the Lost,* available from Delacorte Press.

Read the first two books in the
Dispossessed trilogy.

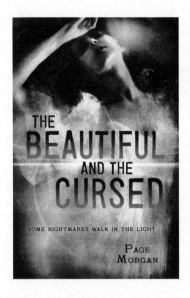

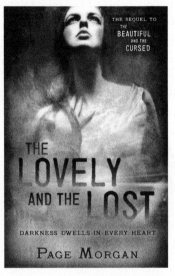